THE AMULET
OF CAORUNN

A Jinx Hamilton Adventure

Book Seven

Also by Juliette Harper

THE AMULET OF CAORUNN

A Jinx Hamilton Adventure

BOOK SEVEN

JULIETTE HARPER

Skye House Publishing, LLC
4517 Ranch View Road
Fort Worth, TX 76109

Edited by Patricia Pauletti

Print ISBN: 978-1-943516-60-5

First Edition: April 2017

DEDICATION

"Who are you?" said the Caterpillar.
This was not an encouraging conversation.
Alice replied, rather shyly, "I . . . I hardly know, sir,
just at present . . . at least I know who I was when
I got up this morning, but I think I must have
been changed several times since then."

Lewis Caroll, *Alice In Wonderland*

ONE

One morning early in November, my best friend and business partner, Tori Andrews, handed me a wrapped package when I came downstairs from my apartment over the store. We have coffee together every day and discuss business, like what variety of beans we needed to order for the espresso bar.

That morning, we had a lot more to talk about than the merits of Hawaiian Arabica versus Brazilian. Her parents, Gemma and Scrap Andrews, just ended their 35-year marriage. The conclusion of the legal proceedings marked the beginning of a kind of migration from our childhood home, Cotterville, North Carolina to Briar Hollow.

Tori's mom, Gemma, and my folks, Jeff and Kelly Hamilton, bought two buildings on our town square—Gemma across the corner from George and Irma's grocery store and my parents two doors past Chase McGregor's cobbler shop.

Throughout the summer, in the months just after I took over the store from Aunt Fiona, I dated Chase, but we faced hurdles worthy of the Complicated Relationship Hall of Fame.

You see, I'm a witch—we all are, except Tori and Gemma use their abilities to study alchemy. Chase and his father, Festus, are werecats and the sworn guardians of our hereditary line, the Daughters of Knasgowa. However,

1

witch and werecat magic aren't compatible when it comes to what they insist on referring to as "mating." The feeling against such unions is so strong; it amounts to a taboo among their kind.

Unfortunately, the McGregors seem to like the strong women my family routinely produces—they like us *a lot*. Festus still carries a torch for my mother, and I think he was sweet on my grandmother, Kathleen Ryan.

Werecats live much longer than humans, which you can either see as a chance for more experiences and adventures or a ticket to greater heartbreak. The more I talk with Festus, I think both are true.

Am I human? That's an idea I struggled with in the beginning. I didn't know about my magic until I was almost 30 years old. I didn't know that there are beings called the Fae who primarily occupy another dimension known as the Otherworld or that sandwiched between that place and the human realm is a no man's land labeled simply the "In Between."

Once, hundreds of years ago, humans accepted magic as just another part of nature. The Fae had great affection for humans and interacted with them routinely. But then a new idea began to sweep across the face of the world, the Christian religion.

As the power of the organized Church grew, humans drove magic into the shadows. Witch hunters hanged the accused, pressed them under massive stones to extract confessions, broke their fingers with thumb screws, and in some instances burned their victims alive.

The horrible truth is that the vast majority of those who died weren't witches at all, a tragedy that caused tremendous pain for the real witches. One reason the Fae go to such lengths to keep their world and their affairs hidden from human view is because they've seen the horrors of human hysteria.

Coming into my magic, I struggled with the idea that I might be something evil. Here's a simple but difficult fact; *different* doesn't always mean *evil*. I am Fae. If I spend most of my time here in the human realm, I'll live a fairly conventional span of years. But the more my powers grow, and the more time I spend in the Otherworld, the longer I'm going to be around.

At first, my powers scared me. I found the affairs of the Fae reality complicated and confusing. Now I'd describe myself as curious and excited. Let me try to explain.

I dated this guy in high school who loved to take pictures of bugs. Like most teenage girls—and even though I would describe myself as a tomboy—I drew the line at creepy crawlies. Not Jimmy.

"You don't have to touch them, Jinx," he said. "Just look at my pictures. These are the eyes of a butterfly, and see that long, curly tube? That's called a proboscis. It works like a straw. The butterfly uses that tube to drink nectar."

Jimmy showed me spider's faces and the veins in the wings of dragonflies. He made me see that underneath rocks or on the bottom side of leaves or way back in the dusty corners of attics, there are alternate worlds. To the fly caught in the spider's web, the monster coming toward it looks just as big as Godzilla up there on the movie screen.

With the lens of his camera, Jimmy changed my perspective on what I saw going on around me and what I didn't. That's how I feel about being Fae. I've been given a different lens to see a part of life most people don't know about and couldn't handle if they did. For me, that knowledge carries extra responsibilities.

Magic, like all life on this planet, sprang from the natural order, but that includes a system of checks and balances. If you've ever heard of Newton's Third Law, you'll have some idea what I'm trying to describe. "For every action, there is an equal and opposite reaction."

Where there is light, there is also dark.

If you're going to fully appreciate the story I'm about to tell you, we need to turn our attention back to the 12th century for just a minute, to two men, Gregorius Chesterfield and Henri de St. Clair. Both were Fae wizards and Knights Templar. They rode together to the Crusades not to fight for the church, but to ensure that the magical artifacts of the "Infidels" were not destroyed or worse yet, used to commit evil acts against humankind.

Gregorius had a son named Irenaeus, and Henri fathered a daughter named Brenna. Neither of those two children possessed hereditary magic and both, in time, made a deal with the darkness to become "made" practitioners—the first Creavit.

Nine centuries later, people like me are still trying to clean up their messes. The Creavit are immortal, ambitious, and prone to play power games with little thought to the collateral damage they might cause.

Just a couple of weeks before Tori handed me that wrapped present, Irenaeus Chesterfield kidnapped my brother. We got Connor back safely, but Chesterfield managed to get his hands on the Amulet of Caorunn, an artifact that might have the ability to sever the realms and set Chesterfield up to rule over the humans as a Creavit dictator.

When I reached to accept the gift Tori was holding out, I spotted Rodney peeking out of the collar of her sweater.

"What's this all about?" I asked. "And I see that we have an audience. Good morning, Rodney."

The black and white domestic rat held up one paw and waved in response. Then he pointed at the packaged and mimed ripping the paper.

"Hold on," I laughed. "Let me at least sit down."

Rodney is something of a mystery. He was left at the front door of the shop shortly before I took over from Aunt

Fiona. Clearly, he has no trouble communicating with us—even to the point of using a computer keyboard—but he remains mum on the subject of his life BBH (Before Briar Hollow).

"He's not the only curious one," Tori said. "You might as well show yourself Darby."

Our in-house brownie immediately materialized by her elbow. Invisibility is only one of Darby's many, many talents. Honestly, I don't know what we'd do without the little guy for all kinds of reasons.

A disturbing amount of my life tends to be lived in metaphysical disarray, But physically? We could be on the cover of *Better Home and Garden*. Darby keeps the store, the lair, and our apartments immaculate—and he cooks for us—which makes him six feet tall in my book. (He actually stands just under 2'11".)

"Well," I said, "and good morning to you, too."

"Good morning, Mistress," he said cheerfully. "We can hardly wait to see if you like your gift. Please do as Rodney says and rip the paper off now."

"Won't happen," Tori said, as I sat down and began to painstakingly apply the edge of my fingernail to the first piece of tape. "She's just like her mother—peels the tape and folds the paper."

I almost had the first piece of tape off cleanly when I stopped. "Wait a minute," I said, "aren't we short one spectator here?"

On cue, a Barbie-sized green witch on a broom banked low over the espresso counter, zipped into the scene, and came to a hovering halt in front of my face.

Glory is a former archivist for the State of North Carolina colorized and shrunk by—you guessed it—Irenaeus Chesterfield. The Creavit wizard sent her into our shop as a spy, with vague promises that he'd restore her to her normal self if she helped him get what he wanted.

That was never going to happen regardless of what Glory did or didn't tell him, something she figured out when her cover was blown. She defected to our side because we enlarged her from 3 inches to her current towering 6.5 inches. Well, that and she's absolutely terrified of Chesterfield.

"I thought you had to be around here somewhere," I said. "You're cutting it a little close flying through the shop just before we open, aren't you?"

Balancing herself perfectly on the broom, Glory put her hands on her hips. "_I'm_ not the one taking forever to open the present," she said. "Get _on_ with it!"

"Yeah, what she said," Tori agreed. "Come on, Jinksy. I bet you're even going to fold the tissue paper, aren't you?"

"Of course," I said, removing the lid from the box, "who in their right mind would waste . . ."

As I drew the first layer of tissue aside, the words caught in my throat. Rodney's eyes went wide, and he put one paw over his mouth. Glory let out with a "wow" that made her wobble in mid-air, and Darby stood on tiptoe to get a better look.

A book bound in dark leather lay nestled in the silver and blue tissue, its hand-tooled cover bearing a majestic tree I recognized immediately; the Mother Oak that grows in the center of Shevington. That's the Fae sanctuary in the Otherworld founded and still governed by my many times great-grandfather, Barnaby Shevington.

The decorative border around the tree panel bore perfect miniature depictions of the flock of dragonlets that greet me every time I pass through the portal to Shevington. My embossed initials appeared in the lower right-hand corner in elegant gothic letters, NJH.

"I designed the cover, but Connor made it," Tori explained. "We had Mr. Pagecliff do the binding and enchantment. Write all you want to, Jinksy. You'll never run out of pages. Every witch needs a grimoire to help her study her magic."

Darby nodded solemnly. "Mistress Tori is correct," he said. "The shelves in the archives hold the grimoires of your ancestors and those of many other great witches and wizards."

Our building sits atop a fairy mound, which resides cloaked in the In Between. If other people go downstairs, they're in a cluttered, dirty space filled with spiders big enough to saddle.

We enter a work area equipped for our needs and elegantly furnished with leather chairs and sofas, lush Oriental rugs, paneling, bookshelves, and a fireplace that never goes out or needs cleaning.

The fairy mound also serves as an archive for Fae documents and artifacts. In Myrtle's absence, Darby tends the collection.

"Thank you," I said to Tori, with tears in my eyes, "both of you. I'll call Connor later and tell him how much I love it."

Tori grinned. "You're welcome," she said, "but there's more. Open the cover."

Gently lifting the grimoire—my grimoire—clear of the tissue, I opened the book, delighting in the intoxicating smell of new leather. Inside, resting in a loop next to the pages, I found a breathtaking black pen overlaid with an intricate design of crimson swirls. It took me a minute to realize the lines formed a great bird. The wings stretched out to wrap the barrel as if the creature strained to reach the golden nib.

"That's from Barnaby and Moira," Tori said. "Same deal as the grimoire. You'll never run out of ink and if you need to draw something, just think about the image you want to create and the pen will do the rest."

Tori knows me better than anyone. Without magic, I can't draw a straight line with a ruler.

"Alchemy?" I asked.

Moira is the resident Alchemist in Shevington. She and Granddad are in a relationship, which they try and fail to keep secret.

Tori nodded. "The ink contains a formula to aid in the transformation of raw ideas."

Running my fingers over the design, I said, "And this is the Great Phoenix, the bird that rose from the ashes."

As a Daughter of Knasgowa, I also serve as a priestess to the Mother Tree. In Latin, I'm called *Quercus de Pythonissam*, the Witch of the Oak.

Now, before you ask, I don't fully understand the responsibilities of my job—or I didn't then. The complexities of the Fae world and its interaction with the human realm represent a long learning curve. The intricate connections stretch back for centuries.

The Fae lead incredibly long lives. My grandfather, who was born in 1125, will turn 891 this year. Just before Christmas, he confessed to us that his real name is Barnabas Chesterfield. Irenaeus is his younger brother by five years. The dynamics of their relationship are, in modern psychological terms, "dysfunctional" at best.

There's some accouterment that comes with my position as Witch of the Oak—a sentient staff named Dílestos, and an amber amulet encasing a single feather of the Phoenix.

That bit of bling currently hangs around the neck of my second father and dear confidante, Colonel Beauregard T. Longworth. In the interest of full disclosure, I will tell you Beau's technically dead. The amulet allows him to have corporeal form.

"It's perfect," I said, standing and pulling Tori into a hug. "I love it."

"We just thought maybe starting to work on your grimoire would help you get a handle on everything that's happened this year. Consider it an early birthday present."

"Great," I said, releasing her and wiping my eyes, "your birthday is three days after mine, and there is now literally *no way* I'm going to come up with a present for you that is anywhere near this awesome."

"Yeah," she grinned, "but you'll try, which means one way or another, I'll score something cool. That's a win/win in the Tori column."

I was so blown away by the thoughtfulness; I could have easily dissolved into a sentimental, crying lump. Instead, I squared my shoulders and said, "Okay, show's over. Tori and I have to get to work and you three need to get out of here so we can open up."

For Rodney that simply meant burrowing back into Tori's sweater. Darby winked out of sight, and I held the basement door open to Glory could fly back downstairs to the lair.

She hovered in mid-air a few inches in front of my face before making the descent. "Jinx Hamilton," she declared, "even if you do have an awful, terrible, evil, scary wizard trying to get you pretty much all the time, I think you may be the luckiest witch alive."

With that, she zoomed through the doorway, disappearing into the darkness below. As her words sunk in, a feeling of gratitude washed over me. I couldn't agree with her more.

That feeling stayed with me all day and put a spring in my step that night as I carried the grimoire to my new alcove in the lair.

When our friend and mentor, the ancient being we called Myrtle, lived with us, I thought she was responsible for any additions to our subterranean headquarters. But then Myrtle was forced to merge with the Mother Tree to heal from exposure to a toxic artifact, and the lair went right on expanding and improving itself anyway.

With no input from us, the fairy mound anticipates our wants and needs, generally before we realize what those things might be.

The day after my brother's return, I walked downstairs and found an alcove outfitted with a desk, bookshelves, a comfortable, easy chair upholstered in soft fabric, and a tiny private fireplace. An unseen hand tugged at me to investigate more closely.

"Is that for me?" I asked.

In response, a curtain dragged itself across the arched entryway. Woven into the pattern in my handwriting was the message, "Please do not disturb. Thanks, Jinx."

That made me laugh, but when I stepped through the curtain into the cozy space, I immediately appreciated just how considerate the fairy mound had been. The covering didn't just shield me from prying eyes; it substituted the soothing sounds of a forest and running water for any external noise.

When I retreated to the alcove with my new grimoire, I had the curtain open and was sitting in the desk chair looking at the book and thinking. Under the desk, my feet bumped against the leather satchel my mother passed on to me months before. It contained all the private notebooks kept by my matrilineal ancestors.

Next to the chair, Dílestos reclined in a softly padded niche created specifically for her comfort. I knew the staff felt contented because the raw quartz set atop the polished oak pulsated slowly and emitted a barely discernible but completely companionable hum.

I thought I was alone until Festus McGregor sauntered into the alcove, jumped into the easy chair, circled three times, and lay down with a sigh. Festus lives in his small werecat form to better accommodate the limitations of a lame hip. In their large form, both he and Chase are mountain lions.

"Well," I said, eyeing him a little sardonically, "make yourself at home."

"Don't mind if I do," the ginger tom said placidly. "It's nice in here."

"It is," I agreed, "but I don't know why the fairy mound decided to make a space especially for me now."

"Because you need it," Festus replied without hesitation. "That's how the fairy mound works. It sensed you needed some place for private reflection and created it for you. This alcove should come in pretty handy when you're up to something you want to hide from the rest of us."

He delivered the last line with an eye whisker waggle that told me he already had me dead to rights. Trust me, if you need a fast buck, play cards with me. I can't bluff to save my life—at least not with someone who knows me as well as Festus does.

I might have dated the son, but I also cultivated a good friendship with the father. Festus can be an irascible old coot at times, but he's also one of the most honorable men I've ever known—with two legs or four. If I told him what I was working on, the information would never leave the alcove.

I stood and pulled the curtain over the archway.

Festus fixed me with a satisfied cat face. "I thought so," he said. "What are you up to?"

"I asked Hiram Folger to do me a favor," I replied.

This time those ever-expressive eye whiskers drew together in a decidedly feline frown. "You mean the dead guy out at the cemetery? The one who pitches on the baseball team?"

"Yes," I said. "You know that Tori and Beau have ghosts from all over the south wanting to play in the Dead Majors?"

Through an odd series of events, I had a sort of ecto-plasmic, ball-playing Pinkerton Detective Agency at my disposal. After Beau became solid and moved in with us, Tori got him interested in baseball. Soon interest turned to obsession, and the Colonel organized his deceased friends at the graveyard into two opposing teams.

When a trio of local ghost hunters—one of whom was currently employed upstairs as our barista—managed to get footage of a game in progress, the video went viral on YouTube. Although I'm still not sure how, a ghost buried in the Cave Hill Cemetery in Louisville, Kentucky got wind of the incident.

Said spirit happened to be Henry Clay Pulliam, the deceased 1906 president of the National League, who contacted our spirits about organizing a league for players from the other side.

Beau and Tori wanted to do it, but I only got on board after we struck a deal with the local team. The Briar Hollow ghosts could play and even host out-of-graveyard opponents, but in exchange, they had to become our actual "spooks"—as in intelligence agents. When you're constantly the target of outlaw Creavit, you want boots on the ground even if they're transparent.

"Yeah," he said, "I know about the League. Me and Rube are planning to make book on the season."

Rube, a raccoon, works as a containment specialist with the International Registry for Shapeshifters and does undercover work for the Division for Grid Integrity. I know Rube through Lucas Grayson and his partner, Greer MacVicar. The Mother Tree recently assigned the two DGI agents to work with me, and they've become lair regulars along with the rest of us.

Holding up my hand to stop Festus, I said, "Don't tell me. Ignorance is bliss where you and Rube are concerned."

"Fine," Festus sniffed, "but I was going to offer to cut you in."

"Moving on," I said. "I asked Hiram if he could get me in touch with someone inside the Raleigh ghost community. He talked to a dead player for the Raleigh Capitals and came up with a name."

Festus eyed me with an odd mixture of suspicion and admiration. "Are you trying to recruit outside the legal process and run in a ringer? Because if you're into game-fixing that sophisticated? I have serious respect for you."

"What? *No*! Festus!" I said. "Could you get your mind off gambling and listen to me? I'm trying to get us a lead on where Chesterfield went the night Connor and Gareth got away from him."

Chesterfield kidnapped my brother, but Connor escaped aided by a somewhat hapless amateur alchemist named Gareth who had been trapped inside a chess set since 1890. Gareth managed to transport them both inside Chesterfield's fountain pen and back out again when the wizard absent-mindedly left the writing instrument in his Raleigh hotel room.

We believe he went to meet with a thief named John Smyth to arrange to buy the Amulet of Caorunn, another Fae pendant, but this one crafted from amber derived from the Mother Rowan and encasing three rowan berries.

"Do Barnaby and Moira know about this?" Festus asked.

"No."

"Lucas and Greer?"

"No."

"That uptight boy of mine?"

"No," I said, with exasperation. "Let's not turn this into a game of twenty questions. You're the only person I've told."

"What's up with that?" he asked, with genuine curiosity.

"I'm tired of running around like some little kid asking permission from the grown-ups," I said. "Does everything have to be some major coordinated plan all the time?"

"It does not," Festus said, with a note of approval.

I started to thank him and then realized that would more or less contradict my little declaration of witchly independence. I swear to you the old cat read my mind and bailed me out.

"So," he said, "who did the dead guy tell you to see?"

"Mary Willis Mordecai Turk," I replied.

Festus' eyes expanded. "That can't be her real name," he said.

"I'm afraid it is," I replied. "She haunts a place called Mordecai House that dates to around 1758."

"When you say 'haunt,' exactly what do you mean?" he asked warily.

"What's the matter, fraidy cat?" I said. "Since when do you have a problem with ghosts?"

From time to time the spirit of Festus' father, James makes an appearance in the lair, usually to have a conversation with Beau. The two of them are Lodge brothers. James found Beau's body on the battlefield back in 1864 and arranged for him to have a Masonic funeral. That act of kindness created a bond between them that no form of death can shatter.

"For your information," Festus said, "I've gotten enough ectoplasm in my fur from hacked off haunts to last me through all nine lives and then some. If this one is a slimer, I'm not your cat."

"Who said I wanted you to go talk to her?" I asked, feigning innocence."

"Oh, please," Festus scoffed. "How are you supposed to take a hop through the Raleigh portal without someone noticing? I go up there all the time."

I sighed. "Okay, busted. Will you do it?"

"Sure," he said. "What do you want me to find out?"

Opening the top drawer of my desk, I pulled out a map of Raleigh and laid it on the ottoman in front of the chair. Festus sat up and leaned over to look at the map.

"This," I said, pointing to a spot, "is the hotel where Chesterfield stayed the night Connor and Gareth escaped, and this is Miss Shania Moonbeam's Divinatory Emporium where they asked for help thinking she was the real magical deal."

"Miss Shania is the real deal alright," Festus muttered, "a real deal nutcase."

"Now stop that," I said. "She's very nice, just a little over the top."

"Whatever," Festus muttered, still studying the map. "This is interesting," he said, pointing with the tip of one claw. "Look how close the hotel is to Chesterfield's old apartment."

"Exactly," I said. "The restaurant where he met with John Smyth has to be close, but there's always the possibility he took a cab somewhere. I'm hoping Mrs. Turk can put the word out on the ghost grapevine. If a spirit saw Chesterfield and this Smyth character, maybe we can get some real information on their meeting."

"As in, did any goods trade hands?" Festus said. "Okay, I like it. I'll go talk to Mrs. Turkey."

"Do not start, Festus," I warned. "You be polite to this woman. She's been haunting the house since 1937. She wears a gray dress and plays the piano. Sometimes she only appears as a mist. Very benign stuff. I figure you can get in and out unseen."

"Of course I can," Festus said, puffing out his chest. "I'm a professional. If she can help us narrow the search, I can talk to the street cats and see what they know."

That took me off guard. "Street cats?" I asked. "You don't mean other werecats, do you?"

"Don't be ridiculous," Festus said, stretching and yawning. "I mean street ferals. I may be a werecat, but I do speak Felinese with a perfect North American accent. How do you think I talk to your cats?"

"About that," I said, "are you the one who put it in Yule's head that nothing but pâté is acceptable?"

"I just explained to him the delicate art of the protest barf," Festus chuckled. "Did he get your shoes like I told him to?"

"He did," I said, "but I'm a little surprised you eat cat food. I've never seen you eat anything but human food."

"I get hungry for something ethnic now and then," Festus said, "but that crap you're feeding your guys is disgusting. I mean seriously, would you eat anything labeled 'chopped grill' that costs forty cents a can?"

"Well, I . . . I never thought about it," I sputtered.

"I suggest you get on that," Festus said, hopping to the floor and switching his tail. "If your guys don't start seeing some quality tuna and salmon coming through the door, I'm moving them up to advanced regurgitation resistance tactics. You've been warned. I'll get back to you on the Mrs. Turkey thing."

And with that, he slid through the curtain and was gone.

TWO

Still inwardly grumbling from the impromptu lecture about my cat care standards, I drew the drape aside covering the mirror hanging over my desk. Concentrating on the center of the surface, I chanted the words of the calling spell and watched as the silver rippled and spun. When it stabilized, my brother's face grinned back at me.

"Hey, sis!" Connor greeted me. "What's up?"

As part of our search to recover Connor from Chesterfield's clutches, Barnaby revealed the shocking news that I have magic on both sides of the family. Dad descends from a family of Druids who lived in the Orkney Islands called the Skeas.

The first Skea in the New World, Alexander, married the founder of our magical line, a Cherokee woman named Knasgowa, who was Barnaby's daughter by his second wife. Here's the tricky part, though. Alexander wasn't a Skea.

Brenna Sinclair was his mother, which is a big deal because Creavit theoretically can't bear or father children. Enter shipwreck survivor Hamish Crawford.

Hamish and Brenna had a thing, resulting in Hamish being a baby daddy. *Then* he found out he'd been sleeping with a witch. That news might be a little tough for any guy to take, but Hamish was deeply religious.

I assume he decided that you could only fight magic with magic since he went to local Druid Duncan Skea for help. Together they imprisoned Brenna in a cave, and then Duncan took the baby to raise.

Fast forward to that child's grandson, Alexander, who came to this country in 1787 to get away from his scary great-grandmother, Brenna, newly busted out of her cave.

That part of the story I already knew. The revelation came in the form of a "brother," Duncan Skea the Younger, who followed Alexander to the New World. Even though they weren't related by blood, the men were raised together.

Alexander refused to put Duncan in danger from Brenna, so Duncan changed his last name to Hamilton and stayed close by. Eight generations later, my Dad, Jeff Hamilton, married Kelly Ryan.

The magic I have comes from the matrilineal line and is recessive in males. The Skea magic is patrilineal. By combining my blood and Dad's, we used a tsavorite amulet to track Connor to Chesterfield's hidden lair.

But there were side effects. Aren't there always?

The spell awakened Connor's magic and Dad's.

Working with Barnaby and Moira, Connor is making slow and steady progress toward controlling his powers. The first thing he wanted to master was using mirrors to place calls to us in Briar Hollow.

As for our father, he's on a suppression potion to control his erratically emerging abilities.

I know, I know. That sounds like I'm drugging my Dad to control him—because I am.

There was no other way short of letting him burn down this side of the town square. Before the potion, all he had to do was walk in a room for light bulbs to explode and electronics to fry. I'm pretty sure when Dad gets a handle on things he's not going to be a slacker in the hocus pocus department, but right now, he's a total menace.

"Hey yourself," I said to Connor. "You're getting good at this mirror thing."

"Answering calls is easy," he said, "but yesterday when I tried to call Mom, I got through to Mrs. Shinglebutter by mistake. She spent fifteen minutes trying to understand why I would call her when she lives so close to the stables and I could have just walked over."

Behind Connor, a short, round man in a monk's habit stuck his head into the picture. "Hi, Jinx," he said, waving. "I'm on my way to Moira's, but I wanted to say hello."

"Hi Gareth," I said. "How are you and Dewey getting along?"

Dewey, Moira's dwarf assistant, was not amused when the alchemist decided to take Gareth on as an apprentice.

From the way Gareth's face fell, I knew the answer already. "I'm trying," he said, "but Dewey insists on making everything I do a confrontation. I moved a beaker yesterday, and he threatened to take my head off—literally. He was holding an ax when he said it."

I started to point out that Dewey was too short to take Gareth's head off, but decided that wouldn't sound sympathetic. "Did you try what Darby suggested?" I asked.

In one of the great paradoxes of true friendship, my perpetually happy little friend and the ever-contentious dwarf are best buddies.

"I'm stopping by Madame Kaveh's on my way to the workshop," Gareth said mournfully. "But I'm not sure a dozen sugar coated fried pastries will help."

"But they probably won't hurt," I said encouragingly. "Good luck."

Gareth waved good-bye. I heard him cross the oak floorboards in Connor's apartment over the tack room. When the door opened and closed, I asked Connor, "Think the bribe will work?"

"I doubt it," he said. "Dewey doesn't like changes. He

treats me pretty much the same way when I show up for my lessons."

Another face came into view, this one covered in soft gray fur and dominated by enormous sad eyes. "Pretty lady come to Ailish's house today?" the creature asked.

Ailish, an Elven Gray Loris, is Connor's constant companion, but she has developed a major crush on me.

"Not today, Ailish," I said, "but soon."

That won me an enormous sigh. "Soon never come fast," she said, climbing down Connor's arm.

"She does guilt better than our mother," I said, shaking my head. "I feel like I just walked away from an abandoned puppy in a rain storm."

"Try living with her," Connor said.

"Isn't it morning in Shevington?" I asked. "I didn't work out the time difference before I called."

"Mid-morning," he said. "I finished mucking out the stalls and feeding the animals early, so Ellis let me take a couple of hours off to work on a commission for a client. Want to see?"

Connor works for Ellis Groomsby in the Shevington stables, but he does leather work on the side. As I watched, he turned toward his workbench under the dormer window and held up a pair of gauntlets. One bore an intricately tooled family crest at the wrist.

"I just finished the first one," he said. "They're dragon master gauntlets."

The only dragons indigenous to North America, *Draco Americanus Minor*, are about the size of a large dog. Some Fae communities in Eastern Europe still maintain flights of *Draco Europa Major*. I've never seen one, but the pictures look like what you'd expect from a storybook.

"You're working for a European client?" I said. "How'd that happen?"

In theory, a huge rift exists between the New and Old

World Fae, but the more I learn about the politics of the Otherworld, the more the division strikes me as artificial and anachronistic.

In 1584, Barnaby led a group of Fae settlers to the New World ostensibly to colonize Roanoke Island for Sir Walter Raleigh. The ruse hid their escape from the turmoil of the Fae Reformation. The social and ideological conflict pitted "made" or Creavit witches like Brenna Sinclair and Irenaeus Chesterfield against natural or Hereditarium practitioners like my grandfather.

The real English settlers to the New World ultimately made nice with the Mother Country—after the little matter of a revolutionary war. Barnaby and the people of Shevington, however, never reconciled with their counterparts across the pond.

In spite of that, agencies like the DGI, the Registry, and International Bureau of Indefinite Species collaborate globally, and nobody bats an eye. The real political split involves Barnaby and Reynold Isherwood, the head of the Council of Ruling Elders, the Fae governing body in Europe.

Recently the chill showed signs of thawing. The Elders contacted Barnaby to work with them in a diplomatic capacity. He accepted, even going so far as to tell me I would take his place as Lord High Mayor. After that, nothing happened.

I can't decide if that's the usual glacial pace the Fae apply to their affairs or the bad blood between the two men coloring the political waters. So far the situation hasn't called for me to say, "Granddad, you and Reynold need to get over it," but I sensed that might be coming.

"You know that jerkin I made for Rube?" Connor asked.

A jerkin is sort of a sleeveless jacket. Very Renaissance Faire. When Rube wears it, he looks like an extra in an all-critter version of a Robin Hood remake.

"Yeah," I said. "I love that thing on him."

"Me, too," Connor said. "A dragon master saw it and asked him who did the leather work, and Rube referred me. The guy sent me an old pair of his gauntlets, and I used them as a pattern."

"The new ones are going to be beautiful," I said, "and so is the cover of my grimoire. Thank you so much for doing that."

A little blush colored his cheeks, but he didn't turn as bright red as he would have a couple of weeks earlier. We were getting to know each other better through mirror calls, and in-person visits and an easy rapport had begun to develop between us.

"I didn't know when Tori was going to give it to you," Connor said. "I'm glad you like it."

"Not like love," I said. "I have to call Granddad and Moira next about the pen. Oh, and Darby wants to know what kind of cake you want for your birthday. He's making one for each of us."

Connor's birthday is December 3, mine is the 6th, and Tori's is the 9th. Mom and Darby were deep into planning a triple celebration.

"Chocolate," Connor said firmly. "Always chocolate."

"Me, too," I laughed. "We're going to eat ourselves into blissful chocolate oblivion."

"Good!" he enthused, licking his lips. "What did Tori pick?"

"The same thing she's been picking since we were kids," I said. "Red velvet cake."

"What's that?" he asked curiously. "Is it good?"

"It's sort of a second cousin of chocolate cake, and the frosting is made from cream cheese," I explained. "And yes, it's good."

His interest in Tori wasn't lost on me at the time, nor was the little spark of interest she was showing in him.

The first time she saw a picture of my big brother; my BFF labeled him a "major hunk."

Connor and I talked for a few minutes longer. He told me about how fast the new unicorn foal was growing. I helped him with some ideas for Christmas presents for our parents. But then he had to get back to work, and I needed to wrap up my calls to Barnaby and Moira since I had a project brewing in the back of my mind.

A project I had no intention of sharing with anyone just yet.

If that statement sticks out for you like a red flag, then you get a gold star for keeping up. Sometimes the scariest thing in the world is me with a bright idea in my head.

THREE

I finished the last of my mirror calls and stuck my head through the alcove curtain. The lair was deserted. Perfect. I didn't need any prying eyes for what I was about to do. I started to cross the open space to the bookshelves to the right of the fireplace when I saw a light burning in Graceland East. The dollhouse is a replica of Elvis Presley's mansion that serves as Glory's home.

Creeping forward silently, I heard soft snores coming from the vicinity of the tiny living room. Tori wall mounted an iPod Touch for Glory to use as a big screen TV. Most nights our diminutive friend falls asleep watching old movies, hence the snoring. Perfect.

Still moving quietly, I searched the shelves for my Grandmother Kathleen's grimoire, slid it free and carried the book back to the alcove, drawing the curtain behind me. Then I dug through the leather satchel under the desk until I located her private notebook. I set them side by side on the desk and took a deep breath.

My mind was made up. I knew what I was going to do—and still, my inner good girl tried to pitch a fit. "*No*," I told her—myself—firmly, "you do not need to ask anyone's permission. Now get on with it."

I opened both books and started to read, flipping back and forth in search of matching references in the texts.

Grandma Kathleen possessed the same signature power I have,—psychometry—and I needed some advice from an expert.

From the start, I've been able to touch objects and get visions. It doesn't happen every time I pick something up, I just intuitively know how to ask when I want to extract images and impressions stored in the item.

The experiences that come to me feel so real; it's as if I've entered an alternate dimension. Through hours of practice, I can now summon up instant replays and even share them with another person. What I can't do—or couldn't do then—was use an inert object, one with no infused memories or life energy, to search for information.

I had a photo of the Amulet of Caorunn that Chase and Festus retrieved from the law offices of the late Anton Ionescu, Esquire. The same Ionescu who was Chesterfield's attorney and the strigoi who cursed my mother and caused Connor's exile to Shevington.

The strigoi are a type of vampire. They feed on energy, not blood. Anton lived on a vendetta—the belief that Mom and Gemma were responsible for the deaths of his daughter and niece. He didn't like me much better since I was the one who inadvertently raised the girls from the grave as actual bloodsuckers.

Anton redeemed himself prior to his death, but not before he facilitated putting the Amulet of Caorunn in Chesterfield's hands via the meeting with John Smyth.

No matter how much I tried to use that photograph to have a vision about the amulet, all I saw was the inside of Anton's desk and the inner workings of the printer that produced the picture from a digital file.

That left me with the firm assurance that Anton had a thing for binder clips and the printer needed a new magenta ink cartridge. Not exactly vital information.

Then the idea came to me to search Grandma's notes

about her own psychometry to see if I could find a way to fine tune my signal.

No two witches keep their grimoires in the same way. Some of my ancestors recorded nothing but precise spells and incantations. Others made notations in the margins, included diagrams, or composed outright journal entries.

My only memory of my grandmother was of an old woman who went to church a lot. Festus and Mom both assured me, however, that Kathleen Ryan had enough power, as the ginger cat put it, "to curl your whiskers."

After spending an hour with her grimoire and notebook, I could see that Grandma had been a learned magical scholar and a sharp, inquisitive woman. In addition to the sorts of things I would have expected to find in her notes, I was surprised to see that she also cataloged some of the artifacts that found their way into the archive.

One, in particular, jumped out at me—the Casket of Morpheus. In her neat, precise hand, Grandma described an ivory box that contained some type of horn. To my consternation, the writing was smeared, so I couldn't tell if I was looking for a wooly mammoth leg bone or a moose antler.

According to the notes, the bone and ivory together allowed the person in possession of the box to request a specific type of dream. Bingo! Surely someone with my psychometric power could use that sucker like a metaphysical homing pigeon.

(For the record, I chose to ignore what Grandma wrote in the margin. "Artifact produces unpredictable results." In case you haven't guessed, that might have been a poor decision on my part.)

The reference number for the Casket said it was shelved in Section 57, Row FF, Shelf 9. Normally I wouldn't have had a clue how to find that, but Darby and Glory just completed a sort of Google Maps for the lair. In addition to keeping our domestic world in order, Darby knows the archives like the back of his hand.

Pair his knowledge with Glory's archival skills and add a dash of Tori's ability with computers and you get a location finder app for the collection. I switched on my iPad, punched in the information, and followed the pulsating red dot on the screen straight to the Casket of Morpheus, which turned out to be roughly the size of a cigar box.

When I had the item in hand, I returned to my alcove and examined the casket. Grandma didn't leave any instructions on how to use the thing, so I went with a standard approach. I folded the photograph of the amulet, put it inside the casket, laid my hands on the box, and chanted a simple spell asking to locate that which had been lost.

Nothing happened, but since I was working with a dream-based magical item, I expected sleep needed to be part of the equation. I was exhausted anyway, so turning in for the night seemed like a good next step in my big master plan.

That first night my mind conjured up what amounted to a three-dimensional floating hologram of the amber pendant. The detail came through so vividly the three crimson berries glowed. When I reached for the pendant, however, the colors faded. As soon as I drew my fingers back, the hues grew vibrant again.

That was it. No plot. No purpose—and no useful information. Just bling suspended in mid-air like a sleep-induced visit to the Home Shopping Channel.

Still, I recorded every detail in my grimoire. Rather than keep two separate books, I flipped pages toward the center of the volume and started to write the word "Notes" at the top of the page. Then, just for the heck of it, I closed my eyes and envisioned a decorative divider page that looked like something out of an illuminated manuscript.

Barnaby and Moira's pen pushed gently but insistently

against my fingers. I opened my eyes and released the writing instrument, watching with delight as the nib began to draw, changing ink colors spontaneously as needed with no further input from me.

Tendrils of ivy flowed from the gold point, entwining with climbing flowers to encircle the outer border of the page. When that was finished, the pen hovered over the paper for a second as if assessing its work before writing, in an elegant, calligraphic hand, *The Notes of Jinx Hamilton - Witch, in anno domini 2015.*

"Nice touch with the Latin," I said.

The pen turned to face me, bowed, and then gently settled back into my waiting fingers.

"Wait," I said. "Can you draw a picture of the Casket of Morpheus for me on the next page before I start to write?"

Obligingly, the page of the book turned, the pen levitated again, and quickly produced a precise black ink sketch of the artifact.

"Thanks," I said, taking charge again. "I've got it from here."

Even though the first dream didn't tell me much, I wanted to record the details of my experiment—from the methodology I used to the images that came into my dreams. Hopefully, at some point, it would all start to make sense, and I would get the information I could use to recover the amulet.

Unfortunately, I had more or less the same dream three nights in a row. After the last one, I came downstairs grumpy enough that Tori asked me what was going on.

Pulling her into the storeroom, I came clean about what I'd been doing.

"Are you out of your *mind*?" Tori hissed. "Why would you try to find the amulet without coordinating with Barnaby or for that matter, Lucas, and Greer?"

"Because," I hissed back, "I don't need anyone's permission to use artifacts housed in the archive under my own store, *and* I'm trying to let everybody enjoy the holidays. Mom and Dad are over the moon because Connor is home. He certainly doesn't need any more chaos after what he's been through. Barnaby hasn't said a word about the amulet since Connor's kidnapping. Granddad may be content to sit around and wait for his lunatic brother to make his next move, but I'm not."

Tori blinked at me a little dumbfounded. I'd just spit out way more of an answer than she was expecting. "Okay," she said, reluctantly, "I get the thing about the holidays. If you're bound and determined to do this, then count me in. What can I do to help?"

"You're the alchemist," I said. "You tell me. Can't you mix up something to supercharge the effect my spell has on the box?"

"Bad idea," she said emphatically, "bad, bad, and *bad* in case you didn't hear me the first three times," Tori said, shaking her head and backing up. "You do not try to enchant artifacts that are already enchanted. It's just not done, Jinksy. There's no way to tell what the result might be."

That did nothing but make me more insistent. "I'm not asking you to mix magic," I said stubbornly. "I just want you to amplify the box's . . . signal. Stick an antenna on the danged thing. I need a dream that tells me something."

We argued about methodology all day under our breath and in the storeroom—any place where the customers or Mindy, our barista, couldn't hear us. By closing time, I'd worn Tori down—and she'd had enough time to think about the casket and come up with an idea.

We spent the evening in the lair, excused ourselves at a normal workday bedtime, and half an hour later, Tori came upstairs with a small vial of pale greenish blue powder.

"What is it?" I asked.

"Ground blue kyanite," she said. "It's used to amplify psychic powers."

"Sounds good," I said. "So how do we do this?"

Tori examined the casket sitting on my bedside table. "What have you been doing so far?" she asked.

In response, I handed her my grimoire. She opened the book to a blank page and looked at me questioningly.

"Sorry," I said. Then, speaking to the book, I said, "Can you show Tori the notes section please?"

The pages riffled in her hands, and Tori let out an appreciative whistle. "I see you guys are getting to know each other," she said. Then her eyes landed on the illustrated page. "Wow! Did Barnaby and Moira's pen do this?"

In its leather ring beside the pages, the pen let out a tiny, indignant growl. "Sorry," Tori apologized hastily. "Of course you did it. Fantastic work."

She sat on the edge of the bed and read my notes on the first four dreams. "You just put the box on the bed, recite the invocation spell, and go to sleep?" she asked.

"Yep," I said. "That's the drill."

"And you get the same dream every night?" Tori asked.

"Pretty much," I said. "The amulet is either suspended in thin air or lying on a piece of black velvet. Usually the berries in the amber glow. In one dream, the pendant was slowly turning with a light falling directly on it."

"Well, let's just go with that for starters," Tori said. "I'm going to sprinkle the kyanite powder over the top, so the grains sit in the grooves of the carving. You say your spell, and let's see what happens."

As she twisted the top off the vial, I felt my first flicker of doubt about the wisdom of our plan. "You'll stay close?" I asked, a little uncertainly.

"You couldn't blast me out of here with one of those

blue energy bolts of yours," Tori assured me. "I'll be on the sofa in the living room."

As I watched, she dusted the box. I recited the spell. We said our goodnights, and to my surprise, I fell asleep quickly and immediately entered the dreamscape.

This time I found myself standing on a street corner in the middle of a full-blown action movie. Swiveling my head around, I took in the vaguely European style of the buildings. Movement across the street caught my attention. I saw an elderly man wobbling and swaying along the sidewalk. Even at a distance, I could tell he'd been drinking.

As the old gent passed by a shadowed, recessed entrance, a second figure stepped out of the shadows. I tried to call out a warning, but my throat refused to produce any sound. As I watched helplessly, the newcomer held out one hand palm up and blew some sort of dust toward the man's face. He gasped and inhaled the powder.

Unfortunately, I did the same thing.

A reeling maelstrom of confusion slammed into me with such force I woke up with a startled cry. Tori was instantly by my side. "Easy there, Jinksy," she said. "It was just a dream. Are you okay?"

Through gritted teeth, I managed to get out the word, "Dizzy."

"Lie still," she said. "Let it settle down."

When she started to move away, I panicked. "Don't leave," I said.

"I'm not," she soothed. "I'm just going to bring a chair in from the kitchen. I don't want to sit on the bed. The motion might make you dizzier."

"Okay," I said, staring straight up at the ceiling. "Hurry."

I heard chair legs on the linoleum, and then Tori's

returning footsteps. "I'm back," she said, "just breathe. In and out, deep and steady."

"Open the grimoire," I instructed, "and take the pen out of the leather loop."

"You can't even sit up." Tori protested. "How are you going to write anything."

"I'm not going to try," I said, "just put the pen in my hand."

When I felt the smooth barrel between my fingers, I concentrated on the scene I'd just witnessed. "Draw it," I said softly.

The pen tugged against my fingers, and I released it. I lay still, listening to the gold nib scratch against the page. The rhythmic strokes eased my thudding heart, and the spinning stopped.

"What's it doing?" I asked Tori, still afraid to move.

"Drawing," she said in an awed voice. "Every little detail."

"I want to see," I said. "Help me up."

With her steadying arm for support, I managed to get upright and turned slightly to watch the pen dancing over the page of the grimoire. The book was resting beside the Casket of Morpheus on my bedside table.

"Is that what you saw in the dream?" Tori asked.

"To the letter," I replied. "The man with his hand out-stretched blowing the dust just stepped out of the shadows before the old guy knew what happened. When he gasped, so did I and that's when vertigo hit me, and I woke up."

Putting the last strokes on the drawing, the pen turned to face me inquisitively. "Thanks," I said, "that's it for now."

With that, the writing instrument went horizontal, descended slowly toward the grimoire, and smoothly slid itself back into the leather loop.

"I have got to get one of those pens," Tori said. "That thing beats an Etch-A-Sketch all to hell and back."

When I put the grimoire in my lap, she sat down on the side of the bed with me as we studied the scene. "Your green stuff worked," I said. "I wanted more detail. I'd say we got detail."

"And then some," Tori agreed, "but what does it mean?"

Sliding open the top drawer of the bedside table, I took out a magnifying glass and held it over the figure of the elderly man. "Look," I said. "There, under his shirt. Do you see the chain and the top of the pendant?"

Tori took the glass and squinted at the drawing. "Yeah," she said. "He's definitely wearing something under this shirt."

"Not something," I said. "He's wearing the Amulet of Caorunn. I think the dream showed me how it was stolen."

"Okay," Tori said, "but *where* was it stolen?"

"Your guess is as good as mine," I said. "The buildings are old. I'm thinking Europe. Maybe you can go online and try to find some place that looks the same?"

She reached into the pocket of her sweats and took out her phone. "It's a long shot," she said, snapping pictures of the page, "but I'll give it a try. It's not much, but at least it's a start."

"It's more than a start," I said, holding the magnifying glass over the face of the thief. "If I see this guy in real life, I'll recognize him."

"Any chance I can talk you out of repeating this little experiment until we have more information?" Tori asked.

"No problem," I said. "I'm not anxious to get hit with another dream-based whammy of any kind."

Trust me. I said it with complete conviction, but as it turns out, the Casket of Morpheus had other ideas.

FOUR

A Secluded Estate, Location Unknown

Irenaeus Chesterfield removed the jeweler's loupe and regarded his prized pocket watch with a look of infinite regret. The instrument had flawlessly transported the wizard to bookmarked locations in time and allowed him to move laterally across the stream of present hours. But now, under the damnable weight of the natural order, the glittering diamond set in the watch's face was poised to shatter.

Using the loupe's magnification, Irenaeus found fine cracks radiating from the gem's center, already distorting the inclusion at the heart of the diamond that allowed it to focus and channel temporal magic. The stone, acquired in Egypt after the Second Crusade, could not be replaced.

Chesterfield would need a compelling reason indeed to initiate the diamond's ultimate destruction; for now, he returned the gold watch to the pocket of his vest. Rising from his chair, he put on a maroon silk smoking jacket, tying the black belt with studied precision. Finding comfort in the gesture, Irenaeus paused to drink in the elegance and sophistication of his new home.

Although pained by the loss of his apartment and antique store in Raleigh, he had long ago become accus-

34

tomed to casting off one identity for another. Immortality demands sacrifice and subterfuge. At least he was free of his blessedly brief but barbaric sojourn in a dank cavern lying beneath the North Carolina mountains bordering Tennessee. While perhaps not the worst lodgings he'd endured in his long life, Irenaeus far preferred civilization's comforts.

The late afternoon sun slanted across the glass fronts of the cabinets lining the walls of the baronial study. Each contained treasures and curiosities collected over centuries. The objects formed a visual record of Chesterfield's long journey.

Now, as the only Creavit in North America, he stood far distant from his origins as the scorned, defective second son of Gregorius Chesterfield—and yet, an image of his father's scowling face still rose unbidden in Irenaeus' mind.

No matter what the son accomplished, no matter how far he advanced his practice of magic, he could not exorcise that wretched father from his memories or dreams.

Or at least that had always been the case. Soon Irenaeus would be the most feared self-made wizard in the human realm—a fact he alas could not hold over the long-dead Gregorius.

Instead, Irenaeus would exact his familial revenge from the sufferings of his pious brother, Barnaby. The Lord High Mayor of the sanctuary city of Shevington would regret his feigned superiority as would the turncoat, assimilated Creavit of Europe—those lapdogs who had once shared Chesterfield's vision of a new age of made magic. For their sin of collaboration, the fools would pay in equal measure with the Hereditarium.

A knock at the door interrupted his thoughts. Smoothing his lapels, Irenaeus stood away from his desk and stepped across the priceless Louis XV Savonnerie carpet.

Positioning himself to greet his visitor with the air of a gracious gentleman, Irenaeus said simply, "Come."

The carved mahogany door swung silently on well-oiled hinges to reveal a slender, slightly elven man dressed in dark trousers. A tweed vest covered his faded workman's shirt, and in one hand he held a soft cloth cap. "Begging your pardon, Mr. Chesterfield," he said, "but your guest has arrived."

"Thank you, Liam," Chesterfield replied. "Show the lady in."

Stepping to the side, the man ushered an old woman through the entrance. The cold breeze that preceded her accentuated the pale blue tinge of her skin. She wore a long, gray cloak and carried a gnarled wooden staff. With each rap of the wood against the floor, small circles of ice crystals formed.

"Cailleach Bheur," Chesterfield said, bowing. "Welcome to my home."

"What business have you with the Queen of Winter?" the old woman asked sharply, her breath fogging the air as she spoke. "I am not accustomed to being summoned by self-aggrandizing pretenders."

Although he stiffened, Chesterfield's pleasant expression remained carefully in place. "Not summoned," he said, "invited. Would you care to join me by the fire?"

Cailleach turned and regarded the hearth. "It is a myth that I do not enjoy the warmth," she said absently. "I will sit with you."

Chesterfield turned to the servant who still stood, cap in hand, at the door. "That will be all, Liam. Thank you."

"Yes, sir, Mr. Chesterfield," the man said, bobbing his head and closing the door behind him.

"He is not of the human world," Cailleach said, lowering her body into one of the chairs. "Nor is he of the Otherworld. He smells of the In Between. What is he doing here?"

"Working for me," Chesterfield said, taking the chair across from her. "May I offer you anything?"

"You may answer my question," she said. "What business have you with the Queen of Winter?"

Steepling his fingers, Chesterfield said, "You are the Queen of Winter for now, but indolent Spring will soon come knocking at your door sending you into exile, will it not?"

Anger kindled in the old woman's crystalline eyes. "Do not dare to diminish me, wizard," she said. "I am and always shall be Mistress of the Cold. I create a world of icy beauty where the earth slumbers beneath blankets of snow and rivers pause in their course. My voice drives mortals shrinking into their pitiful dwellings to hunker by the fireside. Through my dominion, they find gratitude in their petty hearts for hot food and warm beds."

Chesterfield continued to regard her impassively. "It is upon those truths that my plans depend," he said. "Do you not weary of the yearly transition? Of the need to melt away beneath the incessantly sunny gaze of Brighid?"

Studying him warily, Cailleach said, "I have no love for the Queen of Summer, but the way of things demands the coming of her season and the waning of mine. So it has always been, and so it shall always be."

"Why?" Chesterfield asked.

The crone blinked in confusion. "Do you wish me to tell you any one of the hundred tales the humans use to explain the passing of the seasons?" she asked. "Even a Creavit should know that the winter months have been my dominion since the days when the Tuatha Dé Danann ruled the earth."

Choosing to ignore the pointed insult, Chesterfield said, "The tribe of the gods has long since retreated from the affairs of the human realm. You are not one of the Tuatha Dé Danann, yet you faithfully follow the old order.

Where do you go when the days turn warm, and the earth grows green?"

"I retreat to the far lonely places," Cailleach said simply. "They are my sanctuary."

"And are you not losing that sanctuary?" Chesterfield asked. "Does not the ice at the top of the world diminish each year and with it your place of repose?"

Cailleach nodded slowly. "It does," she said cautiously, "but how is that any of your affair?"

"I, too, have suffered from the superiority of the Fae," Chesterfield said. "The greed of the Queen of Summer seeks to overwhelm your dominion. Brighid, the daughter of Dagda, does not know her place. She is not a faithful servant of the natural order as are you, dear Cailleach. Would you not like to teach this presumptuous child a lesson?"

At first, she didn't answer, but then Cailleach said slowly, "Perhaps. What do you suggest?"

Rising smoothly to his feet, Chesterfield crossed to a cabinet near his desk. Extracting a key from his pocket, he opened the heavy glass doors and carefully removed a flat box covered in black velvet. Returning to his chair, the wizard opened the case and showed the contents to Cailleach.

"I suggest," he said, "that at the stroke of midnight on the Winter Solstice you fasten the Amulet of Caorunn around your neck, thus preventing the fading of your dominion."

Cailleach studied the amulet. "What is its power?" she asked with thinly disguised interest.

"The rejuvenation of that which has faded."

The old woman snorted. "An enchanted trinket will not stop Brighid from pressing her case for the ascendancy of summer," she said.

"Let me worry about Brighid," Chesterfield replied. "I

assure you the amulet will prevent the waning of your powers. I will give it to you in exchange for a small favor."

Cailleach's eyes narrowed. "Now we come to it," she spat. "I do not do your bidding, Creavit."

Chesterfield held up one hand. "Wait until you hear what I ask. All that you must do is plunge the area of the United States known as the Deep South into the clutches of an unrelenting winter storm. In particular, I wish the state of North Carolina to experience near arctic conditions."

Cocking her head, the Queen of Winter said, "And the rest of the world?"

"Visit whatever conditions on the globe suits your purpose," he replied. "Only do as I ask in this one region until I tell you otherwise."

"How long may I keep the amulet?" Cailleach asked.

"Once you take possession of this box," Chesterfield said, "the amulet is yours. If I am successful in my designs, I will rule over a new order of magic in the realm of the humans. I do not require unrelenting sunshine to do so. We can negotiate the state of that world's climate at some future date."

For the first time, the old woman smiled. "You do not require the heat of the sun because the depths of your heart are as cold as my own."

"Colder," Chesterfield said, holding out the box. "Have we concluded an accord?"

Cailleach's blue-veined hands started to reach for the amulet, but the crone stopped. "And if you fail?" she asked.

"If I fail," he said, "I have no doubt the precious forces of the 'natural order' will reassert themselves."

"And if I say no?"

The wizard fixed her with a flat stare. "Then my next conversation will be with Brighid. It matters not to me if the world is plunged into deep winter or hellish summer. The choice is yours."

After a moment's pause, Cailleach took the box.

"Remember," Chesterfield warned, "do not put the amulet on until the stroke of midnight on the solstice."

"I understand," Cailleach said, running her fingers over the smooth amber. "When do you wish cold to fall upon the South?"

"You may begin to deepen winter in the region as soon as you like, but on Monday, December 28th, a storm must paralyze all of North Carolina," he said. "Build the intensity of the event to the turning of the New Year. By that day, I wish to see the state powerless and encased in ice. Can you do that?"

Cailleach's eyes flashed. "I can do that," she said. "I can do that and much, much more."

FIVE

The experiment with double enchanting the Casket of Morpheus didn't leave me in a frame of mind to go downstairs and use magic for anything that day. That's not something I typically do when there are customers in the store anyway, but then a situation landed right in my lap that I couldn't ignore.

Okay, I *could* have ignored it, but I didn't.

When I walked outside to sweep off the sidewalk, I ran straight into Chase working on the same chore.

I've never been the type of woman who refuses to speak to an ex-boyfriend again—unless he's been a total jerk. I can't say Chase handled ending things with me gracefully, but he didn't leave me hating him. Frankly, things would have been easier if he had.

Generally, when a relationship falls apart, there's a post-break-up cooling-off period to allow for closure. That's when you manage to find enough equanimity to speak to the guy you were dating when you see him in the post office and ask him how his grandma's doing.

I should be so lucky.

Chase lives next door, and we've got this whole sworn destiny protection *thing* going on. Getting away from each other hasn't been an option. Now, admittedly, after *he* broke up with *me*, my anger and hurt feelings did win out over my better impulses.

Chase endured the sharp edge of my tongue for weeks, especially when Lucas Grayson showed up and Chase decided it was a good idea to play the jealous ex. Bad choice. Seriously bad choice.

That attitude did not work with me, and Mr. McGregor heard about it in no uncertain terms—from me and finally from Festus who came right out and told his son to grow the hell up.

Since then, things have been better between me Chase and me. But here's the deal. Even though I don't admit it to anyone, not even Tori, I'm still trying to get over him.

Imagine, then, how not thrilled I was to step out my front door, broom in hand, and find Chase talking to Ann Marie Detwiler right there on Main Street. To put it bluntly, the only men in three counties that woman hasn't gone after are the guys on life support over at the Leisure Lodge Nursing Home.

The first words I heard came slithering out of her mouth. "Oh, *Chase!*" she gushed. "Do you really think you can fix them? They're just my *favorite* pumps in the *whole* world."

The fact that I didn't immediately swat her with my broom proves that I have enormous self-control—restraint I almost lost when Ann Marie spotted me and squealed, "Norma *Jean* Hamilton, just look at you! If we weren't in direct light, I'd swear you haven't aged a day!"

Chase coughed into his hand so he wouldn't laugh. I gritted my teeth, and said, "Why thank you, Ann Marie. Is that your original hair color? I honestly don't remember, honey."

"Oh, Jinx," Ann Marie trilled. "You always did try to have a sense of humor."

Chase must have seen something flash in my eyes he took as a warning sign because he dove between us, which was, frankly, an act of raw courage.

"Ann Marie, why don't we take your shoes inside and let me have a closer look at them?" he suggested.

Batting her fake eyelashes until they looked like a pair of epileptic butterflies, she said, "Whatever you think, Chase. You're the professional."

"Go on in and make yourself at home," he told her. "I'll be right with you."

When the door closed behind her, I muttered something dark and entirely inappropriate. Grinning at me, Chase said, "I take it the two of you know each other?"

"We went to school together," I said sourly. "Watch yourself. She collects men like scalps."

"I think I can handle her," he said. "I'm a big boy."

The remark could have been delivered with that particular wording on purpose, or my imagination might have been in overdrive, but the sentiment came across just a tad more wolfish than I liked.

As he disappeared into the cobbler shop, I took a couple of vigorous—okay, vicious—swipes at the concrete with the broom and went back inside myself.

The morning regulars were engrossed in their books and crossword puzzles. Tori was cleaning the espresso machine, and we had Mindy in the storeroom bundling herbs. No one was paying any attention to me.

Making a show of re-folding a stack of t-shirts shelved on the wall we share with Chase's shop, I waved my palm over a hand mirror on display and muttered, *"Revelabit."*

The surface of the mirror swirled and then showed me the interior of the building next door—complete with sound. Chase was sitting at his workbench, practically staring right at me, with Ann Marie hanging over his shoulder.

"Magis praestiterunt silentium," I ordered.

The volume dropped, but not before I heard Ann Marie say, "Why don't we have dinner sometime since you're not seeing anyone?"

I couldn't hear what Chase said in response, but he smiled when he said it. That was enough for me.

"*Extinctus,*" I said, the word cracking around the lump in my throat.

The image in the mirror disappeared. I had no intention of standing there watching Chase make a date with another woman. Especially not a woman like Ann Marie Detwiler.

It was bad enough *knowing* that's what he was doing.

That *was* what he was doing . . . wasn't it?

Something tugged on my pants leg. I looked down to find Rodney staring up at me.

"What are you doing running around out here during business hours?" I asked. "I thought we talked about this."

In response, Rodney quickly scaled the leg of my jeans, hopped to the crook of my arm, and ran up to perch on my shoulder. He shot me a worried, inquisitive look.

"I'm fine," I said. "Eavesdroppers get what they deserve."

Rodney cocked his head in question.

Gesturing toward the mirror, I said, "I used it to look into Chase's shop. He's over there flirting with a woman."

Standing up on his hind legs, Rodney balled his paws into tiny fists and punched at the air. A surge of love washed through me. "If you were big enough, you'd do it, wouldn't you, Sir Galahad?" I asked fondly.

The rat's chest puffed out, and he nodded.

"You don't need to punch Chase out for me," I assured him. "We're not dating anymore. It's none of my business if he decides to take up with loose, trashy women."

It was Rodney's turn to laugh.

"Trust me," I assured him. "Ann Marie Detwiler is a total tramp."

The expression on the rat's face was unmistakable.

"Don't you give me that 'you're not being nice' look," I said. "She *is* a tramp. Just ask Tori."

"Ask Tori what?" my BFF said, coming up behind us.

"If Ann Marie Detwiler is a tramp," I said.

Tori offered up such a colorful description of Ann Marie's morals, Rodney put his paws over his ears. She finished with, "And why in God's name are you talking about that slut anyway?"

"Because she's next door gushing all over Chase," I said.

It was Tori's turn to give me a look. "And you know this how?" she asked.

A guilty blush started across my cheeks. "I ran into them on the sidewalk," I said.

Catching sight of the mirror on the shelf and accurately gauging my growing level of discomfort, Tori put two and two together at the speed of light. "Did you spy on them?" she hissed. "Jinx! Seriously?"

"Just long enough to see her hanging all over him and asking him to dinner," I said defensively. "Then I cut it off."

"Did he say yes?" Tori asked.

"He was smiling," I said hotly.

"But was it an 'I'm letting you down easy because I can see you're trouble' or a 'hot damn, you bet I'll go out with you' smile?" she persisted.

That stumped me. "I don't know," I admitted.

"Then how about you wait to plot the man's murder until you have evidence," she suggested, "and while we're at it, explain to me why you're upset about your ex boyfriend going out if you don't care about him anymore?"

Oh, hell no. We were not going there.

"I have to inventory the essential oils," I said, handing Rodney to her. "I'll talk to you two later."

With that, I stomped off, and I didn't look back. I already knew they were both grinning at me. I didn't need to see it.

Six

Chase McGregor broke two eggs into a frying pan and watched as the transparent liquid surrounding the yolk slowly turned white and solidified. He almost jumped out of his skin at the sound of unexpected footsteps on the hardwood kitchen floor.

Wheeling around expecting to find an intruder, he confronted a much more confounding sight, his father, in human form, wearing gray trousers, a white shirt, and a navy blazer.

"Dad, you scared the daylights out of me," Chase said. "What on earth are you doing shifted and dressed?"

"And a cheerful good morning to you, too, boy," Festus said, pouring himself a cup of coffee. "Don't let my egg yolks run."

"You tell me that every day," Chase said. Returning his attention to the stove, he switched off the heat, deftly slid the eggs on a plate, and picked up a knife and fork.

"Stop!" Festus ordered.

Chase looked at him perplexed and then realized that his father was currently equipped with opposable thumbs. "Sorry," Chase said, putting the plate on the table in front of Festus. "Force of habit."

Sitting down with his coffee, Chase said, "You didn't answer my question. Usually, on a Monday, morning you're trying to decide if you want to nap in the sun puddle at the front of the shop or snooze by the fire in the lair. Why are you going to Raleigh?"

"None of your business," Festus replied, buttering his toast. "You always were bad to ask too many questions around Christmas time."

"Christmas is almost a month away, and you do your shopping online," Chase replied. "What gives, Dad?"

"What *gives*," Festus said, "is that you need to quit being so nosey. I'll be back by supper. Think you can manage without my expert guidance and advice for that long?"

"I'll do my best to muddle through," Chase said, picking up the paper. Then, as if the idea just occurred to him, he peered over the top of the sports section at Festus. "You're not going to do anything illegal are you?"

"Don't be ridiculous," Festus said, licking the back of his hand and scrubbing at his face.

"Uh, Dad," Chase said.

"What?" Festus asked, staring at him.

"That's a hand, not a paw. Humans use napkins."

"Oh," Festus said absently. "I knew that. Don't worry about me. I'm not going to get into any trouble today. When the humans look at me, they just see a crippled senior citizen."

"Wash your face like that again, and they'll see a crippled senior citizen with Alzheimer's," Chase said drily.

Draining the last of his coffee and standing up stiffly, Festus said, "Duly noted. See you tonight, boy."

By the time he reached the downstairs door to the basement, Festus wished he could shift back to his usual ginger cat self. His hip already hurt and he hadn't even gotten out of his house. But, painful or not, this errand demanded human form. The Mordecai Historic Park was closed on Mondays, which created an opportunity to get inside and talk to the resident haunt.

With a little help from Rube and a ferret named Stinky who had a paw for forgery, Festus would be presenting his credentials to the security guard as Dr. F. James McGregor, an eminent scholar studying extant 18th-century southern structures. That and a letter of permission should get him inside long enough to talk to the ghost of Mary Willis Mordecai Turk.

When he walked into the lair, Festus found Beau deep in online research at his roll top desk with Glory serving as his assistant. The Colonel looked up from the screen of his laptop and frowned, "May I ask how you got in here sir?" he said.

From under the desk, Beau's spectral coonhound, Duke, whined.

"Lighten up, Beau," Festus replied. "And that goes for you, too, Roadkill. I got in here the way I always do."

Beau's brows drew together in puzzlement, and then recognition dawned. "Festus?" he said. "Good heavens. I have never seen you in human form."

Glory climbed on top of a stack of books and craned her neck to get a better look. "Well, I'll be danged," she said, "you're handsome. In an older guy sort of way."

Duke, who drew enough energy from the fairy mound to be partially solid, thumped his tail against the desk.

Scowling first at her and then at the dog, Festus said, "You're not bad looking for a dill pickle, either, but I can't say much for the canine cadaver."

That sent Duke's tail wagging even more furiously.

"Yep," Glory said. "That's Festus, alright. No doubt about it."

From one of the chairs by the fireplace, the lilting sound of a woman's laugh brought a smile to Festus' features. "Hey, gorgeous," he said. "I didn't see you sitting over there. Care to give an old man a lift to the Raleigh portal?"

Greer MacVicar set aside the book in her hands and

uncoiled from the chair in one fluid movement. Her deep auburn hair flowed over the shoulders of her black blouse, accentuating the emerald depths of her eyes.

"You always have liked the flight of the baobhan sith," she said, walking toward the desk.

Festus watched her with openly approving eyes. "How can I resist when you go around looking all dark and dangerous like that," he said.

From the desktop, Glory chimed in curiously. "Wait a minute, did you two have a thing?"

"Gentlemen don't tell tales," Festus said, taking Greer's hand and kissing her knuckles. "No matter how good the story might be."

"You old rascal," Greer said fondly. Then she looked at Glory and mouthed, "We'll talk."

The miniature green witch giggled and gave Greer the thumbs up sign.

"Do you have business in Raleigh today?" Beau asked.

"I do," Festus replied. "You need me to pick something up for you?"

"As a matter of fact," Beau said, "an antiquarian establishment in Brightleaf Square has acquired a personal journal relevant to my genealogical research. I can contact them via electronic mail and authorize you to retrieve it for me if you would be so kind."

"No problem," Festus said. "You still working on finding out what happened to your people after the Civil War?"

"I am," Beau said. "It would seem I have a rather elderly bachelor nephew several times removed who may be in possession of some items that belonged to my late wife. It would mean a great deal to me were I able to retrieve some physical remembrance of her."

Festus nodded. "I understand," he said, adding gruffly. "When I'm in Raleigh, I put flowers on my Jenny's grave. You never stop missing them."

"Indeed you do not," Beau agreed sadly.

The two men fell into an awkward silence. Glory dabbed at her eyes with a tiny handkerchief she extracted from the sleeve of her purple cardigan. Greer saved them all when she said, "Shall we, Master McGregor?"

"Yeah," Festus said. "Off to see the wizard."

At those words, Glory let out a strangled cry. "You're not going to see *him* are you?" she gasped.

"Now see what you've done," Greer said to Festus with a reproving glare.

"Geez," Festus grumbled. "It's a line from a freaking movie, Glory. Nobody knows where Chesterfield is now."

Glory's face blanched to a pale jade. "That's what scares me most of all," she said.

"You are perfectly safe here with me," Beau said kindly. "Perhaps I might direct your attention back to the census records on Ancestry.com?"

The question successfully re-engaged the researcher part of Glory's brain. She hopped down and returned to her iPad, but not without a nervous backward glance at Festus and Greer. Before the miniature witch could have another panic attack, they quietly made their escape, nodding at Beau as they exited the lair.

When Greer was sure they could no longer be heard, she stopped and faced Festus. "Now," she said pleasantly, "tell me the truth about this errand of yours."

"I'm just going up to Raleigh to tend to some personal business," Festus said defensively.

"My dear, Festus," she said, laying her hands on his shoulders. "You are shifted and wearing nice clothes. Do not even attempt to lie, not to me. What are you up to?"

Festus frowned. "Don't be pulling any of that baobhan sith mesmerization crap with me."

A lazy smile curved the corners of Greer's lips. "When did I ever need vampiric powers to mesmerize you?"

Swallowing hard, Festus said, "You don't play fair."

"Fair play is rarely fun," Greer countered. "Talk to me, Festus."

When he finished his account of the plan Jinx had to get information on Chesterfield's meeting with John Smyth, Greer sighed. "She can be so adorably young. Does she think that Barnaby and Moira are not actively searching for the Amulet?"

"Her brother's home. She wants everybody to have a nice Christmas, but she doesn't want to shirk her responsibility either," Festus said. "She's come a long way from the scared young woman who went running out of the lair when we told her about the Otherworld and the Fae."

"Is it any wonder she ran?" Greer asked. "You told me you shifted in front of her."

Festus shrugged. "The 2 x 4 upside the head approach seemed to be the right answer at the time," he said. "What are the big bosses in Shevington up to?"

"They have Lucas running around the globe gathering information," Greer said. "Most of it has to do with Chesterfield and Brenna Sinclair."

"Did they not get the memo?" Festus asked. "You know, 'ding dong the witch is dead?'"

Greer laughed. "You are quite full of *Wizard of Oz* references today."

"The movie was on the other night," Festus said. "I laugh my tail off every time I see that thing. How would the humans feel if they knew Frank Baum was Fae and he based that whole story on the Otherworld and the In Between?"

"I suspect in inimitable human fashion, they would break out the torches and pitchforks," Greer replied. "Now, let us get to Raleigh and get about our business."

"You're going to stay with me?" Festus asked.

"My dear boy, you do not look like a visiting professor

regardless of your attempt to strike an academic pose,"
she said. "Your plan is badly in need of some feminine
wiles."

"If you're planning to pose as my graduate student,"
Festus said, "you're a little too hot for the job."

"Thank you," Greer said, "and we will be making a
couple of stops to acquire props before we approach the
security personnel at Mordecai House."

With that, she held out her hand. When Festus took it,
the air around them warmed and began to churn. As the
archive faded from their sight, Greer said, "Hold on Festus,
we're not in Kansas anymore."

They materialized in an alley behind an upscale retail
district. While Festus sat on a bench in the sun and waited,
Greer went shopping. When she was done, they ducked
behind the buildings again. Greer took out a vial of fairy
dust, sprinkled some on the palm of her hand, and then,
chanting softly, tossed it into the air.

"Cloaking spell?" Festus asked.

"Yes," Greer replied, closing the top two buttons on
her blouse. "Of short duration. Just long enough for me to
make some alterations in my look."

She reached into one of the smaller bags and took out
a jewelry box holding a severe black onyx brooch, which
she fastened against her throat. Then she drew a soft, gray
cashmere sweater out of another bag. Next Greer kicked
off her stiletto heels, replacing them with a pair of sensible
Mary Janes. She completed the subtle transformation by
twisting her flaming hair up into a high bun and donning
black horn-rimmed glasses.

"Well?" she asked Festus, who had been watching her
with bemused interest.

"Now you look like a hot librarian," he said.

"But a librarian all the same," Greer replied, stashing
the packages behind a pile of crates. "We'll retrieve these

later when we return so that I can purchase the killer Louboutins I just saw. Those are shoes, by the way."

Pasting on his trademark scowl, Festus said, "I'm a male, not a moron. I know what Louboutins are, but how do you know they'll still be there when you get back?"

"Because I enchanted them to look like unusually ugly Birkenstocks," Greer replied, "and might I add that making Birkenstocks look even worse than their normal hideous appearance is no small feat. Do not underestimate my retail powers, dear boy."

As he took her hand, Festus said honestly, "Darling, I'm not about to underestimate you, period."

Seven

Half an hour later, after a dazed security guard left them standing in the dim foyer of the Mordecai House, Festus said, "Geez, what was I saying about not underestimating you? What the *heck* did you do to that guy?"

Greer shook her head and mouthed the word, "Wait."

She closed her eyes and as Festus watched the ruby ring on her left hand began to glow. Greer's lips moved as she whispered the words of an incantation. Festus felt something change, almost as if some of the weight of gravity had been drawn away.

"Did you just stop time?" he asked.

"Yes," Greer said. "I don't see any surveillance cameras, but I'm not willing to take the risk. We will return to this exact spot when we are finished, take a leisurely walk around the ground floor, and then let ourselves out. If we are being observed, all will look perfectly natural."

Festus let out a low whistle. "Dang, you are good," he said. "I didn't even think about a place like this being wired up with cameras."

"The house is beautiful," Greer said, wandering into the parlor and admiring the original furnishings. "Certainly aspects of the 18th century suffered from regrettable primitiveness, but they were interspersed with touches of elegance and graciousness."

"Where were you in the 18th century?" he asked, running his hand along the polished wood of the box grand piano.

"Many places," Greer said a little wistfully. "In the company of people now long gone. It was a period during which I spent a great deal of time with humans. They are so short lived, these fragile friends of ours."

A voice from the doorway said, "That determination depends on how you choose to count the years of our consciousness. In the mortal realm, I lived 79 years, but I have already been granted that much time again on my current plain. Welcome to my home."

Greer approached the woman. "Mrs. Turk?" she asked.

The ghost, who wore a long period dress with a high collar nodded. "I am Mary Mordecai Turk," she said. "Pardon me for being forward, but what are you?"

"Like you," Greer said, "we are not creatures of the human realm. I am Fae and my friend, Festus McGregor, is a shapeshifter."

Festus stepped beside Greer and offered Mrs. Turk a half bow. "My pleasure, ma'am," he said. "Thank you for seeing us."

The spirit's gray form rippled uncertainly. "I do not think I had a choice," she said. I do not show myself in the daylight hours, but when you came inside, you brought power with you. What have you done to the house? The motion of the passing years has stopped."

"A mere bit of magic to ensure that we are not detected," Greer said. "We would like to ask your help with a matter of great importance."

Mrs. Turk frowned. "I have not left these premises since my death," she said. "What help could I be to you?"

"A few weeks ago someone like us, a person with power, concluded a deal in a local restaurant," Festus explained. "He bought something that could hurt a lot of

people, and now we don't know where he is. We're trying
to find out where that deal happened. Can you appeal to
the local spectral community for information on our
behalf?"

"Oh," Mrs. Turk said. "Is that all? Of course. We have
a number of spirits associated with local restaurants and
establishments that sell alcoholic beverages. If you'll
excuse me briefly, I'll ask now."

"By all means," Greer said. "We would be most grateful."

As they watched, Mrs. Turk's form faded to near invisibility. All that was left was a cloud of vague, wispy fog.
After a minute or two, she came back into focus. "A man
such as you describe had dinner in a small restaurant on
South Wilmington Street near the First Baptist Church. The
deceased pastor sensed his presence and feared a devil
threatened his flock."

"Please assure the late minister that the man we seek
is not a devil, though he certainly does not war on the side
of the angels," Greer said. "Also let the pastor know that
we will be visiting the area shortly and that we mean neither he nor his flock any harm."

Mrs. Turk nodded. "I will do so," she said. Then, with
faltering hesitation, she asked, "Could you not stay a few
minutes? I cannot recall when last I spoke with someone
from the world of the living. Perhaps I could play the piano
for you?"

Festus and Greer exchanged a glance and Festus
inclined his head slightly in agreement.

"By chance would you play something by Chopin?"
Greer asked.

"Oh!" the ghost said, brightening to the point that a
suggestion of color filled in the outlines of her form. "That
would be lovely. I am quite fond of Mr. Chopin's noc-
turnes."

As Mrs. Turk settled herself at the keyboard, Greer whispered to Festus, "You're nothing but an old softie."

"Hmphf," he grumbled. "I'm no such thing, I just figure living or dead, everybody wants an audience now and then."

"I repeat, you're an old softie," Greer said, laying her hand on his arm, "and a very nice man when you get it in your mind to be."

"Hush," Festus said, a blush spreading over his cheeks, "dead lady playing."

When the impromptu recital ended, and they had taken their leave of Mrs. Turk, Greer and Festus returned to the foyer and positioned themselves for possible video surveillance. With a few whispered words, Greer released the stream of time.

As planned, they circled the first floor, stopping periodically to engage in mock-scholarly conversation. Once outside, the pair exited the park onto Mimosa Street without bothering to say anything to the security guard.

"Are you sure that doesn't leave a hole in our 'visiting scholar' cover story," Festus asked as they crossed the empty street and ducked under some trees at the back of a funeral home parking lot.

"Quite sure," Greer said. "I planted the memory of our cordial departure in his mind with the initial mesmerization. If anyone should ask, he will offer up quite a tidy little story about our time at the house complete with earnest assertions affirming our bona fides. Shall we?"

Festus took her hand, and they made a short flight to the First Baptist Church, an imposing red brick structure with a high, cross-bedecked steeple. No sooner had they landed than a ghost in pastor's garb came rushing out of the sanctuary brandishing a Bible.

"Get thee behind me, devil!" he commanded.

Greer shook her head, covering her eyes with one hand.

"My dear fellow," she said patiently, "I kept company with the chief translator of the King James Bible. The phrase you are looking for is 'get thee behind me, Satan.' You have my word that I am not Lucifer nor am I in his employ."

The minister, keeping the Bible raised in front of his chest, eyed Festus. "What about you?" he demanded.

"Me?" Festus purred. "I'm sweet as a pussycat."

Stifling a laugh, Greer said, "We are only here to investigate the previous devil you encountered."

The preacher nodded. "That man was most certainly evil," he said. "He had the smell of brimstone on his very soul."

"Right," Festus said, "brimstone. Got it. Could you point out the joint where he had dinner?"

Pursing his lips in self-righteous disapproval, the minister gestured toward a restaurant a couple of doors down. "There," he said, "that is the den of iniquity."

"Den of iniquity?" Greer asked. "It looks like a perfectly respectable establishment."

"Hardly," the minister replied. "They serve intoxicating beverages."

Craning his neck for a better look, Festus said, with interested eyes, "They do?"

"Indeed," the ghost said, "but I assure you such things did not occur in the vicinity of this house of God when I was alive."

"I have no doubt," Greer said drily. "Thank you for your help."

The preacher turned and floated back through the nearest wall, then stuck his head back out of the bricks. "I will be in the sanctuary should you need assistance in doing battle with the minions of Beelzebub." And with that, he was gone.

"Some people get smarter after they die," Festus said. "That guy wasn't one of them."

"Now, now," Greer said, "he is simply following the faith of his convictions. Shall we speak to the restaurant staff?"

"You go on without me," Festus said.

Greer arched an eyebrow. "You are turning down the chance for an intoxicating beverage?"

"If I go back to Briar Hollow with booze on my breath I'll have to listen to that boy of mine lecturing me about acting my age," he said. "Chase is a good guy, but I'm telling you, he does not take after my side of the family."

"So I gathered," she said. "Very well. I'll make the inquiries. Are you going to wait here?"

"I'll be down there," he said gesturing toward the alley. There are three cats behind that dumpster. I want to talk to them."

Greer peered into the dim space between the buildings. "I don't see anything," she said.

"Of course not," Festus replied, already limping away, "they're in invisible mode."

"I thought you said these were street cats, not Fae creatures," Greer frowned. "How can they be invisible?"

"Shows how much you know," Festus said. "All cats can disappear at will. It's one of the mysterious feline superpowers. Now scat. They won't talk to me if you're around."

As he approached the dumpster, Festus called out a greeting in Felinese. After a few seconds, a black cat looked out cautiously. "Do you truly speak our language?" she asked.

"What," Festus said, "you thought I was just some crazy old human wandering down the alley meowing?"

The black cat stepped into plain view, followed by a calico and a gray, tiger-striped tom. "It's been known to happen," the black cat said. "Humans are a most peculiar lot."

"They are indeed," Festus agreed.

Craning her neck to look over her companion's heads, the calico spoke up. "What are you?" she asked. "You smell like us, but you look like them."

Festus stopped about six feet in front of the trio. "I'm a werecat," he said. "In my small form, I'm a ginger tom. My name is Festus McGregor."

"If you are a werecat," the black cat said, "you know we do not give our true names."

"I do know, Little Sister," Festus said. "I don't need to know your name, I just wondered if you sensed anyone pass by here recently who gave off an aura of power?"

The gray tom arched his back and hissed. "We did," he said, "and he was with the deer man."

"The deer man?" Festus said. "Some guy was down here with deer?"

The black cat drew her whiskers back in disdain. "Are you sure you're not human?" she asked. "Because that's about as bright as something a human would say."

"Hey!" Festus said, pointing an accusing finger at the gray tom. "I'm not the one talking about 'deer men.' I'm just trying to figure out what ole Hissy Fit over there means."

At that, the gray tom let out with a menacing yowl, which Festus returned in kind.

"That's enough!" the black cat said. "I will never understand why you toms feel the incessant need to have these ridiculous face-offs!"

"He started it," Festus growled sourly.

"What*ever*," the black cat said. "He meant the man who was with the powerful one smelled like deer."

"You mean he smelled like he'd been around deer?" Festus asked. "Like he was a hunter?"

"No," the cat replied, "he smelled like he *was* a deer."

EIGHT

Thankfully we had enough customers for the rest of the morning that Tori didn't give me any more grief about using my magic to spy on Chase—or for instantly jumping to the conclusion that he'd accepted Ann Marie's invitation.

I spent a lot of time telling myself he had higher standards—or that he better. The idea that I had gone out with a man who would go out with Ann Marie did not sit well with me.

And then, when I realized just how high school that sounded, my annoyance at myself only grew. Staying busy seemed the best antidote for my runaway thinking.

A little before closing time, Mom and Gemma came through the back door juggling paint cards, tile samples, and carpet swatches. Both of the newly acquired buildings included upstairs apartments currently under renovation and redecoration.

After we locked the front door and turned the "Closed" sign over, Tori and I settled in to listen to the imaginary merits of "Minced Onion" versus "Calming Aloe" before pronouncing the near identical paint shades "pale green."

"Do you need to get your eyes checked?" Mom demanded. "Can't you see that Calming Aloe is darker? I want the kitchen to be light and airy."

"Then paint it white," I said.

Yep, you guessed it. I do not while away Sunday after-
noons glued to the Home & Garden Channel.

"Just like your father," Mom muttered darkly. "If Jeff
had his way, every room in the house would be white, and
we'd have beige carpet. Beige carpet with six dogs."

I let that one slide. They were still working out the
logistics of housing my father's canine pack in an apartment. He'd commandeered what had been the laundry
room to serve as a kennel. In exchange, Mom got a
knocked-out front-loading washer and dryer set, even
though it meant figuring out how to run plumbing into an
extra walk-in closet.

The move won Dad a state of truce, but at best I'd term
it "fragile." Don't get me wrong. Mom loves the dogs, but
she was going to have to see the arrangement in action to
believe it could be made to work.

Since Dad routinely uses my four cats as an argument
in favor of his dogs, I could easily find myself on the wrong
side of the ongoing debate. But the thing is, cat owners
have a major advantage called "litter boxes." Not to mention the one time I tried to put a harness on Winston and
take him for a walk, he collapsed under the weight of the
straps and refused to stand until I removed the hideous
contraption disarranging his fur.

Thankfully, before Mom could get started about the
dogs, Tori emerged from behind the counter with a tray of
bear claws. We made room on the table and Tori went back
for beautifully frothed lattes all around—vanilla for me,
cinnamon for Mom, and caramel for Tori and Gemma.

"So, what hideous color are you planning to paint your
kitchen?" Tori asked her mother.

"I am going with white," Gemma said. "The kitchen in
my place was redone last year with retro black and white
tile, so it's in good shape. I am, however, taking that as an
excuse to buy all new appliances in red."

Brochures for KitchenAid Mixers and Keurig Coffee Machines immediately joined the growing pile of decor-themed detritus in the center of the table.

Leaning back and sipping my latte, I savored the moment. There they were, Mom and Gemma, color coordinating with ruthless efficiency while Tori tossed out her usual running string of off the cuff quips. Being with them made me feel safe and distinctly non-magical. It wouldn't last, but that tiny bubble of normalcy soothed my still jangled nerves.

Not jangled from the encounter with Chase and Ann Marie, but from the dream vision of the theft of the Amulet of Caorunn. That thought, however, I kept strictly to myself.

The conversation veered off to plans for our Thanksgiving dinner at Uncle Raymond's and then moved to the triple birthday celebration we'd have the first week of December for Tori, Connor and me.

Watching my mother plan a party for her son filled me with quiet joy. If Connor and I had grown up together, we probably would have experienced typical sibling jealousy, but I feel nothing of the kind now. I want my parents to have every joyous occasion with him possible after the long years they lived without him.

The sound of boot heels on the hardwood made me look toward the basement door. Beau crossed the space toward us, offering the group a half bow. "Is this gathering strictly confined to the ladies, or might a hungry soldier claim a pastry and join your company?" he asked.

Mom and Gemma scooted over and made a place for Beau, who snagged a chair from an adjoining table. "I fear," he said, reaching for a bear claw, "that I have become nearly as addicted to these confections as you have, Miss Jinx."

"Hey!" I said. "I am not an addict. I prefer to think of myself as an appreciative consumer."

"Tell yourself that when your jeans start getting tight," Tori said, taking another pastry for herself.

"And you're immune to calories?" I asked.

Actually, she is. Tori eats like a horse and never gains an ounce. She came back with the response I expected since I'd heard it a million times. "I'm blessed with a high metabolism," she replied, biting into the bear claw and depositing a neatly glazed frosting mustache on her upper lip.

In a thoroughly motherly gesture, Gemma reached over with her napkin and wiped her daughter's face.

"Mom," Tori complained, "I am not three years old."

"That," Gemma said, "depends completely on how you are behaving at any given moment. Grown or not, I am not having my child go around with a dirty face."

The banter continued back and forth until Dad came wandering in with a stack of fishing supply catalogs under his arm. Even though we'd been munching on the bear claws, Darby materialized and asked if everyone would be staying for supper.

I suddenly realized this is how our new family life would look—a constant round of spontaneous gatherings and shared time both in Briar Hollow and in our other home, the Valley of Shevington.

That, much more than our combined powers, would always make us stronger than an embittered man like Irenaeus Chesterfield. The realization warmed and comforted me.

My state of cozy familial awareness was so strong; I even called Chase and asked him to join us for supper in the lair. We'd just pulled our chairs back when Greer and Festus, in human form, came walking out of the stacks.

"Hey!" Festus crowed. "Is this good timing or what? I'm starved." The words were barely out of his mouth before he shifted back to his ginger tom self, jumped clear of his discarded clothes, and landed on the table with a resounding *thump*.

"What does a cat have to do to get a plate around here?" he demanded. "Give me some of everything, and somebody cut up my roast beef."

Shaking his head as he filled a plate, Chase said, "So glad to have you back Dad. There was far too much civility around here in your absence."

Flicking his tail and narrowly missing the gravy boat, Festus said, "I'm perfectly civil, but I'm also hungry. Get a move on, boy."

"Where have you two been?" I asked lightly, knowing danged well Festus had gone to Raleigh that day and apparently taken the baobhan sith with him.

"Christmas shopping," Greer said, right on cue. I picked up a hint of a conspiratorial gleam in her eye.

Reaching for the rolls, I said, "Get any good buys?"

"I did," she said. "I picked up a little something for myself."

She took out a Louboutin shoebox and displayed a pair of black stiletto pumps that sent Glory into a paroxysm of shoe envy, which also served to deflect any further questions about the purpose of the Raleigh trip.

"You people have *got* to help a girl out!" Glory wailed. "You're all witches for heaven's sake! Can't one of you shrink a pair of those *heavenly* shoes down to my size?"

That's when Greer delivered the coup de grâce. "This pair," she said, "belong to me, but *these* are for you. An early holiday gift."

Glory took one look at the pink glitter mesh pumps with the six-inch heels and almost fainted into the mashed potato bowl.

"*Really*?" she gasped. "Greer! You bought those for *me*?"

"I did," Greer said, taking her place at the table, "and

I feel quite certain that after we dine someone in this company has the magical ability to make them a perfect fit."

For the rest of the meal, Glory never took her eyes off
the shoes—well, almost never. She spent a good deal of
time glaring at every forkful that went into our mouths,
willing us to eat faster and get on with the Louboutin transformation.

While Darby was cleaning up the table, Dad, Beau, and
Chase spread out the fishing tackle catalogs and instantly
became deeply involved in a conversation on the merits of
live bait as opposed to lures.

By virtue of his 19th-century birth, Beau adopted the
pure position that worms, in the end, are the most "entic-
ing piscine inducement." Chase argued for something
called a jig, and then Dad got on his fly fishing soapbox.
We could have tossed a bottle rocket in the fireplace, and
they wouldn't have noticed.

Mom, Gemma, Tori, and Glory got right on the shoe
thing, which rapidly devolved into a complicated debate
over the correct incantation to use. All were in agreement
that under no circumstance should any Louboutin be
harmed in the execution of the reduction spell.

Lucas, who hadn't shown up until we were done eating, planted himself in one of the leather wingback chairs
by the hearth. Greer joined him and listened patiently to
a long recitation of his day in Cairo. With Lucas none the
wiser, she caught my eye and gave an imperceptible nod
first toward Festus and then in the direction of the alcove.

Festus picked up on the gesture as well and proceeded
to disappear under the table. The curtain over the entrance
to my private nook rippled slightly, and I caught a rapid-
fire glimpse of a yellow tail before the old cat was hidden
from view.

"If anyone wants me, I'll be reading," I said.

No one even noticed I'd said a word.

As I closed the curtain behind me, I said to Festus, "Talk fast. I don't know how much time we have. How did things go in Raleigh?"

I listened in silence until he got to the part about the figure we assumed to be John Smyth smelling like a deer.

That bit of information drew a groan from my throat. "You are *not* getting ready to tell me there's such a thing as weredeer, are you?"

Festus made that cat face. You know the one. Like he just ran straight into a pile of the foulest substance on the planet.

"For Bastet's sake," he said, "you've seen too many bad movies. No, there's no such thing as weredeer. What the heck would a weredeer do anyway? Sprout antlers on the full moon and run around trying to get himself shot?"

He had a point there, but I wasn't ready to give up my skepticism. "Seriously," I said, "you want me to believe that these street cats smelled this guy all the way down the alley?"

"For your information, Miss Superior Humanoid," Festus growled, "the feline sense of smell is roughly fourteen times better than yours. We have twice as many receptors in our noses than you do. And while we're on the subject, there are days when you could step up your game in the deodorant department."

"Back off," I said. "You don't have to get personal about it."

"You started it insulting the street cats," he said, laying his ears flat.

"Okay, okay, fine," I said. "My apologies. If the street cats say they smelled deer, they smelled deer. So what do you think is up with that?"

Festus still regarded me with pursed whiskers, but his ears came back to normal. "I have no idea," he said, "but if you want me to, I'll run it by the triplets at the Registry."

He meant Merle, Earl, and Furl, three Scottish fold brothers, who work with the Registry investigating cases of shapeshifter misbehavior in the human world. They fix what they can and cover up what they can't. We called them in, for instance, when a rogue werecat halfling, Malcolm Ferguson, left a dead man on our front doorstep.

"Okay," I said, "but tell them to keep it quiet. I don't want anyone to know I'm digging into this."

"I know," Festus said, jumping down. "I'm on it. Now let's get back out there and act normal. The last thing I want is to get grilled by Chase when we get home."

"Trust me," I said, getting up, "I don't want to deal with my mother being suspicious any more than you want to deal with your son."

We timed our re-entry perfectly. As I drew back the curtain, a cheer went up from Tori and Gemma's alchemy work area as Glory took her first wobbling steps in the Louboutins. Festus and I slid right back into the scene in the lair like we'd been there all along.

By the time I climbed into bed later that night, I wasn't thinking about Chase and Ann Marie, or even my unpleasant attack with vertigo from the night before. If anything, I had come to the conclusion that the experiment was a total success. We'd put a face on John Smyth, and Festus had come up with the intriguing detail that the man smelled like a deer. That alone might be enough to help narrow our search.

The Casket of Morpheus still sat on my bedside table, but I didn't chant the invocation spell or use any of Tori's green dust. I needed a decent night's sleep, not another wild trip down the rabbit hole. So I shut out the light, shoved the protesting cats over enough to make room for myself, and fell asleep.

You ever think about how we say that—"fall" asleep? If you've ever fallen through a black void in the unconscious depths of slumber, you'll never hear it as a benign turn of phrase again.

In my dream that night, I fell—with flames surrounding my body and searing my flesh. My chest felt as if something had been driven through my rib cage. I don't know what I feared more—dying when I hit bottom or living to endure more agonizing pain.

Without warning, however, my momentum slowed and the air around me cooled. As I passed through a cloud of light mist, the flames went out. I did touch down, but with a feather-light impact.

A voice to my left said, "Lift her carefully," followed by the rhythmic sound of beating wings. In the dreamscape, I lost consciousness, but in my world, I came awake with a start.

My first impulse was to open the grimoire and reach for the pen. Dispensing with formalities, I just said, "Draw it for me."

The pen did as I commanded, creating an impressionistic image first of a woman falling through a swirling voice, her body encased in flame. Then, on the opposing page, the nib began to work on a different scene. The profile of an eagle emerged from the strokes against the backdrop of a rocky cliff. The bird sat beside the fallen woman, who was being tended by a small creature with pointed ears and—horns?

Reaching for the magnifying glass, I studied the drawing more closely. Definitely horns. But then I choked on a strangled breath. The woman lying on the ground with a bloody wound in her chest was Brenna Sinclair.

"Are you sure about this?" I asked the pen, which had returned to its leather enclosure.

My question met with an outraged chirp. "Okay, okay," I said, "you drew what I saw in my dream. Sorry."

Glancing at the clock on the bedside table, I saw it was

almost 2 A.M., but I didn't care. Tori had to see this latest sketch—now.

I went downstairs with the grimoire and the magnifying glass. When I knocked on her apartment door, several seconds passed before my bleary-eyed bestie opened it and looked at me with confusion.

"World ending?" she mumbled.

"Not exactly," I said, pushing past her and plopping on the sofa. "But close enough."

"Come in," she said, as the sarcasm center in her brain woke up. "What happened?"

"You know how you said double enchanting an artifact wasn't a great idea?"

She joined me on the sofa. "This ought to be good," she said. "Say it."

"You were right," I answered automatically. "We kicked the Casket of Morpheus into high gear alright, but we definitely did not find the off switch."

"Why do you say that?"

"Take a look at this," I said, holding out the open book and the magnifying glass.

First, Tori squinted at the woman's face when I pointed it out to her, then she went completely still before flipping on a second lamp and looking again.

"Oh, hell no," she said finally. "What is she? The freaking Energizer Bunny from the dark side?"

NINE

"I continue to have reservations about this, Barnaby," Moira said. "You know that Jinx does not react well when she believes that information is being withheld from her. Given the rapid advancement of both her skills and her understanding, this subterfuge does not seem necessary."

The Lord High Mayor of Shevington sat at the desk in the Alchemist's private study surrounded by piles of books and papers. Beside him, a block of quartz projected images of assorted objects in a holographic array several inches above its polished surface.

"Thank you, Vicus," Barnaby said to the stone. "Please work on cross-referencing the latest information."

"It will be my pleasure, sir," Vicus replied obediently.

Barnaby placed the quartz in his pocket and began fussing with the notebooks spread out on the desk.

"We are not withholding information," he replied stubbornly, avoiding Moira's gaze. "We are merely attempting through careful research to delve more deeply into how my brother's fascination with magical artifacts led him to the Amulet of Caorunn. When we have something to share with Jinx, we will."

Moira moved to stand behind him. She rested her hands on his shoulders, kneading the tense muscles. "Would this have anything to do with your grandfatherly desire to let your family enjoy a proper Christmas?" she asked.

Closing his eyes and leaning back, he said, "Is that such a bad thing?"

"No," Moira said, "but you did make rather a point of emphasizing the urgency attached to recovering this artifact. Do you think that it has escaped Jinx's attention that you have not mentioned it in her presence since?"

Barnaby reached up and caught hold of her hand. "Restoring Caorunn to its rightful place *is* a matter of urgency," he said. "You understand that better than anyone, but the problem is that we cannot predict how Irenaeus will use the amulet unless we have some sense of what other objects he has amassed. Had I known of his acquisition of enchanted timepieces and navigational instruments, perhaps I could have halted his experiments into temporal magic."

Moira's hands stilled. "So now you are gifting yourself with the powers of prognostication?" she asked.

"Please do not let us quarrel," he pleaded.

"Barnaby, in the several centuries we have known one another, I can use the fingers of one hand to count the times we have quarreled," Moira said. "You know that your brother used some means to suppress his powers when we examined him in 1936. Temporal magic is a rare and esoteric skill—one I would have said was completely beyond Irenaeus' abilities."

"But that is just it!" Barnaby said. "He wants us to believe that he has no skills, and yet time and time again he proves that to not be the case. For now, the eleven remaining amulets are safe in the hands of the designated guardians. Colonel Longworth is in possession of the Phoenix. The most pressing question at the moment is what can Irenaeus accomplish with only one amulet."

Moira moved around to perch on the edge of the desk

facing him. "My darling," she said, "you must know that sending Lucas Grayson on errands all over the world is not the answer to that question. Even if you do amass a record of every artifact your brother may have acquired, you cannot fully anticipate how he will use them or the Amulet of Caorunn to further his ambitions. Scholarship has its limitations, Barnaby."

The wizard scrubbed at his face in frustration. "I know him too well, Moira," he said. "Irenaeus ignores the cautionary principles of hereditary magic with complete impunity."

"Your brother does not possess hereditary magic," she pointed out. "Irenaeus follows no rules save for those he creates for himself."

"That does not change the way the forces of magic work!" Barnaby cried in frustration. "There are natural rules! No good has ever come of attempting to marry the powers of individual artifacts. This is precisely the sort of thing he did as a boy when father set him to studying alchemy. I cannot tell you how many times Irenaeus blew up his laboratory or set the castle on fire. He was incorrigible!"

Ignoring the force of the outburst, Moira held out her hand and said simply, "Come."

"Come where?" Barnaby asked with surprise.

"Beyond the confines of these walls," she said. "You have been inside too long. Walk with me in my garden. Allow the fresh air to calm your nerves and clear your mind."

"But snow has begun to fall," Barnaby protested.

"Yes," she said, "and the flakes are large and lovely. This is snow we can enjoy, not the blizzard we've just endured. It is a beautiful winter day. We have our magic and one another to keep us warm. You said you do not wish to argue, so do not argue."

She emphasized the last words with a beguiling smile that erased the frown creasing Barnaby's features. "Very well," he said. "We will walk."

On the third circuit of the garden, when she felt the rigidness of his body begin to soften, Moira said, "Now, are you ready to discuss with me the political motivations behind your decisions to search for the amulet in this manner?"

Barnaby sighed. "Am I so transparent?"

"Only with me," she said. "I know you are not anxious to work with Reynold Isherwood and the Ruling Elders on this matter. It would be far easier to simply present them with the recovered amulet as a fait accompli."

"It most certainly would," he agreed.

"Your concerns do not run to Reynold alone, do they?"

"No," Barnaby admitted. "I am unable to bring myself to trust the motivations of the assimilated Creavit of Europe. They sit among the Elders, Moira. They occupy positions of power and influence in the Fae world on the Continent. These are the very things that led us to leave our home and come to the new world. Perhaps these sentiments mean I am a bigot, but the thoughts remain in my mind."

They made another turn of the garden in silence. Then, as they approached the bench under the arbor, Barnaby said, "Shall we sit?"

When Moira nodded, he used his gloves to brush away the accumulated snow. Once they were settled, Moira reached for his hand. "Forgive me for saying so, Barnaby, but you have only truly known two Creavit, Irenaeus and Brenna. You do not know those who live now in Europe. Many have even intermarried with the Hereditarium."

"I would say that together my brother and the Scottish sorceress have provided me with rather a complete education," he grumbled.

"And I would argue that they have not," Moira replied.

"The means by which a Creavit is made does involve striking a deal with the Darkness, but that does not erase free will from the soul of the created practitioner. Is it so impossible to believe that given time and circumstances, a Creavit might not see the wisdom of genuinely aligning themselves with we of the Hereditarium?"

"A generous viewpoint, my love," Barnaby said.

"I think you can offer a better response to my assertion than that," she chided softly.

Barnaby sighed. "You are a relentless woman," he said. "Very well, then. Your viewpoint is also a fair one, and mine perhaps is not. I must return to City Hall now, but I promise I will think about the things you have said and we will talk more this evening."

Moira leaned in and gave him a lingering kiss.

"Your nose is cold," Barnaby said when she pulled away slightly.

"But my heart is made warm by you," she said. "Now, go to work."

He stood and offered her his hand, but Moira shook her head. "I'm going to sit out here for a bit," she said. "I have not yet meditated today."

"Won't you be too cold?" he asked with concern.

"Not if I meditate properly," she smiled.

Barnaby laughed. "Very well," he said. "I will see you at dinner."

Moira watched him let himself out through the garden gate, his shoulders square and erect. The sight transported her back to a country manor in Kent in 1580 when she watched those same shoulders heave with tortured sobs as Barnaby cradled Adeline's lifeless body in his arms.

His grief unleashed an anguished torrent of uncontrolled magic, so intense the ground beneath the house shook. Moira learned later that the earthquake toppled chimneys in London and damaged the highest parts of

Westminster Abbey, even opening a new section of the White Cliffs at Dover on the coast.

Only Moira dared approach Barnaby that day, kneeling by his side and laying her hand on his back. "We must take her to the Druids," she said in a strangled whisper. "She is a priestess of their order. There are certain rites that must be performed."

"Damn the Druids!" Barnaby cried out, pushing her away. "She is my _wife_!"

Choked by her grief, Moira whispered, "Yes, she is your wife and the dearest friend of my heart. We are bound by those obligations of love to do as she would wish. We must take her to her people, Barnaby. They will prepare her soul for the next stage of its journey. It is their way, and it was Adeline's belief."

Unable to meet her eyes, Barnaby only nodded. Beyond where they knelt, in the shadows of the great hall, Moira saw the house brownies huddled in small clumps, sobbing for their mistress.

"Cornelius," Moira called, "are you here?"

"I am here, Alchemist," the brownie said, stepping into the light.

"Send a messenger to the Druid priests and tell them we are bringing Adeline home," she directed. "Then go to my brothers, the forest elves, and say that I have need of their services."

"Yes, Alchemist," Cornelius said. "And please, what may we do for Master Barnaby?"

"I will stay with him," Moira said. "Hurry now and do as I have bade thee."

Within the hour, the elves of the forest came to the manor, forming a circle around the fallen woman. At Moira's behest, the elves took the great shield of a Templar knight from the wall, laid Adeline's body upon its surface, and lifted the burden to their shoulders.

Dusk fell as the solemn procession exited the manor and crossed the fields, hidden from prying human eyes by Moira's softly chanted incantation. Passing through the nearest portal and into the forest of the Otherworld, they took Adeline to the Druids where, by the light of the full moon, her soul was given flight.

When the chief Druid told Barnaby, "She is at peace," it took four elves to restrain the distraught wizard who lunged in fury at the startled old man. Finally, when there was no other way to calm him, Moira put Barnaby into a deep sleep.

"Forgive him," she said to the Druid. "He is not himself."

With infinite compassion, the elderly priest replied, "Take care that he does not lose himself forever."

At the time, Moira had not fully understood the warning. That insight came only after she watched Barnaby hunt Adeline's killer with the ruthless passion that carried him to Brussels where he contemplated betraying his very soul.

Moira had loved him then just as she loved him now, but she did not speak of her feelings. She loved him when she followed him to the New World, and she loved him when she stood in the Shevington square and watched him marry a Cherokee woman named Adoette. Moira loved him as he raised his baby daughter, Knasgowa, and she loved him when fate again made him a widower.

Then, after a wait of almost 200 years, and following a decent interval of mourning for Adoette, Moira took Barnaby's hand and explained that the time of her patience had come to an end.

"You do not know the truth of who I am, Moira," he'd said, tears welling in his eyes. "You will not love me when you know."

At the end of his confession, he sat before her with head bowed.

"Is that all?" she asked.

"Yes," he replied brokenly. "Is that not enough?"

"I care not if you are Barnaby Shevington or Barnabas Chesterfield," she said quietly. "I stood with you at the brink when you stopped yourself from repaying murder with murder. Your name does not measure your worth as a man to me."

But now, the dark legacy of the Chesterfield name once again haunted the man she loved. Moira feared the long-postponed reckoning of the two brothers might be at hand. Irenaeus threatened not just those whom Barnaby loved, but also the natural order to whose service her beloved had dedicated his life.

She had only one consolation. If Irenaeus was gathering amulets and artifacts to make a bid to control the human realm, he at least no longer had the Sinclair witch by his side. Moira had always believed Brenna goaded Irenaeus to kill Adeline and was the real force behind his ambitious plans.

Wily, intelligent, and powerful, the red-haired sorceress let nothing and no one get in her way—which is why Moira found herself uncharacteristically amused that the great Brenna Sinclair was, in the end, killed by a crippled were-cat, a ghost, and a rat.

Emerging from her reveries, Moira stood up and started back for the house. When Barnaby returned, she planned to have more source material ready for him. If he wanted to find the Amulet of Caorunn without the aid of the Ruling Elders, then so be it.

TEN

The Deepest Reaches of the In Between

The cold blade split her ribs sending a searing flood upward through her throat and out over her lips. As the drops fell toward the restraints binding her body, the witch remembered. The spilled blood reawakened her magic, sending it to rise in a wall of enveloping flame.

Brenna Sinclair awakened with a strangled gasp. She reached for her chest, feeling the ridge of scar tissue through the thin material of her nightgown. Even the healing force of her regenerated powers hadn't stopped the skin from knotting and twisting as the wound closed. Sometimes, when the air grew cold and wet, throbbing pain radiated outward from the scar reminding her of the high price of trust.

Neither nightmares nor physical pain fueled her memories, however. The scenes of her past remained ever present for Brenna, informing and driving her plans for the future.

She had believed Irenaeus Chesterfield when he armed her with the Amulet of the Phoenix and sent her into the fairy mound. He spoke of the alliance they had shared since Brenna, as a frightened young girl, entered the deep forest at his behest to sell her soul and emerge reborn.

Sitting up and running her hand through her hair, Brenna caught sight of her reflection in the mirror beside her bed. The woman who looked back at her was not the abused and scorned daughter of a cruel Templar knight.

Like Irenaeus, a birth defect prevented the blossoming of Brenna's magic, but it also shaped her destiny. Any bitterness over that genetic fault disappeared in the vortex of the Creavit transformation, but no matter how powerful either of them ultimately became, Brenna thought she and Irenaeus would always understand one another.

Both had felt the scorn of their Fae kin who regarded them as mere humans, and both had burned with shame as they retreated to the fringes of a society where magic fairly crackled in the air. But when she became Creavit, Brenna never again endured the scorn or mistreatment of a man—nor had she relied on a man to guide the course of her life path.

With immortality came a confident arrogance. What did minor mistakes matter with an infinite number of potential course corrections lying ahead?

But then, an upstart young witch named Jinx Hamilton robbed Brenna of her cherished acquired magic. For the first time in nine centuries, Brenna felt fear, crying out through the void for the one friend she knew would find her—Irenaeus Chesterfield—and thus made herself vulnerable.

The wizard answered her call, but in his surprise in seeing her so weak, he asked Brenna how long it had been since she was "last human." Stung by the cruel insult, she'd wanted to scream at him, "You know the answer, Irenaeus. You were there!"

But instead, she played along because she had need of his good will. No one loved verbal sparring more than Irenaeus. He'd wanted to hear her say the words—to relive through them her vicious treatment at the hands of her father and brothers.

Cruelty, Irenaeus said, was for the savoring. In remembering, he claimed, they remained strong and focused. It mattered not whether the wrongs were against himself or others. All pain could be used for the same purpose.

When she reminded him that the men in her family paid for their actions with slow, agonized deaths, Irenaeus smiled in satisfaction. He didn't expect Brenna to neatly turn the tables on him in his own game of probing questions.

"Why did you seek *your* powers?" she asked, although she knew the answer.

Irenaeus looked at her, allowing the reflection of the sensitive young man he'd been in the 12th century to rise to the surface. "Women were not the only ones used cruelly in the world into which we were born," he replied.

She knew the story of his bargain with the Darkness, forged from the bitter flames of his family's rejection because it had been whispered to her within the bonds of intimacy. After Irenaeus and Brenna became friends, and before they worked as pragmatic business partners, they'd been lovers.

Brenna foolishly relied on that remembered connection when she allowed herself to be convinced to enter the fairy mound beneath Jinx Hamilton's store in Briar Hollow. The plan Irenaeus devised brought Brenna closer to the Shevington portal than she'd dreamed possible, but on the brink of success, she failed—maddeningly foiled by the Hamilton witch's minions.

Impaled on the blade wielded by a ghost soldier, Brenna's blood ignited the flames that engulfed her body and sent her tumbling through a black and bottomless void. At first, she feared to die, and then she begged for the pain to end—but her release did not come with death.

Instead, the air turned gray and wet, extinguishing the blaze as Brenna's descent slowed.

She came to rest on soft ground. Exhausted and at the brink of unconsciousness, Brenna heard a resonant voice say, "Lift her carefully," followed by the sound of beating wings.

Hours later, she awakened under the oddly gentle gaze of a massive eagle. "You have chosen to remain among the living," he said. "That is good."

Brenna tried to answer, but the words stuck in her parched throat. The eagle's head turned to the side. He spoke to someone Brenna couldn't see. "Bring her water," he ordered.

A small figure appeared beside the bed. Brenna took the newcomer to be a brownie, but then she saw the pointed ears and tiny horns. An imp? Into what strange place had she fallen?

The imp supported her into a half-reclining position. Brenna accepted an offered cup of water, drinking deeply to let the pure, sweet liquid soothe her raw throat.

From her more elevated position Brenna could see that her companion was not a bird at all, but a gryphon, with the head, wings and front talons of an eagle, but the body, tail, and hind paws of a lion.

"Who are you?" she croaked.

"You may call me, Aquila," the gryphon said. "Welcome to my abode."

Brenna's eyes wandered over the room. Rich tapestries covered the rough-hewn walls. There were few pieces of furniture, but an astonishing number of books filled the rows of shelves covering the walls.

"Aquila?" she said. "That's Latin for eagle."

A chuckle emanated from the gryphon's yellow hooked beak. "You could not pronounce my true name," he said. "I opted for something more accessible. And you are?"

"Brenna," she said. "Brenna Sinclair."

The gryphon's head dipped in acknowledgment. "A pleasure to meet you," he said. "Do you like games of strategy?"

Brenna smiled at the memory. Since that first night, she had faced Aquila across many game boards and enjoyed hours of conversation with the erudite and intellectual creature.

The fire of her reawakened magic had sent her into the no man's land of the deep In Between. There, she'd found the only companion she'd ever known other than Irenaeus Chesterfield and Hamish Crawford, the father of the child she lost to those Druid scum, the Skeas.

As the bond between them grew, Brenna told Aquila the story of her long life, and under his probing questions, she began to re-evaluate many decisions and presumptions.

When *he* asked her one cold evening why she had sought her magic, she replied without hesitation, "To seek revenge on those who wronged me."

Aquila cocked his head and studied her with one glittering eye. "And in all these many years, you've found no other use for your powers?"

"Don't be ridiculous," she said. "I've manipulated humans and Fae alike to leverage my acquisition of position, influence, and wealth."

"And yet," the gryphon said, stretching his wings. "You've twice been imprisoned, lost your only son, and been double-crossed by this Chesterfield person. Did it never occur to you that perhaps you were using your abilities for incorrect purposes?"

Brenna's temper awakened, bringing green flame to her eyes.

"Now settle down," Aquila said, unperturbed. "I merely wonder why, when you were told you could not bear children, that you did not trust the father of your child with the true story of how you came to be a witch. The baby you created together was, arguably, a miracle, was he not?"

"Hamish was a religious zealot," Brenna snapped. "He was incapable of seeing me or any product of my body as a miracle."

"His religious convictions apparently did not trouble you until his fear of you caused him to turn against you," the gryphon replied.

Brenna had no answer for that.

"Did you think that when you emerged from that cave in the Orkneys that the best way to establish a relationship with your great-grandson was to murder his father?" Aquila went on. "Or that in following Alexander to America, you might have offered him more than his service as the progenitor of a magical lineage you planned to rule?"

"Alexander had nothing but fear for me," Brenna said coldly.

"Because in your fear of ever being vulnerable again, you gave him and everyone else in your path ample reasons to fear you and none to love you," Aquila said quietly. "Are you truly as evil as you would have us all believe? You have lived these many months in my home and been nothing but a gracious guest."

"You saved my life," Brenna said. "You allow me to remain here because I have nowhere else to go unless this is your way of telling me that I have outstayed my welcome."

The gryphon's beak clacked in consternation. "Now you are the one being ridiculous,' he said. "You are welcome here as long as you like. I am merely suggesting that having been given a second chance at life, perhaps there are positions of mind and heart you might reconsider."

Aquila let the matter drop for that evening, but then, weeks later, as he used one elegant talon to capture her rook with his bishop, Aquila put an intriguing question to Brenna.

"Would you not like to get the upper hand on this man Chesterfield and on the Hereditarium who persecuted your kind?" he asked.

"I thought your argument was that I needed to give people reason to love me," Brenna said sardonically. "Did you show love to those who persecuted your kind?"

Aquila's keen eyes regarded her patiently. "Had I so desired," he said. "I could have killed many humans before coming to this place of exile, but I wanted only to be a teacher, a professor. It was, however, my misfortune to have been born into the age when humans began to turn their backs on magic. My form frightened them. While regrettable, human fear is not a punishable offense."

"Isn't it?" Brenna said. "Were not the humans the ones who tortured and burned witches?"

"Ah," he said triumphantly, "so you do have feelings of camaraderie for natural practitioners."

Brenna set her mouth in a firm line, annoyed at having been talked into such an admission. Finally, she said, "I am Hereditarium by birth. I told you that."

"Brenna," Aquila asked gently, "whom do you hate more? Your father or the humans?"

"Both equally," she said stubbornly. "When my father was not being a tyrant, he worked with the Templars to safeguard the most precious artifacts of the magical world against the rising danger of destruction by the humans."

"And because your magic failed to awaken, he regarded you as little more than human, is that correct?"

"Unlike most Fae, my father never had any affection for humans," Brenna said in a rough voice. "He considered them to be impossibly inferior beings, more trouble than they were worth. His opinion of his defective daughter was no different."

"You are not defective, Brenna," Aquila said. "You have simply been disappointed by those whom you should have been able to trust. It is a deep wound, my dear, but it is not one that cannot be healed."

That single conversation seeded her mind with an intriguing question. One so simple, she wondered why it had never occurred to her before. Was Creavit magic inherently evil by virtue of its source, or could the person who possessed that made power still exercise free will?

Even after a deal forged with the Darkness in the name of revenge, could Brenna still choose a different path? The very thought struck her as ludicrous, but the idea existed in her mind all the same.

As she continued to heal, and as her strength returned, Brenna made a place for herself in the strange territory of the In Between. Armed with her native abilities and aided by those who could help her access the technological rivers of information on which the human world thrived, she devised methods to watch Irenaeus Chesterfield and the Hamilton girl.

It was not long before Brenna discovered that her "death" had not been the consequence of mere bad luck.

Irenaeus used her to plant the Orb of Thoth in the fairy mound to disable the aos si. He'd never intended to break into the Valley of Shevington. His only goal was to deprive Jinx Hamilton of the company and counsel of her mentor. To that end, Brenna was completely expendable.

Since that time, Chesterfield had been quite the busy boy—playing games with vampires, manipulating time, kidnapping Jinx Hamilton's brother. But as Brenna tracked the wizard's movements, she saw, for the first time, that Irenaeus was, for all his great age, still little more than a malcontented teenager with a persecution complex—and rather a bumbling one at that.

This was the weakling to whom she had linked her

plans? Those days were most certainly over, a fact the wizard would understand when he discovered Brenna Sinclair was harder to get rid of than he imagined. Whether she chose a better path for herself in the future or not, Brenna's first goal was to settle scores with Irenaeus Chesterfield.

ELEVEN

Maybe it's just me, but when evil, supposed-to-be-dead sorceresses appear in my dreams? I have trouble getting back to sleep. Tori? Not so much. She conked out on her end of the sofa right in the middle of my elegant theory about Dream Brenna being a metaphor.

Granted, it was a boring theory, but I still almost threw a pillow at Tori when a half-snort/half-snore interrupted my monologue. Seriously, I can't really blame her for falling asleep on me mid-ramble. What I was saying didn't even make sense to me.

I couldn't claim on the one hand to see the Amulet of Caorunn and the thief who took it in my dreams, and then turn right around and deny the vision about Brenna Sinclair. Whether I liked it or not, Brenna appeared to be alive—in some place with giant eagles and little dudes with horns thus adding a whole new layer of strange to the situation.

Still, in the moment, I was annoyed enough at Tori to pick up a pillow and start to launch it at her head. Then I caught myself and just looked at my bestie, dead to the world with her arms wrapped around the comforter that usually stays draped over the back of the sofa.

The pose reminded me of the way Tori used to cling to her beat-up old Teddy bear—the one that still lives on the upper shelf of her bedroom closet. He comes out when no other means of comfort will suffice.

Regardless of the level of drama or danger we face, Tori never quits on me. Letting her get some sleep was the least I could do. We'd have to deal with the Brenna question soon enough, a fact that was likely to cause everyone to lose sleep.

As I got up to go, I thought, "It's not like Brenna's hiding outside the door waiting to grab me."

Note to self. Random mental comments like that in the wake of scary dream visions in the wee hours of the night are seldom good ideas.

It took every ounce of willpower I possessed to go out into the store. The displays threw menacing shadows across the floor that my imagination immediately turned into a lurking wicked witch.

My first impulse was to run upstairs and dive under the covers, but the calm part of my mind said, "You know you won't sleep anyway." Bowing to the wisdom of that inner voice, I decided to have another look at Grandma Kathleen's grimoire instead.

When I came down the stairs into the lair, I found Greer reading by the fire. "Hey," I said. "Mind if I join you?"

"Not at all," she replied, closing the book in her hands. "Please do."

Claiming the chair across from her, I asked, "What are you reading?"

"A biography of Catherine de' Medici," Greer replied. "I'm afraid the human author does not do her justice. Catherine faced no easy task keeping the Valois dynasty intact in France."

It would have made me sound cool if I could have jumped right in with a pithy historical comment, but I had to admit I had no idea what Greer was talking about.

"A small matter," Greer said, smiling. "Incorrect or not,

I find human histories fascinating. The authors' capacity to miss the true nature of events seems bottomless."

"Did you know Catherine de' Medici personally?" I asked.

Greer nodded. "I did," she said, "and I admired her."

Tucking my legs under my body in the chair, I said, "That must be so weird, reading about people you knew from so long ago. When did she die?"

"Fifteen fifty-nine," Greer answered.

Frowning, I struggled with the math in my head, "That was . . . "

"Four hundred and fifty-six years ago," the baobhan sith supplied helpfully, "give or take a few months."

She delivered the last words with a droll smile that made me laugh. The oldest Fae measure their lives in such vast stretches of time, a month must seem like half an hour to them.

"You were in France in 1559?" I asked.

"There," Greer said, "and in England as well."

She got up and crossed to the liquor cabinet. "Elizabeth Tudor ascended the throne that year," she said, "and Good Queen Bess was the match of any man walking."

Pausing to hold up two bottles, Greer asked, "Scotch or brandy?"

"Brandy," I replied, watching as she poured three fingers of whisky for herself in a tumbler and a generous serving of Hennessey in a snifter for me.

When she came back to the hearthside, I accepted the glass she held out.

"What is that Gaelic thing I'm supposed to say?" I asked.

"*Slàinte*," Greer said.

I repeated the word awkwardly and then asked, "What does that mean, anyway?"

"To your health," Greer replied, taking her seat again.

"And the thing Chase says back when Festus says *slàinte?*"

"*Do dheagh shlàinte,*" she replied, "which means basically the same thing."

We sipped our liquor in silence, listening to the crackle of the fire. The brandy felt warm in my throat, and I liked the way it seemed to move out along the nerves in my body. I knew Greer was watching me, but I waited for her to re-start the conversation.

It wasn't a long wait, just enough time for the brandy to start to loosen the tension in my body, something I'm sure Greer, with her vampiric powers, could sense.

"What has you wandering down here at this time of night, Jinx?" she asked after a few minutes. "You're troubled. Does this have anything to do with the visit Festus and I paid to Raleigh?"

I opened my mouth to answer, and without meaning to, I told her everything—Grandma Kathleen's grimoire, the Casket of Morpheus, Tori's green powder, and all of the dreams—in detail.

When I got to the part about Brenna Sinclair, Greer's eyes took on an odd glow. "Well, well, well," she said, with something in her voice that might have been admiration. "I thought Brenna went down just a bit too easily."

The way she spoke those words kicked the connection center of my brain into high gear. "No way," I gasped. "You know Brenna Sinclair?"

"Oh yes," Greer said. "I have known Brenna for centuries. I assure you that it takes one red-haired Scotswoman to get the best of another. Brenna and I have crossed paths and swords—literally—on more than one occasion."

"Did you know her before she became a Creavit witch?"

"I did," Greer said. "Brenna's father, Henri de St. Clair

was if you do not mind my saying so, a thoroughgoing bastard. His cruelties were largely responsible for Brenna's decision to deal with the darkness. You see, Brenna, like Irenaeus Chesterfield, was born into an Hereditarium family but her powers failed to develop."

You think keeping up with the twists and turns in a soap opera is hard? Try sorting out the intricate lives and associations of the Fae. I am talking centuries worth of plot twists.

"Do you think it's possible Brenna has something to do with the theft of the Amulet of Caorunn?" I asked.

"With Brenna," Greer replied, "almost anything is possible, but from the setting you describe, she must currently reside in the In Between. There is no other realm where imps can be found."

That confused me.

"Wait a minute," I said, "aren't we sitting in the In Between right now?"

Greer shook her head. "No," she said, "we are sitting in a fairy mound that resides in the In Between. The Fae are forsworn not to interfere in the affairs of the Middle Realm. There are places like the fairy mound that exist within that realm, but only as a submersible might exist in the ocean."

I'd always thought nothing but . . . well . . . *dirt* surrounded the fairy mound. The idea that beyond the walls of the archive lay a forbidden dimension was going to take some getting used to.

"Somehow," I said, "I don't think a 'Keep Out' sign would mean much to Brenna."

"Likely not," Greer agreed, "but there are virtually no entrances to the In Between, and those that do exist are guarded by intricate security mechanisms. Opening them typically involves facing life-threatening challenges."

"So how did Brenna get there?" I asked.

Greer considered the question. "Understand," she said, "that I am neither a witch nor an alchemist, but if I were to hazard a guess, I would say that since Brenna 'died' within the fairy mound, she was, in some way transported through its boundaries and into the Middle Realm. The journey may not have been one of her choosing, which could explain the sensation you experienced of falling through a vast darkness."

"Have you ever been to the In Between?" I asked.

"I have," Greer said, "but long before the agreement and the safeguards were in place. The Middle Realm is a place of contradictions and illusions. Rather like Lewis Carroll's imaginary Wonderland. Lawlessness and danger exist there side by side with incomparable beauty and mystery."

"Sounds like the perfect place to hide a stolen amulet," I said.

"Perhaps," Greer replied, "but if so, then our elusive John Smyth would also have to be a creature of the In Between, and one violating the agreement to perpetrate his crimes in the human realm."

"Could that explain why the street cats said he smelled like a deer?"

"An intriguing idea," Greer said. "Festus told me, with no small bemusement, that you asked about 'weredeer.' I used the DGI network to reference the Registry computers. There are no specific shapeshifting ungulates in the literature . . ."

The look on my face must have made her rethink her word choice.

". . . no shapeshifting animals with hooves in the literature," she went on, "but I suppose we could be dealing with an individual who possesses hybrid transmogrification skills."

"Meaning?"

"Typically, practitioners with transmogrification powers only alter their appearance within their given species," Greer explained. "That is how the ability differs from genetically based shapeshifting."

If there's one thing I've learned about magic, it's that every "rule" has exceptions—usually major ones.

"But does that mean it's impossible for someone with transmogrification to make cross-species transformations?" I asked.

"No," Greer said. "Infinite potential is the purest essence of magic. How such a creature could cross in and out of the Middle Realm at will, however, is a more complicated matter. Now, may I ask you a question?"

An alarm bell went off in my head. "Sure," I said a little uncertainly.

"How long do you plan to keep all of this information from Barnaby, Moira, and the others?"

Not the conversation left turn I wanted.

"I don't know," I admitted, "but I would appreciate it if you wouldn't tell them what I'm doing."

Greer gave me a penetrating look over the top of her whisky glass. "There is something you should understand about me, Jinx," she said. "My reputation does not include being an informer. I do not work for them. I am in the employ of the Mother Trees, and by extension, you. Therefore the secrets you choose to keep are mine to keep as well."

"Good to now," I said, "but what if the Mother Tree asks you what I'm doing."

"Then I will tell her she must speak to you in person," Greer replied with sparkling eyes.

"Oh," I said, grinning back, "I get it. You won't rat on me to anyone else, but you'll throw me straight under the bus with the Mother Tree."

"In a heartbeat," Greer affirmed solemnly.

Having been put on the spot by the Great Oak more than once myself, I couldn't blame her. Not even a being as powerful as the baobhan sith wanted to deal with the Tree in one of her moods. Somehow knowing that only strengthened the growing sense of friendship I felt for Greer.

"Fair enough," I said, "and thank you for the talk. I came down to look at my grandmother's grimoire, so I think I'm going to spend some time doing that now, if you'll excuse me."

"By all means," Greer said, reaching for her book. "Call me if you need anything."

I found the grimoire on the shelf, started toward the alcove, and then stopped. "Greer?"

"Yes," she said, looking up from the page.

"If Brenna were to get out of the In Between and into the fairy mound . . . "

A flickering green flame instantly kindled in the depths of her eyes. "She'd have to go through me to get to any of you," Greer said.

That was exactly what I wanted to hear.

Carrying the grimoire into the alcove, I drew the curtain behind me. To my surprise, the gentle sound of the bubbling brook began instantly accompanied by chirping crickets. My always-on enchanted sound machine could tell night from day.

Curling up in the chair, I stared contemplatively into the fire for a few minutes. There are all kinds of meditative aids, but I do some of my best thinking getting lost in the wavering light of flames. Between my dream of Brenna and my conversation with Greer, I had a lot to think about.

I can't tell you how long I sat there lost in my musings before I fell asleep. When I woke up, my feet were up on the ottoman, which I could have sworn was longer than it had been the day before. The soft blanket covering my body seemed to emit a comforting warmth, and my head rested against a downy pillow. The alcove and its amenities were starting to grow on me.

Glancing at my watch, I had about half an hour to kill before I needed to get upstairs, fill the cats' breakfast orders, and dress for the day. Grandma Kathleen's grimoire sat on the table beside my chair. I opened the volume to the passage about the Casket of Morpheus and read the description again without finding anything new.

Running the tip of my index finger over the handwritten annotation about unpredictable results from the artifact, I whispered, "Guess, I should have listened to you, Grandma. Now, who do I ask for help?"

Even though I was alone in the alcove, the breath of a whisper swirled around me. I could only make out a single word—*family*.

TWELVE

After my talk with Greer and what I believed to be a ghostly, early morning visit from my grandmother, life just took over for the next couple of weeks. It will do that, even to people like us who lead magically convoluted lives and regularly confront evil wizards and scheming sorceresses.

Now, for the record, everything I just told you is what I *wanted* to believe at the time—maybe even what I was *supposed* to believe.

From a psychological perspective, when you're staring at an impending crisis—the proverbial oncoming train—nothing seems more important than thinking you're in control of everything, including the timetable of events.

So *not* true.

The Fae emphasize one underlying principle over and over again: the natural order.

In one of my more contentious talks with the Mother Tree, I angrily asked why she didn't just step in and clean things up. At the time we were discussing getting my brother home. I had it in my head that the Grid—the Coven of the Woods comprised of the Mother Trees—possessed omnipotent powers.

I guess I thought they could just wave their branches and make stuff happen. The Oak set me straight fast.

She told me that the Trees are responsible for the coherence of time and that they serve as the wardens of magic, but they can't interfere with the natural order. During a quiet moment in the lair, shortly after we rescued Connor, I asked Moira to explain that to me.

Fixing me with the gentle, knowing smile I've come to love, Moira said, "It would be so much easier if the Mother Oak could simply grant our wishes, right all our perceived wrongs, and give us our heart's desire, would it not?"

My eyes instantly filled with tears. "It would," I agreed. "Is that so much to ask?"

"Jinx, there is a Power beyond and above us all, including the Great Trees themselves," Moira said. "Their place in the Natural Order is to ensure the unified, consistent progress of our existence. The roots of the Trees hold the realms in place. Their wisdom anchors our own. They are not gods, but rather guides and friends."

She told me everything happens in the order in which it's meant to happen, which caused my brain to dredge up the remains of some long-distant Sunday school lesson.

"Isn't that called predestination?" I asked.

Moira raised an eyebrow. "You have read St. Augustine?"

"Uh, no," I said, "but I did go to church camp a couple of summers."

"Ah," she said. "Perhaps then you have heard one of Augustine's more memorable quotes, 'Lord, make me chaste—but not yet.'"

"I think I like this guy," I laughed.

"He *is* the Patron Saint of Brewers," Moira said. "A great many more people are in debt to his benevolence than they may realize."

"So am I right on the predestination thing?" I asked.

"Yes and no," Moira said. "Matters of future salvation preoccupied the Christian thinkers sometimes to the exclusion of the life path. Do you remember our discussion about Benjamin Franklin when you first learned of the Strigoi?"

Good ole Ben Franklin, he of the kite strings and the bifocals. Franklin helped a Romanian Orthodox priest named Samuel Damien bring the first Strigoi to the area around Briar Hollow as refugees from a church determined to kill them as cursed servants of the Devil.

Together the men devised a means to feed the Strigoi, who live on life energy not blood, with electricity. Franklin went on, in time, to more or less found the Bureau of Indefinite Species.

"Yes," I said. "I remember we talked about him."

"Franklin was an example of a Deist," Moira said. "He saw the Great Power as a Divine Clockmaker who set in motion the Universe and then sat back to see what mankind would do with it."

"So you're saying that no event occurs before its time," I said. "The Trees can't just make something happen. I get that, but clearly, they know when to put things in motion, or stop us from doing something like the Oak stopped me from seeing Connor. How do they know what to do and when to do it?"

"That," Moira said, "is a matter between the Trees and Mother Earth herself."

Yes, it was a cryptic answer, but somehow it made me feel better. It did not, however, prevent me, a couple of weeks later, from sliding right into my comfortable illusion of being in charge.

Now I can tell you the truth. Nothing major happened during the last few days of November and the first couple of weeks of December because nothing was *supposed to happen*—not yet.

I gave in to that denial because it was easy and it felt good—and I had plenty of other things to occupy my thoughts and actions.

For instance—and it never ceases to amaze me that we pull this off—Tori and I do run a profitable business. Our espresso bar, The Witch's Brew, has become the go-to watering hole for Briar Hollow's caffeine addicts, a fact borne out by our increased revenues.

Once the early morning coffee drinkers come through the front door, we rarely get a minute's peace for the rest of the day. Having a civilian like Mindy Mathis working for us as a barista limited what we could freely discuss during that time, but honestly, I don't think Tori and I could have handled the holiday season without her.

Nothing about my state of mind changed my nightly dreams. The images came fast and furious in living Technicolor on a scale that would make big budget film directors salivate.

There wasn't a single grain of blue kyanite powder left on the Casket of Morpheus, but that didn't matter. The first treatment had been more than enough, and frankly, Tori and I were scared to try anything else. Even returning the Casket to its proper storage box in the archives didn't stop my dreams.

During that time my fountain pen and I did develop a perfect working relationship, which was pretty cool. Every time I woke up the pen quivered in its leather loop, straining to get to work bringing my visions into sharp focus on the pages of the grimoire.

Sometimes rather than open to a blank sheet, the grimoire would, of its own volition, flip back a few pages so the pen could add detail to an existing drawing or remove something it now considered incorrect.

I know. Fountain pens don't come equipped with erasers. Trust me. Mine does.

Anytime I wanted to make an annotation beside one of the pictures, the image would immediately shrink or shift on the page to create ample room. If I didn't feel like writing, I dictated, and the pen transcribed my words.

Developing that close, symbiotic relationship with my new magical tools provided a silver lining to the more disturbing cloud of my dream visions.

On the sly, Festus talked with the triplets at the Registry. They confirmed Greer's research about our mysterious "weredeer." There were no known shapeshifters with hooves, which left the mystery of John Smyth's *Eau de Bambi* scent unsolved.

Tori spent hours staring at Google Earth and finally decided the setting for the scene I witnessed had to be the Royal Mile in Edinburgh, Scotland. That made sense since the Mother Rowan grows in Roslin less than ten miles south of the city. The information didn't get us closer to finding the missing amulet, but it did confirm the content of my vision.

All of this went on against a flurry of activity in our world, starting with Thanksgiving dinner at Uncle Raymond's, an excursion that included Beau and some well-planned stowaways.

Before we left the store, I conducted a final inspection, starting with a stern warning to Rodney who would spend the day in the breast pocket of Beau's sport coat.

"Do not so much as poke your nose out," I told him for the tenth time. "Aunt Faye, Uncle Henry's wife, has a thing about rats. It would *not* be a pretty scene. Understand?"

Rodney nodded vigorously, putting one paw over his heart.

"Do not fear, Miss Jinx," Beau said. "We have devised a plan. With the aid of your mother's seamstress abilities, Master Rodney has openings through which he may observe the festivities while remaining completely concealed."

Leaning closer, I realized there were all but invisible holes in the fabric.

"Get in and let me see," I instructed Rodney.

Beau held out his hand and gave Rodney a lift under his lapel. There was a little squirming in the breast pocket, and then the fabric smoothed back in place.

Only when I put my face six inches from the spot I knew to be Rat Central could I make out a shining black eye looking back at me.

"You two are pretty slick," I admitted.

"Thank you," Beau said. "We believe the device to be a rather clever one. As for Master Rodney's holiday meal, I will covertly slip tidbits to him as the opportunity arises."

At that, Duke let out a mournful whine. "Now stop that, boy," Beau said. "We have discussed this. You may accompany us today, and when we return, I will facilitate your consumption of copious leftovers."

From time to time Beau puts the Amulet of the Phoenix on Duke's collar so the coonhound can assume corporeal form and enjoy a treat, usually an ice cream cone from the Dairy Queen. In exchange for his good behavior at Thanksgiving Dinner, where Duke would be invisible to the other guests, the ghost dog was getting turkey and dressing at the end of the day.

"Okay," I said, "I think you three are good to go. Darby, do you understand the rules?"

A disembodied voice from the vicinity of my knees answered brightly. "Remain invisible at all times," Darby said, "and remember anything your aunts say about you behind your back."

"Perfect. Glory?"

Making sure the miniature witch didn't spend the holiday alone proved more challenging, but Tori came to the rescue. Glory would stay inside Tori's omnipresent messenger bag watching everything that happened through a tiny fiber optic camera poking through the slit in the cover meant for headphones.

"You're sure you're okay with this?" I asked, pulling back the flap and looking at Glory who was ensconced in a shoebox outfitted with the miniature recliner from Graceland East and her iPod Touch hooked up to the camera and plugged into a backup battery.

"*Absolutely!*" Glory enthused. "I feel like a secret agent woman."

My parents and Gemma were already at the farm when we arrived. Festus and Chase opted to spend their holiday in Shevington. Festus knew all the Ryan children from his days guarding Grandma Kathleen. We could have passed him off as a family friend with the non-magical kinfolks, but the old cat wisely thought that might be a bit much for them to handle on top of the news of Aunt Fiona's resurrection.

You see, my aunt faked her death to move to Shevington full-time. She felt it would make the legal transfer of the store to me easier. Now that we all knew about the ruse, however, we weren't going to just cut Aunt Fiona out of family events. It was bad enough that we hadn't come up with a way to explain and thus include Connor.

To account for my aunt's return to life and Briar Hollow, she and Mom concocted up a story about my aunt briefly running away with a handsome traveling tarot card reader who dumped her for a psychic in Vegas. Given Fiona's well-established eccentricities, the family pretty much bought it, although Uncle Bannister's wife Lucille did keep saying, "Tell me again what we buried in that casket?"

All in all, the gathering did go smoothly—until I almost choked on my green beans at the dinner table. That would be the moment when Uncle Milton, Aunt Betty Jean's husband, beamed approvingly at Beau and said, "You sure do know your Civil War stuff, Longworth. Anyone would think you'd been there!"

Mom and Aunt Fiona exchanged a bemused look over the cranberry sauce while Aunt Betty Jean fussed at Milton for talking with his mouth full. Later in the kitchen, she drew me off to one side and said, "Colonel Longworth is a corporeal ghost, isn't he?"

"Yes, ma'am," I said, my eyes going wide. "How do you know that?"

"Emma and I may not be powerful like Kelly and Fiona, but we're Fae too, Norma Jean," she said. "I can't tell you how proud we are that you've come into your powers. Mama would be proud, too, honey. Before I forget, I have a nice leftover soup bone I'm going to wrap up for that sweet ghost dog. Oh, and did the lovely rat in the Colonel's coat pocket get enough to eat?"

There are four Ryan girls—Fiona, Betty Jean, Emma, and my mother—and five boys, Raymond, John, Elwood, Bannister, and Henry. The children did not, however, inherit or cultivate their powers equally. The girls refer to the boys as "dead signals," although I swear Uncle Bannister talks to animals and they talk back.

Betty Jean and Emma are self-described "kitchen witches." Aunt Emma's whiskey and rock candy cough syrup is famous in three counties, but it's not the Wild Turkey that provides the healing power of the "tonic."

As for my aunts and uncles by marriage, they live in cheerful oblivion. If they do see something from their significant others or extended family they can't explain, they look the other way.

On the drive back to Briar Hollow from Cotterville, Beau fairly glowed with pleasure. Careful not to wake Rodney, who was sound asleep in the crook of his arm, Beau twisted his tall frame around in the front seat of my cherry red Prius to address me directly.

"Miss Jinx," he said, "I am most taken by your extended family. Your Uncle Milton is quite knowledgeable about the Late Unpleasantness. He has invited me to inspect the array of accouterment he has amassed for use as a Confederate re-enactor. I am looking forward to the visit enormously."

From the backseat, Glory said, "Now Beau, we've talked about you using that silly phrase."

"My mistake," he said genially, "the War of Northern Aggression."

"Now you're messing with us," I laughed. "And trust me, you and Uncle Milton are two peas in a pod. You know, he shoots the guns and everything."

Beau's smile broadened. "Indeed I do know," he said, "our engagement will include a round of target practice. I would pit myself against the skill of any man when armed with my .36 Navy Colt revolver."

"What about your sword?" I asked. "Are you guys going to do the whole Errol Flynn thing?"

Drawing his brows together, Beau puzzled over my comment before he put it together. "Ah!" he said. "The motion picture actor late of the 1940s. I believe he portrayed Robin of Loxley, did he not?"

"If you mean Robin Hood, yes," I said, "but he also did a lot of movies where he waved a sword around. I'll bet Uncle Milton will love your saber."

Out of the corner of my eye, I saw a strange look pass over Beau's features. "Sadly I was never much of a hand with a blade," he said. "I believe your uncle and I will confine our weaponry enthusiasm to firearms."

Tori leaned forward between the seats. "What's up with the modesty, Beau?" she asked. "I thought you told me you were a master swordsman."

The old soldier shook his head. "I fear you misheard me." With that, he abruptly changed topics, asking, "Miss Tori, have you looked at the roster of recent recruits supplied to us by Mr. Pulliam?"

Tori went ahead and ran with it, but she caught my eye in the rear view mirror, and we exchanged a "what the heck was that about" look."

That night she and I discussed the conversation and agreed that Beau had seemed a little "off" since he started researching what became of his family after his death. That would be enough to upset anyone, so we decided not to make too much of his odd reaction to the mention of his saber—or at least I didn't. More on that later.

Hot on the heels of the Thanksgiving celebration, Mom and Darby pulled off a fantastic triple birthday party. The only thing that injected even a hint of tension in the evening was when Lucas kissed me—and we are talking *pecked* here people—and Chase got his hackles up.

Thankfully said hackles did not come with any verbalizations. I really did not want to have to smack down a jealous ex-boyfriend in front of my brother, who was fascinated with everything about our lives in Briar Hollow. After we had cake, Connor asked me to take him upstairs and show him the store.

Obviously, we had the party after hours, so with no customers in the place, Connor was free to wander around picking up objects from the inventory and asking me about them. Unbeknownst to me, even though this was only his second visit to the human realm since he was taken to Shevington as a baby, Connor has always been fascinated by human cultural artifacts.

"You sound like Mr. Weasley in the Harry Potter books," I said, meaning to tease him and being rewarded with a blank stare instead.

"What are the Harry Potter books?" he asked.

From the vicinity of the basement stairs, Tori let out with an outraged cry. "Oh, hell no," she said, "we cannot allow you to continue to live in that state of ignorance one minute longer. Come with me."

Blushing a little, Connor fell in behind her, and we all went into her apartment where the Harry Potter books sit enshrined on a special reserved shelf.

To my absolute amazement, Tori, who won't even let me touch the hallowed collector's editions, said, "They're about a boy wizard who doesn't know he has magic until he gets accepted into a school called Hogwarts. The first one is short. Would you like to take a couple of them to get started with the series?"

"That's so nice of you," Connor said. "I think I can relate to Harry. I'm just getting started with my magic, too. But at least I haven't blown anything up the way Dad does."

"And you don't have an evil wizard after you," Tori said, before shooting my brother a crooked grin. "Oh. Wait. My bad. You do."

Connor laughed. "It doesn't sound so bad when you say it," he told her.

From my position leaning against the doorframe, I could not believe what I was seeing. My best friend was flirting with my brother, and he was flirting back.

An unexpected surge of little sister protectiveness went through me until I remembered this was Tori. If I had to pick someone to date my brother, her name would be the only one on the list. I knew she would never do anything to hurt Connor.

Retracting my invisible claws, I said, "Better send him the first three. He has more books in his place than you have in here."

"You do?" Tori said, her eyes lighting up. "So do you just read Fae authors or do you know human writers, too?"

Before they could really get started, I jumped in front of the bookmobile. "If the two of you are going to do the whole library nerd thing, could I please get a latte first?"

"Huh?" Tori said like she'd forgotten I was even around. "Oh, yeah, sure. Connor, you like mochas, right?"

"You remembered," he said with an expression that was already well on its way to 'adoring puppy dog.'

Picking up the books like they were made of fragile porcelain, he headed out the door first. As Tori passed me, I whispered, "If you're going to set your sights on my brother, could the two of you please not be that nauseating in my presence?"

"Jinksy," Tori said, flashing me a wicked grin, "I have no idea what you are talking about."

"Yes, you do," I whispered back. "Behave yourself."

"Don't I always?"

There was no answer to that one that wouldn't get me struck by lightning.

We had the party on Saturday, December 12, which immediately threw us into the two-week "Shop Briar Hollow" event sponsored by the Town Square Association. Fresh off the success of the Halloween paranormal festival, the group was determined to keep those tourist dollars pumping into the local economy.

Since we did a banner business, I can't complain, and Tori and Mindy get the credit for making us the flashiest business on Main Street. I swear there wasn't a square inch of the shop that hadn't been hosed down in red and green or festooned with some sort of tinsel.

Tori outdid herself with witch-themed ornaments and gift selections. She even climbed up on a ladder and outfitted the witch on our "Witch's Brew Espresso Bar" sign with a Santa hat.

There just wasn't time for magical drama—or so it seemed—especially since nothing new had developed.

Barnaby and Moira remained silent on the subject of the Amulet of Caorunn. Festus and Greer continued to work on finding out more about John Smyth—without much luck—and my dreams were all repeats that added fine details but nothing substantially new.

That changed in the wee morning hours of Monday, December 21st—the Winter Solstice.

THIRTEEN

Brighid stood at the window looking out over the pond. Ice clung to the shoreline and snow drifted under the trees. Shivering, she drew her shawl closer around her shoulders. Old Cailleach Bheur, the Queen of Winter, had a tight hold on the land this year.

For more seasons than she could count, Brighid had kept this watch through the cold months. With gentle enchantments, she and her sisters drew away any questions that might arise in the minds of the humans who were their friends and neighbors.

No one noticed that the women never aged or that their stone cottage perched on the edge of the pond had no need of upkeep or repair. The people around Kildare didn't ask how the O'Dannon sisters made their living or even thought to question why each was called Brighid, even if the second sister went by Brig and the third was known as Bea.

The old stories called the Brighid, goddesses, but the Daughters of Dagda were members of the Tuatha Dé Danann, that beautiful race of Fae that dwelled in the Otherworld.

Animated by a special love for the Celtic peoples, the Tuatha Dé Danann could not long absent themselves from the realm of man even when their relationship with the mortals proved vexing. Especially here in Ireland, certain of the Fae, like Brighid and her sisters, continued to watch over the humans, to delight in their eccentricities, and, when possible, to save them from their foibles.

Brig of the dancing green eyes and flaming red hair studied the healing arts. Bea, a black-eyed brunette was a poet and historian. But blond Brighid with eyes as blue as the sky took on a more active and ancient responsibility in the realms.

Each year, in her role as Queen of Summer, she oversaw the transition from winter's chill to the renewing heat of spring. This day, the Winter Solstice, marked the turning of the calendar and the slow lengthening of the sunlit hours. Each year, the Solstice awakened within her a deep longing for her time of ascendancy, a hunger that made the cold grate on Brighid's nerves with unbearable intensity.

Behind her on the hearth, Bea struck a mournful chord on her cláirseach, the triangular harp resting on her lap. "You're doing it again, sister," she said. "Old Cailleach won't let go any faster no matter how hard you stare out that window. Come sit by the fire and let me tell you how Brig went chasing after Seamus Hennessy at the pub last night."

"I did not chase after anyone," Brig retorted, tying the bundle of dried herbs in her hands. "Seamus was telling funny stories from work. He has a job with that company that makes those little pills the humans are always taking. Pharmaceuticals they call them."

Bea ran her fingers idly over the strings of her instrument. "All that silly giggling was about pills?" she asked, her full mouth curving in a teasing smile. "That's not the kind of thing I was talking over with Jimmy O'Halleran."

"I don't expect it was," Brig said, "since you played your harp intentionally to turn his head. What would father say if he knew you used magic to toy with the human men?"

Bea smiled at her innocently. "Now sister, what's magic for if not to be used for a bit of fun? What say you, Brighid?"

"I say," Brighid replied, "that you both best be careful about the mortals. No sooner do we get attached to them than their time among us is done."

"Well, aren't you the cheerful one!" Bea cried. "I know the Solstice isn't your favorite day, but you're not usually so dour."

A low, moaning wind circled round the cottage rattling the windowpanes. "Listen to that wind," Brighid shuddered. "I'm sick of the cold and sick of being cooped up inside."

"Then throw a veil of warmth around yourself and go for a walk," Brig said. "It's not as if you must let the cold slice through your bones."

Brighid considered the suggestion. "I think I will," she said, "and when I get back, I'll bake fresh bread to go with our dinner."

Throwing on a long cloak, Brighid stepped out the door, drawing the garment closer as the wind caught and flared the fabric. Centering her thoughts in the heart of her powers, she kindled a fire in her mind, catching its warmth and sending the energy flowing outward to drive back the bitter air.

Surrounded and protected by the radiant glow, Brighid stepped confidently into the snow, which receded at her approach, opening a path before her as she walked. She moved across the meadow toward the smaller pond known locally as Brighid's Well.

Safely encased in the comforting bubble of energy, she found herself able to appreciate Cailleach's seasonal handiwork. The creaking of branches frozen solid with ice played counterpoint with the mournful wind flowing through the monochrome landscape. It was not Brighid's palette of verdant greens, gentle rains, and renewing light, but there was beauty in winter's art.

Some of the impatient tension she'd felt back at the cottage began to leave her, and Brighid's thoughts wandered to her sisters' lighthearted banter. Always competing for the attention of the handsome lads, those two. Let them have Seamus Hennessy and Jimmy O'Halleran, if Brighid were of a mind to play with mortals, which she was not, she'd have set her cap for Michael Donovan . . .

Just then, a blur of motion at the outer limit of her vision made Brighid drop the teasing fantasy and brought her attention back to the here and now. At the edge of the rocks surrounding the well stood a stag holding one foreleg at an unnatural angle.

"There, there now," Brighid murmured. "Are you hurt, my brother? Come with me to the cottage so that my sister might heal your wound."

In response, the deer snorted and shook his antlers, prancing agitatedly on three legs.

"Easy," Brighid said, moving forward cautiously. "You'll hurt yourself more with that nonsense. I mean you no harm."

As she advanced, the stag's nostrils flared nervously. Angling to get herself to one side, Brighid kept talking to the animal in a low, soothing tone. When the cautious advance appeared to be working, Brighid's confidence increased. Still, the stag watched her with suspicious eyes.

Later, when she would tell the tale, Brighid would say she did not know what startled the deer. It never occurred to her that the animal bolted intentionally to lure her onto the frozen surface of the pond.

As the stag's hooves lost purchase on the bank, he plunged into the water. Brighid followed, acting purely on instinct, with no thought to her own safety. Drawing nearer the flailing stag, she extended the shield of protective energy, infusing it with the subtle flavors of comfort and calm.

The deer stilled as the bubble spread over it. Brighid's eyes met those of the wounded animal. Just before they were both pulled under the surface, Brighid heard the words, "Forgive me, Queen of Summer."

The icy water hit me like a spray of needles. I bolted upright out of bed gasping, my hands clawing at the darkness as I tried to dig my way toward air and light. Four sets of glowing eyes regarded me from the foot of the bed.

Yule let out an inquisitive meow, and Winston stepped forward to butt his head against my side. "It's okay," I babbled. "I'm okay. It was just another dream. A really, really, *really* bad one this time."

Leaning over Winston, I switched on the lamp and reached for my grimoire. The pen was so used to drawing my nocturnal visions, it almost started without me.

I watched as the images appeared in a series of panels. First a beautiful stone cottage on what looked like a millpond, then a woman walking through a path in the snow, and finally a second, smaller body of water that appeared to be frozen over.

As the scene grew more detailed, something became visible on the ice. Squinting, I realized it was a flailing animal that had fallen through. The woman in my vision was trying to help the . . . what the heck was that thing?

Reaching for the magnifying glass that had become a permanent fixture on the nightstand, I looked closer and gasped when I realized the pen had drawn a deer.

Before I could process the information, Winston

bumped my elbow, scaring me half to death and breaking my train of thought.

"Okay, okay, *fine*," I said. "Cat food first, transdimensional Fae drama second."

Starting the day with the sensation of choking to death in freezing water didn't exactly make me want to throw back the covers and meet the world, but I wasn't about to risk falling back asleep either.

I ran my hands through what felt like a serious case of bed head and continued to puzzle through the details of the dream as the cats, and I went about our morning routine. One thing I could not shake was the jarring sensation of plunging into freezing water.

While it was still cold in our corner of North Carolina nestled in the foothills of the Appalachian Mountains, we certainly didn't have heavy snow on the ground—and that deer my pen drew was not one of the local whitetails. First, the street cats in Raleigh tell Festus the man who met with Chesterfield smelled like a deer and now a deer shows up in one of my dreams?

That image nagged at me—a woman following a deer into a pond. Had I read something like that? Whatever it was, I couldn't put my finger on it, and I couldn't stop thinking about it.

When I finally dragged myself downstairs, Tori greeted me with the words, "Happy Winter Solstice!"

Feeling like a dropout from the local witch academy, I said, "The what?"

"Uh, hello?" she said. "The longest night and the shortest day of the year? Midwinter? Countdown to spring begins? Any of this ringing a bell?"

"Right," I said automatically, "happy solstice."

Tori gave me a critical, appraising once over. "Bad night?" she asked, conscious of the fact that Mindy was a few feet away behind the espresso counter.

"Yeah," I said, "bad dreams."

"Which one was it?" Tori asked. "Showing up at school naked or missing a big test?"

"Falling through an icy pond," I answered lightly. "Guess I shouldn't have watched *It's a Wonderful Life* before I went to bed."

Right on cue, Mindy said, "Oooh! I love that movie. When I was a little girl, I went around ringing bells to make angels."

"Me, too," Tori said, turning back toward the counter, but not before giving me the we'll-talk-later look. "So Mindy, did that bull about Frosty coming back again some day bug you as much as it bugged me? I mean seriously, the dude *melted*."

The light-hearted banter about the improbability of Christmas song lyrics got my mind off the dream and got us through the morning. It was lunchtime before Tori managed to pull me into the storeroom and hear a full account of my dream.

When I finished, she said, "Again with the deer."

"I know," I replied, "what the heck is up with that?"

"Tell Greer about it," Tori said. "Maybe she'll have some idea."

Greer had an idea alright, but one that made it crystal clear to me I couldn't keep withholding information from my magical elders much longer, holiday or no holiday.

FOURTEEN

The sight of Greer McVicar lounging elegantly on my tacky plaid sofa covered in adoring cats left me slack-jawed with shock. Well, that and the fact that she was dressed head to toe in jet black and seemed to be repelling every piece of cat hair my boys were trying to lay down.

There's magic, and then there's *magic*.

As I watched, Zeke wrapped himself around her neck and buried his face in her thick auburn hair while Xavier flopped in her lap and demanded a belly rub. Yule wedged himself under her right arm, and Winston lay sprawled across her knees.

"Do you want me to get them off you?" I asked.

Using one perfectly manicured crimson nail to scratch behind Zeke's ears, Greer said, "Good heavens, no. I'm quite fond of cats. They're wonderfully intuitive animals and superb company."

"Glad you think so," Festus said, sauntering out of my kitchen and almost giving me a heart attack.

"Don't do *that*!" I scolded. "How the heck did you get in here anyway?"

The ginger tom made a three-legged leap to the top of the easy chair by the window and arranged himself in a sun puddle. Then, fixing me with one of his impassive stares, Festus said, "Wouldn't you like to know."

"As a matter of fact," I said, "I would. I don't think I like you coming in here and corrupting my cats."

At that, four feline heads shot up and a chorus of protesting meows filled the room.

"I'd say that's a unanimous vote in my favor," Festus said smugly, "so unless you want to start finding hairballs on your pillow, I suggest you not insult me in front of the guys again."

"Festus McGregor," I said indignantly, "are you threatening me in my own living room?"

"Now, see," Festus said, "that's what's wrong with you so-called 'pet owners.' It's *their* living room, too, and they want me here."

When I opened my mouth to say something else, the ornery old rascal held up a paw. "Ah, ah, ah," he said, "remember, hairballs."

Only someone who has been awakened in the dead of night by the dreaded sound of pre-hairball yakking will understand why I caved. "Where are my manners?" I asked with saccharin sweetness. "It's *so* nice to see you, Festus. Welcome to *our* home."

"Much better," he said, giving me his contented cat face. "Lovely to be here."

I had invited Festus and Greer up to my place to discuss my latest dream in a private setting. Chase took off earlier in the day to do his Christmas shopping, so Festus could come and go without having to answer any questions, but I could hardly plunk a talking cat down in the middle of the espresso bar.

The lair was out because Beau and Glory had genealogical materials spread out all over the worktable, plus Darby and Rodney were deeply involved in some secret project for our time in Shevington.

When I asked Tori what they were doing, she said, "All I know is that it involves skiing videos on YouTube and they have your Dad helping them with miniature equipment."

"Never mind," I said. "I don't think I want to know."

That only left my apartment for a meeting place. With Festus settled in his sunny spot and Greer weighted down with cats, I launched into an account of my dream about the pond, using the illustrations from my grimoire to point out details.

When I finished, Festus looked at Greer and said, "Are you thinking, what I'm thinking?"

"The well maidens?" she asked.

"Okay, just stop it right there," I said. "This is not going to turn into one of *those* conversations. No vague references and no assuming that I know what you're talking about when I don't. Give me details. Now."

Festus arched an eye whisker. "Well," he said, "don't you get testy when you don't get enough sleep."

"This from a guy who is conscious what, 2 hours a day?" I shot back.

To my utter astonishment, Winston jumped on the coffee table, arched his back, and hissed at me.

"What the . . . " I started, but Festus broke in.

"It's okay, Winston," he said soothingly, "you don't have to defend me. Humanoids don't have manners as refined as ours."

Although his fur was still puffed out, Winston sat down, but not before giving me the feline stink eye.

Meeting his disapproving gaze head on, I muttered, "traitor," much to Festus' amusement.

I could tell Greer wanted to laugh, but somehow she kept a straight face. "My apologies," she said to me. "Festus and I do have a familiarity with Celtic lore that you lack. Let me begin again."

As the baobhan sith talked, the Highland burr grew thicker on her tongue. She spoke of a time when wells scattered throughout Scotland and Ireland served as open passageways from the Human Realm to the In Between and beyond to the Otherworld.

Fae maidens guarded the wells, offering bowls of the enchanted waters for the rejuvenation of weary travelers. Over the centuries, however, greedy humans began to abuse the free connection of the realms and the friendship of the Fae.

Hungry for power, the humans came to believe that the well waters could make them the magical equals of their Fae brothers. When the well maidens tried to protect the sparkling waters, many were abused and even killed.

In response to these crimes, the waters dried up of their own volition. At the same time, the Fae began their long, slow retreat from direct interaction with humans and their kind became the stuff of legends. A body of human mythology grew up around the events at the wells, even linking the kidnapping of the maidens to the search for the Holy Grail. In those stories, when the maidens disappeared, the land itself withered and died.

"There is one myth in particular," Greer said, "that speaks of the wasteland, the tale of the wounded Fisher King. In that story, man's greed and his interference with the laws of nature caused famine and drought that could only be relieved by recovering the Grail. The king himself suffered from a wound that would not heal until he was asked an innocent question from the depths of an unspoiled heart."

Before I knew about the Fae, none of that mythological imagery would have meant much to me, but now I heard the story in a completely different way. "But the real wasteland was the loss of magic in the world," I said.

"In the human world, yes," Greer replied. "In one way or another, the people of this realm have been searching for magic ever since."

"So what do you think is the significance of the pond in my dream?" I asked.

"It is possible," Greer said, "that the pond you saw is one of the few surviving wells through which it is still possible to reach the In Between."

"But I thought you said the wells dried up."

"The vast majority," she said, "but in a handful of enchanted places openings to the Otherworld still exist. They are not used, however, because we no longer enter the Middle Realm."

"You never told me exactly why that is," I said. "What happened?"

Festus lifted one hind leg and scratched at his ear. "That," he said, "is a really long story and honestly, I don't know how much of it is myth and how much is fact. Let's just say the Middle Realm turned into a dumping place for everyone and everything that didn't fit anywhere else."

"Okay," I said, "but what does any of this have to do with what I saw in my dream?"

"In the legends," Greer said, "the well maidens were often lured into danger by beings pretending to be wounded stags."

That's when I realized I knew this story already. "Joseph Campbell!" I cried. "I had to watch an episode of *The Power of Myth* for extra credit in senior English. He talked about this."

"He did," Greer said. "Campbell did everything he could to help humans recapture their sense of magic by reconnecting with the core principles of the natural order that underlie the themes present in the old stories."

I frowned. "Was he . . . ?"

"Fae?" Greer said. "No, but a man of such wisdom and insight should have been."

"Okay," I said, "so this is good. We have a working theory. John Smyth *can* change into a deer, and for some reason, he lured the woman in my dream into that pond. Now, if we can just figure out how she's connected to the Amulet of Caorunn, we should have it made."

Why I insist on thinking I'm winning any game of Connect the Fae Dots, I do not know.

"Uh yeah," Festus said, "not so fast. Smyth may be able to change into a deer alright, but if he can, we have a whole lot more than a common thief on our paws."

Uh oh.

"How much more?" I asked.

Dropping his usual sardonic attitude, Festus said earnestly, "A whole lot more, and I owe you an apology for not thinking about this possibility before. It all happened so long ago; I never dreamed there could be a connection when the street cats told me Smyth smelled like a deer."

When Festus starts getting serious, I start getting worried.

"Just tell me," I said. "How bad can it be?"

"In the days when the Tuatha Dé Danann walked among men," Greer said, "a Fae woman named Sadhbh refused the attentions of Fer Dorich, the Dark Druid."

Dark Druid? One sentence into the explanation and we had already gone from bad to worse.

"In retaliation for her refusal, the Dark Druid forced Sadhbh to live as a doe," Greer continued. "She remained in that form for three years until a serving man told her that if she could reach the castle of Fianna of Ireland, the curse would be broken."

"Did she get away?" I asked.

"She did," Festus said, "but to put it delicately, during those three years, the Dark Druid lifted the curse when it suited his purposes. There was always a rumor, unconfirmed, that Sadhbh gave birth to a son by Fer Dorich, and that the boy suffered the consequences of his mother's curse."

The unfairness of that rankled me immediately. "Why should he suffer the consequences?" I said. "He didn't do anything to wind up cursed. He just got in the way of what the grown-ups were doing."

Festus hopped out of the chair and landed on the ottoman in front of me.

"That's one of the things I love about you, Jinx," he said. "You always lead from the heart, but you have to understand these circumstances from a Fae perspective. Humans aren't the only ones who can give in to prejudice. If this story is true, the boy was an illegitimate child—a halfling—with a possible connection to the Darkness. He would have been feared and shunned."

"There is more," Greer said. "The castle of the Dark Druid lies in the Middle Realm."

Now I wasn't having any trouble connecting the dots at all.

"So you think that if this thief, John Smyth, is the son of Sadhbh and the Dark Druid, he can turn into a deer, and he has enough grudges to be in league with Chesterfield and Brenna, right?" I asked.

"Right," Festus said, "and I hate to tell you this, but we can't continue to keep all of this from Barnaby."

Festus shouldn't have worried. He wasn't going to get any argument from me.

"Agreed," I said. "We're all leaving for Shevington on Christmas Eve. That's just three days away. Let's let everyone enjoy their Christmas dinner, and then we'll tell Granddad and Moira the whole story. Does that work?"

"Yes," Greer said, "Lucas and I must attend to some DGI business in Uzbekistan on Thursday. We will be meeting you in Shevington that evening."

That's when my curiosity got the better of me.

"Can you tell me why Granddad has been sending Lucas all over the world for the last month?" I asked.

I hadn't intended for the question to come out sounding annoyed, but even to my ears, the tone was unmistakable.

Festus' eyes lit up with interest as a wicked grin drew his whiskers back.

"Oh," he said, "now *that* question had some claws in it. Missing your new boyfriend, are you?"

"Lucas is *not* my boyfriend," I said defensively, "and don't you start with me, Festus McGregor. I just wondered where Lucas has been."

In a timely show of female solidarity, Greer stepped in.

"I have been wondering the same thing myself," she said. "The laddie has been uncharacteristically tight-lipped about his special assignments. I rather imagine that when we do talk to Barnaby, both he and Lucas will have as much to share with us as we have to share with them."

Color me surprised on that one, *not*.

At any rate, we had a plan. A best-laid plan, even—and you know what they say about those.

You'll see shortly that we did tell Barnaby and Moira everything—in fact by the time we returned to Briar Hollow from Shevington everyone was up to speed on the whole story. Barnaby and by extension, Lucas, did, indeed, have plenty to share with us as well, just as Greer predicted.

But for as important as those conversations would be, the one thing I did not see coming was the identity of the other person in the room—a person I thought I might never see again.

FIFTEEN

The Mother Oak breathed deeply, enjoying the natural warmth surrounding her trunk and canopy. Even in the depths of winter's cold, that part of her growing in the Otherworld never felt the withering of her leaves.

Safe in the realm of the Fae, the Tree remained strong and green, strong enough to feed and support those parts of herself that crossed through the In Between and reached the world of the humans. There, with the changing of the seasons, the Great Tree's mirror self, grew sparse and bare, retreating within until the birth of summer.

Humans required such markers to steer their course through life. They needed to count and order the hours within a day, the days in a month, the months in the year. Their minds could not grasp the multi-layered reality of time, no matter how complex the theories devised by their scientists.

For her part, the Mother Tree looked both to the future and the past simultaneously like Janus the Roman. Her watchful gaze comprehended the meaning of transitions and transience, she feared not the negotiation of passages, nor the meaning of beginnings and endings.

In the space of a few hours, her beloved fairy friends would fly on the night wind to decorate her branches with their shimmering dust. She would stand outlined with millions of glittering prisms, all in celebration of the Christmas holidays.

The Oak enjoyed the observance as much as the people gathered round her on the green, because, if she was nothing else, the Great Tree was a Watcher.

Beings across all the realms marked mid-winter in their fashion. The people of Shevington took particular pleasure in mingling multiple traditions. Even now, the sounds of workers drifted into the Oak's awareness. She heard their laughter as they built booths for the Yule carnival and assembled mechanical amusements borrowed from the human realm.

As a second presence rose up beside her, the Mother Tree effortlessly conjured the illusion of a cozy sitting room. Had an outsider been able to look within the mind of the Oak, they would have seen two women friends of indeterminate age sitting together enjoying the view presented through an enormous picture window.

"You did not have to create this setting for my benefit," Myrtle said, "but thank you."

A ripple of laughter circled the room. "You are welcome," the Oak said. "We are all happier amidst that which we know best. You and I both comprehend that form is nothing but illusion, but there is no reason that illusion can not be pleasant. Tell me, aos si, what is that great wheel the workers are erecting?"

"It is called a Ferris wheel," Myrtle said, "a device created for the amusement of humans. They sit in chambers affixed to the wheel, going round and round, finding excitement in both the motion and the view afforded to them."

The simulacrum of the Mother Tree clapped her hands with delight. "I so envy them the simplicity of such pastimes. For all the muddled nature of humanity, for their conflicts and misjudgments, there are times when they remember the joy of simply being."

"They do have that capacity," Myrtle agreed. "I only wish they would search for it more often."

The Oak started to answer, but her attention was drawn to the lower valley. "Ah," she said, "the portal has just opened. Our guests are arriving."

The image in the picture window wavered and changed to show Jinx, her parents, Gemma, Tori, Colonel Longworth, Darby, Glory, Rodney, and even Duke gathered amid a pile of luggage and wrapped presents.

"Look," the Mother Tree said, "young Connor has met them in a horse-drawn conveyance. It does my heart good to see them all reunited."

Myrtle sighed. "My heart is also gladdened," she said, "but I do regret I cannot share Jinx's first holiday season in Shevington."

"Do not be so certain that you will not," the Mother Tree said. "The threat posed by Chesterfield's ambitions grows now that he has turned his attention to the amulets."

"Are you suggesting that the time for my return has arrived?" Myrtle asked.

"You have not healed to the fullest extent possible," the Oak replied. "Were you to go back, I could not return you to them as you have always been. The choice to stay with me or to leave rests with you, aos si."

"If I were to go back, what abilities would I retain?"

"That I cannot predict," the Tree said, "it will be yours to discover."

"I do not fear change," Myrtle mused. "Why do you judge that this may be the correct time for me to rejoin the Daughters of Knasgowa?"

Myrtle felt the weight of the Tree's gaze fall upon her. "Because aos si," she said, "I fear they will be called upon to enter the Middle Realm, and that they cannot do without you."

For me, Christmas has always been magical, but that first holiday in Shevington knocked the concept right out of the park. So much so that I've already recounted the experience with you in another story.

As much as I'd like to take the time now to go back over every detail of that weekend, we need to move along. Honestly, when I shared Christmas in the Valley with you before, I left out all the stuff going on behind the scenes because I wanted you to enjoy the time with us. Now we need to dig a little deeper.

For about 24 hours in Shevington, I managed to forget about guys who turn into deer, missing amulets, and Dark Druids. That happened in part because my personal life took something of a turn on Christmas Eve.

Lucas Grayson kissed me while we stood in a shadowed nook on the city wall overlooking the holiday fair below.

Like the way I just tossed that out? Let's back up a little bit.

Lucas showed up alone on Christmas Eve. The moms, Tori, and I were sitting in front of the fire in Granddad's parlor while the men hid behind the study door and discussed their still-to-be accomplished gift shopping excursion.

With some none-too-subtle maneuvering, I managed to get the moms and Tori out of the parlor so I could have a minute or two alone with Lucas. Up until that night, there had been some good-natured flirting between us, but to be honest, I couldn't tell what interested him more—me or getting a rise out of Chase.

From what Festus tells me, the two men used to be friends. He doesn't know what happened between them either, but at any given moment, Chase and Lucas are roughly one wisecrack away from coming to blows.

About all Lucas and I managed to do on that sofa before the men emerged and claimed him, was make a date to have funnel cakes later at the fair.

Funnel cakes turned into a walk atop the wall, which turned into Lucas trying to put his arm around me. On reflex, I stepped away.

Yep, I am just fickle enough to be annoyed over not knowing where the man had been for a month *and* push him away when he's standing right beside me in a willing mood.

"Have I been reading this all wrong?" he asked. "I don't want to be a clueless idiot here."

Keeping my eyes on the crowd below, I said carefully, "You haven't read anything wrong."

"Then what's going on?" he said. "I know we haven't been able to spend any time together these last few weeks, but you have to see I'm interested in you, Jinx. Talk to me."

"Lucas," I said lamely, "we work together."

"We do," he agreed. "And?"

"Chase and I worked together, too, and having a relationship didn't go so well with him."

That wasn't at all what I had intended to say, but sometimes the truth has a way of just popping out.

"Ah," Lucas said, "well, I'm not a werecat. Certified, taboo-free water elf at your service."

He bowed.

The man actually bowed.

Steeling myself against all that charm, I tried again. "The breakup is still pretty fresh."

Any sign of teasing vanished.

"That I get," Lucas said. "Do you still have feelings for Chase?"

At the same time that I didn't want to deal with a question that complicated, the fact that he had the courage to simply ask it made me like Lucas even more. People who confront things head on make points with me fast.

"Oh," I said, "so we're putting *everything* out on the table."

"I generally find that works best," he said. "I have a lot of faults, Jinx, but I don't go stomping around in another guy's relationship."

Also a point-winning statement. I told him the truth— I didn't honestly know how I felt about anything, in particular, Chase McGregor.

"I'm not a pushy man," Lucas said, "so I'm going to make a suggestion, which you can accept or reject. Okay?"

He stepped closer, and this time, I didn't move away. "Okay," I said, "what is it?"

That's when he directed my attention to the mistletoe bough overhead.

"Do you know the story?" he asked. "Of the mistletoe?"

I shook my head.

"Baldur, the grandson of Thor, woke up one day to find that every living thing on earth, including the plants, wanted to kill him. While he cowered, terrified in his room, his wife and mother went to each animal and plant begging their kindness toward Baldur, but they forgot to speak with the mistletoe."

"Bad plan?" I asked.

"Very bad plan," Lucas said. "Just as Baldur began to celebrate his freedom from fear, a mistletoe arrow struck him dead. Moral of the story? Never forget the mistletoe."

Just as he'd intended, I laughed. "If you're trying to tell me that if I don't kiss you, an arrow is going to come flying out of nowhere and kill me, that may be the worst pick-up line ever."

Cupping my face in his hand, he said, "It's not a line. I do want to kiss you. And if you find the experience forgettable, then we go right on being friends who shared a really nice first Christmas together."

"And if it's unforgettable?" I whispered.

"Then you quit throwing up walls and let us get to know each other."

Trust me, I wanted to argue, but he was so close I could feel the warmth of his body. Light and shadows from the scene below played across his handsome features. Without thinking, I reached up and brushed my fingers through his unruly black bangs. What happened next was anything but forgettable.

And then on Christmas Day, Chase invited me for a walk, gave me his dead mother's locket—with our picture in it, no less—and told me he wanted us to get back together.

Guess I was wrong about Ann Marie Detwiler, huh?

Sixteen

Guys who change into deer, Dark Druids, and missing amulets looked pretty good after I took that walk with Chase. Going after evil in its various forms paled beside the state of confusion that is my love life.

Two facts complicated that state even more. First, Chase saw me kiss Lucas the night before on the wall and second, I followed that up by kissing Chase the next day.

Now hold on. I can explain. Sort of.

Chase had just given me the locket, a gift he followed up with a question that quietly broke my heart. "Are we so easy to forget, Jinx?" he asked, anguish filling his eyes.

Nothing about our break up had been easy. I cried myself to sleep for a month, and, as I reminded him, splitting up had not been my idea.

That's when he caught hold of my hands and said, "I deserve that. I was a coward. I made a terrible mistake. Please forgive me, Jinx. Please let's try again."

When I told him he couldn't be serious, he kissed me to prove he was and, well, I kissed him back. What can I say? The aching familiarity of our history just pulled me in. To my credit, I did come to my senses, I did push him away, and then that jealous side of his personality reared its ugly head.

"Because of Lucas Grayson?" he asked, with an edge in his voice.

"That," I said, "will get you absolutely nowhere, Chase. We aren't going to do this because none of the things that made our relationship hard have changed in the slightest. Now I'm going back to Granddad's. You can walk with me or not, it's up to you, but I'm done with drama for the day."

We went back, but Chase made one thing clear—he didn't intend to give up.

By sundown, everyone had essentially slipped into a post–Christmas coma from an overabundance of food and emotion.

Mom was so happy to be with Connor she burst into tears every time she looked at him. Gemma and Tori kept up a good front, but I know their first post-divorce holiday weighed on them both, and then, in one of the most touching moments of the day, we found out why Beau had reacted so oddly at the mention of his sword on Thanksgiving.

The gallant colonel sold his cherished weapon to an online collector to raise money to buy gifts for everyone, including purchasing his late wife's antique cameo for me. As if that weren't moving enough, Tori figured out what he'd done and bought the sword back. I'll never forget the expression on Beau's face when he opened the box and saw the saber.

When Tori said, "A colonel in the Army of Northern Virginia can't be without his sword," I honestly thought Beau was going to cry. Instead, he thanked Tori for reuniting him "with an old comrade" before wrapping her in a hug so heartfelt it brought tears to *her* eyes.

The sun had hardly set when people began to drag off to bed. Ultimately, I found myself sitting in the deserted parlor with only Dílestos for company.

The arrival of the walking stick in Shevington came as

a total surprise, especially since it was delivered by our next door neighbor and fellow witch, Amity Prescott.

Amity spent most of the summer and fall missing in action. She helped with the paranormal festival, but she didn't involve herself in any of the events surrounding Chesterfield's ambitions. Frankly, that ticked me off a little bit. I felt we needed all hands on deck, but Granddad insisted Amity was doing what she was supposed to be doing.

With her usual brusque manner, Amity refused to come to Shevington for the holiday weekend, preferring to stay in Briar Hollow and take care of my cats, which I did appreciate. Amity did, however, show up for Christmas dinner, Dílestos in hand.

"Forget something?" she asked, shoving the oak staff into my hand.

"Uh, not really," I admitted.

"Are you simple minded?" she asked, glaring at me.

"Excuse me?" I said, more than a little put off by her question.

Her response made me feel about three inches tall and dumber than dirt.

"When Chesterfield kidnapped your brother, what was the ransom?" she asked.

"A living branch of the Mother Tree," I said.

"And what is Dílestos?"

Oh, crud. The staff is a living branch of the Mother Tree.

"I honestly didn't put that together, Amity," I admitted.

"Nor did anyone else, apparently," she huffed. "Someone must be with Dílestos at all times. Don't leave her alone again."

So there I sat at the end of Christmas Day holding a stick, one with the ability to enter my thoughts and hold conversations. Dílestos, like everyone else, seemed to have one goal in mind—getting me to talk to the Mother Tree.

I hadn't paid my respects to the Oak since our arrival in Shevington on purpose. It may not have been the most mature position to take, but frankly, I was ticked off at the Tree for refusing to let me talk to Myrtle. That was the deal when Myrtle merged her essence with the Oak to heal—I would get to talk to her. Didn't happen. Not even once.

That night, however, when Dílestos added her voice to all the other people who had been bugging me about having a conversation with the Tree, I gave in. The Lord High Mayor's house sits right across the square from the Oak, and I was out of excuses.

From the way the air instantly warmed when I stepped under the Mother Tree's spreading branches, I knew that she had been patiently waiting for me.

"Okay," I said, "you finally did it. You got enough people to bug me about talking to you, so here I am. Merry Christmas."

The Tree did what any amused parent would do. She laughed at me.

"Are you so very out of patience with me?" she asked. "You are reunited with your brother. Was that not the last thing you asked?"

Plopping down on one of the stone benches ringing the massive trunk, I said, "Yes, it was, but admit it, that didn't happen the way you intended."

Word of advice. Don't try trading verbal barbs with ancient trees. You won't win.

"What do you know of my intentions?" the Tree asked.

And the correct answer would be "nothing," but I did remember my last conversation with the Oak in detail.

"You asked me to find out why Chesterfield started all of this 30 years ago," I said. "I still don't know that."

"That is true," the Oak agreed, "but the course of your investigations was derailed by the Creavit himself. I would not have expected you to do less than save your brother's life."

The Tree wasn't being unreasonable, I was, and the Oak called me on it. "Are you ready to abandon this petulance and talk to me?" she asked.

The problem with people like me who are good at keeping our own counsel is that when we are ready to talk, you can't shut us up.

An hour later, with midnight fast approaching, I finally ran out of steam. I told the Tree about things I didn't even know I wanted to talk about, like my gratitude for becoming a business owner after years in a minimum wage job, how much I loved having Tori for my business partner, what it meant to me to find my magic and through it to get closer to my mother.

I talked about things that hurt me, like the Andrews' divorce, the break-up with Chase, and my constant frustration that Irenaeus Chesterfield always managed to slip out of our grasp. And, of course, I talked about my confusion over Lucas and my real fear that I might still be in love with Chase, too.

I talked until my voice grew hoarse and I didn't think I could talk any more. That's when the night air grew warm and comforting with the scents of spring. It seemed as if the Mother Tree embraced me, sheltering me in the remembrance of hope.

"We do not experience life in the same way," she said, "but I, too know of anger, disappointment, hurt, and yes, I know of love. These emotions stir in the depths of my heart as surely as they stir in yours. But still, you have not named that which joins all these things and for you causes the deepest pain of all. You have spoken of much to me, Jinx Hamilton, now speak of that."

She wanted me to talk about Myrtle, but I had no intention of setting myself up to be told no again. "I don't know what you mean," I said obstinately.

"Ah," the Tree said, "but you do. The common thread that runs through all these concerns is loneliness. You have grown strong and independent these past months, but now you grapple with problems you do not understand, things that haunt your dreams at night. Although you have said the words to no one, you yearn for the aid of your friend and counselor to negotiate these frightening currents. When last you spoke to me of the aos si, I denied your request, so you fear to make it again. Is this not the truth, Jinx Hamilton?"

The words brought tears to my eyes. Like a begging child, I said, "Will you let me see her now? Will you let me talk to Myrtle? Please?"

At the edge of my awareness, the clock above the entrance to city hall began to chime midnight as a heavy, brilliant snow started to fall. The flakes glowed with unnatural luminescence, hanging around the Great Tree in a glittering aura. The light blinded me so that I raised my hand to shield my eyes.

When I took it away, Myrtle was standing in front of me as goldenly beautiful as I remembered.

"Are you real?" I whispered, afraid to even blink for fear she'd be gone again.

Myrtle held out her arms to me. "As real as you are," she said.

I catapulted off the bench and into her embrace. "Can you stay?" I cried. "Please tell me you can stay."

Holding me tight, she said reassuringly, "I can stay. Have no fear about that."

Leaning back, but not letting go, I searched her face. "You're healed? You're back to your old self?"

Myrtle paused, a hesitation that made my heart skip a beat. "Sit with me, Jinx," she said. "There are things I must tell you."

We went back to the bench, and Myrtle caught hold of my hands. "Do not be afraid," she said. "I am well, but understand that I am not as I was. When I could no longer ignore the threat Chesterfield poses to the Grid and to your family and came to understand how much we all failed to piece together the clues he left for us, I asked the Mother Oak to allow me to return so that I might join this fight at your side."

The Oak's voice filled the air around us. "I granted the request, but Myrtle could not come back to you as the aos si. That part of her was not yet healed. To be with you, she gave up who she has always been."

At that news, tears flowed freely down my face. "Oh, Myrtle, I am so sorry."

"Do not be," she smiled. "This is my gift to you. I am here of my own choosing. I would be nowhere else."

As she spoke, she gently cupped my face in her hand. I leaned against the touch.

"If you aren't the aos si," I asked, "then what are you?"

"I do not yet know," Myrtle admitted. "That we must discover together in the new year that lies ahead, but for now, dear Jinx, it is Christmas, and we are reunited. Let that be enough."

Having Myrtle back wasn't just "enough," it was everything—everything for which I'd hoped and everything I would need for what lay ahead.

SEVENTEEN

When we left the Mother Tree, Myrtle managed to keep me from shouting her return to the rooftops of the sleeping city, but just barely. Instead, at her suggestion, we walked together through the silent streets to the bottom of the long hill leading to the Alchemist's workshop.

Dílestos quivered in my hand. She was as excited as I was to have Myrtle back. Even though Amity had made clear to me the staff's importance as a living branch of the Mother Tree, I had no idea the real role Dílestos was meant to play in my life. It wouldn't be long before I learned more.

At Moira's door, I paused before knocking. "Are you sure about this?" I asked. "It must be after one in the morning. Moira will be asleep, and Dewey is not going to be happy."

Dewey only cracks a smile for Darby.

"Master Dewey will be happy," Myrtle said, "he just won't show it. Knock."

The sound of my knuckles striking the massive oak door echoed like gunfire, but no one answered.

"Maybe we should just go back to Barnaby's and see Moira in the morning," I suggested.

Myrtle smiled. "The dwarf approaches," she said, "and judging from the weight of his footfalls, he will be grumpy indeed."

I started to crack a Snow White joke, but before I could get the words out of my mouth, the door opened to reveal a stout, scowling little barrel of a man wearing a striped nightshirt.

"What?" he barked.

"Good evening, Dewey," Myrtle said. "We are here to see the Alchemist."

Blinking, Dewey held the candlestick in his hand higher and squinted at Myrtle. For a flicker of a second, a look of elated surprise crossed his face before he got control of his expression.

"Aren't you supposed to be inside the Mother Tree," he groused, "not waking people up in the middle of the night?"

From the shadows behind him, Moira's approaching voice scolded him sharply. "Really, Dewey! Is that any way to greet the aos si upon her return?"

"It's not my fault she can't tell time," he snapped. "I'm going back to bed."

Turning on his heel, he started to march away, but after about three steps, he turned and looked at Myrtle. "Welcome back," he said brusquely. Then, glancing at Moira, he added, "I'll stir the fire."

The three of us stood silently in the open doorway. Moira took a step toward Myrtle, before stopping to simply look at her, pure joy playing across the Alchemist's handsome features. The two of them made for an interesting tableau.

Moira wore a velvet robe covering her night dress. Her long hair, braided for sleep, hung over one shoulder. Still, she conveyed an air of dark, regal bearing in contrast to Myrtle's golden lightness. Both women are tall and lean. I know they're strong. But Myrtle always seems thin and willowy beside Moira's sturdy presence.

Holding her hands out, Moira said softly, "How fare thee?"

"I come to thee seeking an answer to that question," Myrtle said, taking her hands. "That and to look again upon thy face, dear friend. I have missed our talks."

Before I thought, I blurted out, "The Tree wouldn't let you talk to her either?"

The two women—the most powerful practitioners I know—made an identical and very motherly "tsking" sound.

"I see that you have not cultivated patience during my absence," Myrtle said. "You make it sound as if the Mother Tree held me prisoner. My silence was something upon which the Oak and I agreed, not a thing that was forced upon me."

Every response that rose to my lips would make me sound like a whiner, but that didn't stop me. "*Fine*," I said, "but I still feel better knowing I wasn't the only one getting told no."

Moira laughed. "You were not, indeed," she said. "Now come in out of the cold and let us sit by the fire."

The Alchemist led us across the room, gesturing the wall sconces to life as we passed. By the time we each claimed a chair by the hearth, flickering light drove back the shadows in the cavernous space. It wasn't until the heat of the fire hit me that I realized I was freezing.

Moira saw my involuntary shiver. With another wave of her hand, a thick wool blanket materialized and wrapped itself around my shoulders while a mug of steaming hot chocolate floated in the air before me waiting to be claimed.

The mug felt like heaven in my hands, and the soothing liquid seemed to flow out along every nerve in my body. I didn't have to ask if the drink carried extra enchantment. With Moira, that's a given.

As I watched, she conjured a snifter of brandy for herself and another for Myrtle. Under normal circumstances,

I might have protested being given a blanket and hot chocolate while my companions drank the hard stuff. But, honestly? In their company, I was the child, and there is no situation in which I will turn down chocolate in any form.

"I spoke with the Mother Tree earlier this evening," Moira said. "She gave me no indication that you would be returning to us. Has something happened?"

"Only my realization that I am needed here to help rectify our error in underestimating Irenaeus Chesterfield and his ambitions," Myrtle said. She smiled at me. "And my desire to give Jinx what she most wished for on this Yule night."

"Ah," Moira nodded. "So Jinx finally spoke honestly to the Mother Tree."

I might have guessed she was in on the whole "talk to the tree" campaign.

"Not that I'm complaining," I said, "but why did the Tree give me what I wanted and more tonight? It's not like I haven't asked before."

"On this occasion, you did not ask with words," Myrtle said, "you asked with your heart."

At the time, I thought I understood what she meant, but I seriously didn't. File that one away. We'll come back to it.

Moira, who had been studying Myrtle's face, said quietly, "What bargain did you strike with the Mother Oak, aos si?"

"You know the Tree well," Myrtle said. "To come back, the course of my healing stopped. No further recovery is possible. I fear I am no longer as you have known me. I am not the aos si."

Setting her glass on the table beside her chair, Moira held out her hands again. Myrtle took them silently. A soft opalescence spread from Moira's form. As it undulated toward Myrtle, a low basso hum rose up around them.

As I listened, my eyelids drooped under the weight of a delicious lethargy. It might have been the hypnotic sound or the mojo-spiked hot chocolate, but when I finally struggled awake, sunlight streamed through the windows falling on a breakfast table set before the fire.

"Good morning," Moira said. "Did you sleep well?"

Considering I'd been upright in a chair, I should have had knotted muscles and stiff limbs. Instead, I felt wonderful.

"Like a rock," I replied. "What did you slip me in that hot chocolate?"

"That," Moira said, levitating the pot and expertly pouring hands-free coffee, "is a trade secret."

I accepted the cup cautiously. "Anything I should know about this coffee?" I asked.

Moira's brows knitted in a frown. "That the beans are from Madame Kaveh's private stock?"

"Just checking," I said. Turning my attention to Myrtle, I asked, "How are you this morning?"

"Well," she replied, "and content. Moira was able to give me some of the answers I sought."

Let me tell you something about the oldest Fae. They say stuff like that and then just sit there like they've told you everything you need to know. It's annoying as hell.

"*And?*" I prodded.

The Fae also drop bombshells with complete nonchalance, like what Myrtle said next.

"I am no longer immortal, and I am confined to this single form."

Okay. She's a blonde knockout, roughly six one who, on a bad day, might be forced to buy a size six. There are worse fates.

The immortality thing was a different matter.

"You can die?" I gasped. "Like *really* die?"

"Not easily," Moira said soothingly, "nor any time

soon. Myrtle will now age as slowly as any other Fae who possesses great power, but yes, she will, one day, pass from this life."

"What about her powers?" I asked. "How much have they changed?"

"I think the best way to describe what I have detected so far would be to say that her 'range' has diminished," Moira said. "Myrtle no longer possesses the hyper-aware-ness of her previous form. Beyond that, only time will tell."

When I took a minute to mull that information over, Myrtle said teasingly, "I should think you would find my diminished perception to be rather positive. Now you and Tori can talk about me while you are upstairs in the store and I won't hear you."

I started to protest. "We never . . . "

Myrtle stopped me with an arched eyebrow.

"We never said anything *bad* about you," I amended. "Okay, except maybe that you needed to lose that silly bun with the pencil stuck in it."

In the beginning, when Myrtle appeared to us in human form, she adopted a stereotypical librarian look she thought we'd find more soothing and less overwhelming. Clearly, she'd never sat through study hall in a high school library.

"Transmogrification is now beyond my ability," Myrtle said. "There will be no more 'silly bun.'"

"How do you feel about that? I know you liked to use your various forms to explore the human realm."

"It is something of a . . . disappointment," Myrtle admitted.

"Barnaby would tell you that transmogrification is a double-edged sword," Moira said. "He has not used that particular ability in centuries."

"Why?" I asked curiously.

Moira shook her head. "That is a story your grandfa-ther must share with you. It is not mine to tell."

Suddenly I realized that no one in my family knew where I was. "What time is it?" I asked. "My mother must be worried out of her mind."

"No," Moira said. "I have already sent word that you are here with me. After we've had our breakfast, we will go to the Lord High Mayor's house and share the news of Myrtle's return."

An hour later, amid a riot of tears and laughter in my granddad's parlor, a great rumbling purr emanated from Festus as he gazed at Myrtle.

Since he primarily lives in his small werecat form, Festus hadn't brought any clothes with him to Shevington. He had no choice but to greet Myrtle as a ginger tom cat.

"Forgive me," he said to Myrtle, bowing his head respectfully. "Had I known you were returning, I would have shifted and worn a proper suit."

More than once I'd heard Myrtle give Festus grief for his refusal to move about in human form or to put on clothes. We all knew she was just teasing, but for the first time, I realized Festus hadn't known.

"Steadfast Festus McGregor," Myrtle said softly, "what need has a werecat with the heart of a lion for the silly raiment of man? I have missed thee, my dear, old friend."

Festus raised his head and regarded Myrtle with brimming eyes. "As I have missed thee, dear lady. Pray, do not leave us again. We were poorer for thy absence."

We all choked up when Myrtle gently laid her hand on his head. Nobody—and I mean *nobody* 'pets' Festus unless he's flirting with an unsuspecting human female who thinks he's just a cute old cat.

But this time, instead of one of his usual razor-sharp retorts, Festus began to purr even louder. The sound embodied the feeling of love overwhelming us all.

Myrtle really was home.

EIGHTEEN

Barnaby declared an open door policy when we all arrived in Shevington on Christmas Eve. We came and went as we pleased, so I shouldn't have been surprised when Rube waddled out of the kitchen that morning balancing an enormous, multi-layer sandwich in his paws.

Fae politics can get deadly serious in a heartbeat, which is why you have to love a guy like Rube who supplied us with the funniest moment of the day.

The instant he saw Myrtle, his snowy muzzle split into a toothy grin. "Mert!" he cried joyously. "Welcome back, babe! I knew you couldn't hang out with old Ma Oak forever. Just between us, she can be about as funny as a case of root rot on a good day."

While the rest of us regarded them with varying degrees of shock, Myrtle replied with equal enthusiasm, "Reuben! I see you are maintaining your usual healthy appetite. Does my spot on the dart team remain open?"

"Absolutely, Mert!" Rube said. "Usual time on Wednesday nights. We need you back. The fairies tried to run in a ringer. Some pixie from Philly. Great bod, but if you don't keep an eye on her she cheats like a banshee."

Then realizing what he'd just said, Rube turned to Greer, who was seated by the fire and added apologetically, "Not meaning no implication about present company, Red."

146

Greer nodded tolerantly. "I am only distantly related to the banshees," she said. "As a rule, we baobhan sith have a reputation for more forthright dealings. I personally find all that banshee wailing to be rather melodramatic."

"My point exactly," Rube enthused, approaching Myrtle. They exchanged an elaborate handshake complete with a synchronized elbow bump.

That's when Rube realized we were all staring at them. "What?" he asked indignantly. "I can't hang out with the big dogs? Speaking with metaphors, of course."

"Reuben," Greer said drily, "you wouldn't recognize a metaphor if it walked up and slapped your charmingly insolent face."

"Not true," Rube countered, "I talk immaculate English."

We all laughed at that. Shrugging, Rube took a bite out of his sandwich. Then, shifting the half-chewed salami to one side of his mouth, he said, "Tell'em about you and me Mert."

Myrtle seemed to be enjoying our reaction to the whole exchange enormously. "Reuben and his wrecking crew have been of use to me through the years," she said. "I have always found their lack of awe for my status rather refreshing."

"In other words," Tori said with a grin, "you like slumming with them."

"Hey!" Rube protested. "We don't hang out in no slums."

"You work in sewers," Tori pointed out.

"Hazard of the profession," Rube said. "Besides, Mert always has a blast with us. Everybody around here treats her like this big deal Fae. She can be a dame with us."

Smiling tolerantly, Barnaby said, "Need I point out that Myrtle is a 'big deal Fae?'"

At that, Moira and I exchanged a glance that was not

lost on my grandfather. "What?" he said suspiciously. "Is there something you're not telling us?"

Myrtle stepped in smoothly. "Perhaps we can retire to your study for a few minutes, Barnaby?" she suggested. "There are some matters I would like to discuss with you in private, at least initially."

Mom shot me a questioning look. I mouthed "it's okay," before following Myrtle and Moira into the small room off the parlor.

It didn't take long for Moira to deliver the results of her assessment of Myrtle's altered abilities to Barnaby. He listened without interrupting. When the Alchemist finished, he turned to Myrtle, "How are you taking this news?" he asked.

"I somewhat regret the loss of my transmogrification," she admitted, "but I believe I am still in possession of adequate abilities to be of use to our cause."

Barnaby laughed. "My dear, Myrtle," he said, "at even half of your original capacity, you are more naturally powerful than any of us, not to mention the benefit to be derived from your vast experience."

Inclining her head in what might have been embarrassment, Myrtle said, "Thank you. I do hope that proves to be the case. We've rather underestimated Chesterfield, haven't we?"

Scrubbing tiredly at his face with his hand, Barnaby said, "I am afraid my brother has been underestimated since the day of his birth. The strain of that disparagement twisted what is, undeniably, a brilliant mind."

Myrtle frowned. "You have revealed the truth of your identity to Jinx?" she asked.

"To Jinx and to the others in her immediate circle," Barnaby said. "During your absence, Festus in particular expressed suspicion about my decisions regarding Irenaeus following the incident in 1936. It was best for the half truths and obfuscations to end."

"Agreed," Myrtle said. "We must all learn as much as we possibly can about your brother's motivations if we are to stop him."

"I should have stopped him after he killed Adeline," Barnaby said bitterly.

That was the first time I'd ever heard my grandfather admit that his younger brother was a murderer.

Moira laid her hand on Barnaby's arm. "At the time you had no conclusive proof that Irenaeus was the killer."

"I could have gained that conclusive proof had I been less a coward," he said tiredly.

They were doing it again.

Raising my hand, I said, "Hold on. I realize this is a highly sensitive subject, but I need you guys to fill in some of these gaps for me."

My grandfather turned uncertain eyes to Myrtle and then to Moira. The Alchemist leaned forward and ran her fingers soothingly through the graying hair at his temple. "Tell her, darling," she said softly. "She will not think less of you."

The tenderness of that gesture alone indicated to me how hard this conversation was for Barnaby. He and Moira never display their affection for one another in front of witnesses.

When Barnaby caught hold of her hand, Moira entwined their fingers and drew him out of his chair to sit beside her on the settee. The proximity seemed to give him the resolve he needed.

"You know the story of my first wife's murder?" he asked me.

"Most of it," I admitted. "Chase told me. I hope that's okay."

"Of course," Barnaby said. "I rarely speak of those days, so your foreknowledge saves us considerable time.

In the wake of Adeline's death, I used my power of transmogrification to travel in disguise throughout the Continent seeking her killer. In Brussels, I cornered a young apprentice wizard who had been seen in the vicinity of our home in Kent the day of the killing. When I located him, he was in the company of Brenna Sinclair."

Chase told me that part as well, but at the time, the full implication of it didn't dawn on me. Now, especially in light of my dreams and my conversation with Greer, I understood perfectly, but I let my grandfather tell his story.

"The Norman Templar Knight to whom my brother apprenticed himself during the Second Crusade was Brenna's father, Henri de St. Clair. Our families enjoy a long, convoluted history," Barnaby said. "That day, Brenna would have been quite happy had I forgotten my principles and, like my brother, forfeited my soul."

He turned his eyes toward the fire in the grate, but his true vision went inward to the landscape of a painful memory. "I intimidated that apprentice—that boy— through every magical means possible. Transmogrification allowed me to wear the face of another man. I could do as I pleased without sullying my reputation in the Fae world—or so I thought until Brenna revealed herself. My focus had been so intent, I did not feel her presence concealed in an antechamber. She had more than enough information with which to damn me and aggrandize herself, but she sought to deliver the coup de grâce, goading me to tighten my fingers on the boy's neck and wring the life from him. It mattered not to her, or to me, that he withheld nothing. He simply had no information to give. By that time my rage and grief consumed me to the brink of madness."

"What happened?" I asked softly.

"Moira arrived," Barnaby said, slipping his arm around the Alchemist's shoulder and drawing her closer.

"Adeline was my dearest friend," Moira explained. "She would not have wanted Barnaby to commit a murder to avenge her death. When I learned that he had gone to Brussels to confront the apprentice, I went after him."

"And I thank the Blessed Universe that you did," Barnaby said. "Yours was the voice of reason."

"So that's why you don't use your transmogrification," I said.

My grandfather nodded. "Yes," he said. "I have no right to make use of that ability after so abusing it for my own self-interest."

"You are too hard on yourself," Moira said. "You did not kill the boy."

"But I *wanted* to kill him," Barnaby said. "That is more than enough."

"I hate to ask," I said, "but I just want to make sure that we're all in agreement now that Chesterfield really did kill Adeline.

Myrtle, who had been silent through the whole exchange, said, "The provenance of the Amulet of the Phoenix provides the most damning evidence. Before it surfaced in Brenna Sinclair's possession, it was last seen by Barnaby on Adeline's person the day of her death."

That statement gave me an opening to ask a question that had bothered me for weeks.

"Granddad," I said, "I know you said the Mother Tree directed you to let Beau keep the Amulet of the Phoenix after he took it away from Brenna, but if the last time you saw it was on Adeline, you couldn't have been as calm as you acted when the artifact showed up."

"I wasn't," he admitted, "but the power of denial can be stronger than any chain."

Yeah. I didn't have any comeback for that one.

"The time for denial has passed," Myrtle said. "Now we know Irenaeus may well have acquired the Amulet of

Caorunn, we must take deliberate steps to counter what-ever malevolent plan he has in mind."

"How are we supposed to do that?" I asked.

Myrtle fixed me with a smile that was both tolerant and probing at the same time. "By locating the Amulet of Caorunn," she said. "Perhaps you would like to begin by telling us about these dreams you've been having?"

Nineteen

Remember what Rube said about "big deal" Fae? Three people sitting in my grandfather's study that morning already qualified for the title: Barnaby himself, Myrtle, and Moira. Then Greer joined us, with Festus limping along beside her.

Werecat or not, you might think that Festus would be inclined to show a little respect in their presence, especially since Granddad is the Lord High Mayor.

Here's what the ginger tom actually did.

First, he sauntered across the carpet like he owned the place. Then, he jumped up on the corner of the desk and knocked a stack of papers to the floor, watching them flutter toward the carpet like he'd had no part in their downward journey,

Finally, as the crowning bit of feline arrogance, Festus yawned, sat, and pronounced sagely, "You really ought to clean up in here, Barnaby. This place is a mess."

With decidedly forced tolerance, Barnaby said, "I'll take that under advisement, Festus."

"I'd ask you to forgive him because he's not himself today," Greer said, "but I'm afraid he's completely himself."

The remark cleared the air and even won a half-smile from Granddad. "Festus does have a rather famous incorrigible streak," he conceded.

Licking his paw nonchalantly, Festus said, "I prefer the term 'legendary.'"

"That will be enough out of you, Festus," I warned. "Can you behave yourself long enough to tell everyone about your trip to Raleigh?"

"Sure," Festus said. He lifted his good back leg and gave his ear a hearty scratch in preparation. "Okay, so, when Jinx here decided to start skulking around . . . "

Great. He was on a real roll today.

"Just back up there, buddy," I said indignantly. "I have *not* been skulking around.'"

Until that moment I'm not sure I understood what the phrase "withering" look meant.

"I'm sorry," Festus said, "but did we or did we not have our first meeting about my going down to Raleigh behind a drawn, soundproof curtain?"

"Emphasis on *we*," I said. "You're in this up to your whiskers right along with me."

To my surprise, Festus capitulated—for about 2 seconds.

"I am," he admitted, "but nobody expects *me* to play by the rules."

Now he was starting to get on my nerves.

"You listen to me, you hairball-tossing alley . . . "

Myrtle's happy trill of laughter stopped me mid-insult.

"How I have missed you all!" she said, looking thoroughly delighted by the exchange. "Jinx, you really did not need anyone's permission to seek the Amulet of Caorunn."

I felt like saying, rather defiantly, *"Yeah, what she said,"* but it's good I didn't because Myrtle's next words offered a gentle, well-taken admonishment

"But I do think it might have been prudent had you sought some guidance from a more experienced practitioner before you decided to double enchant the Casket of Morpheus."

Busted.

I hope the look I gave her was nowhere near as petulant as what I said. "I thought your powers were supposed to be diminished."

Regarding me with sparkling eyes, she said, "Not to the point that I cannot have a conversation with my own home. The fairy mound tells me you've installed a big screen television in the lair and that we have matching leather sofas now."

"Those sofas were on sale," I said. "We got them for a total steal."

"The fairy mound wants me to tell you that next time you should just ask and not spend money needlessly on something so easily conjured with magic," Myrtle said.

Oh.

"That never occurred to you, did it Miss Smarty Pants?" Festus asked.

Turning back toward him, I said, "No. Did it ever occur to you when you sat on the hearth watching us lug those sofas down the stairs to mention it?"

"And ruin a show that good?" Festus asked with wide eyes. "Not on your life."

Barnaby cleared his throat. "For as . . . *illuminating* as this conversation might be, perhaps we could return to the salient topic of the investigations Festus and Greer conducted in Raleigh?"

"My pleasure," Festus said, flicking his tail in my direction. "Connor and Gareth told us they got away from Chesterfield when he went to see a man about an artifact. Jinx asked me to take a trip to Raleigh and get one of the local ghosts to put out a call for any area spooks who might have seen anything. Greer offered to come along to keep me out of trouble."

The baobhan sith inclined her head in acknowledgment. "A rather daunting proposition," she said, "but we managed a most successful excursion."

Taking turns adding details and clarifying points, the two of them gave us a full account of their conversation with Mrs. Turk and the information supplied by the street cats—that the man Chesterfield met with smelled like a deer.

When Festus began to talk about the Dark Druid, and I described my dream of the woman in the pond with the flailing stag, Barnaby and Moira both leaned forward and listened intently.

"You are suggesting that this John Smyth person is the son of Fer Dorch and Sadhbh?" Barnaby asked.

"We cannot say so conclusively," Greer replied, "but we do believe it to be a strong possibility. Do you know of any other Fae with the reputed ability to take the form of a deer?"

Moira shook her head. "No," she said. "If this child exists, he would be the only one of his kind. The deer to whom you refer who were used to lure the well maidens of old into danger were bespelled animals with no native magic."

"The Registry records agree with that assessment," Greer said. "Perhaps it would be advisable to make inquiries with IBIS."

(Don't you love Fae acronyms? IBIS stands for the International Bureau of Indefinite Species.)

At the suggestion, Barnaby shifted uncomfortably in his chair, touching off a political warning light in my head. He chose to answer Greer with a non-answer. "IBIS is based in London," he said.

Now, if you don't know anything about Fae politics you might hear that and think, "Of course. It would be silly to drag somebody over from London to look into a guy who smells like a deer in Raleigh, North Carolina."

I, on the other hand, *do* know something about Fae politics, and I'm learning more all the time. Trying not to sound accusatory, I decided we might as well get right to the point.

"Granddad, you've been working on this on your own, haven't you? That's why you've been sending Lucas all over the place for the last month. You're trying to locate the Amulet of Caorunn without involving Reynold Isherwood and the Elders."

The directness of my question took Barnaby aback for a second. Then he regained his composure and his sense of authority.

"You do not know Reynold as I do, Jinx," he said. "The man tends to complicate matters beyond reason."

Summoning every ounce of control I had, I didn't say the first thing that popped into my head. *When don't the Fae complicate matters?*

Antagonizing my grandfather wasn't the battle I wanted to pick.

Instead, I went with, "But if the Amulet of Caorunn is associated with the Mother Rowan and the tree is in . . . "

"Roslin," Festus supplied helpfully, "just outside Edinburgh, Scotland."

Out of the corner of my eye, I saw that the cagey werecat followed the unspoken subtext of the conversation perfectly—as did Myrtle, Moira, and Greer.

"Right," I said. "Scotland. Doesn't that make all of this Isherwood's business?"

My grandfather's jaw hardened into a stubborn line. "Reynold did not feel the need to inform us when the Amulet was taken. Therefore, I see no need to apprise him of our efforts to locate it."

Before I could respond, Moira caught my eye and gave a nearly imperceptible shake of her head. Reasoning that she knew my granddad better than anyone in the room and that I had pushed my luck far enough, I accepted the silent advice and dropped the subject.

"Okay," I said. "I think we've told you everything we've discovered so far. Did I miss anything, Festus?"

"Just that the street cats said Chesterfield came out of the restaurant carrying a flat, black box," Festus said, "which would seem to confirm that he does have the Amulet of Caorunn."

He stopped, appeared to think for a minute, and then said, "Oh, and you dreamed Brenna Sinclair is alive in the In Between."

Greer already knew the story, but the other three heads in the room swiveled toward me.

"Smooth, Festus," I muttered, "real smooth."

The old cat never so much as blinked. "You didn't seem to be getting real busy about telling them," he said. "So I thought I'd help you out."

Help me out?

He might as well have handcuffed me in a straight-backed chair under a single naked light bulb.

So many questions flew at me at once, I can't tell you who asked what when. I was forced to go back over how I originally used the Casket of Morpheus, what Tori used when we tried to amplify the signal, and every dream from start to finish in excruciating detail.

Finally, in complete frustration, I said, "Enough! You know everything I know. When we get back to Briar Hollow, I'll send you copies of the pictures from my grimoire, but I know it was Brenna and I'm pretty sure she's alive. Greer thinks so, too."

That temporarily shifted the interrogation to Greer, who repeated her theory that the force of Brenna's reawakened magic might have propelled her through the barrier separating the fairy mound from the greater in between.

"What would have generated enough force to do that?" Moira asked. "Kelly and Gemma placed Brenna in a binding spell. Once the Amulet of the Phoenix was removed from her person, she had no powers."

The baobhan sith smiled. Not the smile I was used to seeing on Greer's face. This look was something wilder and more primal. "Blood," she said, the word rolling off her tongue with a sensual warmth that was almost shocking. "I think her blood awakened when the tip of Colonel Longworth's sword, infused with the magic of the amulet, pierced her heart."

No one was prepared to dispute that Greer was our resident blood expert.

"That," Moira said, "is a theory I can test immediately."

Rising from the sofa, she walked to the door of the study, opened it, and called to Beau. "Colonel Longworth, a moment please?"

I heard Beau's boots cross the floorboard. He and Moira exchanged a few words, and then Moira closed the door. She held Beau's cavalry saber in her hand.

When she returned to sit beside my grandfather, she slid the blade from its scabbard and placed the sword across her knees. Then reached into the collar of her tunic and pulled out a heavy blank pendant on a gold chain, the Touchstone.

I'd only seen the stone used once before. When I first came to Shevington, Moira had each of us hold the pendant to help me understand the levels of power we each possess. This time, she unfastened the chain and wrapped it around the blade to hold the stone in place against the metal.

Within seconds, the Touchstone turned the color of freshly shed blood. Every few seconds, tiny bolts of lightning shot across its surface.

"Greer is correct," Moira said. "This sword has been used for blood magic."

So much for me and my theories about dream metaphors.

"So Brenna is alive?" I asked.

"It would appear so," Moira said, "which means we have an additional question to consider. Is she once again in league with Irenaeus? Barnaby, what is your opinion on the matter?"

My grandfather stared at the pulsating Touchstone. "The possible connection of the Dark Druid to my brother and now the potential resurrection of the Scottish sorceress trouble me deeply," he admitted, "As does the fact that Irenaeus may have been in possession of the amulet for almost six weeks without making a move."

"Chesterfield planned and prepared for 79 years to launch his first attempt to get into the fairy mound," Myrtle said. "Six weeks seems a trivial passage of time."

"Not if he has made a move coincident with another event," Barnaby said, "for instance, the Winter Solstice upon which Jinx dreamed a scene much like the kidnapping of one of the well maidens."

"Did Lucas find out anything in his travels that would be of assistance to us?" Myrtle asked.

Barnaby shook his head. "No," he said. "Irenaeus has not attempted to acquire any other artifacts on the black market that we can discover."

"So what's our next move?" I said.

That's when Myrtle offered up a suggestion that sent a little thrill of excitement through me.

"I believe we should contact the Witch of the Rowan directly," Myrtle said, "and ask her to give us the details of the amulet's theft. That will give us an indication of the accuracy of the dreams Jinx has been experiencing."

"Who is she?" I asked, thrilled at the idea of meeting another witch in service to a Mother Tree.

"Katrina Warner," Moira said, "and I assure you, she has about as much patience for Reynold Isherwood and Fae politics as your grandfather."

TWENTY

Everyone sat around the fire in the parlor after we came out of Barnaby's study. To my surprise, Myrtle asked me to relate the details of our closed-door conversation. When I started talking about my experiments with Grandma Kathleen's grimoire, I saw my mother's eyes narrow. I knew there was a "talking to" in my future.

Never one to face maternal disapproval alone, I made sure to include full details of Tori's involvement. While I was telling that part of the tale, Gemma turned and stared at her daughter, who mouthed, "She made me do it." Gemma didn't buy that one for a minute.

As I continued, I saw Beau take a slender book out of the breast pocket of his jacket and start to take notes. Glory looked like she wished she had a bucket of popcorn.

Then I dropped the bombshell about Brenna. Audible gasps circulated the room.

"Is this the evil sorceress that your mom and Tori's mom are supposed to have killed?" Glory asked. "The one I saw in Mr. Chesterfield's shop when he plastered me on that cup and set me up on the top shelf for a year?"

Glory tried to steal a lock of Elvis Presley's hair from Chesterfield. She'd wanted it as a talisman to start a singing career, which is when her nightmare began. The hapless woman never made it out of the shop. Chesterfield

161

miniaturized her and imprisoned her until she was so desperate and terrified she agreed to work as his spy.

"Yes, but the killing part was a group effort," I said. "Our mothers bound her in magic, Festus kept her distracted, Rodney snatched the amulet off her neck, and Beau stabbed her."

Glory turned toward Festus who was sitting on the hearth. "*You* distracted her?" she asked.

Without missing a beat, a shimmering wave passed over the yellow cat's body leaving a massive mountain lion sitting in his place. "You were saying, Dill Pickle?" Festus asked with a low growl.

Glory took a couple of steps back on the arm of the sofa, lost her balance, and fell into my mother's lap.

"It's alright," Mom said, helping her sit up, "Festus is just showing off, aren't you, Festus?"

My mother is the only person in the world who can get consistently good behavior out of the cantankerous werecat.

"Yeah," he said begrudgingly, "I don't even like pickles."

"Good," Mom said, "shift back, now."

Ignoring all the grinning faces staring at him, the old cat did as he was told. Once back in his usual ginger tom form, he looked at Mom and said, "Sorry, Kelly."

"I'm not the one you should apologize to," Mom said sternly.

Festus' ears deflated. "Sorry, Dill . . . sorry, *Glory*," he said contritely. "I didn't mean to scare you."

Glory, ever the magnanimous one, gushed with open awe. "You did scare me, and I'll bet you scared that terrible Brenna person something *awful*."

At that, Festus sat up a little straighter and puffed his chest out. "It was nothing," he said with self-deprecation.

"Which is why the story gets better every time you tell it," Chase mumbled.

Mom wheeled on him and snapped, "Chase McGregor, you show some respect for your father. He was protecting the Daughters of Knasgowa with courage and distinction when you were a wet-behind-the-ears kitten."

Chase went white. Opened his mouth to say something. Thought better of whatever it was, and said, "Yes, ma'am. Sorry, Dad."

"No problem, boy," Festus beamed. "No problem at all."

My Dad leaned back on the sofa and put his arm around Mom's shoulders. "Down girl," he said fondly. "You're scaring the menfolk."

"I do not like all this secrecy," she said, staring pointedly at me. "Especially all this talk about the In Between."

It struck me as odd that out of everything I'd said it was the In Between that bothered her most, but so far she hadn't lit into *me*, and I wanted to keep it that way. I let the remark go.

Beau stepped into the breach. "If I am to understand all that you have told us, Miss Jinx," he said, referring to his notes, "we are in agreement that the wizard Chesterfield met with John Smyth, a man who may have the ability to turn into a deer, which has significance in relation to a figure called the Dark Druid. As Chesterfield exited the dining establishment carrying a jewelry box, the assumption holds that he is in possession of the Amulet of Caorunn, which he may have used in a significant way on the Winter Solstice as per your dream. In addition, it would seem Brenna Sinclair lives. Am I correct on all those points?"

"You are," I said.

"Then," the Colonel said, "I have only one query. Given that Myrtle chose this juncture of circumstances to return to our company, might she share with us an account of her time within the consciousness of the Mother Tree?"

"I guess that's for Myrtle to say," I answered, turning toward the aos si. "Do you mind?"

For a second, I don't think Myrtle knew what to say. Then Greer spoke up. "Forgive us, aos si," she said, "but in merging with the Mother Tree, you have gained insight into the workings of the Grid unlike those granted to any other being. I am also curious about your experiences during the time you have been away."

Myrtle nodded slowly. "I understand your curiosity, baobhan sith," she said, "especially given your long years of service to the Trees, and you, Colonel Longworth, you do not want to miss a single piece of information that might aid our search."

"I do not, dear lady," Beau said, "but neither do I wish to invade your privacy. Forgive me if I have done so."

"You have not," Myrtle said, "it is merely a difficult experience to put into words. Remember, I was born in the roots of the Mother Oak centuries ago in the land of the Celts. For me, being with her again felt quite . . . normal."

My mother, who was seated closest to Myrtle, laid her hand on the aos si's arm. "Did you feel as if you were home again?" Mom asked.

"I am home now," Myrtle said, looking around the room, "but I was also home then. We carry home in our hearts, Kelly, is that not so?"

Mom smiled and squeezed Myrtle's arm. "It is," she said.

Even a year earlier, I might not have understood what Myrtle meant, but now her words resonated with me.

"When you were with the Mother Oak, did you know what was happening with all of us?" I asked. She had, after all, nailed me about my dreams and I didn't think all that information came from a conversation with the fairy mound. Myrtle's "range" wasn't as diminished as she and Moira made it out to be.

"Not always directly," Myrtle answered. "I had to recover from the strongest effects of my exposure to the Orb of Thoth. Then, the Mother Oak allowed me to wander in the global stream of data as I liked. You cannot imagine the sense of connection the Trees enjoy with one another and with the realms."

Tori perked up. "So the Grid *is* like a computer network?"

The Grid of Mother Trees provides a structural frame for the Otherworld, the In Between, and the Human Realm. The more we've learned about how it works, the more convinced my nerdy BFF becomes that the whole thing is a metaphysical version of the Internet.

"The Mother Trees share global awareness," Myrtle said, "but it can be quite difficult to distinguish their voices from those of all the lesser trees that add information to the collective whole."

"Chatter," Tori said triumphantly, looking at me with elation. "I told you, Jinksy. *Avatar.*"

She meant the 2009 James Cameron movie about the sentient planet Pandora that kicks the parasitic human settlers right back out into space before they ruin the environment.

Beau, who had been listening quietly, said, "Forgive me, but if the Mother Trees working as a single unit have global awareness, why can they not provide us with the necessary information to apprehend the outlaw wizard Chesterfield or his possible accomplice, the Sinclair woman?"

Every head in the room swiveled in Myrtle's direction. None of us would be happy to discover that the trees were holding out on us, but we would be thrilled if tracking Chesterfield could be simplified.

"The Mother Trees are repositories of vast and ancient

knowledge," Myrtle said. "They do not monitor or police us in an interventionist manner. Their function is rather to counsel and advise."

"But each Tree is associated with an amulet that possesses a specific power, right?" I said. "If the trees are in charge of making sure the amulets end up in the hands of the right people, shouldn't they always be able to locate the amulets themselves?"

"No," Myrtle said, "although that would most certainly make our current problem much more manageable. The amulets are as sentient as the Trees themselves, and like the Trees, they may make free will choices. The amulets can be subject to manipulation and to magic. The Mother Oak and the Amulet of the Phoenix, which you wear, Colonel, communicate openly."

Barnaby looked thunderstruck. "Then why was the Amulet of the Phoenix silent following Adeline's murder?" he asked. "Why, if it was in my brother's possession, did it not seek to break free from its captor?"

"That," Myrtle said gently, "would be a question you would need to put to the Amulet itself."

My grandfather's pale face told me that conversation wouldn't be happening anytime soon, even though Beau immediately said, "You need only say the word, Barnaby, and the Amulet will rest in your hand."

Barnaby shook his head. "Thank you, Colonel Longworth," he said, "but I do not believe I am yet ready to speak to a witness to my wife's murder."

An awkward silence fell over the room until Gemma spoke up. "Myrtle, you said the Phoenix and the Mother Tree communicate. What about Caorunn and the Mother Rowan?"

"Theirs is a more complicated relationship," Myrtle said. "Since its disappearance, Caorunn has maintained its silence."

Great—a magical artifact acting like a runaway teenager, just what we needed.

"Is there anything the Mother Trees can tell us about the missing amulet?" Mom asked.

"Only that they are in agreement that Caorunn must be recovered," Myrtle said.

To my surprise, my father spoke up. "Does it have to be done today?" he asked.

For just an instant, I thought Mom was going to hit him with something. She did let out with a thoroughly disapproving, "Jeff!"

No one else seemed to know what to say until Rube, from his perch in the window seat, rattled his sack of potato chips and voiced his agreement. "Finally!" the raccoon said. "Somebody's brain kicked in gear."

Turning first to my father and then to Rube, Barnaby said, "I regret to admit I am not following the point either of you seems to be attempting to make."

Rube wiped his paws delicately on a napkin, which, to my astonishment, he then folded.

"Not to be rude or nothing Your Lord High Mayorship," he said, "but technical like, it's still Christmas."

"Exactly!" Dad agreed. "I have a date to go ice skating with my son. You ladies are supposed to have a girls' night out at O'Hanson's, and Festus invited all the men to the Dirty Claw tonight. Can't we please put off saving the Grid and dealing with the evil wizard for another 24 hours?"

Currently, we were all running on Shevington time, which moves at a slower rate than the timestream in the human world. We planned to head back to Briar Hollow the next afternoon since Tori and I had to open the store Monday morning. In our world, however, we'd arrive around breakfast and have an entire Sunday at our leisure.

One look at my grandfather's face, however, told me

that even a short delay in getting back to business just wasn't going to happen.

"While I, too, regret the loss of our carefree time together," Barnaby said, "I hardly think the Mother Tree would have allowed Myrtle to return if this matter could be put off any longer."

Everyone in the room more or less deflated until Lucas offered a possible compromise.

"Why don't we call Katrina now?" he suggested. "When we find out what she has to say, then we can decide if we need to head back to Briar Hollow or if we can stay in Shevington one more night."

It was not lost on me that he used the Witch of the Rowan's first name in a way that indicated they knew each other. The frisson of jealousy that moved through me touched off a warning claxon in my brain.

Was I already involved enough with Lucas to be jealous? If so, that just compounded the problem life handed me the day before when Chase announced he wanted us to get back together.

Since then, Myrtle's return had kept Chase and me from having any direct contact, which was fine with me. Given the choice between sorting out my tangled love life and going after a magical amulet to save the world? Point me at the world saving.

Barnaby looked at Myrtle. "What do you think about this proposal, aos si?" he asked.

"I agree with Lucas," she replied. "Without speaking to the Witch of the Rowan, we cannot proceed intelligently. We should allow that conversation to guide our immediate actions."

"Very well," Barnaby said, rising to his feet. "I will fetch the mirror."

He disappeared into the foyer. A few minutes later we heard wheels crossing the wood floor. I opened my mouth to ask Lucas and Chase to help my grandfather with what sounded like a heavy piece of furniture, but before I could get the words out, Barnaby stepped back into the room.

Beside him, an elegant standing mirror of carved mahogany trundled along under its own power. Barnaby was so absorbed in the leather-bound volume in his hands; he completely ignored the ambulatory looking glass.

As we watched, the mirror deftly steered itself around the sofas, then paused and seemed to examine the large bay window currently dominated by a decorated Christmas tree. Judging that to be a bad backdrop, the mirror rolled toward the door to Barnaby's study where it turned and fidgeted right and left before coming to a stop.

Remarkably, the mirror positioned itself, so the lamps didn't create flashes on its shining surface. None of our reflections were visible either. Anyone looking through the mirror from the other side would see nothing in the room but a wingback chair in front of a bookcase.

"Nice driving," I said, not intending to directly address the mirror, but more in the vein of a wisecrack.

To my utter shock, the mirror dipped forward as if taking a bow.

"You're welcome," I said, sounding about as stunned as I felt.

After all these months, I shouldn't still be surprised by enchanted objects, but they get me every time.

Looking up from his book, Barnaby took in the position of the mirror, noticed where we were all sitting more or less rooted in place, and said, "Very well, are we ready?"

I felt like I should raise my hand before speaking, but I stifled the urge and asked, "Who, exactly, is going to participate in this call?"

"I believe Myrtle should place the call since she is acquainted with Miss Warner," Barnaby said. "We can leave it to her to include others of us in the conversation as she sees fit."

Myrtle got up from her place by the fire, and Barnaby took her chair. When she was re-settled by the bookcase, Barnaby began to read from the book now resting on his lap. As he spoke, the surface of the mirror clouded over, the mist gathering into a central swirl that revolved faster and faster until a burst of blue light obliterated the fog.

A lovely blonde woman wearing a soft green cashmere sweater and a tartan skirt turned her head toward what I assumed was her own mirror. She stood in a storeroom surrounded by crates of books. I squinted to make out one of the shipping labels. "Katrina Warner, Rowan Bough Books, The Royal Mile, Edinburgh."

At the sight of Myrtle, the woman's eyes widened, and she dropped into a deep curtsy. She spoke in Gaelic. All I recognized was "aos si" and "urram," which I thought meant, "honored."

Myrtle answered in English. "We have no need of such formalities, Katrina," she said. "You may call me Myrtle."

"Then I am even more honored," the woman said. "What may I do for you?"

"You may tell me of the disappearance of the Amulet of Caorunn."

So much for the niceties.

TWENTY-ONE

The story Katrina Warner told us confirmed the major events I saw in my dream, but in greater detail. The Amulet of Caorunn had been in the possession of her business partner and magical mentor, Findlay Whetstone, for as long as she could remember—back to the days when Katrina's mother served the Great Rowan.

Findlay, like Moira, descends from both elves and druids. He does not practice alchemy, but rather possesses a reputation as one of the foremost scholars of the Fae world and, as Katrina put it, "the man drinks a wee bit."

Every evening, regular as clockwork, Findlay eats his supper at a pub on the Royal Mile, lifts a pint or two with the boys, and then weaves his way back to the apartment below the bookstore he calls home.

"I live above the store," Katrina said. "As soon as I hear his key in the lock, I know the old dear is safe and sound, but that night, he almost beat the door down trying to get in."

Katrina found her friend frantic and disoriented on the doorstep. "He was holding his key," she said, "but he couldn't remember how to use it. When I got him inside in the light and had a good look at him, I found traces of *tumultus pulverem* on his face and clothes."

"Confusion powder," Myrtle said, "a simple but effective trick."

"Indeed," Katrina said. "Several hours passed before he came to his wits, but then Findlay told me a dark figure stepped out of the shadows and blew the powder in his face. His attacker snatched the amulet from around Findlay's neck and was gone as quick as he'd appeared."

Katrina described how she'd immediately tried an impressive range of location and recovery spells to no avail. That night, she drove to Roslin and slipped through the portal to confer with the Mother Rowan.

"I went to her asking for advice," Katrina said, sounding annoyed. "As usual, she was less than forthcoming."

Before I thought, I laughed out loud.

Myrtle gestured for me to come into the mirror's field of view. "Katrina Warner, Witch of the Rowan," she said, "allow me to introduce Jinx Hamilton, Witch of the Oak."

Surprise and then pleasure crossed the blond woman's features. "Finally!" she said. "We've been hearing tales about you, Mistress Hamilton. I take it your Mother Tree has a habit of being vague with you as well?"

"Please," I said, "call me Jinx. And yes, the Mother Oak gives me the run around constantly."

Katrina laughed, a throaty chuckle at odds with her somewhat delicate appearance. "You'll have to join the lasses at the next meeting," she said. "You'll find plenty of commiseration in our number."

"Meeting?" I asked. "Of what?"

Katrina shook her head. "Mercy," she said, "you are new, aren't you? The Women of the Craobhan."

Shaking my head, I said, "I'm sorry, but my Gaelic is pretty bad. The women of the what?"

Myrtle answered before Katrina could. "The Women of the Trees," the aos si said. "The coven of the witches in service to the Mother Trees. Your sisters."

From off to the side, Tori gasped. "There's a *club*? Does she get a decoder ring?"

"That's my best friend Tori," I explained to Katrina. "Please excuse her, she gets a little overly enthusiastic."

"Mine too," Katrina said, "especially about all things sci-fi. She's off at some convention in London as we speak."

At that, Tori sprang up out of her chair and stuck her head in the field of vision. "Oh my *God*!" she said. "She's *there*? Is she going to meet Captain Picard? Hi, by the way, I'm Tori."

"Hi," Katrina said, "and yes, Elspeth reserved some sort of photo appointment with Sir Patrick Stewart."

Myrtle cleared her throat. "Ladies," she said bemusedly, "focus."

"Oh!" Tori said. "My bad. Sorry!"

She quickly ducked out of sight as Katrina re-arranged her face in more serious lines. "My apologies as well, aos si," she said.

"Not at all," Myrtle replied. "I find human popular culture fascinating, and I want Jinx to meet her colleagues, but given the current circumstances, we must stay on track. Now, what, exactly, did the Mother Rowan say to you?"

"She said that the amulet knows where it needs to be and I wasn't to interfere," Katrina replied, "and I didn't, not until Reynold Isherwood rang me up and demanded to hear the whole story."

Barnaby stepped into view beside Myrtle. "Miss Warner," he said, "I am Barnaby Shevington, Lord High Mayor."

Katrina's eyes widened again. I knew how she felt. I'd had days like this when one major Fae after another threw curveballs in my direction.

"It is a great honor, Lord Mayor," she said, dropping another curtsey.

"For me as well," Barnaby said. "Allow me to request clarification on one point. Am I correct in understanding that you did not tell Reynold Isherwood of the theft of the Amulet of Caorunn, but that he possessed this information already when he contacted you?"

"Yes, Lord Mayor," Katrina said. "Elder Isherwood already knew the amulet had been stolen."

"Did he say how he knew?"

"He did not, Lord Mayor."

Then something happened I didn't expect.

Lucas stepped beside Barnaby and said, "Hey, Katrina. I was just wondering, have any official types been in your store before or after the theft of the amulet? DGI? Registry? IBIS?"

"Hi Lucas," Katrina said brightly. "Not that I know of, but those IBIS lads are a cagey lot."

As I listened to the breezy, familiar exchange, any doubts I might have had that Lucas and Katrina already had some sort of existing relationship evaporated. That twinge of jealousy came back full force.

Want a good laugh? I can tell you exactly what I was thinking in that moment, *"What does he do, make the rounds of all the witches, tree by tree?"*

Yeah, not my most mature moment. When Myrtle put a question to Katrina, I forced myself to pay attention.

"When did all of this happen?" Myrtle asked.

"About two weeks before Samhain," Katrina said. Then realizing I might not know what she was talking about, she added, "Jinx, you likely call the holiday Halloween."

The timeline fits perfectly. John Smyth—or whoever he was—had plenty of time to steal the amulet, contact Chesterfield through Anton Ionescu, and get to America for the meeting in Raleigh.

⌖

After the call with Katrina ended, the mirror swiveled toward Barnaby and tilted slightly toward the door.

"Yes," my grandfather said, "that will be all. Thank you."

As the looking glass trundled out of the parlor, I said, "So are we heading back to Briar Hollow tonight or tomorrow?"

"I rather think tomorrow as planned," Granddad said. "I must make some inquiries. I find it rather fascinating that Reynold knew of the theft of the amulet before he spoke to Miss Warner."

Greer, who had remained silent during the entire call, spoke up. "If I may?" she said.

Barnaby nodded for her to continue.

"I think it might be prudent for either Lucas or myself to spend a few hours in London. We have contacts that are . . . outside the bounds of officialdom. Let us see what we can discover."

Turning to Moira, Barnaby said, "What do you think?"

"The baobhan sith offers a good plan," the alchemist said. "If Reynold were to be involved in this . . . incident . . . in ways we do not anticipate, tipping our hand by asking questions openly would not be a wise action."

"Very good," Barnaby said. "Until we have your report, I do not think there is anything more to be done."

When Lucas volunteered to be the one to go to London, I was both relieved and disappointed.

"You're sure you don't mind?" I asked him in the hallway as he put on his coat.

"I'm sure," he said. "I really wasn't up for a night in a werecat bar with Festus and the gang. Those cats have four hollow legs and hollow tails."

When he said "I'll see you in Briar Hollow" and made a move to kiss me, I shook my head and mouthed "not here."

Glancing over my shoulder toward the door of the parlor where the moms and Tori stood waiting, Lucas grinned, tipped his fedora at them, winked at me, and headed out the door.

For just a split second, I thought about following him, but I'd have to face the maternal music sooner or later.

Right on cue when I turned around Mom said, "Norma Jean, we need to talk. *Now*."

Tori did her best to slide toward the stairs and escape, but Gemma nailed her with a stern, "Where do you think you're going, young lady?"

"Uh, nowhere," Tori said weakly.

"Good answer," Gemma said. "Follow us."

Exchanging a joint look of dread, we followed the moms into the library where Innis, Barnaby's brownie housekeeper, had yet another cheerful fire going. I did not take it as a good sign when Mom closed the double doors behind us.

"All right," she said, "both of you sit and start talking."

I opened my mouth to do just that and was cut off by a torrent of motherly disapproval.

"Honestly, Norma Jean," Mom said, dropping beside Gemma on the settee. "I went to bed last night and left you sitting in the parlor with Dílestos. I get up this morning, and you're nowhere to be found. Then you come home with Myrtle, and now I discover you've been playing with magical artifacts and having dream visions about Brenna Sinclair."

Gemma reached over and patted Mom on the knee. "Kelly," she said in a soothing tone. "I second what Jeff said. Calm down. Isn't taming mouthy werecats enough for one day?"

"Don't help," Mom commanded, but Gemma had still managed to get a smile out of her. Sometimes it's uncanny to watch the two of them. Gemma does exactly the same things to talk Mom off a ledge that Tori does with me.

When both mothers looked my way, I took it as my cue to launch into an explanation. I described Myrtle's return at the base of the Mother Tree, our visit to Moira's workshop, and then, reluctantly, gave yet another full accounting of my dreams.

At the mention of Brenna's name, Mom threw up her hands in frustration. "And it never one time occurred to you to *tell* someone?" she demanded.

There was no way I was taking the whole rap for this one.

"I did tell someone," I said. "I told Tori."

Which instantly sent Gemma into Mother Overdrive.

"And that," she said, wheeling toward her daughter, "brings us to you, Victoria Tallulah Andrews."

Ouch! Now we were both getting lashed with the triple Southern name whip.

"What was I supposed to do?" Tori demanded. "Be a tattletale?"

"Yes!" both moms said in unison.

Trying for the emotional save, I said, "If we'd told any of you about the dreams the whole thing would just have gotten out of hand. I wanted us to at least have a nice Christmas together before we had to start running around saving the world—again."

My next words weren't planned.

"And I didn't think I needed anyone's permission to do my job."

That would be the moment when everyone in the room seemed to remember that all four of us were Daughters of Knasgowa.

My words put a gleam of admiration in Gemma's eye, but then she heaved a sigh—which I'm pretty sure was for Mom's benefit—and said, "As much as I hate to let these two off the hook, Kelly, Jinx is right. She was doing her job, and let's face facts. In our line of work, there's always going to be something these girls have to do that we're not going to like. There was a time when we would have done the same thing Jinx and Tori did, and our mothers wouldn't have been happy with us either."

"And that makes what they did right how exactly?" Mom asked stubbornly.

"The apple doesn't fall far from the witch?" Gemma asked with mock seriousness.

Mom tried to scowl. She really did, but she couldn't pull it off. Giving Gemma a half-hearted punch on the arm, she said, "Honestly, Gem. You could have backed me up on this one."

"Sorry, Kell," Gemma said. "But you know I'm right."

"I do," she said with exasperation. Then she looked at me, and for just a second, I thought she would burst into tears.

"Connor isn't going to have to be involved with this Chesterfield business is he, Jinx?" she asked. "He barely managed to escape from that awful man's clutches last time."

You have no idea how much I wanted to tell her no—to assure her that we'd keep Connor as far away from the Creavit wizard as possible—but I knew better than to make a promise like that.

"I don't know, Mom," I said. "I hope not."

She nodded but didn't trust herself to speak.

"So, as soon as we get back to Briar Hollow, it's full speed ahead with Operation Find That Amulet?" Tori asked.

"It would seem so," I said, "which immediately raises a problem. We have to get Mindy out of the store. There's too much going on to have her underfoot."

"Oh!" Tori said, "I forgot to tell you. Mindy sent me an

email yesterday saying she's quitting. She and her buddies scrounged up funding for their web series, so she's going to be doing full-time production work."

"Finally," I said, "some good . . . wait, you managed to get your email in Shevington? How'd you pull that off?"

"I had a talk with Ironweed about how they get the GNATS drones to work trans-dimensionally," Tori grinned. "A little tech. A little magic. Ba da bing, ba da boom— email."

Major Aspid "Ironweed" Istra commands the Brown Mountain Fairy Guard that deploys a nifty, super-micro drone surveillance force called the Group Network Aerial Transmission System or GNATS for short. Each drone is literally the size of a gnat and runs on a single grain of fairy dust. After our most recent encounter with Chesterfield, Barnaby put a whole squadron—twelve drones—at our disposal.

"Okay," I said. "That takes care of the Mindy problem, so yes, depending on what Granddad finds out we'll be going all out after the Amulet of Caorunn, which means figuring out how Brenna is involved in all of this. Actually, we have to figure out where she . . ."

Mom cut me off cold.

"Stop," she said, with an odd edge in her voice. "I'm sorry to pull a Scarlett O'Hara on you, but I refuse to think about any of that until tomorrow. I want to enjoy these last few hours in Shevington, *and* I want a Scotch egg at O'Hanson's tonight. Come on, Gemma, let's go get changed."

As Tori and I watched the two women exit the room, I said, "Is it just me, or was that weird?"

"It was weird," Tori said, "definitely weird."

TWENTY-TWO

Rodney stood upright on the banister in the foyer with paws on hips. I stood on the carpet striking an identical posture.

"*No*," I said, "and that's final. You are not going to The Dirty Claw with the guys. It's a *werecat* bar, Rodney. Emphasis on *cat*. You are a *rat*. Felines *eat* rodents. It's a thing. Look it up."

In response, Rodney jumped down, ran over to Festus, and defiantly smacked him in the nose as if to say, "*See!* He's never eaten me."

Festus, perfectly following the rat's unspoken argument, said, "Do that again, and you'll experience the brief, but delicious life of an hors d'oeuvre."

"You want to help me out here?" I asked the old cat.

Sighing, Festus reached out and tapped Rodney on the shoulder. The rat, who had continued to glare at me, wheeled around and turned his indignation on the ginger tom.

"Look, Short Stuff," Festus said, "as much as it pains me to admit it, Jinx is right. You can't take your rodential personage into a bar full of shifted werecats of all shapes and sizes. Just because I have the self-restraint not to eat you doesn't mean they will, especially if they're drunk. I'm sorry, but you can't go."

My sense of vindication at having Festus on my side warred with my annoyance when Rodney instantly caved and nodded his capitulation.

"What?" I demanded. "When I say it, I'm coddling you, but *Festus* is suddenly the voice of reason?"

Chase, who sat on the last step of the staircase in human form, suggested mildly, "Why don't you just quit while you're ahead?"

"*Fine!*" I said, reaching for my coat. "Far be it from me to get in the way of male solidarity."

"That's good," Chase said amiably, "since we're agreeing with you."

I wanted to smile at him, but I wasn't going there. In his current frame of mind, Chase might have taken it as a sign of encouragement. I needed him discouraged where I was concerned.

"What-*ever*," I grumbled. "Are you riding with me, Rodney?"

In response, the rat strolled across the carpet to Tori with exaggerated dignity. He stopped in front of her as if to say, "Well?"

She offered him a hand. Without so much as glancing at me, Rodney hopped on her palm, ran up her arm, and disappeared into the collar of her jacket.

"You," Tori snickered, "are *persona non grata*."

"Yeah, well, he's *rodentia non grata*. Let's go."

Innis held the door open as we all filed out, directing us to "stay warm, don't drink too much, and find your way home safely."

On the sidewalk, the men broke into a separate group and headed along the side street toward the Dirty Claw while the women cut across the village green and made for O'Hanson's pub.

Even though the entire population of Shevington had jammed into the town square just two nights before and no snow had fallen since, we found ourselves walking on a pristine blanket of white. The explanation became clear when I looked over my shoulder. Our footprints disappeared behind us.

Moira followed my gaze and laughed. "We bespell the snow on the village green for the holidays," she explained. "It's more picturesque, wouldn't you say?"

"I would," I agreed. "In fact, this whole town looks like it's straight out of a Christmas fairy tale."

"Don't let the fairies hear you say that," Greer advised. "They don't like the way the humans have appropriated that term for their bedtime stories. The Fairy Tales of Blood and Valor do not make for good nocturnal reading unless you want to have nightmares."

Your average fairy stands about 6 inches tall. The only one I've ever met, Ironweed, habitually dresses in black commando fatigues and a purple beret. I don't recommend making Tinkerbell jokes in his presence.

The garish beret might highlight his glittering, iridescent wings, but that's not the reason behind the color choice. Only the most elite fairy soldiers win the right to wear the purple beret, and you seriously do not want to mess with those guys.

In spite of his size, Ironweed does go to The Dirty Claw—even in the face of the serious risk that a drunk werecat might mistake him for a moth. The last one who committed that error, however, backed off with a bleeding gash on his nose courtesy of Ironweed's combat knife.

As we stepped through the door of O'Hanson's, the sight of Myrtle brought the patrons to their feet for a sustained round of applause. The aos si held up her hands. "Thank you, beloved friends," she said, "but really, this is too much."

It took fifteen minutes to wind our way through the tables. Everyone wanted to shake Myrtle's hand or reach out and touch her arm. Finnegan O'Hanson himself settled us in front of the fire.

"Drinks and food are on the house tonight, ladies," he said. "What will it be?"

We placed orders all around and settled in for a night of girl talk—well, girl talk plus one guy. Rodney reverted to his usual cordial self when presented with a plate of select cheese in the center of the table for his exclusive enjoyment along with a thimble-sized wine glass.

We interspersed games of pool and a few rounds of darts with the food and drink. At one point in the evening, as I leaned over the felt to line up a shot, I caught sight of Myrtle, the moms, and Greer in what looked like a serious conversation.

"Wonder what that's all about," I said to Tori. "Nine ball, corner pocket."

My cue hit the ball with a resounding smack, nailing the shot. As I stood up, Glory, who was hovering nearby on her broom with a minuscule piña colada in one hand, said, "Want me to fly over and eavesdrop?"

"No, I do not," I said. "I hate to break this to you, Glory, but with your . . . complexion . . . you're not exactly inconspicuous in that outfit."

Looking down at her magenta blouse trimmed in flaming pink, Glory said, "I'm not? I thought this was understated for a bar."

"You look great," Tori said, chalking her cue. "I don't think whatever they're talking about over there is any of our business. Let's leave well enough alone."

~~~∞~~~

Kelly took a sip of Scotch as she watched Jinx and Tori at the pool table. When Jinx turned and saw her mother looking at her, Kelly lifted her glass in salute, an action that momentarily stunned Jinx before she collected herself and grinned back.

"Do you think she'll ever get used to the sight of you with a drink in your hand?" Gemma asked, idly stirring the ice cubes in her bourbon.

"Doubtful," Kelly said.

"Daughters have rather a persistent problem seeing their mothers as living, breathing people," Greer observed. "I would not describe my mother as particularly nurturing, but the first time I saw her in action, I admit to having been rather shocked."

Downing the rest of her whisky and signaling Finnegan for a refill, Kelly said, "I'm probably going to regret asking this, but what exactly do you mean by 'in action.'"

"We showed up at the same Elks convention," Greer said.

Then, when Kelly didn't catch on, the baobhan sith added, "For dinner."

Kelly's eyes tracked back and forth, then stopped as she mouthed the word "dinner."

"Oooohhh," she said. "That must have been awkward."

"Indeed it was," Greer said. "Mother looked smashing in her cocktail dress. It made me feel a total frump."

Gemma snorted. "If your mother made *you* feel like a frump, the rest of us would probably be suicidal around her."

"Katherine MacVicar generally inspires *homicidal* feelings," Greer admitted. "Mum is not known for her diplomacy."

Kelly stared at her glass, running her index finger lightly along the rim. "Does your mother worry about the dangerous things your job requires you to do?" she asked.

"Alas, my mother and I have not spoken in more than a decade," Greer said. "You're worried about Jinx, aren't you?"

"I don't like all this talk about the damned In Between," Kelly said. "No good ever comes from that place."

Myrtle reached across the table and caught Kelly's hand. "There is no reason to believe that Jinx will be called upon to enter the greater In Between," she said. "Do not torment yourself with these thoughts until the problem is upon us."

"No one enters the In Between," Greer said, "but it certainly can be done. Why does the thought of Jinx going there trouble you so deeply?"

When Kelly didn't answer, Gemma spoke. "Because," she said, "the In Between presents some unique problems for the Daughters of Knasgowa."

The next day I squinted painfully in the bright sun of the lower valley and wished I had turned down that last beer the night before. As Beau, Dad, and Chase transferred the luggage from the sleigh through the Briar Hollow portal, I drew Connor off to one side.

"Thank you for everything," I said. "Mom and Dad had a wonderful time. So did I."

"I wish you'd let me come with you," Connor said. "I want to help search for the amulet."

What was I supposed to say to that? He'd barely learned to place a mirror call, and our mother wanted him as far away from danger as possible.

"Connor," I said, "you know I appreciate the offer, but you're just not ready yet, and Mom will have my head if I put you within a thousand miles of Irenaeus Chesterfield."

His gaze wandered over to Mom, who was directing the last of the baggage transfer and fussing at Dad for not being careful.

"Does she know I'm a grown man?" he asked.

I realize the question sounds resentful now that I'm telling you about it, but Connor's tone was quiet and gentle.

"I'm not sure she does," I admitted. "To her, you're still the baby she gave up."

"That was such a horrible thing to happen to her," he said. "Dad, too, but Mom blamed herself for so many years. That's why I wanted her to see where I live and work so she would understand what a good life I have."

"Intellectually, she does understand that," I said, "but emotionally, she just got her little boy back, and she's not ready to have you in harm's way again."

Connor caught my gaze and held it. "Do you think I'm ready to have my mother and sister in harm's way either?" he asked.

There was nothing I could say around the lump that rose in my throat.

"Promise me, Sis," he said, "promise me that if there is anything I can do to help find the Amulet of Caorunn and keep you all safe, you will tell me. I'll be there in a heartbeat."

I nodded, pulling him into a hug. "I think I like having a brother," I whispered.

"I think I like having a sister, too," he said softly, brushing a kiss against my temple. "Stay safe."

So that's how we left our first Christmas in Shevington to go back to Briar Hollow, where we walked straight into a deep freeze.

When she opened the arched doorway, I caught a glimpse of a richly paneled room aglow with welcoming lamps before Myrtle disappeared inside.

As we'd been talking, Chase and Dad worked to ferry luggage and packages to the lair and up into the store proper. I'd just put Glory's tiny suitcase inside Graceland East for her when Dad came clomping back down the stairs.

"Did you forget to leave the heat on up there?" he asked me, going over to the fire to warm his hands. "The store is like ice."

"I don't think so," I said, "but I may have set the thermostat too low. You know, Dad, I don't . . ."

"Own the electric company," he finished for me. "Very funny, young lady. That's supposed to be my line."

Rodney, who was sitting on Tori's shoulder, mimed a shiver and shook his head vehemently.

"God," Tori said, "you are such a drama rat. I know you don't like to be cold. I'll take my stuff up and check the thermostat. We can all stay down here in front of the fire until upstairs gets warm."

Hefting the last of their suitcases, Dad said, "Not us. We're meeting with the realtor in the morning, and I have to pick my dogs up from Leroy's. You coming with us, Gemma?"

"No," she said, "I'm bunking with Tori tonight so I can meet the painters in the morning. I'll ride back to Cotterville tomorrow afternoon with Kelly when she comes over to take the furniture delivery at your place."

Everyone exchanged hugs all around. I followed my folks upstairs to say good-bye. They'd left their car behind the store while we were in the Valley. When I opened the back door to let them out, a blast of frigid air hit us in the face.

"Whoa!" Dad said. "Guess the weather guy was wrong

about spring coming early. It looks like a cold front blew in while we were in the Valley."

"I'll say," I said. "If I'd known that was going to happen, I would have left the heat on. You guys let me know you got home safe, okay?"

"We will," Mom promised, giving me another hug. "Love you, honey."

After I watched them drive off, I climbed the stairs to the apartment to check on my cats. If the store was cold, my apartment wouldn't be much better, and the guys were not going to be happy with me.

I found the four of them in an enormous cuddle pile in the center of the sofa. They didn't even get up when I came in. When I saw the amount of food Amity put out for them, I understood why.

"No wonder you guys can't move," I said. "If you've been eating like that for the last three days you might as well be furry, beached whales."

Winston opened one eye and gave me a reproving look before going back to his nap.

"Good to see you, too," I said, unfolding a plaid wool blanket and settling it around their sleeping forms.

When I came back downstairs, I found Tori staring at the thermostat. "It's supposed to be 70 degrees in here," she said, "but it's actually right at 58. If the store doesn't warm up pretty soon, I'm guessing the furnace is on the blink."

"Great," I said, rolling my eyes. "I don't even want to think what that's going to cost us."

Darby almost gave me a heart attack when he popped out of thin air beside me. "I took the liberty of examining the machinery, Mistress," he said. "I am quite skilled with all things mechanical. The box that makes heat is working as it should."

"Then why is it so cold in here?" I asked.

"Perhaps because the temperature outside is 28 degrees according to the scale developed by Daniel Gabriel Fahrenheit?" he asked.

That would do it.

Taking a page from Rodney's book, we all opted to spend the rest of that Sunday in the lair. Festus wasn't the only one who needed a nap. Even Beau confessed to "having imbibed a bit liberally" at the Dirty Claw.

Chase, sensing my ongoing discomfort in the aftermath of our conversation in Shevington, excused himself to go work in his shop. "Might as well get a head start on Monday," he said. "You coming, Dad?"

In a move reminiscent of what Winston had done with me, Festus opened one eye, which he trained on his son with an arguably malevolent and completely silent glare.

"Okay then," Chase said. "I'm taking that as a no."

He looked at me expectantly, hoping, I think, that I might say something or even walk next door with him. Instead, I said, "Have fun with your work."

His expression wilted a little. "Thanks," he said. "I'm sure I will."

After Chase left, I went into my alcove to read, but it was a losing battle. I kept falling asleep in my chair. You'd think with everything that was going on, we might all have been energized and in a state of high alert, but post-holiday exhaustion can take down the best of us.

Tori and I both made periodic trips upstairs to see how the heat was doing. The furnace finally caught up about 8 o'clock that evening, which was the only invitation I needed to go upstairs and join my cats in their fur pile. Obligingly, they moved the group snooze to the bed once I pulled out an extra quilt.

I fell asleep to the sound of their purring and thankfully had no dreams that night. Instead, I woke up the next day to the Southern version of a meteorological nightmare. Briar Hollow—indeed the whole state of North Carolina— had been plunged overnight into the grips of a freak winter storm.

My first clue came when I woke up, stumbled into the kitchen for coffee, stopped, and went back out in the living room to verify that my mind wasn't playing tricks on me. A thick blanket of snow covered the courthouse square, and jagged icicles hung from the eaves of the buildings. The howling north wind periodically raised clouds of snow, and the sound of ice pellets beat a staccato rhythm on the roof.

Shocked at what I was seeing, I reached for the remote in spite of the cats wrapping themselves around my ankles in outrage that their breakfast wasn't being served. When the picture came on, the words, "Severe Winter Storm Warning" scrolled across the bottom of the screen in big red letters decoratively outlined with ice.

A weather guy with a bad toupee was talking to a perky blonde newscaster doing her best imitation of "serious journalist face."

"Stephanie, this storm is just unprecedented. It literally blew out of nowhere. None of our models forecast this event, which seems to be deepening in intensity. Temperatures continue to fall throughout the state, and rising winds are sending the chill factor plummeting into negative numbers. Unless this storm leaves as quickly as it arrived, we could have a very dangerous, statewide situation on our hands."

A freak snowpocalypse on a Monday? Unprecedented, maybe, but unlike the weatherman, I knew the storm hadn't just come out of nowhere.

Acquiescing to the cats' increasingly yowled protests, I got breakfast in the bowls before throwing on my clothes. Then I created a mountain of blankets on the sofa knowing they'd all be right back in their cuddle pile as soon as their bellies were full.

Tori and Gemma were waiting for me at the bottom of the stairs. "We have a problem," Tori announced.

"Other than the arctic cold front?" I asked.

"In addition to," she replied. "The front door is frozen shut."

What the . . . ? "How does that even happen?" I asked.

Gemma started to explain. "Condensation from too much humidity . . . "

I held up my hands. "Please," I said. "I haven't had enough coffee for a science lesson. Don't worry about the door. Nobody is going to be out in this anyway."

"Fine by me," Tori said. "So what *do* we do?"

"We get to the lair," I replied. "I'd say Chesterfield has made his move."

TWENTY-FOUR

Tori and Gemma went into the storeroom to wake Rodney up and begin the process of relocating his bachelor pad to the lair. I started downstairs, but the instant I opened the basement door, I yelped, and dove for cover as Glory careened past me on her broom.

She banked hard right, executed an impressive barrel roll, and came to a stop inches from my face.

"It's that awful Chesterfield, isn't it?" she shrieked. "We're all going to die, and they'll find our freezer burned carcasses covered in crusty frost like last summer's ice cream!"

Glory can mix hysterical metaphors with the best of them.

Although I wouldn't have put the idea quite as colorfully, I hate to admit I had been thinking much the same thing. Still, I'm supposed to be one of the voices of reason around here.

"If we're all going to die," I said, "who are 'they' and how will they find us?"

That accomplished nothing but sending Glory's mind diving down yet another rabbit hole.

"Oh my gosh, oh my gosh, oh . . . my . . . *gosh*," she exclaimed. "You're right! We'll be like the dinosaurs in the tar pits."

I should have let it go, but some temptations are just too strong.

"Glory," I said patiently, "the tar pits are hot."

"But how do you know the dinosaurs didn't freeze first and then fall into the pits?" she shot back. "It could have happened that way, you know."

And this is how conspiracy theories are born.

"First," I said, "I do think it's Chesterfield, but nobody is going to die. Second, calm down and quit zooming around on that broom before you put somebody's eye out."

The instant I said it, I winced. The words sounded far too much like my mother's famous "don't run with that sparkler" line.

"You're coming to the lair?" she asked.

"I am if I don't have to dodge any more jet-propelled mini witches on the staircase," I said. "Why don't you go see if Gemma and Tori need any help in the storeroom? We should have all hands on board. You know, to get through this."

Don't start with me. I didn't *lie* to her. And no, I didn't exactly pass the buck on dealing with her either. Let's think of it more in terms of "reallocation," and Glory was completely onboard with the idea. She actually snapped me a salute before wheeling around and flying away.

Making a fast exit before Tori could "reallocate" Gory right back at me, I went downstairs to find Beau, Greer, and Myrtle watching the latest weather reports on the big screen TV.

"Good morning," Greer said. "Shall we safely assume Chesterfield has taken up weather manipulation?"

"Uh, yeah," I said. "Is there such a thing as meteorological magic?"

"Of course," Myrtle said, "but rarely on this scale. Perhaps a stray rain incantation or a spell to invoke a cooling breeze on a warm day. Sending an entire state into an impromptu ice age, on the other hand, reeks of Chesterfield's flair for melodrama."

"Do you have any explanation for how he's doing this?" I asked.

"I would like to confer with Barnaby and Moira before I attempt to answer that question," Myrtle said. "Since the initial conversation may be a bit esoteric, I will initiate the call from my quarters."

"Okay," I said. "I'm going to get in touch with my folks and get them back over here."

"And I will ring up Lucas," Greer said. "I believe he's in Patagonia at the moment, but he will want to return to Briar Hollow immediately when he learns what is happening."

"Beau, can you coordinate with Darby to make sure everyone has a place to sleep, and that we're good with food and essentials?" I said.

"I would be delighted to do so," Beau replied. "It has been some time since I have been called upon to provision an army, but I certainly have not forgotten how to accomplish the deed."

The feeling that we were all doing something eased some of my anxiety over the sudden crisis in which we found ourselves. As I stepped into the alcove, Tori and Gemma came down the stairs carrying Rodney's bachelor pad with Glory flying alongside. The rat, who was perched on Tori's shoulder, didn't look too happy about the move.

"You'll be safe and warm down here, Rodney," I heard Glory say. "Jinx won't let Mr. Chesterfield get us."

The earnest faith in her voice put a lump in my throat. I had absolutely no idea how to reverse the effects of something as massive as what we were facing, but the fact that Glory believed I did somehow made me feel stronger and more resolute.

Stepping into my alcove, I took out my phone.

Mom answered on the first ring. "Norma Jean," she said, "is everyone over there okay?"

"We're fine," I replied, "but I think you and Dad should come back. I'm pretty sure Chesterfield is behind this storm."

She paused for just a heartbeat and then said. "We have to bring the dogs. There's no way your father will leave them at Leroy's in this weather."

"Duke will be over the moon," I said. "We're all moving to the lair where it's warm and safe. Gemma and Tori are bringing Rodney's stuff down now. The dogs will be fine. They can romp all over the place. We'll make it work. I promise."

I neglected to mention that I would be transferring my cats to the lair as well. Surely someone in the group could figure out how to keep the two species separated and Rodney safe from all critters present.

"Don't be so quick to make promises like that, young lady," Mom said. "If this forced visit goes well, you may be babysitting your father's dogs on a regular basis after we move. You know, he does use your cats as justification for the idea of keeping a pack of hounds in an apartment."

Technically only one of Dad's dogs qualifies as a hound, but I decided to let that distinction slide.

"That's fine," I said, "just get on the road before the conditions get any worse."

She assured me they'd be over before nightfall. I called Amity next.

"Good morning," I said.

With her usual acerbic incisiveness, Amity snapped, "What's good about it? I'm freezing my backside off, and God only knows what this is going to do to my bottom line for the month. My New Year's sale is supposed to start today."

"Amity, nobody is going to be making any money during a storm like this," I pointed out.

"Tell that to the generator salesmen," she said.

Crud. Power outages. I hadn't thought about that. "Hold on, Amity," I said. "I'll be right back."

Setting my phone on the desk, I exited the alcove and walked to Myrtle's door. Hesitating for just a second, I started to knock. Myrtle's voice stopped me.

"Come in, Jinx," she called out. "The door is not locked."

Who needs a video doorbell when you're an ancient Fae being?

Turning the knob, I stepped into what I can only describe as a storybook vision of a home in which a forest elf might live. The architecture was vaguely Old English, but the fanciful lines of the furniture and the curious objects sitting on the mantle and in the cabinets made the room both exotic and warm. A fire crackled in the round fireplace, and oil lamps glowed in brass sconces on the walls.

Myrtle was seated in a comfortable high-backed chair talking to Moira in a rectangular standing mirror.

"Hi, Moira," I said, waving. "Sorry to interrupt, but I have a quick question for Myrtle."

"Of course," Moira said. "We have only just begun."

Turning to Myrtle, I asked, "Is the fairy mound self-powered?"

The aos si frowned. "I'm sorry," she said. "Self-powered?"

"Is there any chance we're going to lose electricity?" I rephrased.

"Oh," Myrtle said, "no, not at all. In modern times we have paid the electrical generation company so as not to raise suspicions regarding our identities, but no, there is no actual necessity for external power."

"Thanks," I said. "That's all I needed to know."

I let myself out and returned to my conversation with Amity.

"Sorry about that," I said when I picked up the phone. "If the electricity goes out, join us in the lair. The fairy mound . . ."

"Makes its own juice," Amity said. "For heaven's sake, Jinx, I'm hardly new at this."

I really wanted to tell her I might remember that if she ever came around and participated in what was going on, but that would only serve to make her crabbier.

"Right," I said. "Well, there's also the added wrinkle that we think Chesterfield is behind this storm."

The silence on the line stretched out so long I thought the connection had broken.

"I'm still here," Amity said as if reading my mind. "I'll pack a few things and be over later."

Well, that was an abrupt change of heart, but dropping Chesterfield's name does have a way of doing that to people.

No sooner had I put the phone down than Chase and Festus walked into the Lair.

"Enjoying the tropical heat wave?" Chase asked.

"Very funny," I said. "Did Tori call you?"

"She did," Chase said, "but we were just about to come over anyway. I think you're right about the Chesterfield connection, but I'm going to have to leave you all to sort that out without me for a few hours."

"Why?"

"Sheriff Johnson called," he said. "His office is organizing volunteers to check on old folks around town. The temperature is still dropping. The mayor is working on getting the high school gym set up as a community shelter. Right now, they can't find a big enough generator to power the whole place."

No pun intended, but a light bulb flipped on in my head.

"I can take care of that," I said. "I'll call in a favor with

Cezar Ionescu. The Strigoi have enough generators up at their place in the mountains to light up the whole town."

Greer, who had been typing on a laptop while we were talking, looked up from the keyboard. "They have the generators," she said, "but the Strigoi require electricity to feed. I don't think you want both an arctic blizzard and a host of hungry Romanian vampires on your hands at the same time."

"Will two generators do it?" I asked Chase.

"They will," he said. "And I'd like to use the GNATS drones to help ensure everyone in town is safe."

"Sure," I said. "Just leave one drone to keep an eye on the store."

That's pretty much how the rest of the day went—high organizational mode. I called George and Irma at the corner store to make sure they were okay.

"Lord yes, honey," Irma said, "but every shelf in the place was emptied out by 9 o'clock. We're hold up in our apartment with plenty of food and a good space heater. Our boy, Elwood, is coming to get us and take us to his house before the sun goes down. We'll be fine. You all doing okay?"

"Yes ma'am," I said. "We're going to ride it out here. There's a . . . uh . . . emergency generator in the basement."

"Well, imagine that," she said. "That was real smart of Fiona. Is it vented good, honey? We don't want to come back and find you and Tori all blue and asphyxiated."

She said that last part like it would be a shame, but perfectly normal for two irresponsible young women trying to operate machinery that only a man should touch. "It's a very safe system," I assured her. "You won't find us asphyxiated."

Chase returned just before nightfall half frozen to the bone. We settled him in front of the fire under a blanket with a stiff glass of Scotch and a bowl of beef stew Darby produced.

"So far everyone we've checked on is well provisioned or has plans to go somewhere else," Chase told us between bites, "but the electric company is already dealing with iced over lines breaking. Cezar came through with the generators. He and some of his people are helping get everything connected and working over at the gym. He said to tell you that if more generators are needed, the Ionescu Clan will provide them."

Sometimes the greatest displays of humanity come from the folks other people have branded as "monsters."

And speaking of monsters, that would be the moment when Mom, Dad, and the dogs showed up.

TWENTY-FIVE

You want to talk apocalypse? Consider this equation:

$(6 \ dogs + 4 \ cats + 1 \ rat) \ x \ 1 \ troublemaking \ old \ werecat^2 = chaos$

Earlier in the day, Myrtle took the news of the impending critter influx calmly. She assured me that containment would not be an issue—but did point out Glory might not be all that safe either. Given her size, she could easily be mistaken for a snack or a dog toy.

My free floating anxiety over the bigger picture—you know, the whole coming of the second Ice Age—had to go somewhere. It settled on matters of animal control, conjuring up one disaster scenario after another.

Myrtle listened tolerantly and then suggested we build the zoo in stages. "Bring your cats down first," she said, "and we will make arrangements for them."

Her strategy was solid. Just wrangling the recalcitrant felines into their carriers provided more than enough distraction for my worried mind. Their general attitude seemed to be, "Oh, hell no, we are not going to vet jail in this weather."

When I finally got them downstairs, their native curiosity kicked in, however, and the yowls changed in tone to, "let us out of here so we can explore."

"I don't want them getting lost in the archive," I told

the aos si. This place is huge. We'll never find them again."

"A small matter," Myrtle said, inclining her head toward the ceiling and listening again. "The fairy mound assures me the cats will not be allowed out of sight of the lair."

Slightly mollified, I said, "Okay, and how about keeping them and the dogs separate?"

"That," Myrtle said, "is my job. Please release the individual cats simultaneously if possible."

Tori, Greer, and Beau stepped in to help me. We each took a single carrier and counted off the release. As soon as the doors opened, Myrtle conjured up what looked like an enormous soap bubble.

The enchantment covered all of us, but we were able to step beyond its borders. The cats couldn't, running into the soft barriers with consternation.

"They may move around as they please," Myrtle said. "When the dogs arrive, they will be placed in a similar flexible enclosure. The two species may not cross into each other's space, and neither Rodney nor Glory can come within more than two feet of either of them. Is that satisfactory?"

Satisfactory? The whole set-up was brilliant.

The cats didn't take long to acclimate to their new surroundings. Even by lazy cat standards, no one will ever accuse my guys of being athletic. They forgot about the bubble entirely once they spotted the fireplace and became intent on staking out places for themselves on the hearth.

When Yule tried to claim Festus' favorite spot, the old ginger tom nailed him with a menacing hiss. I decided to let them settle the problem between themselves with the unspoken rules of cat-to-cat diplomacy. It worked because my boys obviously have come to see Festus as the head cat in charge.

(Not to mention that he had gifted them with a massive stash of catnip for Christmas. Honestly, I think in the end their capitulation to his "authority" boils down to not wanting to tick off their dealer.)

Everything seemed to be going great until Dad and the dogs arrived. You see, we all forgot one highly salient factor. Dogs bark.

The pack bounded down the stairs with their usual boisterous enthusiasm, spotted the cats, and made a beeline for the group howling like the hounds mom accuses them of being.

When Festus bellowed, "Stop right there!," Bobber, Dad's favorite, and the brightest of the bunch screeched to a halt, tilting his head to one side uncertainly. I imagine if you're a dog, a talking cat gets immediately filed in the "worst nightmare" column of life experiences.

That bought Myrtle enough time to envelop the dogs in the enchanted Bubble, but Festus wasn't done yet.

"Good," he said. "I see one of you mutts has a functioning brain. Sit!"

To everyone's amusement, Bobber's backside instantly hit the floor. "Excellent," Festus said. "Down!"

Again, Bobber complied. The rest of the dogs glanced at each other uneasily and decided to opt for a "follow the leader" approach to this unexpected turn of events, all lying down as well.

That's when Winston sat up and meowed at Festus who answered at length in felinese.

"What are you telling him?" I asked suspiciously.

"I'm just explaining the boundary system," Festus said innocently.

"Explaining how?" I said.

"You'll see," Festus replied smugly. "Go on, Winston, give it a try."

As I watched, Winston hopped off the hearth, walked right up to Bobber, and hissed in his face thereby causing the dog to lose his mind.

Bobber lunged at Winston, who didn't even twitch a whisker. The dog hit the invisible barrier separating the two of them, scratching furiously at empty air but unable to reach his tormentor. I swear to you, Winston grinned, put out a paw, and delicately shot Bobber the claw.

The whole pack erupted into a cacophony of frustrated howls and barks that escalated markedly when Yule, Xavier, and Zeke joined Winston for the doggy tauntfest.

"Norma Jean!" Dad commanded. "Control your cats!"

"Me?" I said. "How about you do something with your dogs!"

Amity picked that exact moment to walk in the lair. "What in the name of Merlin's beard is going on in here?" she yelled. Dropping the suitcase in her hand with a heavy thump she made a slashing motion with her hand. "*Silentium!*"

Thunderous quiet fell around us. The dogs' mouths were still moving, but no sounds came out of their throats.

Dad's jaw dropped in outrage. "What the *hell* have you done to my dogs?"

"Nothing," Amity snapped. "I like animals much better than people. I would never harm one in any way. Your dogs are still barking, we just can't hear them anymore. Am I the only one here who knows how to use practical magic?"

Feeling the need put blame where it was due, I said, "Festus egged them on."

"And you didn't expect that to happen?" Amity asked acerbically. "You do *know* Festus, don't you?"

I opened my mouth to protest, caught sight of the smirking old tomcat's face, and stopped. Amity was right. I should have seen the whole thing coming a mile away.

"You're sure you didn't hurt my dogs?" Dad asked, still sounding belligerent.

"Positive," Amity said, "but I might hurt *you* if you question my use of magic one more time."

Before the two of them could start an even bigger dog-fight, I said brightly, "*So!* You're here! Hi Mom, Hi Dad. Glad you're okay. Driving must be murder out there."

Still babbling, I started steering them out of the lair proper. "Let me show you where you'll be sleeping. Oh, and Dad, the fairy mound made a grassy patch just down there through the stacks where the dogs can take care of their business."

The notion that an indoor comfort station had been created for the convenience of his beloved pack seemed to satisfy my father.

Rising to the demands of the emergency, the fairy mound did more than just create a mini dog park though. In addition to Myrtle's quarters and Beau's bachelor digs on the other side of the stairs, the lair now faced a row of six small, but thoroughly well-appointed guest rooms.

Greer doesn't sleep, and Festus prefers to snooze on the hearth, but my parents, Gemma, Tori, Amity, Chase, and Lucas (when he returned from London) would all be afforded some privacy during our forced cohabitation.

As for my sleeping arrangements, the alcove simply expanded itself to include a recessed space with a comfy mattress and piles of quilts and pillows opposite the fire-place.

Not long after the initial rumble with the dogs, my cats discovered that secluded haven and claimed the private sanctum. That allowed the dogs to settle enough to accept a shy invitation from Duke for a raucous game of chase.

The fairy mound obligingly shoved several rows of shelves farther back into the shadows to make a play-ground for the dogs and Beau. Yes, the sedate Colonel waded right into the middle of the pack, throwing tennis balls, and allowing himself to be tackled by the ecstatic canines.

"Can you believe what we're seeing?" Tori asked, handing me a cup of coffee from the rather impressive mini espresso bar that had materialized under the stairs.

"Beau told me that before the war he had half a dozen dogs that followed him around all day on his plantation," I said. "Apparently Mrs. Longworth wasn't any more thrilled about them being let in the house than Mom is, but she put up with it."

As we watched, Dad joined the game of fetch in progress, sending a fresh round of ecstasy through the pack. The picture of two grown men—one of them roughly 196 years old—playing like boys with their dogs put a happy grin on my face in spite of everything.

"You know," I said, "if the whole world weren't freezing over our heads, camping out down here like this would be fun."

Tori put her arm around my shoulder. "I think we have to let it be fun anyway, Jinksy," she said. "If we don't, Chesterfield wins."

I told you my BFF is the smart one in the bunch.

After supper, everyone assembled around the fire to watch the latest weather reports on the big screen TV. To say that the humans were confused doesn't even begin to describe the befuddled reporting dominating the program on every station.

"Dan," one newscaster said in a serious tone, "we have never seen a weather phenomenon quite like this. Across the border in Tennessee temperatures are in the mid-50s, but right at the state line, the mercury plunges into the single digits. The same is true on the border with South Carolina and Virginia. North Carolina has been plunged into a geographically precise meteorological anomaly."

"Geographically precise meteorological anomaly?" Tori repeated. "What does that even mean?"

"It means they don't know what the hell is going on,"

Festus said, "but they get paid to talk, so they're talking—without saying a damned thing."

That assessment pretty much summed up the majority of the "breaking news" alerts, although the journalists did provide us with scary details on the spreading power outages and the proliferation of emergency shelters.

Chase called up the video feeds from the GNATS drones. The snow had stopped, for the time being, allowing us to see that all of Briar Hollow had gone dark. The only visible lights were those at the high school gym. The Ionescus were making good on their promise.

As we watched, however, jagged bursts of static interrupted the drones' video transmission.

"They're having trouble with the cold," Chase said. "The pilots are telling me that even fairy dust can freeze in these kinds of temperatures. We may have to ground the drones."

"How cold is it out there?" Gemma asked.

Tapping commands into his tablet, Chase's face paled. "Right now, it's 2 degrees."

We didn't even have a chance for that news to sink in before Myrtle's mirror came rolling into the lair.

"It seems we have a call," she said, softly chanting the words of the reception spell.

When the swirling silver glass coalesced into a solid image, my grandfather's grim face looked out at us.

"I'm afraid this crisis has reached a new and quite severe level," he said without preamble. "The Mother Tree feels the cold."

TWENTY-SIX

Barnaby's statement didn't scare me at first. After all, the Mother Trees make up a global grid. Didn't it make sense that the Great Oak would be able to feel the cold gripping North Carolina?

That naive reasoning shows how little I understood about the interaction of the realms and how together they create a coherent whole.

To explain the importance of Barnaby's words, Myrtle conjured a 3D model of the Great Oak, but where the roots of the tree should have been, there was another tree—or at least the top of one—upside down.

The image reminded me of the way the Tree of Life is sometimes drawn. When I said as much, Myrtle smiled. "Human artists have devised variations on this model for centuries," she said. "Unwittingly, they have recreated the intricate structure of the Mother Trees. Once, before they turned away from magic, even the humans understood the role the Trees play in the composition of all reality."

As she talked, the different parts of her model changed colors. Myrtle described the Mother Trees as they stand in the Otherworld, every one a majestic example of their given species and each the living embodiment of the qualities long associated with their history.

The Mother Oak, for instance, is equated with strength,

stability, healing, protection, and wisdom. The Mother Rowan, on the other hand, enhances psychic powers and can locate precious metals. She is so deeply steeped in magic that the wood of her children is often given for the crafting of the most powerful wands.

"As the mighty trees descend into the soil of the Otherworld," Myrtle said, "their trunks pass through the In Between, anchoring with their bodies the connection and relationship of the realms."

She went on to illustrate how the trees break through again in the human world to sit at vortices of power on the global network of ley lines.

"Some of our human brethren are aware of the existence of these geographic lines of power," Myrtle said, "but the Trees exist over and above those common convergences. They mask their greater role in this place, doing as the humans expect them to do, suffering the annual shedding of their leaves and seeming to be at the mercy of the elements."

As I stared at the revolving model of the Mother Oak, I remembered the things Greer told me about the In Between.

"How do the Trees protect themselves in the Middle Realm?" I asked. "Isn't it supposed to be a lawless frontier?"

To my surprise, Mom spoke up. "Stop being so curious about the In Between, Norma Jean," she said sharply. "There are good reasons why no one goes to the Middle Realm."

Greer, of all people, laid a calming hand on Mom's arm. "One does not have to cross the deepest ocean to study a map of its waters," she said softly. "Be at peace, Kelly."

For just a second, I thought I saw anguish in my mother's eyes before she gave Greer a wavering smile and said, "Of course, you're right. I'm just letting this weather get on my nerves."

Myrtle, who had watched the exchange with an unreadable expression, returned her attention to me. "The people of Wales, in a medieval poem called *Cat Goddeu*, recount the tale of the wizard warrior Gwydion," she said. "He enchanted the trees of the forest to fight at his side in a legendary battle."

Next to me, Tori let out a sharp exhalation of air. "No. *Way!*" she said. "The Ents were real?"

Myrtle nodded. "Tolkien was quite skilled in weaving the stories of the Fae world for the delight of the humans. He includes in his trilogy a variation on the Battle of the Trees."

"Tolkien was Fae?" Tori asked.

"He was," Myrtle said, "and save for that ridiculous Tom Bombadil passage, a thoroughly engaging story-teller."

The only time I've seen Tori more shocked was the first day we walked into Shevington, and she found out unicorns are real.

"In gratitude for the aid of his forest brothers, Gwydion and his men guard the trunks of the Mother Trees in the Middle Realm to this day," Myrtle went on. "No creature dares run afoul of their swords, which they wield in utter devotion to the Great Trees."

"Okay," I said, "so what's the big deal about the Mother Oak in Shevington feeling the cold? Part of her does exist in the Human Realm. It makes sense she'd be aware of what's happening outside."

From the looking glass, Moira cleared her throat. "If I may," she said, "the Great Oak was not speaking of the cold in the world of the humans. The frigid winds that touch her trunk do so in the depths of the In Between."

Gemma sat up. "You're saying that the cold has reached across the barrier between the realms?" she asked. "That's not possible."

"It should not be possible," Barnaby agreed, "but that is what is happening. As each hour passes, the cold moves farther up the trunk of the Great Oak deep in the reaches of the In Between. It seeks out her heart here in the Otherworld."

His words carried such an ominous tone I said the unthinkable, "You're telling us the Tree's life is in danger."

"I am," Barnaby said.

You'd have to see the Mother Tree to realize the impact of that statement. The sheer weight of her presence gives the Oak an air of invincibility. She looks as if she could stand against any force, but now the chill hand of death crept toward her inexorably from below.

"Can't this Gwydion and his men do something?" I asked. "Build a bonfire and drive back the cold?"

"They are doing just that, stoking the flames around the clock," Barnaby said. "The fires have done nothing but slow the progression of the cold. If the climate in your realm is not restored to normal soon, the killing frost will reach the Oak and no power will be able to drive it back."

I may not be good at bluffing, but I don't back down even when I'm holding a hand full of rotten cards.

"You're actually telling me there's nothing we can do?" I asked indignantly. "Come on! I don't believe that for a minute. We're sitting in an archive packed to the gills with magical stuff, and we don't have a single enchanted space heater?"

The corners of Barnaby's mouth quirked in a smile. "I did not say that, granddaughter. There is an artifact housed in the fairy mound, the Jar of Prometheus, which would provide ample heat to protect the Mother Oak, but someone would be required to deliver the object to Gwydion and his men."

"Okay," I said. "Great. We can do that, right?"

The force of my mother's voice almost knocked me out of my chair. "Wrong!" she said vehemently. "No one, most especially you, Norma Jean, is going into the Middle Realm and that's the last I want to hear about it."

An uneasy silence fell over the group. Finally, Amity took the bull by the horns and faced my mother.

"So just like that you decide your girl will fail like all the others?" she said. "I thought you'd found a particle of courage, Kelly Ryan, but I'm not seeing any of it right now."

Festus instantly bristled, arching his back at Amity. "That will be enough out of you, witch," he hissed. "It is not your place to speak so insolently to a Daughter of Knasgowa."

"Really?" Amity said, raising her hands menacingly in response. "I'm the last practicing member of the Briar Hollow Coven, and I will not endure insolent back talk from you, Festus McGregor."

Without warning, the telltale ripple passed over Festus as he shifted into his mountain lion form. I saw Chase tense, but Greer was faster. In a blur of motion, she placed herself between the werecat and the irate witch.

"You're developing bad habits in your old age, laddie," the baobhan sith said tightly. "If there is to be a dance, Festus, then dance with me—if you dare."

Festus didn't shift back, and he didn't say anything, but he did sit.

Gemma turned tolerant, loving eyes toward my mother and said, "Now see what you started?"

In all my 30 years, I've never seen Mom and Gemma fight. Not once. I thought this was going to be the first time. Then the tears started—heavy, hot rivulets that spilled over Mom's cheeks and stained her blouse.

"My girl isn't going into the Middle Realm," she said, her voice breaking. "Not because I think she can't, but because I will not have another of my children pay the damned price that magic always exacts."

Dad, who couldn't have possibly been more out of his element in a conversation of this type, turned to Myrtle with appealing eyes. "I have no idea what's going on here," he said, "but I don't like it. Somebody explain it to me."

"You began this, Amity," Myrtle said curtly. "Tell the tale."

It was a tale, all right. In 1815, on the Island of Sumbawa in Indonesia a volcano threatened to erupt—not just any volcano, a seriously big one called Mount Tambora. Two of the Great Trees, the Ficus and the Eucalyptus, appealed to the Mother Oak for help.

The Oak directed Myrtle to locate an artifact stored in the fairy mound that could diffuse the pressure building up under Mount Tambora. Awenasa, Knasgowa's daughter, volunteered to enter the Middle Realm to deliver the item—the fastest route to reach the endangered region.

Once inside the Middle Realm, however, the people of the Moss Forest, the Golem, confronted Awenasa as a trespasser and presented her with a test to gain safe passage. If she merged their hidden lights into the single white beam, they would allow her to continue on her way and even illuminate the next perilous stage of her journey.

When Awenasa failed, the Golem exacted their stated revenge laid out in the terms of the test, taking from her the thing she loved most, her husband, Thomas Page. Awenasa was left alone with a four-year-old daughter to raise, Sarah, who was my great-great-great-great-grandmother.

The icing on the cake, however, was that the Golem told Awenasa that no Daughter of Knasgowa would ever be welcome in their land again. Apparently, they get insulted when people fail their test. If one of us tried, the consequences might be even more severe than those Awenasa suffered.

On April 10, 1815, Mount Tambora did erupt—an explosion so violent it shrouded the planet in ash for three years, ushering in an event in far away New England in 1816 called the Year Without a Summer. Crops failed, famine and disease set in, and the people turned to religious revivalism and witch hunting in search of answers.

"That's why you won't even let me try?" I asked Mom as gently as I could. "Because of something that happened 200 years ago?"

"Yes," she said. "Unless you're prepared to lose the one among us you love the most."

I looked around the room. I wasn't prepared to lose any of them. Not even to save the Mother Tree. There had to be another way.

TWENTY-SEVEN

Before we did anything else, we had to locate the Jar of Prometheus. Just to brush you up on your Greek mythology, Prometheus was one of twelve primeval deities known as the Titans. As the human legend goes, he stole fire from the gods on Mt. Olympus and gave it to mankind.

Prometheus was a Fae being who aided mankind in "discovering" fire and harnessing its potential to further refine their developing civilization. For the record, humans might have been better off staying in the cave, at least according to the Paleo diet folks, but that's a whole other conversation.

Anyway, remember that beach scene in the movie *Castaway* around the bonfire? Tom Hanks pounds his chest and says, with proper caveman intonation, "I have made fire!" For him, stuck alone on that island, the ability to light a fire was one of the factors standing between him and death. According to Charles Darwin, the two greatest innovations in human history are fire and the development of language.

For most people, the extent of our analytical reaction to fire runs toward good, old-fashioned caveman simplicity: "Fire hot. Fire burn. Ouch!" We don't stop to consider that not all fire is created equal.

Flames burn at different temperatures, which are perceived by the human eye along a set color range. The pretty yellow-orange flames in the lair fireplace along with the glowing red embers in the grate create temperatures of 1,200 to 1,500° F. Throw in the effect of air circulation, and that drops to around 1,000° F.

Blue-white flames, however, can burn at temperatures of *9,010 °F.*

As we set out to locate the Jar of Prometheus, we were looking for something even hotter—something that did not come up on Tori's nifty location finder app for the archive when I typed the request on my iPad and hit "Find."

"What gives?" I asked Myrtle. "There's no record for this thing."

"Of course not," she said, crossing to the fireplace. "The Jar is in Special Collections."

Myrtle pressed a hidden button in one of the braces under the mantel, releasing a trap door in the bricks. Reaching into the recessed panel, she came out with an enormous ring of rusty skeleton keys.

"Shall we, Jinx?" she said.

The way she phrased the question left her meaning fairly clear, but I wanted to make sure anyway.

"Just me?" I asked.

"Yes," she said. "Only the Witch of the Oak may enter the Special Collections area."

With that, Myrtle set off at a brisk pace, and I followed—past the temporary guest rooms and into the stacks where we wound through a maze of shelves and larger freestanding artifacts.

The farther we moved into the lair, the more our footfalls echoed in the vast silence. We passed rows of crates labeled "Library of Alexandria," and I barked my shin on what looked for all the world like the Rosetta Stone.

"Isn't this thing supposed to be in the British Museum?" I asked.

"Heaven's no," Myrtle said. "There's a *version* in the British Museum, but we can't have the humans knowing everything, now can we?"

Before I could say anything else, she announced, "This is it."

We were standing in front of what looked like a bank vault decorated with a myriad of magical sigils or symbols that glowed faintly in the dim light. As I watched, Myrtle selected a key, inserted it into the lock, and then made precise quarter turns accompanied by four incantations.

As she progressed toward a full circle, the sigils moved through the colors of the spectrum, stopping when they reached violet. The lock tripped, and the heavy door opened.

Looking past Myrtle, I saw the interior of the Special Collection. We were standing on an elevated platform above an endless sea of shelves, cabinets, and storage bins that made the main archive look like a backyard garden shed.

"*Wow*," I said. "That's pretty much all I've got. *Wow!*"

"Indeed," Myrtle smiled, "an understandable reaction."

She directed me to step clear of the door, which closed behind us.

"Do I even want to know how far we have to walk now?" I asked.

"Not far at all," she said. "The Jar is kept at the front of the collection in a special room for volatile objects."

Volatile objects. Plural. So *not* what I wanted to hear.

We descended a short flight of stairs and Myrtle led me into a small, bunker-like chamber set in the same wall as the door. Extracting another key from the ring, she opened a box that looked like it could withstand a nuclear explosion and took out a cylindrical vessel inlaid with transparent panels. Pale blue, roiling flames filled the interior of the tube.

"The Jar of Prometheus," she said. "Forged on the anvil of Hephaestus to contain the elemental fire."

Myrtle held the artifact out to me. I took it reluctantly, surprised by how cool it felt in my hands.

"This is supposed to warm up the Mother Tree?" I asked turning the cylinder over. The living fire inside flowed with the motion of the vessel.

"Do not let the Jar's benign appearance deceive you," Myrtle said. "When the lid is opened and the inner core exposed only a fraction, this small vessel emits the radiance of the hottest summer day."

"And if the whole core was exposed?"

"It would rival the heat of the sun."

Scared and fascinated, I continued to stare at the Jar as an idea formed in my mind. "If we took it upstairs," I said slowly, "couldn't we stop this whole winter apocalypse? Save the state *and* save the Mother Tree?"

Myrtle shook her head. "Would that so simple a solution lay at our disposal," she said. "This is the fire Prometheus kept *away* from man. It cannot be released in the human realm. Even to do so in the Middle Realm risks breaching its containment, but the life of the Mother Tree must be saved."

"You're telling me that the fire to end all fires is in this *jar* and we've been keeping it right here in the basement?" I asked.

Myrtle looked puzzled. "Where else would we keep it?"

Well, of course. What was I thinking?

We retraced our steps, locking the Special Collection behind us and picking our way through the archive back to the lair. Myrtle returned the keys to their hidden niche, and I gingerly placed the Jar of Prometheus in the center of the work table where it pulsated ominously.

"So that's it, huh?" Tori said, bending down to get a better look.

"Yep," I said. "Myrtle says it's pretty much the power of the sun in a bottle."

"Cool," Tori said, unflappable as always.

Okay, then. So we were going for calm and collected. I could fake that with the best of them, even if we did have a mythological atom bomb currently serving as our centerpiece.

Inquiring about the weather was out, so I went with work progress. "How's the research going?" I asked, throwing the question out to the room in general.

Everyone at the table—even Rodney—sat amid a clutter of books and ancient documents. They were looking for some way to deliver the warming fire in the Jar to the Middle Realm that did *not* involve me being the delivery girl.

"Slowly," Greer said. "We are attempting to ascertain if any of the other openings to the In Between come with less stringent entrance requirements."

She made it sound like they were trying to get me into some toney witch's finishing school.

After that, there was no more conversation. Everyone was too engrossed in what they were doing for chit chat. Leaving them to their work, I quietly sneaked upstairs.

After 24 hours in the lair, I wanted to see for myself what the storm was doing to Briar Hollow. The first piece of information Chase had given me when Myrtle and I returned was that the GNATS drones had all been forced to return to Shevington.

"They just can't take this level of cold," he said. "It's below zero out there, and the wind chill makes it even colder. The electrical grid went about two hours ago. Pretty much the only power in town is at the gym. The Ionescus have added the third generator so some of the people can overflow into the classrooms, and they took two more generators over to the nursing home."

"Has anyone . . ., " I almost couldn't get the word out, but the reality of the situation could no longer be denied. "Has anyone died?"

"Not yet," he said grimly. "At least not here in Briar Hollow."

The rest of the details he shared overwhelmed me. People on the borders had started to try to get out of North Carolina altogether and into neighboring regions where the temperatures remained normal. Cars jammed the major highways and gas supplies were running low.

In areas like ours where the mountain roads made travel too dangerous, the National Guard wanted to do supply drops, if the winds died down enough to allow the helicopters to fly safely. I felt like we were in a war zone.

Going upstairs wasn't just to see what things looked like outside, I needed away from the constant stream of horrible news coming over the television.

When I stepped into the shop, the cold hit me so hard it took my breath away. Myrtle had taught us how to use a simple spell to envelop our bodies in protective warmth, but I didn't plan to be in the store long enough to need it.

That idea lasted less than five minutes. I muttered the words through chattering teeth, sighing in relief as the incantation washed over me. It felt like crawling under an electric blanket on a winter night. If only we could do that for every single person trying to live through the storm.

As I stared out over the courthouse square, which was completely entombed in ice, that inner voice of wisdom we all possess, spoke to me quietly. *"You know you have to go to the Middle Realm."*

Even if it meant losing the person I loved the most, I

couldn't just let the rest of the world literally freeze to death. Now, as we neared the end of the second full day, the TV newscasters no longer sounded excited to be covering a big story. There was fear in their voices. Conditions were so serious, even the federal emergency teams were having trouble getting into the state.

Lost in my thoughts, I didn't hear Tori come up beside me. The same gentle glow of warming magic engulfed her form.

"Can you believe this?" she asked in a hushed voice. "I half expect to see a wooly mammoth come walking around the corner."

"How's it going down there?"

"We're striking out, Jinksy," she said honestly. "You know it already, but I might as well be the one to say it. You have to use the door in the fairy mound if you're going to do this thing."

"I know," I said, still staring out the window.

She let a couple of heartbeats pass and then said softly, "Jinx, look at me."

When I faced her, my tears started to fall. "I believe in you," she said. "You'll get through the Moss Forest and into the Middle Realm. Nothing bad will happen."

"And if I don't?" I said, my voice thick and rough. "What if you're the one I lose? Or Mom? Or Dad? Or your mother? It's one thing when I have to risk my life. It's different when I have to risk others."

"I get that, but what about their lives?" Tori asked, gesturing toward the window. "Everyone out there is an innocent bystander in this whole mess. They think it's climate change, or some secret Russian weapon, or God being ticked off. We know exactly who did this and if he kills the Mother Tree, whatever is next on the Chesterfield hit parade will be worse. You have to go, and before you even think about saying no, I'm going with you."

"Does that mean you'll tell my mother?" I asked hopefully.

"Uh, no," Tori grinned. "I might be willing to die for you, but there's not a chance in hell I'm facing Kelly with this news."

As it turned out, we were both spared facing the maternal wrath, thanks to an unexpected mirror call—from the In Between.

TWENTY-EIGHT

Back downstairs, we found the research brigade camped out at various spots around the lair. Darby hummed cheerfully to himself as he set the supper table. By the fire, Greer, and Festus, once again on good terms, periodically exchanged chess moves when they looked up from the ancient tomes they each were examining.

I was amused to see Festus, who was sitting on the hearth, lick his paw before he turned the page of the book lying in front of him. Then he extended a single claw and used it as a pointer while he scanned the lines of calligraphic type. I wasn't used to seeing the old scoundrel look so scholarly.

Beau and Glory worked together at the rolltop desk. Someone had carried Glory's iPod Touch down from Graceland East. The device sat propped up against an ink bottle playing *Viva Las Vegas* on the screen. From time to time, the movie caught Glory's attention. As she watched, she silently mouthed the lines along with the cast. Clearly, she didn't need sound to keep up with her idol, the King.

The Colonel had removed his jacket and draped it over the back of the desk chair. His rolled up sleeves and ink-stained fingers testified to his intense concentration. Beau liked most of the amenities of the 21st century, but nothing would induce him to give up his fountain pen.

While Tori and I paused on the landing, surveying the scene below, Dad came walking back from the comfort station with all six dogs at his heels. Visibly excited about something, he almost grabbed Mom as she came out of their temporary bedroom pulling on a heavier sweater.

"Kelly!" he said exuberantly. "They poop, and it just disappears. Darby says he can give us the same set up at the apartment. Isn't that great, honey?!"

You have to remember that as a fisherman's wife, my mother is used to responding enthusiastically to statements she doesn't care about in the slightest. She murmured something like, "That's wonderful, Jeff," but then the full import of what he'd said sunk in.

"The poop *disappeared*?" she said. "There was *nothing* left behind?"

For the record, there are virtually no circumstances under which a girl is going to be thrilled to hear her parents having a poop discussion, but this qualified as an exception. The relieved expression on Mom's face gave me hope that my parents' ongoing canine housing argument might be headed for a possible resolution.

"It's amazing, isn't it?" I asked Tori.

"What?" she grinned. "The disappearing poop?"

Bumping her good-naturedly, I said, "Wise ass. Yes, the poop, but I meant this." I waved my hand over the scene below. "Right in the middle of this massive catastrophe, everything down there seems perfectly normal."

"That's what people do when they want to survive, Jinksy," she said. "They adapt."

She was right. Even in circumstances not of our choosing, we had instantly built a new routine. Beau would probably say something about how that proved the "cohesiveness of our troop," and granted; we were safe and comfortable in the fairy mound. But while those factors certainly helped, living underground while the world froze over our heads wouldn't have been our first choice. Yet there we all were, doing it—and appearing to do it well.

"We need to get back to work," Tori said. "Mom's in the stacks looking at alchemical texts on bilocation. I'm going to go see how she's doing."

"Okay," I said, as we descended the last few steps, "but it looks like Darby's about to put supper on the table."

"When have I ever willingly missed a meal?" Tori asked, looking at me like I'd taken leave of my senses. "We'll be right back."

As she headed off between the rows of high shelves, I walked over to Chase who was standing near my magical target range. He had his cell phone up to his ear. As I approached, he held up the index finger on his free hand to indicate I should wait.

"No, John," he said, "I promise, we're fine. Fiona outfitted the store with an emergency generator several years ago. Jinx and Tori have been nice enough to let me and my cat come over here. We have plenty of food and water. You let me know if you need me to pitch in and help your deputies."

As he signed off the call, I said, "Sheriff Johnson?"

"Yes," Chase said. "Everyone in town is accounted for. No fatalities yet and the Ionescus have things running smoothly over at the shelter. To quote John, 'Strange folks, those I-on-es-cues, but not nearly as uppity as I always figured.'"

Although the Ionescus are certainly "domesticated" as Strigoi go, they've still kept to themselves for decades to hold any possible temptation to feed on humans at bay. Not surprisingly, that's made them the subject of all kinds of wild rumors around town.

"How does it look up there?" Chase asked.

So, someone other than Tori had noticed I was gone.

"Frozen solid," I said. "The wind's blowing hard, but

it's not snowing right now. What are the news reports saying?"

"The same," Chase replied. "Lots of speculation about the freak nature of the storm. The newscasters are trotting out everyone from climate change experts to preachers trying to explain the whole thing."

"Hopefully they won't need to for much longer," I said.

Chase's brow furrowed, but before he could ask any questions, Darby called us to supper. The conversation at the table ran toward reports on individual research projects, most involving alternate ways to get an object into the Middle Realm that did not involve human delivery. Let's just say the results were not promising.

As I listened to Gemma discussing the transdimensional challenges of bilocation with Myrtle, I decided I'd let everyone finish eating and then announce that Tori and I had decided we were going through the door in the fairy mound. You can think I was considerate if you like, but truthfully, I needed more time to work up the courage to face what I knew would be massive resistance from my mother.

The two of us hadn't been avoiding one another, but we had most *certainly* avoided discussing the danger a Daughter of Knasgowa would face entering the In Between. While I understood her fear, and I never wanted to hurt her, Mom was going to have to confront the same truth I'd already forced myself to accept. We were out of options.

Before I could initiate that conversation, I was literally saved by a bell.

After her first consultation with Moira when we returned to Briar Hollow, Myrtle positioned her floor length looking glass in the lair for the duration of the crisis. She reasoned, correctly, that there would be frequent calls back and forth with Barnaby and Moira.

When the friendly chime sounded indicating an incoming transmission, I was the one standing closest to the mirror. I answered the call, assuming it would be one of them. Instead, I found myself staring dumbfounded into the bright, intelligent eyes of an eagle.

"Uh, hello?" my mouth managed to say, while my brain grappled with whether or not it's possible for someone to dial a wrong number with a mirror.

The uncertain tone in my voice made everyone stop and look up from what they were doing. The stunned faces all around me gave me some assurance. No one else in the room saw this call coming either.

"Good evening," the bird said, speaking with a slight English accent. "Please forgive me for contacting you without warning. Do I have the honor of addressing Mistress Jinx Hamilton, Witch of the Oak?"

A talking eagle. Well, that was par for the course given how things had been going over the last few days.

"You do," I said. "How may I help you?" I pitched my voice at the end of the phrase to indicate I wanted to know his identity in return.

"I would give you my true name," the eagle said pleasantly, "but I assure you no human tongue can sort out the pronunciation."

Myrtle stepped beside me. "My tongue, however," she said, "should have no problem."

Without hesitation, the massive bird let out with a series of clacking chirps and hisses that sounded worse than the dragonlets' language. Coming from his powerful yellow beak, the vocalization only sounded more unnatural.

I don't know why I should have been surprised when Myrtle repeated the sounds—perfectly. "Are you not the scholar and university professor who wrote the definitive treatise on medieval Fae political relations with the courts of Europe?" she asked.

The creature inclined his head. "I am," he said, "but that was a long time ago in a vastly different lifetime. And you are, if I am correct, the aos si known as Myrtle."

"There are some who still regard me as such," Myrtle replied. "As for you, Professor, the common belief is that you no longer exist among the living."

Letting out something I thought was a chuckle, the eagle said, "I assure you, madam, I am quite alive, but for many centuries past I have been a resident of the Middle Realm. A creature with my unique physiology regardless of my repute as an academician does not always receive a warm welcome, even in the Otherworld."

"You're an eagle," Tori said. "What's wrong with that?"

The bird cocked his head to get a better look at her. "And you are?" he asked.

"Tori Andrews," she said, hooking a thumb in my direction. "Alchemist. I'm with her."

At that, our caller moved farther back from the looking glass until we could see that only the front portion of his body took the form of a bird. The hindquarters were those of a lion.

"Now do you understand?" he asked. "I am a halfling. A gryphon by birth. My status as a scholar did not save me from the prejudices of either the human world or the realm of the Fae. For me and others like me, the Middle Realm affords sanctuary."

"Well that sucks," Tori said.

The gryphon chuckled. "I think I like you, Alchemist Tori," he said.

"Back at you, Bird Guy," she said.

At that, the eagle let out with a hearty cackle. "You may call me Aquila," he said. "Or Bird Guy, as you please."

"I'm sticking with Bird Guy," Tori grinned.

Their exchange took away much of the awkwardness

of the call, and I felt the tension in the room ratchet down a notch or two. That wouldn't last.

"What business have you with us?" Myrtle asked.

Aquila literally ruffled his feathers, smoothed them out, and then said, "I call on behalf of one who wishes to speak with you, but who fears the reception she might endure. Aos si, I swear to you on my honor, this being is not as you have known her and poses no threat to you and yours. I beg you to listen to her words."

"Who is this being," Myrtle asked, "and what news would she bring us?"

Aquila drew his head up. "The sorceress, Brenna Sinclair," he said. "She would speak to you of the kidnapping of the Queen of Summer."

Twenty-Nine

Aquila stepped away, leaving me face to face with Brenna Sinclair. I didn't know exactly what she'd been through since the night our mothers fought her, but I saw on the woman's thin face the effects of prolonged pain. The high cheekbones etched harsh lines into her angular features, and Brenna's green eyes betrayed a sense of age that had not been there before.

"Thank you for agreeing to speak with me," she said quietly.

Without thinking, I said, "I'm not sure that I did."

For the merest fraction of an instant, something like anger warred with her calm demeanor, but then it was gone again. "Your reaction is completely understandable," she said. "You have no reason to trust me."

"Damned straight we don't," Tori muttered.

Brenna turned toward her with a look of longing tinged with unrequited affection.

"Victoria, I know you have no desire to be my grand-daughter," she said softly, "but that does not alter the connection of our blood. I sincerely regret the circumstances of our initial meeting, and I apologize for the manner in which I treated you. I hope, some day, that you will find it in your heart to forgive me."

The last thing any of us expected to hear was an apology from Brenna Sinclair.

"Do you honestly think I'm going to buy that for a second?" Tori said. "You tried to kill my mother!"

This time the sorceress made no attempt to control her features. The sadness I saw there seemed real. So real, a bolt of empathy shot through me.

"I have tried to kill many people and succeeded with far more than I care to admit," Brenna said. "If I am granted the span of ten lifetimes, I cannot atone for the things I have done. I can, however, help you stop Irenaeus' mad plan to sever the realms—if you'll let me."

Mom and Gemma came forward to stand beside Tori and me. Their body language conveyed all the subtlety of a pair of angry mama lions.

"Why would you want to help us?" Mom asked hotly. "You broke into the fairy mound and held us prisoner. You tried to force us to open the Shevington portal so you could steal the secrets of made magic from Moira. Good God, you wanted to create a master race of your followers. You're Creavit, Brenna. The truth isn't in you."

At that outburst, Aquila rejoined the conversation. The sorceress gave him a look filled with so much relief; I saw immediately that the two shared a close bond.

"I know this is difficult for you to believe," the gryphon said, "but when I found Brenna, she lay near death from a sword wound to the chest and burns she suffered from passing through the membrane of this reality without the benefit of protective magic. For days she lay unconscious. It has taken her many months to recover her strength. During that time, we have spent hours in conversation. She understands the Power That is Above Us All gave her a gift that is not to be abused."

"What gift?" Myrtle asked.

This time when Brenna's emerald eyes looked at us full force, I knew in my gut she was telling the truth.

"My deal with the darkness was broken in the crucible of my death and resurrection," she said. "I cannot lie. The force of my anger did keep me alive these many months, but under Aquila's tutelage, I have slowly come to question the nature of my revived powers. At first, I thought I had been given only the gift of free will, but now I know that I am no longer Creavit. The Hereditarium magic that is my birthright has awakened."

The silence that followed her words stretched on well past the point of our comfort, but I don't think either Myrtle or Brenna was aware of the passage of time. When Myrtle did speak, the words came out slowly and with measured weight.

"Even an hereditary practitioner exercising free will can perform acts of evil," she said. "The motivation of pure magic arises in an unstained heart."

"Or in a heart willing to suffer the burden of true healing," Brenna replied.

Aquila made a sound I took to be clearing his throat. "If I may," he said, "I possess a touchstone. If Brenna were Creavit, the stone would remain black as night, would it not?"

"It would," Myrtle said.

Lifting one massive talon, he held a pendant out to Brenna. It was identical to the one Moira wears beneath her tunic. When the sorceress accepted the stone and held it in the palm of her hand, it warmed to ruby red and pulsated gently—the same color Moira's pendant displays for me.

"You see?" Aquila said. "Only natural magic flows in her veins now."

Greer moved up to stand with us. "Brenna," she said in greeting, "many a long day has passed since last our eyes fell on one another."

"Greer MacVicar," Brenna said, a dancing smile bringing some life to her pale face. "What a day that was. We tried our best to kill each other. An ambitious goal on your part since I was then immortal."

"Indeed," Greer agreed. "I've told the tale more than once."

"As have I," Brenna said. "What says the baobhan sith of my truth?"

A ripple of power flowed over Greer's lean frame, and flickering flames filled her eyes from within. "I say that if you are lying, I will finish that fight, and this time, given your changed circumstances, I will not stop until you are dead."

Brenna didn't so much as flinch. Her manner remained completely unchanged as she spoke to Greer in Gaelic. I didn't understand the words, but I knew they were far older in form than any I'd heard before. She and Greer were, in those minutes, creatures out of time. Even Festus seemed to be straining to follow the conversation.

When the sorceress fell silent, Greer turned to Myrtle and said, "She speaks the truth."

"She does," Myrtle agreed.

Mom looked at both of them with an incredulous expression. "So that's it?" she said. "Out of nowhere a gryphon shows up with *Brenna Sinclair* claiming to be a born again Hereditarium and you just *believe* her?"

"The touchstone cannot lie, Kelly," Myrtle said. "Brenna is Hereditarium again."

"Fine," Mom said, "she's Hereditarium, but that doesn't mean she isn't lying to us."

This conversation could go on forever if we let it. Sometimes you just have to step off the cliff. That's why it's called a leap of faith.

"That's enough," I said. "If Myrtle and Greer think this is legit, then we're going with it. You said you wanted to talk to us about the kidnapping of the Queen of Summer, so talk."

Mom didn't interrupt again, but disapproval fairly radiated off her small form.

"Shortly after the Winter Solstice," Brenna said, "rumors began to circulate in the Middle Realm that the son of Fer Dorich had kidnapped a Fae woman. She is being held in the Dark Druid's castle. Given the winter storm currently plaguing North Carolina and the description of the prisoner that I have been able to obtain through Aquila's contacts, I believe the captive to be Brighid, the Queen of Summer."

That had to be the woman I saw fall into the pond in my dreams.

"How was she kidnapped?" I asked.

"The Dark Druid's son, who goes by the name Liam Cleary in the human realm, took the form of a wounded stag and lured her into Brighid's Well in Ireland," Brenna said. "It is one of the few remaining passages to the In Between in the world of the humans."

Tori and I exchanged a look, and she mouthed the word "bingo."

Myrtle considered the information. "The taking of Brighid would be enough to delay the coming of spring," she said, "but not to create the world of ice and snow that has descended upon us."

"True," Brenna said, "but if Irenaeus has acquired the Amulet of Caorunn, a fact also rumored in this region, what if he were to give it to Cailleach Bheur?"

This is where I'm supposed to tell you that the "plot thickened."

"Who is Cailleach Bheur?" I asked.

"The Queen of Winter," Myrtle replied, "she whose powers are meant to begin their waning on the Winter Solstice."

Wane. A synonym for fade. The condition the Amulet of Caorunn corrects.

Ladies and gentlemen, we have a winner.

Tori, who is even better at word games than I am, put it all together just as fast as I did.

"So, we get the Queen of Summer back, and this whole thing ends, right?" she asked.

"To an extent," Myrtle said. "Traditionally, every year on the first day of spring, the Queen of Winter and the Queen of Summer meet and complete the transition to the changing of the seasons. In the weeks that follow, Brighid's powers grow with the warming of the days as Cailleach retreats to the high, cold places. However, Cailleach cannot refuse to meet with Brighid at any time after the Solstice so long as they are in the same realm. What I do not know is how such a meeting would be affected by Cailleach's possession of the Amulet of Caorunn."

As far as I was concerned, we'd file that part under "cross that bridge when we come to it."

"We have something we have to deal with first," I said. "The Mother Oak is feeling the cold from this storm. First, we have to deliver the Jar of Prometheus to her guardians. Then we worry about springing Brighid from the Dark Druid's castle and getting this Cailleach person into a meeting."

(I know. Sometimes I can't believe the things I'm saying either.)

"You must save the Mother Tree," Brenna said. "If Irenaeus breaches the Grid, he will have taken the first step toward severing the realms."

"Yeah," I said. "We got the memo."

"Do you have a plan?" Brenna asked.

When I hesitated, she accepted my reticence with a grace I wouldn't have thought possible from the Brenna Sinclair I knew.

"You do not have to tell me now or at all," she said. "Confer amongst yourselves and decide if you truly believe what we are saying. If you do, and if you will accept our help, we will do everything in our power to aid in the delivery of the Jar of Prometheus and the liberation of the Queen of Summer."

She made a move to terminate the call, but my Mother's voice stopped her. "Hold on," she said, "what's in this for you? And don't talk to me about redemption because I'm still not buying it."

"Redemption is not an event," Brenna said quietly. "It is a process—a lengthy one. If we work together and accomplish these deeds—and if in doing so, I earn your trust, I ask only to be allowed to leave the In Between with you and for Aquila to come with me."

Only? Ancient sorceress or not, Brenna needed to work on her vocabulary.

THIRTY

Lucas showed up just after the call with Brenna ended. Greer filled him in on all the big reveals from the conversation as he demolished a double helping of leftover roast chicken. When she got to the part about the Queen of Summer, he hastily washed down a mouthful of food and verified the information.

"Brenna Sinclair is telling the truth about that part," he said. "John Smyth or Liam Cleary or whoever the hell this guy is, did kidnap the Queen of Summer."

Earlier, when Lucas walked into the lair looking all rakish in his long leather coat and lopsided fedora, I resisted the urge to give him a kiss. Chase had been standing right there and I just didn't want to deal with the two of them. But after what Lucas told me next, I was peevishly glad I'd been restrained with my greeting.

"How do you know about the kidnapping?" I asked.

Aiming another forkful of food at his mouth, Lucas said, "Katrina told me."

I instantly bristled and just as instantly tried to hide it. Lucas was so engrossed in his meal, he missed the reaction. Tori didn't, and shot me her "don't go there" look. She was right. I couldn't claim to be avoiding trouble between the two men and then turn right around and go all green-eyed jealous monster at the mention of Katrina's name—especially when I knew absolutely nothing about the true nature of her relationship with Lucas.

Summoning up my best reasonable adult impersonation, I said to Lucas, "You talked to Katrina in the mirror again?"

"Nope," he said, complacently diving into a thick slice of pecan pie. "I went to Edinburgh to see her."

So much for being a grown up. Among the other handy magical tricks at my disposal, I am armed with telekinesis. In that instant, I wanted to grab that fork right out of his fingers and stab him with it.

Instead, I said, "Oh, really."

Smart men know that when a woman says "fine," she isn't—and neither are they. The phrase "oh, really" indicates an equal threat level, especially if it's not couched as a question. In case you didn't catch on either, I wasn't asking him a darned thing.

"Yeah," he plowed on. "I wanted to get a look at the spot where Findlay was robbed. Right before I arrived, Katrina talked to Dagda and his other two daughters, Bea and Brig. They're Brighid's sisters."

I managed to keep my mind on business, but I planned to have a talk with Mr. Lucas Grayson and get to the bottom of this whole Katrina Warner thing. If he was some witch-hopping-playboy-water-elf, my name wasn't getting added to his list of conquests.

"Who is Dagda?" I asked.

Myrtle answered, and judging from the look on her face, Tori wasn't the only one who picked up on my silent little hissy fit. My wise, all-knowing Fae mentor looked distinctly amused.

"Dagda is also a remnant of the Tuatha Dé Danann," she said. "He has always preferred to remain among the Irish, however. In their mythology, he is seen as a father figure, a Druid chieftain who concerns himself with matters of time and the seasons. His eldest daughter, the first Brighid, was long ago entrusted with the transition to and from the warm months of summer."

Tori frowned. "There's more than one Brighid?"

"Each of Dagda's girls bear the same name," Myrtle explained, "so that individually they embody different qualities of that identity."

All I could think of was the guy who sells those grills on TV, George Foreman? He has five sons and they're all named George Foreman. Of course, I'm named for a blond bombshell starlet who had an affair with John F. Kennedy, so I guess I don't have much room to criticize.

Even though I might have been in a snit over how Lucas obtained the information, the confirmation of the kidnapping sealed the deal for me. We had two good reasons to enter the Middle Realm. Save the Mother Oak and rescue the Queen of Summer.

"Okay," I said, steeling myself for what I knew was coming. "We're all here and there's never going to be a good time to say this. I've come to a decision. I'm going to use the door here in the fairy mound to enter the In Between. Tori is coming with me—that's her idea, not mine. We'll deliver the Jar of Prometheus and then work with Brenna and Aquila to rescue Brighid."

In the same instant, Chase and Lucas both said, "I'm coming with you."

Then they looked at each other and leaned in like a couple of junkyard dogs spoiling for a fight.

"The two of you can just *stop it*," I said. "Right now."

Both heads swiveled toward me as each man prepared to argue for his position and against the other.

"Don't. Do. It." I warned them. "You're both welcome to come with us, but not if you're going to act like Neanderthals. Either agree to work together peacefully or stay here with the others."

Neither man wanted to be the first to give in, which only irritated me more. Greer, as she has a habit of doing, stepped in to smooth things over.

"These lads will be just fine, won't you?" she said. "Because I'm coming, too, and if there's any misbehavior from them, I'll settle it myself."

She smiled when she said the words, and nothing about the statement conveyed the overt level of threat she'd laid out for Brenna, but the effect was much the same. Chase and Lucas backed down and agreed to play nice.

After that, an uneasy silence fell over the group. I could barely look at my mother, whose face had gone ashen.

When no one else mustered up the courage to speak, Beau cleared his throat. "And what of the rest of us?" he asked.

"I'm sorry," I said, "but you're all just going to have to wait this one out. If our plan doesn't work, someone has to be here who can help Barnaby and Moira to stop Chesterfield."

At one time, I would have expected Myrtle to argue with me. Instead, she nodded her head and said simply, "A prudent plan."

That was too much for my mother.

"*Prudent*?" she gasped. "We're all sitting here blithely talking about sending Jinx into the Middle Realm like it's just the easiest thing in the world. Am I the only person here who remembers that if she doesn't answer the Golems' questions correctly one of us is going to die?"

Maybe she didn't mean it *exactly* the way it sounded, but her apparent lack of belief in my abilities stung. "Mom," I said, "if I don't do this, a lot of people may die. Have some faith in me."

All that accomplished was making Mom look like I'd just slapped her in the face. After several seconds and a couple of abortive attempts at responding, she threw her hands up in frustration and stormed out of the lair.

I expected Dad to go after her, but instead he looked at Gemma. "Go talk to her, Gem, please," he said. "You're the only one who can make her listen when she gets like this."

Gemma took a few steps toward the stacks, then came back and stopped in front of Tori. "Young lady?"

I saw Tori swallow hard, but she stood up to face the music. "Yes, ma'am?"

"I've never been prouder of you in my life," Gemma said. "You've turned into a fine, brave woman. You and Jinx won't fail. I know it."

Impulsively, Tori threw her arms around her mother. Gemma held her hand out to me, and I joined the group hug, grateful that one of the moms believed in us and saw we had no choice but to go ahead with the plan.

"Don't worry, Norma Jean," Gemma said. "I'll deal with your mother. She didn't mean what she said. You girls start getting ready to go."

With that, she released us both and went after Mom.

I watched until Gemma disappeared from sight, then I spoke to the group with what I have to admit was false bravado. I didn't want to go into the Middle Realm and leave things unsettled with my mother, especially since her life was one of the ones I was placing in danger, but we were also running out of time.

"Okay, everyone," I said. "Let's figure out what we need to take with us on this journey. I want to get going as soon as we possibly can."

Right up until that point, I felt completely in charge. Then Myrtle asked a delicate, but pertinent question. "Are you going to speak with Barnaby about this?"

Letting my confidence waiver at this point didn't seem like an option. Aunt Fiona always says, "In for a dime, in for a dollar."

"Yes," I told Myrtle, "I'll talk to Barnaby, but only to let him know that we're going, not to ask his permission."

Thankfully, she totally had my back. "You do not need his permission," Myrtle replied, "but your grandfather is due the courtesy."

On that part, I agreed.

"I'll go in the alcove and make the call now," I said.

Amity, who had been uncharacteristically quiet during everything that had happened, including Brenna's call, chose that moment to get back in the game.

"I'm coming with you to make that call," she said, in a tone that indicated she wasn't interested in arguing the point.

The annoyance at Lucas that I'd managed to stuff down came bubbling out. "I didn't invite you," I snapped, much to the shock of everyone in the room.

"I know," Amity replied, just as acerbically. "I invited myself. You can start the call on your own if you like, but as soon as Barnaby hears what you've got it in your head to do, he's going to want me there anyway."

The *nerve* of this woman. She sits on the bench for everything we'd been through for months, and *now* she thinks we can't win the big game without her. Uh, no.

"If that happens, I'll come get you," I said, completely confidant that my grandfather wasn't going to do any such thing.

Uh, yeah. I don't eat crow often, but when I do, I like it served feathers and all.

THIRTY-ONE

Kelly stared disconsolately into the fireplace that had appeared out of nowhere along with the settee and the lap robe draped over her legs. As she'd walked farther and farther away from the lair trying to escape her whirling thoughts, an involuntary shiver had wracked her small frame. An awareness of the cold crossed her thoughts, and just like that, around the next corner, the warm sitting area appeared.

"Thank you," she said to the fairy mound. "You're certainly in a generous mood these days."

In response, the flames in the oil lamps flanking each end of the mantle flared, and then Kelly was alone. Only the crackling of the fire interrupted the silence until she heard the approach of familiar footsteps.

Jeff had sent Gemma to find her. He wouldn't know what to say himself, not in a situation involving magic at this level, but he'd never want his wife to be by herself.

The steps stopped, and Kelly knew her friend was standing behind her surveying the setting.

"Nice digs," Gemma said. "Mind if I join you?"

"You don't have to ask," Kelly said. "Come. Sit with me."

Gemma claimed the opposite end of the settee. "Where'd this come from?" she asked.

"The fairy mound," Kelly replied woodenly. "Magic giveth and magic taketh away."

Sighing, Gemma said, "That's a little melodramatic."

"Is it, Gemma?" Kelly said hotly. "Is it really?"

"Okay," she said, "are we in venting mode or talking mode? Because if you want to vent, I'll just sit back and listen until you run out of steam. If we're going to talk, then you know where I have to start."

Kelly covered her eyes with her hand. "You have to tell me the girls are right and that I have to trust Jinx to know what to do when she meets the Golem."

"Oh, good!" Gemma said brightly. "You are still in there."

Kelly didn't look up, but her shoulders shook with suppressed mirth. "Do not make me laugh," Kelly warned darkly. "There is nothing to laugh about."

"Then there's nothing to live for, honey," Gemma said softly, "and I know that's not how you really feel."

Kelly shook her head, drying her damp eyes with the back of her hand. "No," she said, "it's not, but you've read Awenasa's grimoire. You know as well as I do what she wrote. You can't possibly have forgotten."

"I haven't," Gemma said. "I remember her exact words. *'I did not know who I loved most until he was taken from me.'*"

"Exactly," Kelly said. "Jinx might think that losing me or her father or Tori is the worst thing that can happen to her, and maybe it is, but she won't know until the Golem exact their revenge. *'They inflict the wound that will never heal.'* That's what Awenasa wrote at the bottom of the entry. If that happens to Jinx, what will become of my girl?"

Gemma ran a tired hand through her short, unruly hair and stretched her long legs toward the fire.

"Kelly, we can't control any of that," she said. "Don't think for one minute that I haven't considered the collateral damage. If someone dies, it's going to affect every one of us, but the girls are going. Period. The only thing you can fix is to make sure Jinx doesn't enter the Middle Realm thinking her mother doesn't believe in her. I know you're scared, but you have to do this for your daughter."

"Have you talked to Tori?" Kelly asked in a small voice.

"I have," Gemma said.

"What did you say?"

"That I've never been more proud of her in her life."

From behind them, a voice said, "Which is exactly what Jinx needs to hear."

"I wondered when you'd show up," Kelly said without bothering to look toward the speaker. "How long have you been spying on us?"

Festus, back in his small cat form, limped around the settee and turned his bad hip toward the fire. "You know as well as I do that cats don't have any better hearing range than humans," he said. "It's all about frequency. I didn't follow the sound of your voices, I followed the scent of your perfume. Still Chanel, eh?"

"Jeff bitches to the high heavens about how much it costs," Kelly said, "but he never lets me run out."

The ginger tom scratched absently at his ear, and then said, a little tentatively, "I'd apologize for butting in, but you know me, I butt in at will. Like I said, I agree with Gemma. You can't let the kid go into the Middle Realm the way you two left it back there. You have to talk to her, Kelly. If she thinks you're expecting her to fail, you're kinda stacking the deck against her. Is that what you want?"

"Of course not," Kelly said. "I don't *want* any of this."

"Want isn't in the deal, darling," Festus said. "You can't stop what's about to happen, good or bad. Make it right with Jinx before she goes through that door."

Kelly looked at her old friend with tears in her eyes. "Your son is going through that door, too, Festus," she said. "What if he's the one to die?"

"Then he will have died doing his job as a McGregor," Festus replied. "I don't want to lose my boy, but he has to answer the call of his destiny the same way Jinx does. The same way we all do."

"Don't you ever think destiny asks too high a price from us," she asked.

The old cat bowed his head for a second before he answered. "Of course, I do," he said at last. "My wife died protecting what we are. I sacrificed my . . . dreams, to do the work I was born to do, but this is who we are, Kelly."

"I'm sorry for that, Festus," she said, in a tone that told him they were no longer speaking of their children and the danger they faced.

Never taking his eyes away from hers, Festus said, "I'm not sorry, Kelly. Not for one second. I'd do it all over again, just the same way."

∾

Before Granddad sent me out to get Amity, I have to say that he took the news about my decision to enter the In Between and Brenna's sudden reappearance better than I thought he would.

"I do not like Brenna Sinclair's involvement," he admitted, "but I know this gryphon, Aquila. Like Myrtle, I thought him to be dead. He has an excellent reputation as a scholar and a gentleman."

"Oh, yeah?" I said. "Then why has he had to live in the Middle Realm all these years?"

"The precise details of that story would have to come from Aquila himself," Barnaby said, "but I will tell you what I know."

As I listened, my grandfather described the days when the Fae began to retreat from the human world. Obviously, creatures with physiology as distinctive as the gryphons were among the first to leave the company of man.

"Even in their absence, however, these creatures live on in the mythology of the humans," Barnaby said. "Their images decorate the pages of storybooks and the heraldic shields of the noble families of Europe. The real gryphons went into the Otherworld where they continue to work as scholars and physicians. It is little wonder Aquila nursed Brenna back to health. The healing abilities of his kind are legendary."

Even during our short conversation, I recognized a being of distinction in Aquila's patrician bearing. Everything Barnaby was telling me made sense, except the gryphon's exile.

"Aquila told me he wasn't welcome in the Otherworld," I said. "Was he lying?"

Granddad shook his head. "No," he said, "gryphons are also renowned for their honesty. Many believe that they are incapable of telling a falsehood. In his conversation with you, Aquila simply chose not to go into the political intricacies of the Fae Reformation, I expect for the sake of expediency. During those days, I know for a fact that Aquila ran afoul of Reynold Isherwood.

Him again? I was starting to think my grandfather had a point about this guy.

"What happened?" I asked.

"Aquila offered an interesting theory in counterpart to the rise of the Creavit," Barnaby said, "one that he may have proven with the rehabilitation of Brenna Sinclair. He held that we who opposed the Creavit should not so quickly dismiss their capacity to exercise free will. As his line of thinking went, although the Creavit bargained with the darkness to gain power, they themselves were not inherently evil and could choose how to use their new-found magic."

"But isn't that what Isherwood has been saying to you all along?" I asked. "Isn't he trying to get you to trust the assimilated Creavit in Europe?"

"There is a difference, Jinx, between assimilating into a society in which you desire to advance your interests and exercising free will to use acquired powers in the pursuit of just ends," Barnaby said. "I am intrigued by Aquila's argument now, as I was then, but I am not convinced. Reynold, however, was, in those days, a zealot who branded Aquila a traitor for collaborating with agents of the darkness. It was not until the abilities of the Creavit to play power politics captured Reynold's imagination and lined his pockets that the first made practitioners found their way into the halls of the Ruling Elders. Shortly thereafter, I washed my hands of the whole business and brought the first settlers to Shevington."

So, add another layer of intrigue to the Fae Reformation. No wonder Granddad hadn't been back to Europe in centuries.

"Do you believe Brenna is reformed?" I asked.

"I believe Aquila, Myrtle, and Greer," he said. "Moira will have to confirm alchemically if blood magic could have awakened Brenna's native dormant powers. But even if that is the case, do I think Brenna has abandoned her evil ways? She was an angry young woman bent on revenge when she became Creavit. Only time will tell if that has been exorcised from her soul. Like you, I think we have no choice but to work with her, but I would reserve absolute trust until actions have proven the purity of her motivations."

I laughed. "Isn't that a fancy way of saying that right now you wouldn't trust her as far as you could throw her?"

Granddad smiled. "I so love human idioms," he said. "I have not heard that one before, but the concept seems to correctly match the topic we are discussing. Now, if you don't mind, could you please ask Amity to join us?"

That's when I had to go out and eat crow. I found Amity waiting with a smug expression.

"Barnaby wants you to join us," I mumbled.

"I'm sorry," she said cheerfully. "I didn't quite hear that."

"Seriously, you're going to make me repeat myself?" I groused.

"Just once," Amity said, smiling sweetly.

Gritting my teeth, I said, "Barnaby would like for you to join us, please."

"Of course," Amity said. "I'd be delighted to."

When we stepped into the alcove, two chairs now faced the mirror, both filled with sleeping cats.

"Guys, come on," I said. "I was gone for five whole minutes."

After I relocated the snoozing felines to my makeshift bed, Amity and I sat and Barnaby got right to business. "Amity," he said, "I think the time has come for you to explain to Jinx what you've been working on for the last few months."

I'm not sure what I expected to hear, but I can promise you it wasn't what she said. "With the aid of Dílestos, I've been interviewing witches to reconstitute the Briar Hollow coven."

THIRTY-TWO

The conversation that followed Amity's surprise announcement broadened my understanding of the interlocking structures that support and disperse the power and influence of the Mother Trees.

Without a full coven in Briar Hollow, the Great Oak had been operating from a weakened position within the Grid for years. Only the impressive strength she embodies made it possible for her to continue to function as part of the greater whole.

The prolonged strain she endured might explain, in part, why Chesterfield's plan to attack her from the human realm seemed to be working.

"Why are you telling me all this now?" I asked.

Barnaby seemed almost reluctant to answer me.

"While we did not foresee the necessity of your entering the Middle Realm," he said slowly, "or a possible confrontation with the Dark Druid, we did understand the need to repair this weakness in the Grid."

That seemed pretty obvious. What the heck was he trying to get at?

"And?" I prodded.

Never one to beat around the bush, Amity blurted out the truth. "Some of the witches I've talked to about joining the coven have expressed skepticism about your lack of training," she said bluntly.

All this time the people around me had been telling me I was special and destined. I guess I'd bought my own press. The idea that some witches I'd never even met were running around dissing me instantly put me on the defensive.

"Really," I said testily. "Did any of *them* volunteer to wade into this mess and fix things?"

Amity clicked her tongue. "Don't get in a snit," she said. "I'm on your side. I happen to think you're going to be just fine in the Middle Realm."

Well, wasn't she just full of surprises today. "Oh," I said. "Uh, thank you."

My grandfather cleared his throat. "We are not seeking to add to the pressure under which you are already working," he said, feeling carefully for his words, "but when you return from the Middle Realm . . . "

"Those same witches are going to be lined up out the door trying to get into your coven," Amity finished for him. "So knock their striped socks off."

I blinked. "We don't really ever have to do the striped socks and pointy hats, do we?" I asked.

"Only on formal occasions," Amity said serenely.

She was kidding . . . I think.

When Amity and I came out of the alcove, Tori, Darby, Chase, and Lucas were working on packing four backpacks while Myrtle offered suggestions. Greer had an elegant leather satchel open beside her chair, which she was filling with various small items I couldn't make out.

"Barnaby's good with the plan," I said. "I'm going to call Aquila back and set up a meeting with him and Brenna. If anyone has anything to say before I do that, now is the time to say it."

From off to my left, Mom said softly, "May you and I talk, Jinx?"

The fact that she didn't use my double Southern name was promising.

"Sure," I said. "You want to come into the alcove?"

"Why don't we take a walk instead?" she suggested.

Myrtle laid her hand gently on my arm. "Go with your mother," she said. "I will speak with Aquila."

I fell in beside Mom as we walked away from the lair. Neither of us spoke until the sound of the voices behind us faded away.

"Honey," Mom said then, "I owe you an apology. You're doing the right thing—the brave thing—and I know you'll be fine."

Looking at the floor, I said, "Do you? Or do you just not want me to go into the Middle Realm with this hanging between us?"

Mom stopped walking and caught hold of my hands. "Both," she said. "Of course, I'm scared, Jinx. For you. For us. But this is who you are. This is what you do. I *am* proud of you and it was very wrong of me not to say so sooner."

"Thank you," I said, allowing the tears I'd been holding back to flow freely. "And just so you know? I'm scared half to death."

Drawing me into her arms, Mom whispered, "I'd be seriously worried about you if you weren't."

⸺⸺

When Mom and I returned to the lair arm in arm, I think everyone breathed a sigh of relief. Dad bounded up off the sofa and pulled us both into one of his big, wonderful bear hugs. "How are my girls?" he asked.

"We're fine," Mom wheezed, "but we can't breathe."

He loosened his hold, but he didn't let go. "That's more

like it," he said, kissing me on the forehead and Mom on the lips. "I don't like discord in the family."

"Nor do any of us," Myrtle said. "Jinx, I have spoken with Aquila."

She outlined a simple plan. We would enter the Middle Realm from our side, which directly accesses the Moss Forest. There, we would be met by the Golem who would test me. Assuming I passed, which I intended to, we would then cross a chasm to the adjoining mountain range and descend to the Valley of Quivira.

At that point, Beau interrupted her, "Quivira?" he asked. "Is that not another name for Cibola?"

"It is," Myrtle replied.

That sounded vaguely familiar. "What's Cibola?" I said.

"A land much sought after by the Spanish Conquistadores in the 16th and 17th centuries," Myrtle replied.

Conquistadores? My mind flashed back to seventh grade history class. "The Seven Cities of *Gold*? That Cibola?" I said. "For real?"

"Very much for real," she said. "Aquila and Brenna will be waiting for you at the first of the seven cities, which lies at the foot of Mt. Quivira."

From there, we would journey with the pair to the base of the Mother Oak and deliver the Jar of Prometheus to Gwydion in person. Next stop? Castle of the Dark Druid.

"So what are we going to do once we get there?" Tori asked. "Knock on the door and ask if Brighid can come out and play?"

"Not in so many words," Greer answered, taking a sip of her Scotch, "but Brenna and I are both acquainted with Fer Dorich. He will speak to us and hopefully we can come to an accord without things getting . . . complicated."

Complications involving Dark Druids, the baobhan sith, and a questionably reformed Creavit sorceress? Yeah, I was up for avoiding those.

So—that was it. The bags were packed. We had a plan.

"What are we waiting for?" I asked.

"Midnight," Myrtle replied. "It is the most opportune time to cross into the Middle Realm. There, you will arrive just as the sun is rising, the time of day when the Golem are most inclined to deal favorably with travelers."

I glanced at my watch. That's when I realized I didn't know if it was day or night, or for that matter, the day of the week.

"Being down here has made me completely lose track of time," I admitted. "What day is it?"

"Tuesday, December 29," Chase said, "and it's about 6 o'clock in the evening."

That would explain why I was starving.

"Sounds good," I said. "What's for dinner, Darby?"

The brownie laid out a feast fit for royalty, which I tried not to regard as my last meal. Everyone at the table tried to keep the conversation light, which was pretty tough under the circumstances. The muted TV over our heads displayed a constant stream of scrolling headlines. Water pipes frozen solid. Power lines down. Emergency shelters filled to capacity. Impending food shortages. We needed to get this thing done—*fast*.

When we were all sitting around the fire again, Myrtle explained that like the transition into Shevington, time in the Middle Realm flows along a different stream. "For us," she said. "You may be gone only a matter of hours, but for you, days could pass. There will be no way to communicate with us until you reach a place with access to a mirror."

"Can't they carry a pocket mirror?" Kelly asked.

"They can," Myrtle said, "but a device that small will most probably lack the power to initiate or receive a signal."

"And when we're ready to come home?" Tori asked. "we get back out the same way we got in?"

"Precisely," Myrtle said. "Once you have passed the test of the Golem, they will not trouble you again."

I honestly can't say if time crawled or raced after that. Sometimes I looked at the clock shocked to see only five minutes had passed since the last time I checked, and then a whole hour would fly by in the space of a minute. No matter where I went in the lair, I felt my parents' eyes following me.

Rodney refused to budge from his place curled around my neck. He understood he couldn't come with us, but he was getting every second with me that he could.

Around 11:30, I asked Beau to step into my alcove. Drawing the curtain behind us, I said, "I want to ask you to do something for me."

"Anything, Miss Jinx," he said. "You have only to say the word."

"First," I said, "I need you to take care of Rodney and my cats. I know it's a weird combination, but they know not to eat him."

Gently prying the rat away from my neck, I cradled him lovingly in my hands. "You stay with Beau, you hear me?" I said. "And none of your bright ideas. When I get back, I want to hear you were on your best behavior. Got it?"

Rodney's eyes filled with tears, but he nodded and crossed his heart. When Beau reached for him, the little guy ran up the colonel's arm and dived under his sweater without looking back.

"Okay," I said, drawing in a shaky breath. "Second, will you please look after my folks, too? I don't know what's going to happen in there. Even if I get past the Golem, there's no guarantee I'm coming back."

Beau had started to shake his head before I even finished speaking. "There is no need of this," he said fiercely. "You are coming back."

I caught hold of his hand and made him look at me. "You're a soldier, Beau," I said. "I may not get through this alive and you know it. Please promise me that you will be there for my parents."

He didn't like it, but Beau was not a man to deny the request of a friend.

"On my oath," he said. "I will care for your parents as if they were my own. But Jinx, you will return. Of this, I have no doubt."

"Let's hope you're right about that," I said shakily. "Do you happen to have any words of advice for me?"

"'*This above all: to thine own self be true,*'" he said. "'*And it must follow, as the night the day, Thou canst not then be false to any man.*'"

Shakespeare. First time that stuff ever made a lick of sense to me.

THIRTY-THREE

As soon as Beau and I emerged from the alcove, Myrtle stood up and announced, "We must go to the doorway now." She held the Jar of Prometheus in her hands.

Mom instantly got to her feet, clearly intending to come with us, but stopped when Myrtle said gently, "Only those taking the journey may approach the entrance to the Middle Realm, Kelly. I am afraid you must remain here."

I know Mom wanted to argue, but when Dad put a hand on her shoulder and shook his head, she accepted that this was the moment she'd been dreading.

Since she seemed rooted in place and my father wasn't budging either, I went over to join them.

"Don't worry," I said. "We'll be back before you know it."

Mom's lip quivered, but she didn't cry. "Stay safe," she said. "I love you."

"I love you, too," I answered, pulling her into a hug. "Please don't worry. We're going to be fine."

She nodded. "I know," she said in a choked voice, "but I'm going to worry anyway."

Dad's arms came around us both. "Knock 'em dead, kiddo," he said. "You've got this."

When we stepped apart, Gemma waved me over to

where she and Tori were standing. She had one arm around her daughter and drew me close with the other.

"You two have been getting into trouble together since before you learned to walk," she said. "What one of you couldn't think of, the other one did."

"She's the troublemaker," I said, leaning into Gemma. "I'm the innocent party who gets blamed for everything."

Her laughter vibrated comfortingly against my body. "That's debatable," she said before her tone grew more serious. "Keep each other safe, girls. Trust your instincts, and trust each other."

"Yes, ma'am," we both said on cue.

Glory pulled up in front of us on her broom, hovering at eye level. "Darby made sandwiches and put them in your packs," she said, "and I insisted he put chocolate chip cookies in, too. I don't think anybody should ever do anything scary without chocolate chip cookies on hand."

"Dang straight," Tori agreed. "Thanks."

"You're welcome," Glory said. "And please come back okay. You all are my family now."

I'd managed not to cry with my parents and Gemma, but the mini witch's earnest sincerity took me to the edge of tears. "We feel the same way about you," I said. "We're counting on you to keep an eye on things here until we get back. Can you do that?"

Glory sat up straighter on her broom. "You bet I can," she said. "Don't you worry about a thing."

Across the room, I saw Chase approach his father who was sitting as usual on the hearth.

"You're a credit to the clan, boy," Festus said, holding out his paw. "Your mother would be proud. *Go mbeannaí Dia duit.*"

May God bless you. If I wasn't choked up already, that would have done it.

Chase accepted the gesture. They shook "hands," and he said, "Thank you, Dad. That means a lot to me."

Festus saw me watching them and winked.

When Tori went over to say goodbye to my parents, I caught hold of Gemma's hand. "Take care of Mom," I whispered. "She's not okay with this and if anything . . ."

"Nothing is going to happen," Gemma said, "but I will take care of Kelly, the same way you're going to take care of Tori for me. Deal?"

"Deal."

At the edge of the lair, Darby stood next to Beau with Duke hovering close by. When I stopped in front of them, the brownie regarded me with enormous eyes.

"You and Mistress Tori are doing a great and courageous thing, Mistress," he said. "It will be a story we will tell many times in years to come."

"That we will," I said, bending down and kissing him on the cheek and pausing to scratch Duke's ghostly ears.

When I straightened up, Rodney was sitting on Beau's shoulder.

"I know you don't like this," I told the rat, "but you need to stay here. You don't expect these people to think for themselves, now do you?"

Rodney grinned, shook his head, and gave me the thumbs up.

"Good man," I said. "I'll be back soon, I promise."

Careful not to dislodge Rodney, Beau embraced me and whispered, "I will keep my word to you, but please do not give me cause to do so."

That just left Amity, who wasn't exactly the hugging type. Thankfully she forestalled any awkward parting by handing Dílestos to me and repeating her stern admonition to, "Knock their socks off."

With that, I joined Myrtle, Tori, Chase, Lucas, and Greer. We clasped hands and took the flight of the baobhan sith. The last thing I saw in the lair before the swirling winds obscured my vision, were Mom and Gemma watching us go, wishing they could take our place.

Greer brought us to an open space in the fairy mound that faced an ancient stone wall. In the center, bound in iron and secured by chains and locks, a massive oak plank door waited. Cobwebs obscured the hinges, and a thick layer of dust coated the hardware.

"So that's it?" Lucas asked, dropping his pack on the floor beside his feet. "The doorway to the Middle Realm?" He moved closer to examine the entrance. "Does it work like a portal?"

"After a fashion," Myrtle said, taking out the rusty ring of keys she'd used earlier to get us into the Special Collection. "If you and Chase will be so kind as to remove the locks and chains, I will explain."

Chase took the keys from her and stepped next to Lucas. "We're going to raise a cloud of dust getting those things off," he said.

Even though she was at least six yards away, Myrtle absently waved her hand, instantly brushing the cobwebs and dirt aside.

"Damn," Lucas said. "Neat trick. You need to visit my apartment and do the same thing."

"Hah!" Greer snorted. "It would take more than magic to clean up that pigsty. Have you considered blasting powder?"

"Very funny," Lucas muttered.

He reached for the first lock, then stopped and looked back at Myrtle. "Any chance you can open these with magic, too?" he asked.

"Those locks were forged with dwarvish iron and enchanted by the Druids of old," she replied. "They will answer only to the keys to which they are bound."

Lucas sighed with resignation. "That," he said, straining to lift the first heavy lock, "is the thing I never get about magic. Just when you need it to make things easier, it chooses the hard way."

Both men wrestled the heavy chains and locks, heaving them to one side with a series of resounding clangs so the door could freely swing open.

When the way was clear, Myrtle handed me the Jar of Prometheus. I opened my pack to stow the artifact. "Is there anything else we need to know about how to use this thing?" I asked.

"No," Myrtle said. "Recite the unlocking spell I gave you and expose the core in fractional stages. Open your mind to the Mother Oak, and she will tell you when the cold begins to recede."

I'd already decided that warming up the Mother Tree was going to be the easy part of this trip. Actually getting to her was what had me worried.

At Myrtle's signal, we all shouldered our gear and stood in a loose line in front of the door.

"Any idea what we're going to run into first?" Tori asked.

"The Moss Forest," Myrtle said. "A green space of lush beauty. The door will open onto a smooth path. Walk it until you are approached by the Golem. They will appear when they sense your presence and put their test before you."

I didn't want to ask, but I had to know. "What happens if we fail? I mean immediately. Do we just get zapped back here or something?"

"You will be forced to return to the fairy mound," she said. "You will find the door open and waiting for you. Though you will see nothing but darkness, step through. I will sense your presence and come for you."

"And the other part?" I asked, reluctant to even say the words.

Myrtle put her hand on my arm. "Should you fail, you will immediately understand the consequences," she said. "The loss will strike through your heart like the blade of a knife. Awenasa wrote that she did not wish to live when that knowledge infused her being, but no matter what happens, Jinx, you must live, and you must return. Do you understand?"

Nodding numbly, I said, "Yes, I understand."

Myrtle stepped away and began the spell to open the doorway. Tori caught my eye. "No hill for a climber, kiddo," she said. "Maybe the munchkins will be waiting for us."

Beside her, Lucas muttered, "Those munchkins always annoyed the hell out of me. Squeaky little voices and bad hairdos."

Okay, I might be suspicious that he was a tree-witch-hopping playboy, but it's hard to stay mad at a man who likes *The Wizard of Oz*, especially when he sounded as scared and nervous as I felt.

On the other side of me, Chase stared straight ahead, his jaw set in a rigid line that told me he was none too happy either. Only Greer seemed relaxed, but then she had entered the Middle Realm before.

As Myrtle's voice rose, the lyrical passages of the incantation took physical form, the words hanging suspended in the air before us. The dips and swirls of the individual letters interlocked until the lines formed into a great hand. When the final stanza fell from Myrtle's lips, the fingers grasped the rusty handle and drew the heavy door open an inch at a time on protesting hinges.

A shaft of light appeared around the edges of the wood, growing wider and brighter as the opening broadened. Shielding my eyes against the glare, I began to discern rolling hillocks covered in soft moss. Gnarled trees draped in curtains of verdant green tendrils dotted the landscape.

As Myrtle had promised, a gentle, graded path wound off toward the horizon where the first rays of the rising sun turned the sky orange and violet.

"Go quickly," Myrtle said. "Use the dawn to your advantage with the Golem."

I wanted to say something profound, but all I could do was nod. My first step faltered, but then I squared my shoulders and walked with confidence into the unknown. The others fell in behind me. There was no sensation of moving from one reality to another, but when I looked back, I saw nothing but blackness where the fairy mound and Myrtle should have been.

Just as slowly as it had opened, the doorway creaked shut, leaving us standing in the Middle Realm. Right up to the second when the lock clicked, I fought the urge to dive back through, but then Tori, who was watching me, went for the obvious line.

"Toto," she wisecracked, "I don't think we're in Kansas anymore."

"I know," I said, looking over her shoulder, "and I'm pretty sure they're not with the Lollipop Guild."

THIRTY-FOUR

Physically, the Golem occupied that place where the Pillsbury Doughboy meets an Ewok, and they give birth to a gingerbread man—made of dirt. Silhouetted against the rising sun, the creatures cast long shadows as they shuffled toward us leaving muddy trails on the damp moss. I tried not to think about how much the dark smears looked liked blood.

The Golem's ominous approach seemed incongruous with both their size and the quiet setting. There were seven of the creatures, and none of them could have been taller than four feet. They moved across a landscape that rose and fell like ocean waves. The moss tendrils draping the trees swayed softly in the morning breeze, and I could hear birds singing high in the branches.

When they were roughly three yards away, the group stopped, and a single Golem stepped forward. I assumed he was their leader, but something about the way he planted his feet reminded me of a pugnacious little boy. The stance struck me as oddly endearing.

"Daughter of Knasgowa," he demanded in a thick, raspy voice, "how dare you and your minions enter the land of the Golem after Awenasa's insult?"

The way he said it, the incident might have happened only the day before. Myrtle told me time runs erratically in the Middle Realm. For all I knew, the Golem, in their perception, might have experienced the encounter with my ancestor much more recently than 200 years ago.

That certainly would have explained the outrage in the leader's tone—either that or the Golem were great at holding ancient grudges.

"Forgive me," I said, adopting the formal, respectful speech Myrtle suggested. "We have pressing business with Gwydion and his men at the trunk of the Mother Oak. We humbly ask to pass through the Land of the Golem in peace."

That should have touched off the first question in the test everyone had been freaking out about, but to my shock, the creature said simply, "No."

Myrtle and I hadn't gone over a game plan for an outright refusal.

"That's not how this works," I blurted out. "You're supposed to test me so we can pass through your land."

The Golem planted his fists on what I assumed were his hips and gave me an evil grin worthy of that creepy Chucky doll from the movies.

"*You*," he said, "do not tell us what to do."

Beside me, Tori muttered, "Now what?"

Good question. "Guys," I said, "any suggestions?"

Lucas, who was standing to my left said, "How about we just keep walking? It's not like they're big enough to fight us."

Famous last words.

The Golem leader's eyes glowed like coals in his sooty face. "Insolent elf," he spat. "We do not have to fight you; we will take from each of you that which you love most. If you follow the witch, then you may share the witch's pain."

Escalation. Never a great negotiation tool.

"Okay, okay," I said, "everybody just calm down. We have no intention of charging across your land. Forgive me if I questioned your authority. What can we do to be granted permission to travel through your forest?"

"Nothing," he spat. "We do not deal with Fae scum."

Arguing with him clearly wasn't going to work, and something about his manner bothered me. Nobody is that angry without good reason.

Among the papers in the satchel Mom gave me, I found a leather notebook that belonged to my grandmother. In it, she copied out quotations and passages from books that must have meant something to her.

When I showed it to Beau, he said, "This is a commonplace book. People used them as a way to compile and ponder the knowledge they gained from their reading and other scholarly pursuits. I, myself, keep one to this day."

On the first page of her book, Grandma transcribed, *"Be kind, for everyone you meet is fighting a hard battle. - Ian Maclaren."*

The phrase reminded me of the advice an elderly waitress gave me the first day I worked at Tom's diner. "When some old boy comes in here and snaps at you, honey," she said, "don't snap back. You don't know who got to him before you did."

I took the advice to heart, and it changed my life. The old man who complained that his eggs were runny even when the yolks were hard as a rock? He missed his wife's cooking. She'd died the year before.

The old maid who demanded we trim the crusts off her sandwiches? She wasn't being impossible; she longed for the social status she'd enjoyed in her youth when her father was one of the wealthiest men in the state.

Everybody has a story, and at some level every story involves pain. That had to be true for the Golem as well, otherwise, why would they be so determined to fight for no good reason? Maclaren was right, sometimes kindness is the only magic you need.

"What happened?" I asked softly. "Who hurt you and how can we help?"

All seven of the creatures gasped so loudly Tori and I both jumped. The leader took a faltering step toward me, then stopped. Summoning what I now understood was false bravado, he barked, "Come closer, witch. I would speak with you."

I crossed to stand in front of him and then went down on one knee so I could look into his strange red eyes.

"What did you say to me?" he asked, sounding completely shocked.

"I asked who hurt you," I said. "All of you. You can't have started out hating the world this way."

"No one who has entered our realm from yours has ever asked us such a thing," the Golem leader said.

Melodious sweetness replaced the previous harshness of his voice, tinged with something lonely and inconsolable.

"The people from your world ripped away the heart of this land centuries ago," he told me mournfully. "They left us as we are now, without the One Light. If you can return to us that which was taken, you may pass unharmed."

My first impulse was to give him a big hug and tell him I'd fix everything—never mind that I had zero idea how to pull off the miracle he wanted.

Instead, I said, "May I talk with my friends so we can figure out how to do that?"

"Yes," the Golem said, "you have treated us with courtesy. We will respond in kind."

When I stood up and turned back toward the group, the expression on Lucas' face told me he couldn't believe I was trying to psychoanalyze a metaphysical mud man with anger issues.

I always wondered what football players talk about in

the huddle. Now I was convening one of my own, but as we gathered in a tight circle to talk, I realized the Golem weren't our only problems.

Chase looked awful. His face had no color, and from the rigid lines of his body, I thought he might be in pain. Laying my hand on his arm, I said, "Hey, what's wrong?"

Then he looked at me—with the glowing amber eyes of a cat.

"My body wants to shift," he said tightly. "I'm trying to control it."

Shapeshifters aren't like werewolves in horror movies. They don't transform against their will on the full moon or at any other time, for that matter, nor do they become mindless beasts after the change.

"Has this ever happened to you before?" I asked.

"No," he said, "it's this place. Can't you feel the weight of it pressing down on you?"

That's the trouble with questions. They tend to lead to answers—not necessarily the ones you want.

"I can," Greer said, in an equally strained voice.

Before I even turned my head, I knew we had double trouble. Her green eyes weren't just alight with the inner fire that animates her magic, they burned with something wild and insatiable. An aura of power rippled around her body, fighting to be set free.

"Let me guess," I said. "Hunger pangs?"

She nodded, fixing me with the primal, feral gaze of a hunter. "Do not be afraid," she said. "I will not allow it to overcome me. I have had many centuries to practice self-management."

"But do you *need* to feed?" I asked.

The baobhan sith shook her head. "No," she said. "I attended to that requirement before I came to Shevington for the holidays. That was only five days ago."

Five days? How was that even possible? With all the complications we'd faced since the Christmas celebration seemed nothing but a dim memory.

"Okay," I said, "I know this isn't what we prepared for, but I really don't believe the Golem want to hurt anyone. I think they're reacting to having *been* hurt. Any ideas on how to give these guys back their One Light?"

Lucas scrubbed at his face with one hand, pushing his fedora higher on his head in the process. "Isn't merging the lights of the Golem supposed to be the point of the test you were to take?"

"Yes," I said, "according to what Awenasa wrote in her journal."

"Then," he said, "the One Light has to be that beam. Won't a prism do that?"

Tori shook her head. "No, a prism breaks up light so you can see the individual colors of the spectrum."

Never one to be slowed down by science, Lucas said reasonably, "So what happens if you run it through backward?"

Tori stared at him. I could see the wheels in her mind turning at top speed. Finally, she snapped her fingers and said, "Newton!"

"As in Sir Isaac?" I asked.

"Yes," she said. "When he was studying at Cambridge in the 17th century, he figured out how to break light into the visible spectrum with a prism. Then, he took a second prism, turned it upside down, and merged the spectrum back into white light."

"So you agree with Lucas about the One Light?" I asked.

"It makes sense," she said. "There are seven colors in the spectrum, and we're dealing with seven Golem. When you ticked off the leader, his eyes glowed red. What if the others each represent a color?"

"You're saying we need a prism so they can look at it with their laser eyes or something?" I said.

Tori shrugged. "Anybody else have a better idea?"

"That's not the important question," I replied. "More to the point, does anybody have a prism?"

In my hand, Dílestos began to vibrate. The In Between seemed to be heightening all of our senses because the others picked up on it as well.

"The crystal atop the staff," Greer said, "could it not act as a prism?"

"I can't give Dílestos to the Golem," I protested, "it's a living branch of the Mother Tree."

In my mind, the voice of the staff rose clear and resonant. "*It is not I who must remain with the Golem, but that which I have guarded these many years.*"

Tori, who was watching me closely, said, "It's talking to you, isn't it?"

Nodding, I put my hand on the hunk of crystal embedded in the top of the staff. At my touch, the four gnarled fingers of wood that had held it in place opened like the petals of a flower, allowing me to remove the stone before they wove themselves together again in an intricate Celtic knot.

"The Mother Tree strikes again," Lucas grinned.

Turning back to the Golem, I drew in a deep breath and held out the quartz. "I don't want to lie to you," I said. "I'm not sure we can give you back what was taken from you, but we offer this in its place."

The Golem leader cocked his head to one side, the red light returning to his eyes. "Put it on the ground before me," he ordered.

I did as he asked and then stepped back with the others. As we watched, the Golem formed a ring around the crystal. The leader reached forward and put his hand on the stone, then nodded to his nearest companion. The second Golem's eyes turned orange, and he put his hand on top of the leader's—and so it went from one to the next— yellow, green, blue, indigo, and finally, violet.

As the last Golem's hand came to rest on those of his companions' a shaft of white light shot up out of the quartz. I threw my hands up to shield my eyes just as the Golem exploded into a cloud of dust. When it settled, a single figure stood before us with skin the color of coffee and eyes like jeweled facets.

"Daughter of Knasgowa," he said, "with the impulse of your heart, you have repaired the broken nature of my being. I am *the* Golem, made of the earth of this place and entrusted with the white light of creation to guard this entrance to the Middle Realm and the way to the chasm that lies beyond. From this day forward, you may pass through my land in perfect peace."

Don't get me wrong. I was more than happy with the answer, but I still had to ask.

"That's it?" I said. "All this fear about the curse of the Golem and all you needed was for someone to ask what you needed?"

The Golem threw back his head and laughed, a sound filled with such pure joy, I found myself wanting to laugh with him.

"Do not underestimate the power of authentic concern," he said. "The crystal was but the tool. Your heart was the catalyst. Of all who came before and failed, none did what you have done this day. You asked a question born of earnest concern for another living creature. You, Jinx Hamilton, saw beyond the urge to fight and embraced the first principle of love—to heal. Without that, the crystal you laid before my severed parts would have been nothing but a cold piece of stone."

As we gathered up our packs to continue our journey, Greer caught hold of my arm. The inner battle for control still raged in those haunting green eyes.

"Remember?" she said. "The Grail knight? This day you asked an innocent question from the impulse of your own unspoiled heart. You have won the right to the Siege Perilous."

THIRTY-FIVE

Many days would pass before I had the luxury of looking up that phrase. Merlin held one seat open at the Round Table—the Siege Perilous—to be occupied by the knight who found the Holy Grail.

For the record, no mystical cups were recovered on this adventure, but I did learn that most of the answers we seek can be found within our own hearts if only we have the courage to trust our inner voice.

In her unstable state, Greer didn't want to risk taking the flight of the baobhan sith, so we had a hike ahead of us. We walked out of the Moss Forest and onto a rocky path beside a gorge that would give a mountain goat vertigo. That's when I should have listened to my instinct instead of dropping my guard.

You'd think after all the suspense movies Tori and I have watched, I would know that you never say things like "that was easy" or ask "is it over?" You don't even *think* that kind of stuff. Why? Because the instant you do, everything goes wrong in a big way. Still, I admit, when the clean mountain air hit my face, I let myself breathe a sigh of relief.

Leaving the forest or not, we weren't out of the woods.

The range we entered presented us with vistas of towering snow-covered peaks. The Golem told us that if we followed the path, it would lead us over a suspension bridge and down the far side of the massive gorge to the first of the seven cities of Cibola.

I have no idea if that suspension bridge was the scary kind you see in the movies. You know the one. The hero gets out there in the middle. The rope frays. The boards start breaking. The bad guy is on the other end hacking at the supports with a sword. It's a classic.

Why don't I know? Because our disaster hit before we ever made it to the bridge.

Magic didn't have anything to do with what happened. It was just an accident. A stupid accident. Tori thinks she stepped on a round rock. One minute she was walking beside me talking about the craggy landscape and how it looked like something out of a movie, and then she was over the edge.

We didn't find out until later that the pocket mirror she was carrying had been activated the moment we entered the Middle Realm or that the people back in the Lair heard bits and snatches of everything that happened.

They were still listening when Tori went over the ledge. They watched the mirror spiral out of her pocket and fall with her toward the rock ledge where she landed. And just before the glass shattered, they saw the blood that gushed across its surface.

I had a different perspective on the fall, one that may have been even more terrifying because the instant Tori plunged downward, Chase went after her. He moved so fast, I had no time to call out, only to lunge for the cliff myself. I might have been the third one to go over if Lucas and Greer hadn't caught me and held me back.

Instead, I went to my knees, the weight of the world crashing around me. I couldn't imagine losing Tori or Chase, but both of them at once? That I could not survive.

Not trusting me to stay where I was, Greer kept hold

of me while Lucas cautiously crept to the edge. When he looked over and exclaimed, "Bloody hell!" I didn't know if it was good or bad. Then he said, "Greer, get that rope from my pack."

"They're alive?" I choked.

"McGregor is," Lucas said, "I can't tell about Tori. She's on a ledge about 50 feet down."

When I joined him, he put out a restraining arm. "Don't get too close, we don't need you down there with them."

Peering cautiously over the lip of the gorge, I saw Chase clinging to a gnarled, weather-worn tree that appeared to be growing out of the rock itself.

"Chase!" Lucas yelled. "We're throwing down a rope. Grab it! We'll pull you up."

Over the wind in the chasm, a resounding "No!" traveled up to us.

"What the hell are you talking about, man?" Lucas shouted. "Grab the damned rope."

"I will," Chase yelled back, "but I'm going down to Tori. She's alive."

Equal parts relief and terror washed over me. "Do you have enough rope to reach her?" I asked.

Lucas nodded. "Yes, but just barely," he said, throwing the coil over the edge.

The rope unwound as it went. Chase leaned precariously away from the tree and caught the end. Quickly tying a makeshift harness, he called up. "I'm starting down. Brace me."

"Wait!" Lucas answered. "We have to find something to belay the rope."

In the end, they had to settle for a boulder. Lucas and Greer prepared to play out the slack against the surface of the rock while I shouted directions from the edge. In those moments, I learned the meaning of the word "eternity."

When Chase landed on the pitifully narrow ledge where Tori lay crumpled, the only prayer I could summon was "please," over and over again in my mind like a mantra. I saw him unbuckle his belt and use it on the blood-soaked leg of her jeans as a tourniquet, and then we tried to raise them.

The weight was too much, even for all three of us.

I guess that was my "listen to the Force" moment. It was certainly a crossroads at learning about my power and *knowing* what I could do with it.

Focusing all of my attention on Chase and Tori, I cleared my mind and summoned my magic. When it answered, I saw Chase look up as if he'd heard me call his name.

"Try again," I said quietly.

This time when Lucas and Greer strained against the rope, my telekinesis strained with them. Everything else faded from my consciousness. I became one with the tension in that thin tether to the people I loved. My strength reached out for the sinews in Chase's arms and legs—for the bond I shared with Tori—and told her to hang on. And so, one agonized step at a time, we raised them out of that canyon and back onto the path.

In a blur, I registered Lucas gently taking Tori from Chase and then I threw my arms around Chase's neck and held on for dear life. "Thank you," I whispered against his ear. "Thank you for going after her."

Chase's arms tightened on my body, but I didn't push him away. If I could have in that moment, I would have disappeared into his strength and let him do every hard thing that lay before us. Tori's weak voice calling my name snapped me back to reality.

Releasing Chase, I fell to my knees beside my friend. "I'm here," I said. "You're safe now."

Blood welled up through the cloth Lucas was pressing

against the wound in her thigh. His eyes caught mine and I did not like what I saw there.

Some unknown portion of my brain kicked in and I heard myself say, "Loosen the tourniquet."

Chase reached past me and released some of the tension on the belt. Blood flowed steadily from the wound, which stretched the length of her upper leg, but it didn't spurt. The femoral artery wasn't severed. We had a chance.

I'd like to tell you I remembered that from health class or that I trained as an EMT, but honest to God, the knowledge came from M*A*S*H re-runs. I'd have given anything to have Hawkeye and Hot Lips there with us.

Tori, still clinging to consciousness, had been watching my face. "Am I on the way out, Jinksy?" she asked in a voice so low I had to bend down to her what she was saying. "Because if I am, you gotta promise me some stuff."

"You are *not* on your way out," I said firmly, "and we're not going to start talking like you are. Just lie still."

"My arm's broken," she said, sounding oddly detached. "It hurts worse than the leg."

"I'll rig some kind of sling," Lucas said, rummaging in his pack. "We need to immobilize the arm before we try to move her."

"Move her?" Chase said. "How the hell are we supposed to get her down off this mountain?"

This was not the conversation they needed to be having in front of Tori when she was already scared she was going to die.

"Shut. Up." I said. "Just get her ready to travel and quit arguing like a pair of idiots."

I knew exactly how we were all getting off the mountain.

"I'll be right back," I told Tori. "You let Chase and Lucas take care of you."

Even though my own clothes were now drenched in

my best friend's blood, I crossed the narrow ledge toward Greer who had positioned herself as far away from the scene as possible.

As I drew nearer, she turned and hissed at me with her fangs bared. "Get back, Jinx," she warned. "I can no longer control the hunger."

"The hell you can't," I snapped, without breaking stride, stopping just inches from a creature who wanted to rip out my throat.

Greer's breath rose and fell in heavy gasps. All traces of green were gone from her black and bottomless eyes. She inhaled sharply, drawing in the scent of the red gore staining my shirt and licking her lips in thirsty anticipation.

A smart person would have stepped back, but I didn't have time to be smart.

"I trust you," I said, never looking away from those searing eyes. "Do you hear me, Greer? I trust you. You're our friend. You won't hurt us. We need the flight of the baobhan sith. You have to get us to the Inn where we're meeting Brenna and Aquila. If you don't, Tori will die."

Then, jumping off a cliff of my own, I said, "Get Tori to people who can help her, and you can feed on me."

Something liquid and alive flowed through Greer then and like veins in marble, cracks of green shot through the ebony death in her eyes.

"*That*," she said with effort, "will not happen."

My gamble paid off. It was tenuous, but she was back in control.

"Then let's get this done," I said.

She gave me a jerky nod and walked back with me to where Lucas and Chase knelt beside Tori. When we approached, both men stood up warily.

"Red?" Lucas said. "You good?"

"Pick her up," Greer told him. "Be gentle, but secure her body. This may be a rough passage."

Rough didn't begin to cover it. We flew through a maelstrom, clinging to one another and shielding my injured friend as best we could. The landing came without warning. I hit hard on solid ground, catching myself with my hands and knees. Miraculously, Lucas stayed on his feet, and he didn't drop Tori.

"Get her inside. Now!" a woman's voice commanded. "Make way!"

Raising my still reeling head, I saw Brenna Sinclair pushing back the crowd milling around the entrance to a two-story wooden building with a gabled roof and bright red shutters. The sign hanging over the door read, "Travelers Welcome. Brigands Beware."

I tried to stagger upright to follow, but I fell drunkenly backward into Chase who cushioned my fall. At the doorway, as Lucas swept past Brenna with Tori in his arms, the red-haired sorceress' eyes locked with mine. Then she turned on her heel and disappeared inside.

THIRTY-SIX

"Why doesn't Tori take the mirror out of her pocket?!" Gemma groused. "I wanted to *see* these Golem creatures, and now they're in some Middle Realm version of the Alps. We're missing all the good stuff."

Kelly patted her hand consolingly. "Be glad we can at least hear the girls," she said. "It's more than we expected. Tori doesn't even know the mirror is transmitting."

"This is like the old timers sitting around the radio," Jeff said, leaning toward the mirror. "Right down to the static."

Myrtle chanted the soft phrases of an amplification spell, but bursts of interference still marred the signal. "The device is simply not powerful enough," she said. "Kelly is right. We are fortunate to hear this much."

"The *fortunate* thing is that we know they're safe," Kelly said. "I feel like I can breathe for the first time in . . . "

The words died in her throat as a blinding burst of light shot across the surface of the mirror. Everyone turned toward the glass, now filled with roiling, tumbling images of blue sky and jagged rocks.

Gemma came up off the sofa, her hand reaching helplessly toward the mirror as the glass on the other side shattered. Just before the signal went dark, blood sprayed over the screen.

Wheeling on Myrtle, Gemma cried, "Get it back! Get the picture back!"

"I cannot," Myrtle said, rising and taking the distraught woman's hands. "When the pocket mirror shattered, its magic shattered as well. You know that, Gemma."

Grabbing the Myrtle roughly by the shoulders, Gemma said, "Don't tell me what I know. You're the aos si. Get the picture back. Now!"

From beside her, gentle hands covered her own. "Gem, turn loose," Kelly said. "Myrtle would get the signal back if she could. You know that. Let her go."

Gemma turned wild eyes on her friend. "I lost Scrap," she said. "I'm not losing my only daughter. I'm not, Kelly. I'm not."

"I know," Kelly said soothingly. "I know. Come sit down. Jeff, pour her a drink."

Allowing herself to be led back to the sofa, Gemma sat down woodenly. "What . . . what are we supposed to do now?" she asked.

"Honey," Kelly said, "there's nothing we can do. We wait."

Chase caught me when I fell and held me down when I attempted to stand again.

"Damn it, Chase," I wheezed. "Turn me loose. I have to get in there."

A fine-boned, slender hand wearing a ruby ring appeared in my field of vision. Greer.

Squinting against the bright sunlight, I looked up at the baobhan sith. Her eyes had returned to normal, and she seemed as unflappable as ever. I took her hand and allowed myself to be pulled to my feet.

"Go," she said, "We will be behind you."

I gave myself just a second to look down. Chase's eyes

were normal again. As soon as that information registered, I bolted for the doorway, bursting into a bar, not unlike O'Hanson's. A bartender, rag in hand, didn't wait for me to ask. "Upstairs," he said. "End of the hall."

Taking the stairs two at a time, I ran the length of a long hall, skidding to a stop when I saw Tori lying on a bed with Brenna Sinclair on one side and Aquila on the other. Lucas was nowhere to be seen. Without thinking, I raised my hands and ignited twin balls of blue energy.

In response, Brenna held her palms outward in placation. "Please," she said, "we wish only to help. Your friend has lost a great deal of blood. The wound must be closed."

"If you hurt her," I said evenly, "I'll kill you."

"Understood," the sorceress replied. "Please, you may observe everything we do, but let me work."

Extinguishing the energy, I crossed the room to the bedside. Tori's eyes were open.

"Look at you," she whispered. "Going all Assassin's Creed on their butts."

Catching hold of her hand, I said, "I have no idea what that means, but I'm not going to let anyone hurt you."

My voice broke on the words and true to form, Tori comforted *me*.

"It's okay, Jinksy," she said. "Let Grams here do her thing."

I looked at Brenna and nodded. "Go ahead."

On the other side of the bed, Aquila used a single razorsharp talon to slice open Tori's jeans. I thought I'd throw up when I saw the damaged flesh below the soaked denim.

"That bad, huh?" Tori asked weakly.

"Don't be ridiculous," I said. "You won't even have a scar to brag about."

"Liar," she shot back.

As we watched, Brenna brought her hands within a few inches of the gaping wound and closed her eyes. Her lips moved silently, and yellow gold light radiated from her fingertips. Moving slowly, a few centimeters at a time, the tissues below her hands began to rebuild themselves.

"What is she doing?" Tori asked. "That tickles."

Then she passed out.

And then I panicked.

"Lift her head," Aquila ordered, holding out an open bottle filled with clear liquid.

That part didn't bother me. The smoke rising off the liquid did.

"What is that?" I asked suspiciously.

Annoyance flickered across his black eyes. "Either you trust us, or you do not," he snapped. "She has lost too much blood. If she does not get this potion now, the effects may be irreversible."

I did as I was told.

Hours later, I was still holding Tori's hand. I'd only let go long enough to get out of my blood-stained clothes and into a clean shirt and jeans at Greer's insistence.

"This is not a land where one should wander about smelling of blood," she said. "You will have to take my word on this point."

After that, Chase came in and rested his hands on my shoulders. "You should eat," he said quietly.

"I'm not leaving her," I replied in a tone that told him not to even think about arguing with me.

When his strong fingers began to knead at my muscles, I allowed myself the luxury of leaning back against him. "Thank you for what you did today," I said quietly.

"It wasn't just me," he said. "Without Grayson, Tori and I both would have died."

Tilting my head back to look up at him, I said, "That's awfully gracious of you."

As he smiled down at me, Chase brushed a stray lock of hair away from my face. "I can be a good boy when I want to be," he said.

The words sent a thrill through me I couldn't deny, but this was neither the time nor the place to sort out my feeling. "Be good now," I replied, with just a suggestion of entreaty in the words. "Please."

Chase has always heard the things I say and the ones I leave unspoken. "I'm going to go fix a plate for you," he said smoothly, "and you're going to eat it. Deal?"

When I nodded, he took his hands off my shoulders. I instantly missed the reassuring weight of his touch and the warmth of this proximity. Even though I wouldn't have admitted it to anyone, I was still shaking inside.

He returned after a few minutes with a tray, but then left me alone with my food and my thoughts. I'd just finished eating when a voice from the doorway asked, "May I join you?"

Brenna Sinclair stood behind me, a tentative expression on her face.

"Come in," I said, "but be quiet. She's still sleeping."

The sorceress pulled a chair next to mine and sat down. "The after effects of the magic I used to close her wound and the potion Aquila administered will not wear off for several hours," she explained, "but I assure you that your friend will make a full recovery."

"I don't know what to say," I said, my eyes going back to Tori's pale face. "I thought I'd lost her and . . . well, you're the last person I ever expected to be thanking for anything."

To my surprise, Breena chuckled. It was a warm, throaty sound that I confess I instantly found appealing.

"I envy the two of you the closeness of your friendship," she said. "That is not an experience with which I have great familiarity."

What could I say in response to that? *"If you hadn't gone around playing political games and trying to kill people for several centuries, maybe you would have lived a different life?"*

Even though I didn't speak the words, Brenna seemed to know what I was thinking. "I know that my singular existence is of my own doing," she said. "I do not expect commiseration."

The fire crackled in the grate and outside the rising wind whistled against the pane.

"Why did you do it?" I asked suddenly. "Why did you choose to become Creavit?"

A cloud of pained retrospection fell over her features. "That," Brenna said, "is a question I have asked myself many times since I awakened here in the Middle Realm and realized the Fates had chosen to allow me a second chance."

"Barnaby told me that your fathers and brothers were cruel to you," I said. "Was that why you did it?"

"In part," she said. "In those times women, even Fae women, were regarded as little more than property by the men in their lives. When my magic failed to develop, my father saw no reason to treat me well. I could not be used to broker a favorable marriage that would cement any of the alliances he cultivated to better himself in the world."

I shook my head. "I'm sorry to say I really don't know much about Fae history or culture," I admitted. "This is all still pretty new to me."

Brenna smiled—a real smile that lit up her eyes. "Most people can be forgiven these days for not being familiar with things that happened in the 12th century," she said. "I won't hold it against you."

As shocking as this may sound, I realized I was starting to warm up to her.

"If you would like to rest a little," Brenna said, "I will sit up with her. The innkeeper can bring a cot into this room."

I hadn't even been thinking about sleep, but as soon as the thought of lying down entered my head, a wave of fatigue crashed over me. Trying to shake it off, I said stubbornly, "Not until she wakes up."

From the bed, Tori croaked, "*She* is awake, and you look like roadkill."

Even with dark circles under her eyes and no color in her face, I could see she was back. The tears I'd been holding back for hours spilled out, running in rivers down my cheek.

"Yep," she said, "I knew it. Here come the waterworks. Get this woman a bed."

Smiling, Brenna went to the door and called to someone waiting in the hall. In seconds a pair of servants carried in a narrow camp cot and a pile of quilts.

"You're sure you're okay?" I asked Tori, stifling a massive yawn.

That actually won me a smirk. Wavering, but a smirk all the same.

"Yeah," she said, "considering I fell off a cliff, busted my arm, and went to the eagle free clinic. I'm good. Get some sleep, Jinksy. I'll be here when you wake up."

"As will I," Brenna said. "If Victoria will allow it."

Tori's eyes tracked to her reincarnated ancestor and then back to me. "Grams has got this," she said finally. "Sleep. That's an order."

The last thing I remember before exhaustion claimed me was the look on Brenna Sinclair's face as she and Tori talked quietly. Joy.

THIRTY-SEVEN

When I woke up, Brenna and Tori had shifted to chairs by the fire, a breakfast table between them. Before they noticed me, I just lay still and watched, taking in the nuances of their conversation as well as the details of the room.

If the events of the day before hadn't been so fresh in my mind, I might have thought we were still in Shevington. The furnishings had the same elvish curves I'd glimpsed in Myrtle's quarters mixed with the vaguely Elizabethan architecture so common in the Valley.

Someone had already been in to change the linens. The enormous four-poster bed was freshly made, and any evidence of Tori's treatment was gone. A vase of fresh flowers set in the center of the mantle, an odd cross between the compact beauty of a tulip and the effulgence of a blooming rose.

Truthfully, the women seated at the table seemed more out of place than anything else around me. Brenna like Greer preferred to dress in black from head to foot, but with her mane of deep auburn hair tied back, she looked surprisingly youthful in the early morning sun streaming through the latticed windows.

Outside, I could hear the sound of a community waking up—neighbors calling out greetings to neighbors, the clopping of hooves on cobblestones. I almost had myself convinced the In Between's reputation had been oversold when a shadow crossed the window and I saw what looked very much like a Spanish galleon floating placidly by—over the rooftops of the adjacent buildings.

Still not in Kansas.

My eyes drifted back to Tori, who was listening to Brenna tell a story involving monks and wizards in 15th century France. As the sorceress talked, her graceful, manicured hands emphasized the major plot points with elegant gestures. She had Tori caught in rapt fascination, and my bestie looked almost normal, especially when she let out with a, "No. Way! Really?"

Brenna, who must have felt the pressure of my eyes all the while she was talking, turned to me and said, "Good morning, Jinx. Come, join us. There's plenty of food and Tori tells me you're not 'worth shooting' until you've had your first cup of coffee."

Sometime while I'd been sleeping, the two of them had not only made friends but "Victoria" had become "Tori" in Brenna's vernacular.

Tori has a superpower. She can spot a phony a mile out before one lying word can fall from their lips. The night before, when she'd called Brenna "Grams," I had an inkling that even in her weakened condition, Tori's radar wasn't detecting any warning signs, but the current relaxed atmosphere between them confirmed for me that we were in safe waters.

"Not worth shooting, huh?" I said, sitting up and stretching. "Don't let her fool you. She's not exactly precious and darling first thing in the morning either."

My feet came to rest beside a pair of soft, furry slippers. Without the warming layer of quilts, my body registered the cool air in the room and shivered.

"There's a robe there at the foot of your bed," Brenna

said. "Days in Cibolita always dawn cold, but that will change by noon."

Pulling on the robe, I went over to join them in front of the fire. Now that I was close enough to give Tori the once over, I could see lingering fatigue in her face, but the black smudges under her eyes had faded to pale shadows, and her cheeks had color.

"You," I said, taking her hand, "may be the most gorgeous thing I've ever seen."

"Aw, thanks Jinksy," she grinned, squeezing my fingers. "That's sweet. You still look like three-day old road-kill."

Yep. Tori was back all right.

Brenna laughed at our good-natured banter as she reached for the large silver coffee pot. "Perhaps we can take steps to improve that assessment, Jinx," she said. "May I?"

The fragrant coffee fumes hit my nose, and I tried not to start panting like a junkie in need of a major fix. "Please," I said, "and thank you.

The red-haired woman handed me my cup and lifted the domed lid of a serving dish. I recognized the potatoes and what I thought were sausages, but the bluish tinge of the meat put me off a little. The remaining item had the consistency of scrambled eggs, but again, I wasn't sure because well, in proper Dr. Seus fashion, they were vaguely green.

Sensing my reluctance, Brenna said, "Roast potatoes, Archaeopteryx eggs, and sea cucumber sausage. I assure you the flavors are similar to those with which you are familiar."

My grumbling stomach convinced me to push my reservations aside and just eat. As I filled my plate, I said, "Your patient seems to be doing much better. Is it all mouth or is her recovery real?"

"She will have to answer that for herself," Brenna said. "But she seems to be improving by the hour. I suggest you take as much food as you want now before she indulges in her fourth helping."

A three-plate breakfast was a good sign, strange food or not. I could have dealt with plague, famine, pestilence, and hell minions, but if Tori had refused to eat, the world would indeed be on the brink of ending.

Still, mother hen that I am, I asked as I loaded up my plate, "Okay, how are you, really?"

Reaching over with her fork to snag another sausage, Tori said, "Sore and my arm is stiff, but Brenna says that should go away after about a week."

I'd been so concerned by the gash in her thigh, I'd completely forgotten about the broken arm, also mended by Brenna's magic.

"And the leg?" I said.

Biting into the sausage, Tori said, "Well, you were wrong about the scar. I can't *wait* for Shark Week on the Discovery channel this year."

Stopping with my fork in mid-air, I said, with complete confusion, "What does Shark Week have to do with anything?" I asked.

Tori seemed astonished by how dense I was being in the moment. "Jinksy!" she said. "This baby is getting sold as a Great White shark bite. Total *Jaws* plot line and I have the scar tissue to prove it. My Instagram feed is gonna explode."

Brenna looked to me for an explanation. Tori's statement sagged under so many pop culture references I didn't even know where to start.

"*Jaws*," I began, "It's a movie about . . . never mind. She's definitely better."

"That much I did manage to piece together," Brenna said, smiling across the table.

If I'd had a choice in the matter, we'd have spent the rest of the morning right there drinking coffee, finishing the food—maybe even ordering more, but that wasn't in the books.

"Can she travel?" I asked.

A flicker of sympathetic understanding showed in Brenna's eyes before she said briskly, "That should not be a problem, provided Greer and I have a successful morning. The baobhan sith checked on us late last evening. We devised a plan to merge my magic with her own to amplify the power of her flight. I am to meet her shortly. If all goes well, together we can transfer the entire party to Gwydion's camp."

She excused herself. I waited until the sound of her footsteps faded in the hallway, and then I turned to Tori. "Two things," I said.

"Just two?" she grinned.

Grabbing her hand again and holding on tight, I said, "Don't you ever, ever, *ever* scare me like that again."

"No problem," she said, letting me glimpse a hint of the fear I already knew she'd felt. "Wasn't much fun for me either. What's number two?"

"Did we really just have our morning coffee with Brenna Sinclair?"

Tori snorted. "I know, right?" Releasing my hand, she reached for another piece of toast, bit into it, and then announced, "Brace yourself. I like her."

"You feel it, too, don't you?" I asked.

Still munching on the bread, Tori nodded. "I do," she said, "but I don't know what *it* is exactly."

"The evil," I said. "It's gone."

The problem with knowing something like that is explaining it to someone else. About an hour later, I found Lucas sitting at the bar downstairs plowing through his own breakfast plate and knocking back coffee.

"Where have you been?" I asked, sitting down on the stool next to him.

"Hey," he said. "Word has it Tori is on the mend."

"I'd say she's mended, past tense," I replied, nodding at the bartender who had just set a cup of coffee in front of me.

Something about the man seemed odd, but I wasn't sure what. Then he came out from behind the bar to start wiping down the tables, and I saw that from the waist down he had the body of a goat.

While I tried not to stare at the man's nimble, tiny hooves clacking on the floorboards, Lucas said softly, "He's a Satyr. You're going to see a lot of halflings around here. I went out this morning to get the lay of the land, and a Hatuibwari almost ran me over."

"I'm sorry," I said. "A what?"

"They're native to the Solomon Islands," Lucas said. "Honestly, I thought they were extinct. Head of a man, body of a serpent—but with arms and claws. Oh, and bat wings."

Right. Don't want to forget the bat wings.

Changing topics like we'd just been discussing the most normal thing in the world, Lucas said, "I saw Brenna come downstairs a little while ago. What's your take on her?"

That's when I tried to explain—four times—that the sorceress was no longer evil only to finally throw my hands up in frustration when Lucas said, yet again, "How do you know it's not an act?"

"Because I just do," I said through gritted teeth. "You're just going to have to trust me on this one, okay? Do you really think Greer would be off flying with the woman right now if she thought Brenna wasn't on the up and up?"

Shoving his fedora back on his head, Lucas said, "You haven't met all of Greer's friends. She knows some pretty shady characters."

"Which, according to your logic, means I shouldn't trust you either," I countered.

"Yeah," he grinned, "but you have a soft spot for bad boy water elves. Admit it."

On reflex, I started to flirt right back, but then the visceral memory of Chase's hands on my shoulders hit me, and I clamped my mouth shut. Even a guy as prone to ignoring subtleties as Lucas Grayson couldn't miss the change in direction.

"Hey," Lucas said, softening his tone, "did I say something wrong?"

Men. Just when you need them to stay clueless, they get all aware.

"What? Uh, no," I stammered. "It was just a long night, and we have a lot to do. Meet me halfway on this one, okay? We can trust Brenna."

His brows drew together in a frown, but he apparently decided to press me for an explanation wasn't a good idea. Scratch what I said about awareness. Sometimes it can come in handy.

"Okay. I'll trust her if you say so, but I'll still be watching."

That made two of us.

"Watch away," I said, "but don't let it get in the way of what we came here to do."

As I started back upstairs, I spotted Aquila in the building's rear courtyard. He was sitting on a bench, reading a book held delicately balanced in his talons. Remembering our exchange the day before, I realized I owed him an apology.

I let myself out through a pair of double doors and paused to look up at the flawless blue dome overhead. The gryphon heard me come out and looked my way. "Good morning," he called out, snapping his book closed. "How is your friend this morning?"

As I crossed the flagstones to join him, I said, "Much better. Aquila, I owe you an apology for yesterday. I was scared. "

He shifted on the bench to make room for me. I sat down and studied the regal arch of his beak and the soft shimmer of light that moved through the pristine white feathers covering his head. Something in Aquila's bearing reminded me of Beau, which I found comforting. What I told Lucas at the bar was the truth. It had been a long night, the latest in several long nights.

The gryphon sat patiently under my scrutiny until I realized what I was doing, and blushed. "I am so sorry," I said. "I'm being incredibly rude."

"Do not apologize," he replied. "Either for your fear for your beloved friend or your curiosity about me."

His voice was so kind and understanding, my next words spilled out in a tumble of emotion. "I wasn't just scared," I said. "I've never been more terrified in my life."

"In the heat of battle," Aquila said, "the most dangerous companion is the man who claims to have no apprehension. Fear tempers all true courage."

"If that's true," I said, "I must be a whole lot braver than I think I am."

I meant the words to be a joke, but instead, the gryphon nodded sagely and said, "That you are, Mistress Hamilton, that you are indeed. In this place, that quality will serve you well. The Middle Realm constantly challenges one's equilibrium."

By the end of that day, those cryptic words would become crystal clear.

We left for Gwydion's camp a little after noon without seeing any more of Cibolita than the Inn. As the swirling winds of the flight of the baobhan sith began to obscure my vision, I had a brief impression of other cities spread out across an immense, flat plain. Then Greer and Brenna took us to a land so different from where we'd awakened, my mind struggled to comprehend how the two could exist within the same realm.

The In Between doesn't deal in constants or points of reference. You may walk out of a desert and straight into a lashing typhoon. Endless, cloudless skies overhead can give way to impenetrable cavern walls or murky ocean depths. None of the rules or conventions of what we regard as reality apply. If you leave one land on a Tuesday, it may be Thursday at your next destination, and the previous Sunday when you find your way home again.

Where Greer and Brenna set us down, there was no sky overhead, only a vaulted roof studded with mazes of dangling roots. Then I realized that what I had taken to be the stark skeletons of trees surrounding us were more roots reaching *up*. For the first time since we'd entered the In Between, I truly had the sense of being in the middle.

In the distance, a high palisade surrounding the unadorned trunk of the Mother Oak. The living column of wood stretched from floor to ceiling, joining the two halves of the Great Tree to her existence in both the Otherworld and the Human Realm.

In the few seconds I needed to register all those impressions, something else assaulted my senses—the cold rising from the ground beneath my feet. It resurrected in my mind a lost fragment of a poem long ago memorized and forgotten—"the wind came out of the cloud by night, chilling and killing."

The Mother Tree was running out of time.

THIRTY-EIGHT

From his perch on Beau's shoulder, Rodney stared fixedly at the door to Gemma's temporary bedroom in the lair. His whiskers twitched nervously as he let out with a worried string of rodent chatter.

Festus, who was sitting on the hearth, said, "Calm down, Rodney. Kelly will take good care of Gemma."

The rat turned and looked at Festus with wide, worried eyes.

"Yeah, yeah," the old cat answered. "I know. I don't like what I saw in the mirror either."

Jeff, who also had his eyes glued to the door, asked absently, "Do you actually understand what he's saying?"

"Sure," Festus said. "Rodney's a big picture kind of rat. I like that about him. He sticks with the major themes of a situation."

Beau rested his hand on Duke's head and idly rubbed the ghost hound's ears. "That is life's gift to creatures like Rodney and our dogs," he said. "Creation has blessed them with forthright simplicity. But as for the concern, Rodney currently expresses, I concur. The women have been in there quite a long time."

"Kelly knows how to talk to Gemma," Jeff said. "They've been through a lot together. It'll just take as long as it takes."

Fidgeting in his chair, the colonel said, "That may well be true, but am I the only one of our company feeling horribly superfluous at the moment?"

"No," Festus and Jeff said simultaneously as Rodney shook his head vigorously.

A dissenting, disembodied voice spoke from the vicinity of the desk. "I do not feel superfluous."

"Shorty," Jeff said, "why on earth are you in stealth mode? Get visible with the rest of us."

Darby winked into sight. "I am sorry, Master Jeff," he said earnestly. "Sometimes I forget."

"Why do you not feel at a loss for something helpful to do, Darby?" Beau asked. "Are you engaged in some fruitful project of which we are unaware?"

The little brownie shook his head. "No," he said, "I am sending all my energy to Mistress Tori and our friends in the Middle Realm, so they will come back safely. That counts as doing something, does it not?"

None of them seemed to have an answer for his simple expression of belief. Finally, Jeff said, in a ragged voice, "It sure as hell does, Shorty. Keep at it."

Gemma paced the length of the small space trying to get away from the growing terror that haunted her every thought. Had she just witnessed her daughter's death in the inaccessible reaches of the Middle Realm?

"Honey," Kelly said for the tenth time, "please sit down. You're only making yourself more upset."

Instead of doing as she asked, Gemma wheeled on Myrtle again. "There has to be *something* you can do!" she demanded. "Why don't we just go after them?"

"That," Myrtle said, firmly but gently, "would be a terrible mistake. The Golem directed his largesse specifically at Jinx. If we were to disturb that newfound peace, we could hamper her ability to lead the others out of the Middle Realm through the Moss Forest."

Not backing down, Gemma said, "There are other entrances. You said so. Why can't we use one of those?"

"Because we would have no way of knowing how to find our people," Myrtle said patiently. "There are no maps of the In Between by which we might navigate. You must have faith, Gemma. We know only that Tori fell. Surely you must know that Jinx would move the stars themselves to save her."

That touched off another restless round of pacing. When Gemma passed by her the third time, Kelly pulled her down onto the edge of the bed.

"Stop!" she ordered. "Myrtle is right. Those girls would do anything for each other, just like we would. Gem, honey, I'd make this better for you if I could, but we have to do what Jinx said and stay here. They'll get in touch with us when they can."

"Don't you dare tell me one more time that I just have to wait!" Gemma said hotly. "Don't you dare."

If the outburst was meant to be intimidating, it didn't work.

"I love Tori, too," Kelly said quietly, "like she was my own. You're not the only one waiting and praying, Gem."

She started to protest, but then all the fight bled out of her as she slumped forward holding her head in her hands. "I know you do," she said brokenly. "I just can't stand feeling this helpless when my girl is in danger."

"I know," Kelly said, rubbing Gemma's back consolingly, "I hate it, too."

"As do I," Myrtle said. "Let me place another call to Barnaby and Moira, perhaps they can tell us something."

Glory, who had been sitting on the end table watching, hopped on her broom and flew up beside Gemma. "She's going to be okay," the mini witch said. "I just know it."

Gemma looked up, tears staining her face. "How do you know?" she asked.

"Because Jinx and Tori are everything I ever wanted to be and couldn't," Glory said. "They're who I want to be if I ever get big again. They're smart, and they care about people and each other—and about doing good. People like that can't go away because we need them too much to be here fighting bad guys like Mr. Chesterfield. I know it may sound simple and foolish, but I have way more faith in my friends than I do in some silly Middle Between place."

In spite of herself, Gemma smiled. "You have to pick," she said. "It's either the 'In Between' or the 'Middle Realm,' not both."

"I know," Glory grinned, "but I got you to quit crying, didn't I?"

Gemma laughed, wiping her tear-stained cheeks. "You did," she admitted. "And I appreciate it." Then, sitting up straighter, she said, "Let me fix my face so we can go back out there. I imagine the men are worried half to death by now."

When the women came back into the Lair, Jeff stood up and pulled Gemma into a hug. "How you holding up?" he asked.

"Better," she said. "The girls gave me a good talking to. How about you boys?"

Releasing her, he said, "Worried, same as you."

"Then we'll all be worried together," Gemma said, claiming one of the chairs by the fire. "It's an occupation best shared with friends."

"Correction," Festus said, "best shared with friends and Scotch. For the love of Bastet, would somebody with opposable thumbs please pour?"

Beau stood up and opened the liquor cabinet.

"Delighted to be of service," he said, "but I myself prefer Kentucky bourbon."

"Ditto," Jeff said. "Three fingers for me."

As the colonel served as bartender, Myrtle went to the standing mirror and placed a call to Shevington. Barnaby answered almost before she'd finished the spell.

"Is there any further word?" he asked, foregoing a greeting.

"We had hoped you might have news for us," Myrtle said. "Has the Mother Tree yet begun to feel the heat of the Jar of Prometheus?"

Barnaby shook his head. "Not as of yet. How are the conditions there?"

In response, Jeff reached for the remote and lowered the big screen TV. Together they all watched the latest news report, which termed the crisis "stable but highly dangerous."

"Temperatures are no longer falling," the meteorologist said, "but neither are they warming appreciably . . . ."

A burst of static fractured the picture, replacing the weather map with the smiling visage of Irenaeus Chesterfield, a development that sent Glory zooming into the shadowed stacks to hide.

"Oh, my," Chesterfield said. "It would seem Miss Green has not yet recovered from our encounters. Such a nervous creature. How are the rest of you enjoying this fine weather?"

Across the distance that separated them, the images of the two brothers confronted one another.

"Have you gone mad, Irenaeus?" Barnaby asked tightly. "First you toy with the structure of time, and now you threaten the integrity of the realms? Surely you must know we will stop you."

"Ah, my dear elder brother," Irenaeus said. "I see that you have inherited father's penchant for pedantic lectures.

In fact, I do not know that you will stop me. I frankly think such action far beyond your abilities in a situation where I possess all the trump cards."

Barnaby regarded his sibling coldly. "Don't be so sure of that, little brother."

Flinching slightly at the insulting diminutive, Chesterfield said, "Play your games as you like, dear brother. Send your minions scurrying into the Middle Realm in a vain attempt to warm the Mother Oak. It won't work. This storm is a harbinger of things to come. What has begun in the state of North Carolina will spread the world over at the stroke of midnight signaling the coming of the new year. The Mother Trees will die, one by one, and I will plunge first the realm of the humans and then the Otherworld into a new Ice Age."

"And gain what, Irenaeus?" Barnaby said.

"Initially, the pleasure of watching all you have built and those you have guarded freeze and shatter," he replied. "And then? The rise of a new order predicated on made magic and directed solely by me. It's not too late to join me, Barnaby. Do you think father would not relish the prospect of his sons united to rule the world?"

"Father would wish me to stop you," he replied coldly, "and stop you, I will."

"You'll have to kill me," Chesterfield said, "and your high-minded moral principles won't allow you to seek that expediency."

Barnaby stood up and walked closer to the mirror, allowing his features to fill the glass pane. "You are mistaken about that, brother."

A slow smile spread over the Creavit wizard's face. "I will look forward to the day when you attempt to make good on that threat."

"As will I."

With that, both signals went dead.

THIRTY-NINE

When the palisade gates swung open, a world of flames greeted us. Enormous braziers filled with glowing coals surrounded the Oak's trunk. Farther back from the tree, sweating men in belted tunics and high, soft boots tended a second ring of bonfires stoked with logs the size of 50-gallon drums. We had entered a Renaissance Faire set in hell.

A broad-shouldered man of medium height detached himself from the work crews and approached us with long, swinging strides that conveyed confidence and authority. When he greeted Aquila, I instantly liked his thick, Welsh accent and rich baritone voice.

"Aquila, my brother," he said. "You have arrived just in time."

The gryphon inclined his head in acknowledgment. "Gwydion, allow me to present Jinx Hamilton, the *Quercus de Pythonissam* and her band of followers."

Beside me Tori muttered, "If we're getting a band together, I call dibs on the bass."

"Would you just get with the program and role play already?" I said under my breath as I stepped forward to greet the principal defender of the Mother Trees.

I had a handshake in mind. To my considerable embarrassment, however, Gwydion drew his broadsword, planted it in the earth and fell to one knee. "M'lady," he said, "my blade and my men await your command."

Ignoring Tori's half-hidden snicker, I said, "Please, Gwydion, there's no need to kneel. We're on the same team."

As he obediently rose to his feet, I did hold out my hand—which Gwydion promptly kissed. No matter what I did, this guy was not going to loosen up with the chivalric manners.

"May I know the names of your companions?" he asked courteously.

As I made the introductions, Gwydion acknowledged Tori, Greer, and Brenna each with deep bows, saving decidedly manly handshakes for Lucas and Chase. He didn't seem to know anything about Brenna, but his bushy eyebrows did go up when he realized Greer was the baobhan sith.

"Forgive me, M'lady," he said. "Even with all I have seen in this world and the Other, I had thought you to be a myth."

Greer answered with a thoroughly dazzling, sexy smile that only put the man more off balance—exactly the effect she intended. "I do not mind being thought of as a woman out of legend, Lord Gwydion."

Even though both she and Chase had regained their normal level of control once we got out of the mountains adjacent to the Moss Forest, the Middle Realm seemed to naturally amplify the woman's already considerable charisma.

I've never been able to decide how much of Greer's ability to mesmerize men stems from her vampiric powers and how much of it is just *her*.

Blinking to clear his mind, Gwydion turned back to me. "Forgive me, *Quercus de Pythonissam*," he said, "but do you have the Jar of Prometheus? Our fires grow weaker in the face of the cold assaulting the Great Lady. I fear she will soon be damaged beyond recovery."

It took me a minute to realize that when he said "Lady" he was talking about the Tree. "Yes," I said, shrugging off my backpack and tugging at the zipper. "I have it. Let's get started."

When I brought out the Jar, Gwydion's curiosity won out over his manners. He stepped forward and stared into the glass panels of the cylinder in my hands. "The elemental fire," he breathed in a hushed whisper. "I had never thought to look on such a wonder in my life."

This, from a guy who has lived in a skyless, no man's land, guarding a sentient magical tree for centuries. Clearly, I hadn't been giving the Jar of Prometheus the respect it deserved. In my head, I still thought of the artifact as just what I'd called it first—a magical space heater—but to the warrior standing beside me, I was holding a mysterious aspect of Mother Earth herself.

With the dim blue glow of the jar's inner flames coloring his face and beard, Gwydion looked up at me. "How do we release its power?" he asked.

"There's a spell to open the inner chamber in increments," I said. "Myrtle—the aos si—told me we should start at the base of the trunk and let the Mother Tree herself direct us from there."

Gwydion turned and called to two of his soldiers. "Aidan, Harri, see that our guests' belongings are safely stowed in their quarters."

After that, we advanced as a group toward the Great Oak, passing through the ranks of soldiers who dropped their heads respectfully as we went by. Some of them cast sidelong looks at Aquila. I understood why.

Backlit by the flames and standing six feet tall at the shoulder, Aquila held his massive wings slightly away from the rippling muscles of his lion's body. The majestic effect conveyed exotic, formidable power.

At the base of the tree, I opened my mind to the Mother Oak. A violent shudder instantly wracked my body. Chase and Lucas both stepped forward, but I shook my head. "I'm all right, I said, trying to keep my teeth from chattering. "I can feel the cold in her body."

Brenna instantly took off her cloak and settled it around my shoulders. The wool, woven in the Sinclair tartan, rested lightly, but warmly on my body. As I knelt to place the Jar against the Tree, the fabric pooled around my feet and for just an instant, I did feel like a priestess performing an ancient rite.

Reaching into my pocket, I took out the scrap of paper bearing the releasing spell penned in Myrtle's precise, elegant script. The sight of the handwriting sent a pang through me. I would have felt far more confident about what I was doing if the aos si had been with me.

As if they sensed my doubt, Brenna and Greer both stepped forward and knelt beside me. When Greer turned and held her hand out to Tori, I knew what they were doing. Coven magic. The baobhan sith had used it with us once before, merging our powers with those of our mothers to look back in time and determine the role Irenaeus Chesterfield played in a fateful car accident.

"Remember?" Greer asked. The emerald fire had returned to her eyes but controlled and under her direction.

"Yes," I said, taking her hand and reaching for Brenna with the other. "I remember."

The sorceress held her hand out to Tori, who, like Greer, closed the circle by laying her free hand against the rough bark of the Oak's trunk. As I spoke the words of the spell, the inner core of the Jar slid open a fraction releasing a pale tendril of fire that wove a hot trail up my arm and around my shoulders like a molten snake.

When I tensed, Brenna said softly, "Do not fear the fire. Tell it where to go."

Myrtle hadn't suggested such a thing, but within the current of our merged powers, I knew it was possible. *"Find the cold,"* I said to the fire. *"Drive it back."*

Just like the serpent I imagined it to be, the elemental fire drew away and seemed to look at me, before winding back on itself and flowing into the Mother Tree. Somehow I knew it no longer needed my direction. Drawing away gently, I broke the connection, first with the flame, and then with the women kneeling beside me.

All I could hear was the hiss of the coals in the braziers and the crackling of the bonfires, but when the Oak sighed in contentment, a great cheer rose up from Gwydion's men. The Tree felt the warmth.

In that strange way the Middle Realm has of bending time to its will, night had begun to fall when the four of us stood away from the tree. Yes, I know I said there was no sky, which meant no sun overhead, but still, a settling darkness moved through the land.

One look at Tori's face and the way she favored her leg told me we needed to rest for the next several hours. Gwydion apologized for the military nature of the encampment before showing us to a perfectly comfortable pair of outbuildings where we'd be sleeping—the women on one side, and the men (including Aquila) on the other.

Loaves of fresh bread and hard cheese waited for us on the table, and then I remembered what Glory had said about sandwiches in our packs.

"Do you think they'll be any good after all this time?" Tori asked, digging through her possessions and coming up with what looked like a generic plastic food container. She cautiously popped open the lid, and the smell of warm roast beef filled the room.

She looked at me and shook her head. "I might have

known Darby had a trick up his sleeve. My sandwich is still hot, and so are the fries."

Unearthing my own container, I found the same meal waiting for me. Resisting the selfish urge to wolf down the food in front of the others, Tori and I sliced our sandwiches into quarters and pooled the fries so everyone could share. Between that and what Gwydion's people left out for us, we had more than enough.

To my astonishment, when Lucas said he wanted to inspect the camp and its defenses so he could include the details in his report to the DGI, Chase stood up and said, "I'd like to come with you if that's okay."

"Sure," Lucas said. "You coming, Red?"

Greer shook her head. "The two of you could use some male bonding time," she said. "Do you think you can take a turn around the camp without being at each other's throats?"

"I think we can manage," Chase said with a genuine smile. "Kinda hard to dislike a guy who hauls you up a cliff."

Under normal circumstances, I would have pointed out that my telekinesis played a large part in said "hauling," but if Chase McGregor was in the mood to bury the hatchet with Lucas Grayson? I wasn't going to say a blessed word to derail the peace process.

After they were gone, Greer produced a silver flask from her leather satchel and four small cups. "May I interest you ladies in a libation?" she asked.

"Let me guess," Tori said, "single malt?"

"Not this time," Greer said. "It's brandy."

"Then deal me in," she said. "I don't know about the rest of you, but I could use a drink."

The baobhan sith filled the cups, which we all passed around and raised in a silent but heartfelt toast.

The liquor burned going down my throat but in a good

way. Tori wasn't the only one suffering the effects of the last 48 hours. Unfortunately, there was no time to give into that.

"So," I said, "we've bought ourselves some time with the Jar of Prometheus. Next stop, the Castle of the Dark Druid."

Greer rolled her cup back in forth in her slender fingers. "Fer Dorich," she said, lingering over the words with an almost sultry purr, "now there's a bonnie bad boy if ever I met one."

"That he is," Brenna agreed in a way that told me she, too, had more than a casual familiarity with the man in question.

I wasn't sure what I dreaded most: asking just how well these two women knew the local villain or asking and getting *way* more detail than I wanted.

"I take it you both have . . . history with this guy?"

Just imagine two essentially immortal, green-eyed Scottish redheads letting out with twin bawdy laughs. I didn't even know what, specifically, they were laughing about and I blushed anyway.

"That's a delicate way to put it," Greer said. "Fer Dorich pre-dates my history as a reformed baobhan sith in the employ of the DGI. Our dalliance was sometime in the 10th century as I recall."

"Thirteenth for me," Brenna said. "There was all that nasty fighting in Spain, remember, Greer?"

"I do," she said. "The French took the Kingdom of Aragon in . . . "

"1213," Brenna said. "The whole continent was a mess, so I came home to Scotland for a bit and had a fling with Fer Dorich for the fun of it. I found his indestructible nature refreshing after the fragility of human men. "

The conversation was as casual as two old friends at a high school reunion trying to remember who took who to the prom—or two professional killers sharpening their switchblades. Six of one, half a dozen of the other.

"Any idea how we get him to release the Queen of Summer?" I asked.

Greer and Brenna exchanged a look that spoke volumes I was pretty sure I had no desire to read.

"If there's one thing we can guarantee you about the Dark Druid," Greer said, reaching for her flask again, "it's that he'll have a price in mind. The only question will be, are we willing—and able—to pay it?"

FORTY

The next morning, Brenna and Greer went out early—we assumed to reminisce about their long-running acquaintance or maybe to compare notes on Fer Dorich. I found Tori sitting at the table by the fire polishing off a plate of perfectly normal looking fried potatoes. To my considerable relief, the food was even the right color.

"Did you leave any for me?" I asked. "And is there coffee?"

"If you want to call it that," she said, pointing toward the fireplace where an ancient tin pot on an iron hook dangled near the flames.

"Greer made it before she left by basically throwing a handful of ground coffee in boiling water," Tori explained with a shudder. "Be prepared to strain it through your teeth."

Crunchy coffee. Not my idea of a great start on the day either.

"Heard anything from the guys?" I asked.

"They're over at the base of the Mother Tree with Gwydion," she said. "Our magical space heater is holding back the cold, but it's not stopping it. Whatever we did to the elemental fire, it's self-adjusting now. According to Chase, the central core opened at least another inch over night. Like you said, all we did was buy ourselves time."

Gingerly reaching into the fireplace with some wadded up rags that would have to do as a potholder, I managed to get myself a steaming cup of muddy-looking coffee. When I took a sip, I almost choked. "Seriously?" I said. "You can stand a fork up in this stuff."

"The potatoes are better," Tori said.

Thankfully, she was right.

It might have seemed like we were malingering, but we'd agreed not to leave until we were sure the Jar of Prometheus was stable. Honestly? I was glad to have the time. Sitting there with Tori drinking coffee and talking, it almost felt like the way we started any normal day back in Briar Hollow. We both needed that, I think because neither one of us brought up the urgency of the day's impending business.

We were dressed and packed by mid-morning when the others returned. Chase and Lucas confirmed that the Jar of Prometheus seemed to be symbiotically responding to the level of heat the Mother Tree needed. For now, that had to be enough. It was time to take the flight of the baobhan sith to Fer Dorich's castle.

Gwydion walked with us to the palisade gate. "If we're successful," I told him, "the cold should stop, and you won't need the Jar of Prometheus anymore. These are the words you'll need to break the enchantment and close the core."

He took the folded piece of paper I held out, shaking his head all the while. "I'm no wizard, M'lady," he said. "This is beyond my abilities."

"No," I said, "it's not. We designed the spell so it can be broken easily. Just recite these words and the core will close."

"And what of the Jar after that?" Gwydion asked.

"We'll figure out some way to get it safely back to the archive," I replied. "Let's tackle one problem at a time."

Once we were outside the palisade and on level ground, Greer said, "Are we ready?"

Everyone nodded and joined hands—or talons in Aquila's case—and watched as the scene around us dissolved into a whirling maelstrom of blurred colors and fleeting impressions.

We landed outside the walls of Fer Dorich's castle in a clearing adjacent to a thick grove of trees. Somewhat belatedly, we ducked under the sheltering branches to conceal our arrival. We had a plan, worked out the night before, about what to do next.

Greer, Brenna, and I would present ourselves at the gate and ask for an audience with the Dark Druid. Everyone else would hang back and wait—an idea Chase and Lucas hadn't liked when we came up with it and still didn't like.

Brenna shut them up pretty fast. "I assure you that Greer and I have ample experience in handling Fer Dorich," she said, allowing her eyes to flash brazenly.

The suggestiveness in her gaze rendered Chase more or less speechless while Lucas chose to appeal to Greer. "Come on, Red," he said. "Help a guy out here. You have to see this is a bad plan."

"Not this time, dear boy," she said. "If you and Chase come with us, it will only serve to ignite the competitive side of Fer Dorich's nature. We do not need any . . . " She turned to Tori. "What is that rather colorful term you used earlier?"

"Pissing contest," Tori said evenly.

Aquila let out with a cackling laugh. "Two powerful witches and the baobhan sith are more than equal to the task of negotiating with the Dark Druid," he said. "And, would it not be wise for us to be *outside* the walls should they face difficulties inside?"

The logic of that point won Lucas and Chase over, but neither one of them liked it.

Just before the three of us stepped out onto the road that sloped down to the castle, Tori gave me the thumbs up and mouthed "you've got this." Still, once we were out of the sheltering trees, I felt horribly exposed. Anyone watching from the castle would literally see us coming a mile off.

All this time I've been using the word "castle," because that's what everyone else said. Truthfully, the compound we approached looked like an expensive English country manor surrounded by a high stone wall.

"So are we looking at armed guards down there or what?" I asked.

"Fer Dorich has a security detail," Brenna said, "but they are hardly armored knights, at least not anymore. In these more modern times, the Dark Druid apparently considers himself to be something of a businessman."

Which would be why an elf in a shiny black suit and dark glasses met us at the gate. "State your business," he said brusquely.

"For heaven's sake, Tarathiel," Greer said. "You know perfectly well who I am, and I suspect you recognize Brenna as well."

The elf removed his glasses revealing eyes as light as a sled dog's. "Greer Macvicar?" he grinned, completely shattering his tough guy persona, "Is it really you? How long has it been?"

"Roughly eleven centuries," she replied.

"We heard you went to work for the Mother Trees," Tarathiel said. Then turning to Brenna, he added, "And you're supposed to be dead."

"The reports of my demise were greatly exaggerated," she said smoothly.

Then it was my turn to be scrutinized.

"And you are?" he asked.

"Jinx Hamilton, Witch of the Oak."

"Do any of you have an invitation?"

Greer sighed. "Please don't be tiresome, Tarathiel," she said. "Just tell him we're here."

The elf slid his sunglasses back in place and planted his fists on his hips in a posture of consternation. "And say what?" he demanded. "That the three of you were just out walking and decided to come calling?"

At that, the baobhan sith let out with a burst of Elvish that pretty much pinned Tarathiel's pointy ears back. When she finished, he gasped, "You wouldn't!"

"Try me," Greer snapped.

The remaining color drained from his thin face. "Forgive my bad manners," he stammered. "We don't have many visitors. Please come in while I tell Fer Dorich you're here."

"What was that all about?" I asked Greer as we followed Tarathiel into the house.

"I merely explained that I have always had a fondness for the flavor of Elven blood, but rarely get an opportunity to indulge myself," she said. "He apparently took a purely epicurean remark literally."

Wonder why.

While Tarathiel disappeared toward the back of the house, we waited silently in the entry hall, a massive space paneled with dark wood and tiled in pink marble. I turned at the sound of approaching footsteps, expecting to see someone . . . well . . . Druidic. Instead, a slender, handsome man in a business suit came striding toward us. With his close-cropped beard and immaculately combed hair, he could have been a GQ cover model.

"Greer! Brenna!" he said, embracing each of them in turn. "I cannot believe my good fortune. And you, Mistress Hamilton. The Witch of the Oak in my humble home! This is indeed an honor."

Humble home? Who was he kidding?

"I see you keep up with the times, Fer Dorich," Greer said drily. "When last I passed through your door the atmosphere was a tad more . . . medieval."

Fer Dorich laughed. "Well, dear, when last you were here, it *was* the Middle Ages. I may find myself unnecessarily confined to the In Between, but I don't have to live like a savage. Please, let's go into the den."

He ushered us into a room roughly the size of a football field. At roughly the 50 yard line, a grouping of comfortable furniture sat arranged on a lush Persian carpet in front of a fireplace large enough to barbecue a water buffalo.

"Didn't this used to be the grand hall?" Brenna said as she sat down on one of the sofas. "

"It did," Fer Dorich said, claiming a throne-like wingback chair for himself, "but banquets are so tedious. All those people running about flinging food and chasing wenches."

Something told me this guy had never complained about chasing a wench in his life.

"Now," he went on, rubbing his hands together, "I assume you're here to talk about my house guest, the Queen of Summer."

Fer Dorich might be a Michael Corleone wannabe, but he did know how to get down to business.

"Did you actually take part in Brighid's kidnapping, Fer Dorich," Brenna asked conversationally, "or are you merely an accomplice?"

Laying a hand dramatically over his heart, the Druid said, "You wound me. My only son, a troubled lad who insists on calling himself Liam Cleary, appealed to me for help. What is a father to do? He asked only that I provide secure lodging for the Daughter of Dagda. Would you have had me leave her to her own devices in a land as unpredictable as the Middle Realm?"

"Certainly not," Brenna said, "but are you aware of why she was kidnapped?"

This time the Dark Druid's smile reminded me of a timber rattler getting ready to strike. "I believe Irenaeus Chesterfield is conducting some meteorological experiments in the Human Realm, is he not?" he said pleasantly.

"He is," I said, "and he's threatening the life of the Mother Oak. We need to take Brighid back with us."

Still affecting fake benevolence, Fer Dorich said, "Of course you do, and I certainly do not want to be party to a severing of the realms. That would be rather bad for my personal business interests, but surely, Mistress Hamilton, you understand that I cannot betray my promise to my son unless I am compensated on a level impossible to ignore."

In other words, he wanted to make a deal I couldn't refuse.

"What do you want?"

"A simple accommodation," he replied. "I want the Agreement limiting travel to and from the Middle Real lifted."

Before I could answer, Greer caught my eye. The look she gave me was unmistakable. *Let me take this.*

"Fer Dorich," she said, "perhaps you misunderstood. Jinx is the Witch of the Oak, not a member of the Ruling Elders."

The man's eyes hardened. "She is Barnaby Shevington's granddaughter and in a position to wield considerable influence. If the Daughter of Dagda is to leave my home in your company, my price is an end to the oppressive Agreement. That is not open for negotiation."

"What's to stop us from saying yes and then doing as we please?" Brenna asked.

That's when the true measure of the man became apparent.

"If Brighid was kidnapped once, she could be taken again," he said smoothly. "Or she might meet with a most unfortunate accident. The human realm is quite vulnerable

to temperature fluctuations, is it not? I am not an unreasonable man. You may have six months to effect the lifting
of the Agreement before my patience grows thin."

Greer and Brenna both looked at me. They were here
to protect me, not to make decisions. That responsibility
rested solely on my shoulders, and I was fresh out of bar-
gaining chips—plus, I knew next to *nothing* about the existing agreement.

"Hasn't this arrangement with the realms been in place
a long time?" I asked.

"It has," he said.

"So why are you suddenly so interested in seeing it
lifted?" I asked.

I didn't expect Fer Dorich to tell me the truth, and he
didn't disappoint me.

"Let's just say that I have business interests I would
like to pursue trans-dimensionally and leave it at that," he
said smoothly. "If it makes you feel any better, Irenaues'
mad little plot to set himself up as a Creavit dictator
doesn't interest me."

That, at least, was something. Granddad was going to
have a fit, but I didn't see any other option. We had to get
Brighid back to Briar Hollow to confront Cailleach Bheur.

"Okay," I said. "You've got a deal."

FORTY-ONE

Fer Dorich kept his word. Tarathiel escorted Brighid into the cavernous den, and the Dark Druid took it upon himself to make the introductions all around.

"Are you okay?" I asked Brighid, searching her face for signs of mistreatment.

The blonde woman smiled. It was a good smile, the kind that made the corners of her blue eyes crinkle with humor. "As kidnappers go," she said, "Fer Dorich has been a most convivial host"

"Not a kidnapper," he said disingenuously, "at most an *accessory* to kidnapping."

It's hard not to like a scoundrel who owns up to his crimes so openly.

"Forgive us, Fer Dorich," I said, "but we have to get back to the human realm."

"I completely understand," he said, taking my hand and kissing it. "By the way, I'm sure your companions are quite tired of hiding in that tedious copse of trees. Do bring them along to the house next time."

So much for stealth. I didn't tell him I devoutly hoped there wouldn't *be* a next time.

When we exited the "castle," Brigid walked beside me as we climbed the hill.

"I suspect," she said, "that you've gone to a great deal

of trouble to find me. Entering the Middle Realm is not
something undertaken on a whim. Thank you."

"You're welcome," I said. "You're right that getting
here took some doing, but we had to find you. The Queen
of Winter has been busy while you've been down here."

Brighid shook her head. "I don't know what's gotten
into Cailleach Bheur. The order of the changing of the seasons is as old as the earth itself."

"Well," I said, "in all fairness, we can't blame her
entirely for this whole mess. The real villain is a crazy
Creavit wizard who wants to take over the human realm.
He talked Cailleach into freezing North Carolina solid."

That stopped Brighid in her tracks. "Cailleach does not
have the power to do such a thing," she said, "and most
certainly not after the waning of her powers has begun on
the solstice."

I gave her the short version of the Amulet of Caorunn
story. "The artifact has the power to restore that which has
faded," I said. "In this instance, I think it actually *prevented*
Cailleach's powers from fading on schedule."

"That explains a great deal," Brighid said. "Cailleach
grows stronger until the exact moment of the Solstice,
which signals the beginning of her yearly diminishment.
If that natural cycle were to be interrupted, she might well
be able to achieve the effects you describe."

"Can you stop her?" I asked.

"Yes," Brighid said. "Cailleach cannot deny me the
passing of the season when I summon her, but we must be
in the same realm for me to issue the call."

One trip to the Human Realm coming right up—but
not before Aquila made a surprise announcement. He
wasn't coming with us.

"No way," I said. "We have a deal. You and Brenna
both get to the leave the In Between."

The gryphon titled his head in what I'd come to recognize as a smile. "An arrangement I know you will honor," he said. "I can easily access the Moss Forest, and we can speak via mirror until I am ready to leave. I must pack my books and papers and conclude my business affairs here. I'm afraid I am not nearly so mobile as Brenna, and, of course, there is the matter of placing one such as myself in the Otherworld. That will not be an easy matter. I would prefer to live somewhere with access to scholarly materials."

The sorceress laid her hands on his wings. "You are coming, Aquila," she said, her voice cracking. "You promised you would not leave me."

"And I will not," he said softly, "but we must be practical, my dear. My form presents challenges. Arrange a place for me to settle, and I will follow you."

I don't think any of us realized the depth of the bond between the two of them. The genuine distress on Brenna's face was painful to watch. When I touched her arm, and she turned to look at me, there were tears running down her cheeks.

"I'll talk to my grandfather," I said. "Shevington is a sanctuary city. He will make a place for Aquila there."

"But I am not allowed in Shevington," she protested.

"You weren't allowed in Shevington when you were Creavit," I said. "No one will stop you from going there now. I'll take you myself."

"Our separation will not be a long one," Aquila assured her. "Go now. Take up the fight with these valiant souls against the wizard Chesterfield. He has harmed you as he has harmed them. You are no longer alone, Brenna. You have comrades in arms."

No one said anything as the gryphon lifted his massive wings and rose into the air. Brenna watched him until he disappeared into the distance with her arms folded tight across her chest.

"Are we ready?" Greer said quietly.

"Brenna?" I asked.

With a curt nod and a last longing look toward the horizon into which Aquila had flown, she came to stand beside me. We all joined hands and Greer flew us to the Moss Forest.

True to his word, the Golem didn't bother us; in fact, he didn't even show up. As we approached the spot where our confrontation with him occurred, the doorway to the fairy mound materialized. That's when Brighid balked a little.

"We are to step into that blackness and trust that it will return us to this fairy mound you tell me is your home?" she asked.

I couldn't blame her. She had been dragged into an icy pond by a stag and plunged into the Middle Realm against her will. If I were in her position, walking straight into a jet black rectangle wouldn't have been high on my list of fun things to do either.

"Nothing bad is going to happen," I promised. "It's just like walking through any doorway." I held out my hand to her. "Come on. We'll go together."

Myrtle was waiting for us as promised, with my mother and Gemma at her side. Brighid and I came through first, followed by Greer and Brenna — then Chase, Lucas, and Tori.

At the sight of her daughter, Gemma rushed past us all and engulfed Tori in a tight embrace. I couldn't hear what Gemma said, but Tori's muffled voice kept repeating, "I'm okay. I'm okay."

When I hugged my mother, I said, "What's that all about?"

"The pocket mirror," Mom said. "It started transmitting when you entered the Middle Realm. We heard most of your exchange with the Golem, and we saw Tori fall.

The last image before the glass shattered was her blood. We didn't know if she was alive or dead.

Poor Gemma. She'd had to live with that for . . .

"How long have we been gone? I asked. "For us, it was two days."

"About twelve hours," Myrtle said. "The Mother Tree began to feel the heat from the Jar of Prometheus approximately six hours ago."

Brighid, who was still standing next to me, dropped into a low curtsy. "Aos si," she said formally, "thank thee for coming to my aid."

"Arise, Daughter of Dagda," Myrtle said, "and welcome to my home. We have need of your assistance."

"Which I will gladly render," Brighid replied, "but first, may I be allowed to contact my father and sisters?"

"Of course," Myrtle said. "I will give you access to the mirror in my quarters."

From behind me, I heard Tori say, "Mom, let me go. There's someone I want you to meet."

As we all watched, Tori introduced Gemma to Brenna. "Mom, this is Brenna Sinclair."

Gemma pursed her lips. "We've met," she said.

"No," Tori said, "you haven't. That Brenna doesn't exist anymore. Grams here saved my life, and she's kickass cool. Give her a chance."

I'm not sure which part shocked Gemma more, the idea that Brenna helped Tori or that Tori called the sorceress "Grams."

Brenna has a tremendous capacity to stay cool under fire. She held her hand out to Gemma and said, "May we begin again?"

"Did you really save my daughter's life?" Gemma asked.

"Not alone," Brenna replied. "Her friends rescued her after the fall and brought her to a safe place where my friend and I were able to heal her wounds."

"She's just being modest," Tori said. "My leg was gashed open all the way down to my knee. There was blood all over the . . . "

Tori was so wrapped up in her story, she didn't notice the way all the color drained out of Gemma's face. "Tori," I said, "back off on the gory details."

"Huh?" she said. "I'm just getting to the good part."

Brenna intervened. "I think your mother has grasped the essence of the story without having to hear an embellished version. Am I correct?"

"Completely," Gemma said, "and thank you . . . Brenna."

Not exactly effusive, but I knew Gemma well enough to know the thaw in her feelings toward her living ancestor had started.

While Chase and Lucas chained and locked the doorway to the In Between, the rest of us followed Myrtle back to the lair. Before my father even had a chance to say hello, Rodney jumped off Beau's shoulder, hit the table twice, and vaulted toward me. I caught him mid-air.

"Whoa!" I said laughing. "You're getting a little acrobatic there aren't you?"

Rodney's whiskers twitched in delight as he ran up my arm and instantly buried himself inside the collar of my shirt.

Beau regarded me with open pride. "I knew you would be victorious, Miss Jinx," he said. "Welcome home." Beside him on the floor, Duke's tail wagged wildly.

"It's good to be home," I said, as all four of my cats appeared out of nowhere, wrapping themselves around my ankles purring loudly.

Darby winked into sight beside me and threw his arms around my waist, hugging me fiercely. Glory hovered just over his head. "Tell me *everything*!" she said breathlessly. "And don't leave out a single detail."

Festus, who was sitting in his usual spot, tried to sound casual, but I heard the worried tone in his voice when he asked, "Where's the boy?"

"Securing the door to the In Between," I said. "He's fine."

"Harumph," the old cat grumbled, trying to hide his visible relief, "never occurred to me that he wouldn't be. He's a McGregor, isn't he?"

"You okay, kiddo?" Dad asked, finally managing to get past everyone, including his wildly excited pack of dogs, to get his arms around me.

"I'm good," I said, kissing his cheek. "We all are. Everybody, this is Brighid, the Queen of Summer."

After the introductions had been made, and Brighid spoke with her family, we were ready to summon Cailleach Bheur. From what Dad and Beau told me, conditions over our heads remained unchanged.

"So," I said, "where are we going to have this confrontation with Cailleach?"

To my surprise, Myrtle said, "Here in the lair is fine. Cailleach is an old woman. She is no physical threat to any of us."

Brighid moved into the open space between our work table and the temporary bedroom, closed her eyes, and began to sing. The words were in a tongue I didn't recognize, but they filled my ears with the sound of buzzing bees and my nose with the scent of blooming spring flowers. The light in the lair warmed to the golden hue of a sunny afternoon, and suddenly an old, wizened crone leaning heavily on a gnarled staff stood a few feet away from Brighid.

"Cailleach Bheur," the Queen of Summer said in a voice, redolent of a meadow in full bloom, "my time has come, and thine has ended."

"Do not be so sure of thy ascendency, Daughter of

Dagda," the old woman cackled. "The scales do not rest so evenly between us this day as in days of old."

We could all see the reason for her brazen confidence. The Amulet of Caorunn rested against the rough fabric of her gray cloak.

"That artifact doesn't belong to you," I said, stepping beside Brighid. "I'm giving you the opportunity to surrender it willingly."

In my peripheral vision, I saw Mom, Gemma, Tori, Brenna, and Greer join me in a ragged line. I'll give Cailleach credit. Even facing four witches, the baobhan sith, and the Queen of Summer, she remained defiant.

"I had no hand in the acquisition of this amulet," she said. "It was given to me."

Honestly, I don't know what would have happened next if the Amulet hadn't decided to settle the matter itself. It broke away from Cailleach's neck, shot across the space between us, and found a new home—with my mother.

When the amber pendant touched her body, and the clasp of the chain closed around her neck, she simply became . . . more. Her hair rippled as if caught in an invisible current. The few gray hairs that had begun to show at her temples darkened and the fine lines around her eyes and mouth smoothed away.

"Mom?" I asked uncertainly. "What just happened?"

When she answered me, I saw the strong, confident line of her body and the light of newfound strength in her eyes.

"The Oak and the Rowan have become one."

EPILOGUE

We came back to the lair the day before New Year's Eve. Brighid could have warmed the weather instantly, but we all agreed that would only create more confusion for the human population. As is, entire meteorological careers are going to be built around studying "the Freak Freeze of '15."

As North Carolina slowly thawed, the citizens of Briar Hollow began to return to their homes, and the life of the town edged toward normal. That's when we started to understand how terrifying the incident had been for people at the mercy of the elements.

The customers who came into the Witch's Brew those first couple of weeks in January, talked like converts at a "prepper" convention. They felt like they'd seen a rehearsal for the end times and were justified in laying up survival supplies in case it ever happened again. We sold them hot coffee and listened to their stories, unable to tell our own.

We'd taken a risk and entered an unknown realm to save the lives of not just the Mother Tree, but also the Grid that holds the realms together. We served the higher purpose of the Natural Order and put our lives on the line doing it. Beyond all the magical outcomes you already know about? No one in Briar Hollow died. I wish we could say the same for the rest of the state.

Gemma and I kept a close eye on Tori to the point of annoying the hell out of her. Although she protests that she can barely even remember getting hurt, I see the slight limp when she's tired and the way she rubs her arms at the end of the day when the mended bone aches.

We aren't the only one who watch her. Brenna Sinclair is living with us for the time being. The fairy mound obligingly merged two of the temporary bedrooms to make a small apartment. Everything else in the lair shifted back to normal, although the comfort station for Dad's dogs is still in place. He drops them off here while he and Mom are working on their new place so Duke can have some play time with living contemporaries.

As for Brenna, when we have to make an introduction, we tell people she's Tori's aunt. Truthfully, they are building a relationship. The sorceress has an affinity for computers and Tori is teaching her more. I have to say I've grown to like our former enemy, too.

Now that the weight of the Creavit bargain has been lifted from her soul, there's an oddly youthful curiosity to Brenna's nature. She and Greer are a riot together. The two of them cut a wide swath through the courts of Europe in their day and often regale us with tales of their exploits during evenings around the fire in the lair.

On New Year's Eve, while we were still iced in, Lucas took me off to one side and told me he thought we needed to slow things down between us. "I'm not a blind man, Jinx," he said. "When we were in the Middle Realm, I saw that you still don't know how you feel about Chase. Figure it out. I'll be here one way or the other."

The grace with which he handled what could have been my second nasty breakup, is a blessing. For that matter, Chase is behaving himself, too, which I also appreciate. He's not pressuring me, and the awkward politeness between us has gone back to easy camaraderie. Where is all of that going? I don't know, and I'm not forcing myself to figure it out just yet.

As predicted, Barnaby was not happy with me for striking a bargain with the Dark Druid to repeal the Agreement isolating the inhabitants of the In Between. Thanks to me, my grandfather can no longer put off getting involved in the affairs of the Ruling Elders. I have been warned that there are convoluted Fae political negotiations in my future.

But, by the same token, Barnaby also came through with allowing Aquila to settle in Shevington. Workmen are remodeling a house near Moira's workshop to accommodate the special needs of a gryphon. Brenna can't wait to be reunited with her friend, although I think she's still nervous about going to the Valley for the first time.

When we told Katrina Warner what happened with the Amulet of Caorunn, she took the news in stride. "The amulet has a mind of its own," she said. "If it's chosen your mother in the name of an alliance between the Oak and the Rowan, then that's how things will be."

I'm looking forward to meeting the Women of the Trees at their next gathering in Edinburgh. As for the two Mother Trees, they haven't announced the terms of their alliance to us mere mortals, but they will, in their own sweet time.

In private Dad told me that the transformation in my mother since she was chosen by the amulet isn't so much something new, as the return of the qualities she had as a younger woman. "She's like she was before the accident and before we lost Connor," he said. "She's like her mother."

When I related the conversation to Festus, he agreed, reminding me again that Grandma Kathleen had enough power to "curl your whiskers."

As for Chesterfield, we haven't heard a peep out of him. Cailleach Bheur retreated to the high lonely places, and Brighid is back with her sisters, going about the business of warming the earth as it moves toward real spring.

When most of the snow had melted, and temperatures had returned to the mid-40s, I took a walk high in the mountains. It felt good to be outside, breathing the clean air and not worrying about the next metaphysical catastrophe.

I found myself standing on a bluff overlooking a rocky ridge line. In another couple of months, I will have been living in Briar Hollow an entire year. I came here to take over my aunt's eclectic general store and instead, have discovered new worlds and new challenges.

People make New Year's resolutions and break them all the time, but standing there that day on the mountainside, I made a promise to myself I intend to keep. To live every adventure that comes my way to the fullest. Something tells me I won't be running out of chances to do just that anytime soon.

ABOUT THE AUTHOR

Juliette Harper is the pen name used by the writing team of Patricia Pauletti and Rana K. Williamson. As a writer, Juliette's goal is to create strong female characters facing interesting, challenging, painful, and at times comical situations. Refusing to be bound by genre, her primary interest lies in telling good stories.

Six of Juliette's series are currently available. *The Jinx Hamilton Mysteries* opens with *Witch at Heart*, a lighter paranormal tale featuring a heroine who possesses powers she never dreamed existed. Jinx has been minding her own business working as a waitress at Tom's Cafe and keeping up with her four cats. Then she inherits her Aunt Fiona's store in neighboring Briar Hollow, North Carolina *and* learns that her aunt has willed her special "powers" to Jinx as well. They say admitting you have a problem is the first step and Jinx has a major problem. She's a new witch and she has no earthly clue what that means — until she's given the opportunity to use her magic to do a good thing.

In Book 2, *Witch at Odds*, Jinx accepts her new life as a witch and is determined to make a success of both that and her new business. However, she has a great deal to learn. As the story unfolds, Jinx sets out to both study her craft and to get a real direction for her aunt's haphazard approach to inventory. Although Jinx can call on Aunt

Fiona's ghost for help, the old lady is far too busy living a jet set afterlife to be worried about her niece's learning curve. That sets Jinx up to make a major mistake and to figure out how to set things right again.

By Book 3, *Witch at Last*, A lot has changed for Jinx in just a few months. After the mishaps that befell her in *Witch At Odds*, she just wants to enjoy the rest of the summer, but she's not going to be that lucky. As she's poised to tell her friends she's a witch, secrets start popping out all over the place. Between old foes and new locations, Jinx isn't going to get her peaceful summer, but she may just get an entirely different world.

Book 4, *Witch on First*, has Jinx walk out the front door of her store in Briar Hollow on a Sunday morning only to find her werecat neighbor and boyfriend, Chase McGregor, staring at a dead man. Under the best of circumstances, a corpse complicates things, but Jinx has other problems. Is her trusted mentor lying to her? Have dangerous magical artifacts been placed inside the shop? Join Jinx and Tori as they race to catch a killer and find out what's going on literally under their noses.

Book 5, *Witch on Second*, opens just a week before Halloween. Jinx and Tori have their hands full helping to organize Briar Hollow's first ever paranormal festival. Beau and the ghosts at the cemetery are eager to help make the event a success, but tensions remain high after the recent killings. Without a mentor to lean on, Jinx must become a stronger, more independent leader. Is she up to the task in the face of ongoing threats? Still mourning the loss of Myrtle and her breakup with Chase, Jinx finds herself confronting new and unexpected foes.

Book Six, *Witch on Third*, begins just where *Witch on Second* left off, the last night of Briar Hollow's first annual paranormal festival. With Chase still stinging from the breakup and Lucas Grayson more than a little interested,

Jinx has plenty on her plate without a new evil trio in town. As the team works to counter Chesterfield's newest scheme, something happens in the Valley that changes everything for the Hamilton family.

Six volumes of the best-selling *Lockwood Legacy* are currently available. The story chronicles the lives of three sisters who inherit a ranch in Central Texas following their father's suicide. The titles include: *Langston's Daughters*, *Baxter's Draw*, *Alice's Portrait*, *Mandy's Father*, *Irene's Gift*, and *Jenny's Choice*. The seventh, *Kate's Journey*, will appear in 2017.

Descendants of the Rose is the first installment of the Selby Jensen Paranormal Mysteries. The second book, *Lost in Room 636*, will also be available in 2017. Selby's business card reads "Private Investigator," but to say the least, that downplays her real occupation where business as usual is anything but normal.

And don't miss the hilariously funny "cozy" *Study Club Mysteries*, a light-hearted spin off of *The Lockwood Legacy*. Set in the 1960s, this series takes on the often-absurd eccentricities of small town life with good-natured, droll humor. The first book, *You Can't Get Blood Out of Shag Carpet*, is already listed in the Amazon store with *You Can't Put a Corpse in a Parade* will be coming in 2017.

Juliette has also made forays into the arena of short fiction arena with *Before Marriage*, a light, sweet romance and *Langston's Ghost*, a short-story companion to *The Lockwood Legacy* books.

Fermata: The Winter is the first in a four-novella post-apocalyptic survival series. Five years after an unknown virus divided the world into the living and the dead, four survivors stumble into a winter sanctuary. Brought together by circumstance, but bound by the will to stay alive, a concert pianist and a girl from South Boston forge a friendship and a purpose to cope with their new reality.

*Want to know more about
author Juliette Harper?*

*Visit Juliette Harper's home on the web at
http://www.julietteharper.com*